I0674182

Other Works

The Hive Queen Saga

Queen & Commander – IPPY award silver medal winner for
Best Science Fiction, Fantasy, or Horror eBook (2013)
Hive & Heist (2014)
"The Robot Who Stole Herself" (2014)

Standalone Works

These Convergent Stars (2013)
Cracked! A Magic iPhone Story – First Place Category
Winner for the Cygnus Awards (2015)

A sightseeing trip to a space station garden goes horribly wrong!

Rhiannon had lost any sense of perspective. The garden had been blotted out by walls. She could reach out her arms straight at 180 degrees and touch metal sheets on both sides. Two people would be cozy—she and Wenyan would be cozy—and four would be cramped. "How do we get out?"

"It is a safety measure," said Wenyan, voice gentle. "In case of an air leak, cells slam down from above. The central garden is so intricate that the life-pod cells here must be small to avoid damaging the architecture or the plants. Further out, the rooms are larger."

Rhiannon's breath came faster. Her toes dug into the empty spaces between pebble spikes. "Air leak!" Her stomach pushed at her skin and blood pounded in her ears. "We need to get to the emergency spacesuits."

Wenyan laughed. "This is nothing. It is normal, just an experiment. Come sit with me."

He was delusional. "Emergency spacesuits," she said again. The pounding in her ears could have been her pulse. Or it could have been her Devoted banging on the other side of the wall. They could be trying to get to her. They could be in their vacuum-sealed death throes.

She splayed her hands against the metal prison. Trapped!

Reign & Revolution

Book Three of the Hive Queen Saga

by Janine A. Southard

MARTIAN
CANTINA

Copyright © 2016 Janine A. Southard

Cover by MaeIDesign and Photography
Editing by Cat Rambo
Copyediting by Rachel Lynn Solomon
Print Edition Layout by Stacy Booth
Print Edition ISBN: 978-1-63327-021-3
Ebook Edition ISBN: 978-1-63327-202-6

Acknowledgements

This series has been a process. (There may be more books in this universe, but the triptych has been my plan from the start.) So many people have been supportive and excited about the Hive Queen Saga from the very beginning, and I'd like to name a few here.

First, special thanks to Jeremy Barton, my "main investor" and spouse. He has been unfailingly encouraging whenever I was unsure about this whole professional writing thing. Also, he's brilliant at brainstorming through my blocks. Many of my favorite scenes are traceable to his original suggestions during a brainstorming session. I would be lost without him.

Next, there's my best friend, Tiffany Lutnick-Coleman, who has always listened to my geebling about whatever projects I'm working on. She was also the original inspiration for the character of Gwyn... who isn't in this book. Sorry, Tiffany.

And, of course, I'd like to thank my editor Cat Rambo, who is not only a marvelous editor and wordsmith, but also pushed me for more everything. (More books, more character development, more worldbuilding on the page. Seriously. We were in a car once, driving to a reading, and she was like, "When's the next book, Janine? I want to read it.")

As with the previous two books in the Hive Queen Saga, my Kickstarter backers deserve gigantic thanks. Thank you for believing in this novel and for sharing my passion for ensemble space opera. In particular, I'd like to thank the following backers for their contributions (in alphabetical order by first name because you have to order things somehow):

Alan J.	Matt Ellis
Autumn Harting	Melissa Pagonis
Cassiel	Mike Kenyon
Chad Bowden	Parental Units
Don, Beth & Meghan Ferris	Stevie Carroll
James Truher	Tiffany Lutnick-Coleman
Jon Lasser	

For this particular novel, I also need to thank Jordan and Graham Blair, whose willingness to share their observations about everyday transgender differences gave greater dimension to the gender-switching robot.

Chapter One

Locking Up and Heading Out

The Ceridwen's Cauldron, *airlock*

If Rhiannon had known how much time she'd spend in her ship's airlock, she might have decorated. As it was, the place was small and bare aside from the bright spacesuits of its current occupants. Grey metal covered the walls and the un-adorned floors. A spoked wheel—in the same grey metal—blended into the door that would open the ship to the outside.

The vestibule barely had enough space for her Hive to cram inside.

Would the wheel be hot or cold to the touch? Rhiannon would never know, only coming here when she was already kitted up. Hands slick in her spacesuit's recycled air.

The staging room where she'd donned her red crackle-painted suit—*I still wish I knew whether the paint was supposed to lock like this*—was barely better. Banks of grey metal lockers held full-body suits that might protect a wearer from the void.

For the moment, she left off her hood-like helmet. *If*

someone asks, I'll say it's to save oxygen. Her nose would itch the second she couldn't touch it, made worse by the sweat-scent of everyone who'd ever worn the red gear. Her fingers and toes were already clammy in their rubber casings. She'd spritzed the inside with perfume to combat the rankness, and she hoped to find herself ensconced in a cocoon that was still human-humid, yes, but also vital with amber notes, like a thick waft from a nightclub. This next outing would prove the idea's worth.

All five of her Devoted readied themselves beside her. Gavin flexed his knees to check his black suit's range of motion. Luciano had chosen the bright yellow rubber that made him look like a deformed chicken, not that she'd tell him that. Victor wore a grey suit that matched the rest of his clothes, and Alan poked at his pad with a blue-coated finger.

Mel, of course, had chosen to go *au natural*—aside from his regular vest—since his metal body held up well in vacuum. He wouldn't have been able to fit all his limbs into a human-shaped spacesuit anyway.

Rhiannon had to try one more time: "Mel, could you ping the station for me again please?"

After weeks in transit, Rhiannon and her Hive had reached Yin He Yuan *("Silver River Garden"), the station in Mandarin space, where her own Alan would be giving a presentation about his near-miraculous engine. As soon as they'd arrived in communications range, the station had provided a docking location for the* Ceridwen's Cauldron and promised a local guide to answer further questions. They'd seemed accommodating.

Since then, however, they'd been silent. Whenever Rhiannon reached out to Yin He's station authorities—to confirm a docking time or ask for an oxygen top-up or check whether she'd have leave to return to her ship on her own schedule—she got the same recorded message in English.

Mel played it again now through his own speaker, wry head tilt showing exactly what he thought of the sounds coming from his mouth area. "Thank you for contacting Garden Station. Please leave all weaponry and subversive materials behind before entering the airlock. We hope you enjoy your stay."

Not that they'd added an information packet about what "subversive materials" might be.

It was up to Rhiannon now. They'd suited up while they waited on information from the station and extended their docking accordion. *I didn't even get to ask whether their airlock is compatible with the* Cauldron's *accordion bridge.*

Without knowing whether they'd be allowed to travel back and forth during Alan's conference, the entire Hive had prepared to go across. Which meant they were leaving the ship alone. Unguarded. Open to attack and plunder.

Back on the American station, from whence they'd most recently come, local authorities had cut them off from their ship. While they'd settled into their accommodations on John Wayne in good faith, the administration ransacked the *Cauldron* and stole Alan's experimental tensor jet.

Oh, they'd got the jet back, but they hadn't made any friends doing it. And they'd left behind Rhiannon's best friend in the process. Separated forever.

Rhiannon shivered and contemplated ordering Alan to retract the docking accordion. They didn't have to visit Garden Station (or "Silver River Station" or whatever they wanted to call it) and Alan's conference. They could find another place to purchase supplies, another group ready to laud Alan's achievements, and maybe even a school where her young Hive members could train in their specialties.

But that would mean crushing Alan's excitement. She couldn't do that. She was Queen, with all the responsibilities to her Devoted that entailed. She needed to be smarter and bolder than her potential enemies.

"I could set some proximity alarms," Mel suggested, knowing exactly what Rhiannon was afraid of. Of course he did. He'd been there on John Wayne. "They're the kind I used to have on my own ship. They'll let me know if anyone tries to breach the *Cauldron*." His fingers tapped against his vest with a plinking noise.

Then again, Mel's ship was taken by the Americans—his own people—so how good *were* those alarms? *No, that's not fair.* Mel had abandoned his ship in order to join her Hive and avoid a mob. It hadn't been stolen during his watch. Like Alan's tensor jet had been during hers.

Gavin cleared his throat. "I might have set traps for anyone who opens the outer airlock without me."

Alan waved his arms, tight blue sleeves flying in and out of her field of vision. "Nice of you to warn us before we tried to leave the ship."

Gavin sneered. "I just did."

Victor pointed a sharp finger in Alan's direction. "I don't see *you* protecting our home, even though it was your thing that got stolen last time."

Alan went still, face and arms unmoving.

Luciano sighed. "You've all got salt in the pumpkin, all right? Let's just be pleased we can make sure any unauthorized visitors are both noted and possibly deterred."

He's coming back to us. In the weeks they'd traveled, Luciano had spent ever more time with his Hive mates and his Queen. Penitent, perhaps, after his near-defection on John Wayne. She still surprised a frown on his face whenever he looked away, however, usually during some druidic moment like a prayer to the gods for safe passage.

Alan and Gavin grumbled at his peacemaking effort, but they smiled at each other all the same. *Crisis averted.*

"Thank you," Rhiannon said. "Let's not trust these strangers too much." The last time she'd been in this position, the strangers had saved her life and offered her full run of their home... right before they'd sundered her privacy, stolen her ability to leave, and chased her Hive out of town.

Gavin hummed in agreement. "'Trust but verify,'" he quoted. *Yes! I knew that one!*

"Lock it down," she ordered.

It was the work of moments, Mel and Gavin both hunched over their packs, before they reported their success at setting traps. With that, the entire Hive slipped on their hood-helmets and out the exterior door.

Inside the accordion, Alan tapped at the airlock controls that sealed the edges. Too late to change her mind now. Not that she would. This was Alan's moment, his turn to show off his inventions and learn from other experts in his field. She couldn't deny him.

She still planned to be cautious.

He waved his arms and shook his hips like he was dancing, but... *That's less coordinated than his dancing at Victor's birthday party two weeks ago.* The mystery bewildered her until he pried his pad from his waist clip, an impressive feat in a spacesuit whose gloved fingers were covered with half a centimeter of material.

Rhiannon's suit had done its duty so far, as had everyone else's. This was especially noteworthy for a crew who had yet to learn what maintenance their cold-space equipment required.

The six Hive mates were almost to the station's door when a staticky voice said. "You will declare any sicknesses, animals, or plant matter before coming across." Well, *that* was an untimely notice. Rhiannon was practically to Yin He now and wouldn't have turned around for a mere cold.

Her heart slowed and fever-hot sweat cooled on her skin. Calm. The station's lack of foresight probably meant they'd be terrible at stealing anything off her ship. Too disorganized to break in. Or salvage it for parts. Or hold her hostage to against docking fees.

Her heart sped once more as she listed possible dangers in the silence of her suit. *How did they broadcast that message? I* knew *these suits had speakers. If only I could figure out how they worked...*

She drifted towards the station door, willing momentum to work faster. Three body lengths away from her destination, her stomach swooped. She could see stars. She shouldn't be able to see stars. That was the whole point of the docking tube: safety from the elements plus freedom from tethers. But here was a two-foot gap between the entrance and her accordion. More bad planning?

Her breath picked up, shallow in her chest and making the carbon dioxide scrubbers work overtime. Her skin warmed and eyes tunnel-focused on the exterior view. *Well, at least we're not dead yet.*

Mel gripped her arm, a welcome bulwark against space's infinite ocean. She smiled at him, hopefully visible through her faceplate, and saw that he held on to all the others with his remaining three arms as well. All the others except Alan who had already flown ahead.

She forced her breathing to slow. Mel wouldn't let anyone get lost. She could trust her Devoted.

Alan tapped again, on his own pad this time instead of the airlock controls, and the door slid open. At the head of her Hive, Rhiannon entered the Mandarin station's airlock.

Digital image screens covered the airless safety chamber, except for the blank wall directly ahead. The screens were pinned into boxy basket frames made of painted white metal.

Most screens showed close-ups of chrysanthemums. *Chrysanthemums!* Here, seven orange petals bled dark at the center and edges to nearly yellow in between. There, a pink maw unfurled tongues to reveal a black hole. A white-and-yellow bunch could have been a wedding bouquet, except that Rhiannon had read white was a death color in Chinese culture.

She fancied she could smell them through their screens and her hood, sweet and floral and rich, but that was probably the perfume she'd sprayed into her suit.

Across three screens sprawled a blooming triptych—a scraggling plum branch that bowed with tiny buds all shades of pink. A riot of pink.

The opposite wall remained bare of flowery imagery. A flat sheet of burnished steel stretched from all corners into an impenetrable surface. It was intimidating. It was lifeless. It couldn't be the exit because, being made of one sheet, it had no door.

Rhiannon looked right and left and back the way she'd come, but the other directions had no apparent doors either, except the return to the boarding accordion (which had probably retracted by this point).

A light flashed overhead. Once, twice.

The chrysanthemum images inverted color. Once, twice.

And then the blank wall raised itself completely into the ceiling. Rhiannon watched it go up, her suit making disturbing snapping noises with her movement. *It was a door after all.*

With the door-wall thing gone, the airlock was open onto the station. She removed her helmet, reveling in the sweet, cold air.

Now revealed, another wall stood just behind where the airlock wall had once been. No more thick grey steel, this wall was made of plaster with a cutout doorway, which couldn't be closed, framed in wood by a stone and tile border. Off to the right, bamboo plants rose high—almost like a miniature grove—with some branches bearing chrysanthemum bulbs peeking through the shoots at eye height. Tracking backwards, the branches came through a square window with carved poles in an intricate lace pattern. The "window" didn't have any way to shut either.

Gavin pulled off his helmet and cleared his throat. "This displays a shocking lack of vacuum safety."

Then again, so did their spacesuits.

He added, "But it's very pretty."

At this point, they really should have taken off their spacesuits. The bulky things were hot. Rhiannon opted to continue wearing her suit, just in case, and to hold the helmet under her arm. With all the cold and the lack of doors, well, it was better to be prepared for an emergency. Even if it did mean that her feet squished in their own sweat and the fine hairs between her crown and her crown— *haha!*—stuck to her forehead, where they didn't frizz like crazy. Her cheeks flushed, and she was glad of the breeze.

"Whoa," Victor said, breath misting white with the exhalation.

Inspired by her choice to stay suit-clad, the rest of her Hive (less Mel, of course) did the same.

To the right of the doorway, the bamboo mini-grove grew around a grooved and cavernous rock taller than Rhiannon herself. Spikey vines climbed the wall and infiltrated the window. From the left-hand side of the doorway, ferns peeked in as if to beckon visitors into the station proper. Was that a pebbled path leading off at an angle?

Rhiannon wanted to touch the maybe-banana-leaves at the very edge of the frame, to feel their connection to the life running through all the residents. All these plants! All this nature! She and her Hive were going to fit better here than they had on John Wayne Station. Maybe it would be as good as home. Even if the plants themselves were different.

"Gwyn would have loved this," Rhiannon said. She kept forgetting to call her old friend *Lois*, but at least the other woman wasn't here to hear the slip. With Gwyn's affinity for plants, she'd stayed behind to be an expert for the Americans.

Victor shrunk back against a digital chrysanthemum— twice the size of his head—at the mention of his ex-girlfriend's name. His hands flattened against his thighs, pressing as far away from the sound as he could. Rhiannon tapped a rubber-coated finger to her lips, and the smooth material caught on them. *Victor needs to talk about Gwyn-Lois eventually.* Maybe they could remember her together, do some of the things she used to love. Victor may have lost a girlfriend, but Rhiannon had lost her *best friend* in the same Hive change.

Sometimes it hurt to think that Gwyn left Rhiannon behind. Other times it was a comfort to remember the things Gwyn had loved. And this airlock entry... this would have thrilled her. Whoever had thought of putting so many plants on a space station in such an eye-catching arrangement?

Luciano came up beside her and tentatively poked Rhiannon's shoulder. "Why is it cold?"

Mel's vest slapped against his chest with a quiet ring. Rhiannon was sure that if she hadn't knotted her hair into a braid-like weave to fit beneath her low crown, she'd have frizz flying everywhere.

Alan took her other side. "It says something over the door. What does it say? I can't read that!"

As though I can. The inscription was carved into stone, which hung on the plaster wall over the doorway, and it certainly wasn't in English or Cymraeg. "Clearly it says, 'Welcome, friends. Enter here!'"

Alan's arms waved over his head, as best his spacesuit would let them, and his mouth opened in a half gape and half sneer that showed off a few top teeth. "Where does it say that? How did you read that? I'm not prepared enough for this."

Rhiannon walked forwards to pass the doorway and the little gate stones, her limbs loose. A devious smirk formed on her lips, though nobody could see it—specifically Alan—since she'd strode to the front. Somehow, mock-tormenting her most excitable Devoted made her feel more like a part of her Hive. And with his attention focused on refuting her words, he wouldn't have the energy to worry about his upcoming presentation or his inability to read the local language. "Didn't you study the language packet that Mel made for us?"

There had been no such language packet.

Alan shrieked.

Mel made a throat clearing noise from the rear of their caravan. "Ah, my lady?" he asked in that impossibly smooth voice he'd affected.

Rhiannon waved a dismissive hand, letting Mel know he didn't need to vocalize his objection.

Gavin, playing peacemaker, made the obvious observation. "Oh, my," he said. "Look at all these chrysanthemums."

For there were chrysanthemums everywhere along the winding path. Real this time, not digital. The station air tickled her nose with a peppery green scent, and she rubbed the tip with her gloved hand.

A few feet ahead, another wall loomed with a flower-shaped door of four petals—or a circle gently pinched in four places—coming up on the right. In front of the wall sat a bench, a potted yellow chrysanthemum upon it. To the left, a bushel of ferny trees added a touch of green near a lacquered brown screen. And, of course, chrysanthemums had been interwoven with the ferns.

It was a colorful wonderland of leaves and petals, stems and wood. If she shimmied out of her suit, she could stroke the folded florets. Yellow and orange, blue and white, all had healthy leaves. They'd be dewy against her skin, perfectly maintained.

How did they do that? It looks like a chrysanthemum tree. A beast which, of course, did not exist.

Alan scoffed. "They're so fake," he said. "I don't like them."

On the rightmost wall, closer to the blossom-shaped gate, a set of wooden panels opened to reveal a closet of hanging jackets. Rather than investigate the cunning chrysanthemum trees, she went for the practical and pulled a jacket out.

It was bright purple, plastic, and looked far too big for her. Was it intended for the gardeners, perhaps, who would need to water the plants but might get too cold out here so close to space? Because it would make sense to keep the far reaches of a space station cooled by the exterior weather, and let circulation temper the inner areas.

She hung up the large jacket and pulled out another. It appeared exactly the same—bright purple, plastic, too big for her. "Are we supposed to do something with these, do you think?" she mused.

Mel made a throat-clearing noise. How she loved the way he displayed some human peculiarities and skipped over others. "There's an inscription between the lockers and the gate." He translated:

The silver river inspires awe, shaded by mountain and misty rain

The plants hide and bloom again in their warm houses

"The first line is an homage—or plagiarism, depending on your opinion, that plays on the station name—to a famous poem by Su Shi," he added.

Which didn't help Rhiannon to interpret the inscription at all. Still: poetry. And where were these shading mountains?

Victor sighed happily. "I could get to like this place."

They all could. It had so much in common with home.

Alan's pad trilled, cutting into their appreciation, and the physicist looked down at his screen in surprise. "A new message from Professor Cantor," he said. Like an excuse and a divulgence at once. "Do you remember him, my lady?"

"*Well i mi go*—" Sometimes, talking with Alan, her one Cymraeg-first Devoted, made her drop into her other native tongue. "Yes, I think I do. Is it anything important?"

Alan tapped a few times before tucking his pad into the helmet under his arm. He leaned away from the helmet as though it might attack if he moved wrong. "No, no." His normally deep voice flew nearly into Gavin's baritone range. "I'll read it in more depth later."

She let him close the conversation down. She'd revisit it if he didn't bring it up with her in a few days. Her duty was to care for her Devoted, to look out for their well-being, to shield them even against old friends and mentors. Not to force them into uncomfortable situations.

A young man strode through the blossom gate, arms open to the sides. *Oh.* He reminded her of Cinna on John Wayne Station in that they both dressed to accentuate their features and displayed confidence of both body and attitude. But, unlike the American woman, Rhiannon couldn't look away from this newcomer.

He was about Alan's height—taller than Rhiannon but shorter than Victor or Gavin—and twig-thin. He was dressed all in blue. Unlike the spacesuits her Hive still sported, though, this was no single-piece jumpsuit. He wore a cable-knit sweater with a silk collar peeking out the top and a wool tie flapping in the station's wind. His trousers were leather or vinyl and short enough to display argyle socks under snakeskin booties.

It was at once more sedate and more outlandish than any outfit Rhiannon had ever seen.

"Hello, honored guests. Welcome to Yin He Yuan. *You* may call it Garden Station."

Chapter Two

Meanwhile, Back on Dyfed – Cantor's Lament

42 days earlier: Planet Dyfed,
Professor Cantor's office—summer

Professor Maximilian Cantor had gone through the records thirty times, and he had to admit it: his favorite physics protégé was nowhere to be found.

Alan Jones was missing.

His elbows jarred against his stony desk and he slumped his head between them. *How can I negotiate for his time if I don't know where his Hive is?* He checked the forms for the thirty-first time. The data was the same: Alan had applied for the year-and-a-day trial Devotion, but he hadn't left a forwarding address for his leave of absence.

Let's take a look at the basic facts. He knew Alan had "defected," leaving the department in order to Devote to a Queen. This meant he was no longer a free resource, but subject to said Queen's whims. Cantor was pleased, proud even, that his young graduate student found a Queen to match, but he had the perfect project lined up, with exciting mathematics in it, and he wanted Alan back.

Even if he had to pay him. Even if he had to negotiate with a Queen for his time.

Professor Cantor glared at his four computer monitors. The public(-ish) record of springtime Devotions should have been updated and complete at this point, and Alan's name wasn't on it. Which meant Cantor couldn't find this mysterious Queen and track her movements.

There was only one reason a Devoted wouldn't show up in the public database... because he was only in a classified database. Cantor took a fortifying sip of coffee and rooted through the pads on a side table. The pads sprawled in haphazard piles that came up to his waist and intermixed with some *actual* printouts. He was mature enough to admit his office was getting out of hand.

Aha! He slid the pad he needed from its camouflaging companions, knocking essays and lab reports and last semester's final exams to clatter on the flagstone floor where his threadbare rug ended.

He would sound out his former coworkers in the intelligence division. He hated to do this, really, but it was the only way he could think to find Alan.

All right, he didn't hate to do this at all. *Let's test out my old skills.* He'd been hoping for a chance to use his old, pre-professorial contacts for, gods, fifteen years. Sure, he still got together with his old mates for a pint every now and then, but that wasn't the same as *working* together every day.

Once upon a time, "university professor" had been his cover identity; these days he had to make the role fill his life. When one has protected one's planet by means of intelligence and subterfuge, one does not easily find fulfillment in one's syllabus for Introduction to Electromagnetics. *Maybe when I retired as a field agent, I should've taken a desk job with the division.* But collating his former colleagues' reports hadn't appealed at the time.

He arranged himself in front of the pad so that only his closed office door was visible in the frame—an oar from his rowing days, mostly obscured by a winter/dinner blazer that had been hanging there a few months. Nothing that would make his general location obvious. Of course, everyone involved would *know* whence the call came, but he saw no need to demonstrate atrophied skills.

He tapped the pad's dark surface, then jostled it in a seemingly random fashion, until the screen came to life with an old colleague's face so close up so that Cantor could see nothing behind Dylan Pughe. The device's edge even cut off the top of Pughe's head.

"Max!" Pughe exclaimed. His debonair grin brimmed with white teeth. "This isn't about that hideous bout last week, is it? Because chance is as chance does."

Was this an actual friendly greeting—they *had* gone down to the pub last week—or was he missing some hidden detail in the words? If there was one thing Cantor didn't miss about being a spy, it was not knowing where you stood.

Well, he didn't have to play all the games anymore, and if Pughe was trying to play games, Cantor's straightforwardness was going to put him right off. "Hi, Dylan. I understand that you're using my protégé, Alan

Jones, in some capacity. I'd really like him for a project with my department."

Pughe's face went through contortions that showed he was appalled, bewildered, and displeased with his control over the conversation. Probably the legal-name usage had done it.

Cantor smirked and continued. "If you can't give him up, that's fine, and I'm so proud he's with you, but I'd love it if you would check for me."

Moments of silence passed. Pughe was likely looking through his own files, off screen and as surreptitiously muted as he could manage. With the breeze whistling through Cantor's windows, as well as through the trees outside, any muter's effect were lost on him.

Finally Pughe tilted his head. His wide-set eyes formed a brown-and-white dashed line on the screen. "What makes you think we have your young man?"

So *that* was how Pughe wanted to play this. "Oh, I shouldn't have said anything. It's just that he's so brilliant and he finally Devoted this year." Cantor could finesse with the best of them. The old-fashioned cloak and dagger had been the best thing about his spy days. "His Hive must have captured your people's attention. Their Queen impressed me with her self-possession when I met her, even if she was a bit young." If he made it seem as though he already knew all there was to know, Pughe would have no reason to hide that last little detail from him: where Alan actually was.

But Pughe didn't go for it. "I'm sorry, Max. We honestly haven't got him on file."

Only the dishonest had to emphasize how honest they were. "Of course you do. He's important to me as well, and his research will transform how we look at the universe. Do you know what his off-time project is?"

"I've looked in all our databases for you. I don't see his name anywhere, nor anything that looks like a young and newly Devoted Hive. If I can't find him, he's been kidnapped."

Cantor rolled his eyes. "I met his Queen, remember. They must be in some tiny registry that hasn't updated your office."

Pughe's pink lips went flat. All joking gone. "You know how important the registry is to society. I have every listing as soon as it comes in."

"Society wouldn't *collapse* if you didn't count and recount everybody."

Pughe snorted. "Besides, we've got to give them their special vaccinations." He waggled his eyebrows, good humor returning.

"I never understood those vaccinations."

"I think they were supposed to protect against some virus, like, a hundred years ago," Pughe speculated, "and now it's the way things are done. We have to do them— even if the old virus was eradicated—because we have to do them."

"Ever think about not doing them?"

Pughe laughed. "Talk to your MP."

Well, this had been a dead end. "I'm sure the local MPs have better things to worry about, and you probably do too. I'll let you go."

"All right," said Pughe, leaning back so Cantor could see all of his face and the pink tunic beneath that made his brown skin glow. Pughe was always vain. "I'll meet you for darts next week?"

"Prepare to buy another round."

"We'll see."

And like that, Cantor's most promising lead disappeared. The conversation didn't *necessarily* mean that Alan wasn't on a classified project. But, if he was, he was so far buried under aliases and codenames that Cantor wasn't finding him. Alternatively, Alan and his Queen had purposely run off together, and nobody had filed a missing persons report.

Either way, it wasn't a kidnapping, and Alan had seemed happy enough when he left. Should Cantor really go hunting for a man who didn't want to be found? Especially since Alan had most probably become embroiled in a deep-government project so far down that Cantor no longer had the clearance to even hear whispered rumors about it?

No. No he shouldn't.

Good for you, Alan. Cantor would have to find another assistant.

He misfiled the special pad among its brethren and returned to the cold coffee at his desk. As he did every time he sat down there, he checked his messages.

- Student asking for an extension
- New TA request form
- *Don't forget the departmental ice cream social!*
- A TA application
- Something about a symposium

He reread the symposium message. It came from a rival "colleague" at the University of New Cardiff. Apparently, there was an Advances in Magnetics and Aeronautics conference out on a Chinese station. And, for once, "Chinese station" wasn't a euphemism. The message started with all the usual stuff about getting together at the bar and maybe collaborating on a vague paper sometime in the unspecified future.

The interesting part came when this rival professor explained why he thought Cantor would be attending. "I see your protégé is giving a talk," he wrote. "We'll have to catch up over drinks... unless you're letting him go alone."

The ellipsis contained more than a hint of judgmental derision.

What was Alan doing all the way out in Chinese space? If he was using his name and expertise so publically, he wasn't on a deep-cover project. Nor could he be running away into anonymity.

Alan shouldn't have been able to evade Cantor's multiple spheres by *accident*, and yet... and yet.

He booked a charter for the month-long journey to Garden Station. If he left on a ship coming in five hours, he'd arrive in time for the conference. Lucky timing, that. Which may have been his rival's intent.

Cantor shut his monitors, threw a few pads into his carryall, and headed out. He sent a last hopeful message to Alan:

Alan, I'll see you at the AMAA conference. We'll get together, and I'll convince you to join me back at the university. I've got a project that's absolutely perfect for you.

There, that didn't sound too much like a curious child or an angry parent about to rein in a willful imp. It would catch up with his once-student—and hopefully soon-to-be-subordinate—whenever Alan arrived in a place that took mail packets.

Cantor looked forward to seeing Alan again and meeting his Queen more formally this time. After which, he *would* bring Alan home.

◥ Chapter Three ◢

Welcome to Garden Station

*Now: The Mandarin Station
(AKA Yin He Yuan AKA Garden Station), airlock*

Rhiannon introduced herself to the newly arrived guide first, as was her right and her duty. "I'm Queen-Commander Ceridwen, and this is my Hive."

She'd expected someone older, but their new associate was around their own age (and clearly interested in being a fashionable dresser with his multi-layered and multi-textured clothes). She introduced each Devoted and doubted he would remember them all. He'd likely be overwhelmed by six names at once. She only had to remember the one.

"I'll be your host, Wenyan Lu. You can call me Wenyan." He shook each of their hands, setting his myriad metal and plastic bracelets jangling—these in silver instead of navy like the rest of his clothes.

Gavin said, "I like your style." Her most flamboyant Devoted *would* like this inexplicable mixture of fabrics.

Victor held out an oversized jacket—a purple plastic monstrosity—to his Hive mate. "Is this your color?" he teased. Being in this place, surrounded by all these plants and poems, was good for him. It might be so good that he would do what Gwyn had done, choosing to stay on this station when Rhiannon moved on next. It might be good for all of them.

Any of them could abandon her.

"I see you've found the complimentary jackets." Wenyan's eyes sparkled and his pink lips formed a soft smile....then he lost all semblance of sophistication and peppered them with words. "Don't your space stations have seasons? It's winter in China on Earth."

Luciano engaged the guide. "I've only been on two stations before this, and neither had its own weather."

Snorting, Alan corrected: "*Simulated* weather."

Wenyan didn't notice or simply wasn't put off by Alan's comment. "Here's a secret. If you can handle the cold until you reach your room, you should use your own jackets. They'll be much more fashionable. These are kind of... unstylish?" The advice felt more personal than professional, though he'd delivered it in a gentle manner.

Rhiannon shrugged and looked over her Devoted for their reactions.

"As long as I match the rest of you." Mel was the only one to worry.

"We won't leave you behind, Mel," said Victor. Those two had a bond that none of the others yet matched. Forged in the heat of danger.

Mel's visor went a paler shade of blue, which Rhiannon had observed to mean he was happier. The lighter blue his eye visor went, the more pleased he was. With the exception of flashing white. That, she'd only seen once, and nobody had been in a good mood at the time.

"Wonderful," said Wenyan. "Let us walk."

Rhiannon fell into step beside him, leader of her Hive. Gavin shadowed her, close enough to hear the spacesuit's whisper-squeak. He'd been a bit clingy on the American station too. Was that because he'd been insecure, or because he had an actor's sense of personal space?

The halls and corridors were much like the airlock and entryway. The walls looked like plaster, with vines growing over them. Through permanently open windows she glimpsed more walls, more bamboo plants and ferns, more chrysanthemums than anyone could use for teas and fever remedies. Poetic inscriptions—she assumed—hung beside offset doors, and smaller stones hung over them.

They wended their way right and left, crossed a small bridge that overlaid a water pipe with painted waves on its surface. *Is this the silver river the station is named for?* As they traveled, she watched Wenyan move. His shoulders were astonishingly still for someone walking. From nerves over meeting his foreign guests or to keep his bracelets from jangling?

"So, which of you is Alan?" he asked. "It's you, right?" He didn't point, but nodded his head in Alan's direction.

Rhiannon wanted to pout. Shouldn't he be paying attention to her? She was Queen, after all.

But she didn't. Because that would be foolish.

Alan's eyebrows flew upwards to free his hazel eyes for wateringly wide circle-making. "Ah, yes. That's me. Alan."

Bracelets clinked, metal on plastic, and their guide dropped any pretense of stuffy officiousness. "I was impressed to see someone my age on the schedule. Are you a genius? Of course you are! Never mind. Silly question. Are there many physics geniuses where you're from?"

Rhiannon's lips quirked. Praise for her Hive was always welcome.

Alan blew out a derisive breath and wrinkled his nose to make his wide nostrils flare even further. "Are there many physics geniuses anywhere? We don't grow like fake chrysanthemums, you know."

Thankfully Wenyan was not put off by this mocking rudeness. In fact, he was yet more excited, and he skipped backwards to be in Alan's physical space. "Where did you train? How did you decide to get into physics? Are you famous on your own planet?"

The pair—Wenyan and Alan—proceeded to wave enthusiastic arms at each other. Rubber met fabric more than once. They made an amusing pair, all barely controlled flurries and flushing faces, one interested in learning and the second hiding his nerves over the upcoming presentation and language barriers.

As though he knew what Alan was thinking, Wenyan said, "Don't worry. I'll be here to navigate you through everything. And all the attendees have translators. You were lucky to get me, you know. Everyone else is super old."

Rhiannon giggled, surprising herself. It was so shallow, but she couldn't help being charmed by his energy.

Mel spoke up from the back of their pack. "I could translate."

Rhiannon hadn't realized Mel might feel slighted by a native guide.

It was true, though. Mel could pull up the station schematics for directions, and he could speak any language so long as he had some base materials to work with.

Wenyan paused, stopping their group in the middle of a twisting hallway lined with spikey plants of varying heights. He clutched a lacquered railing and rattled off something that Rhiannon couldn't interpret.

Mel said something in reply. The fry at the end sounded more unsure than interrogatory.

Wenyan smiled brightly, mouth wide open and pleased. "We should practice together," he said in English for the benefit of everyone in the party. Rhiannon appreciated the consideration. "But I don't think you can learn the station topolect—more than a dialect, less than a fresh language— in time for the conference. We don't have any teaching materials."

Mel dipped his head in graceful defeat, headlamps blinking down then back up again. "What else do you speak?"

Laughing again, Wenyan clasped his hands in front of him. "Oh, we'll have great fun. I'll send you a list."

Luciano broke in, "I don't suppose you speak Italian. *Parla italiano*?"

Wenyan shook his head, hanging it overdramatically like Gavin might. His attention returned to Rhiannon. Her chest felt a little tighter, but that was probably an effect of wearing the spacesuit for so long. It would explain her heating neck too.

"So, you're a Queen, then," he said. He took a deep breath and got out the next bit all in one go. "China doesn't have royalty anymore. We're too focused on getting everybody to the same standard of living. It's a long process. But it means we don't have queens like you. What's that like? Were you born like that? I hear there are many Queens. How do you all interact?"

Alan answered for her. "With avoidance and explosions."

"*Metaphorical* explosions," Gavin said.

Rhiannon wanted to be annoyed with this excitable guide. She'd been looking forward to settling in quietly, surrounded by her friends. But Wenyan was so genuinely curious about her home and her Hive, so unlike the last strangers they'd met.

She said, "We negotiate with each other so that our Hives"— she gestured to her Devoted—"can get what they need to live fulfilling and productive lives." Her hand ran into Gavin's chest, and he caught the offending extremity before lowering it to her side and safely away from him.

She rolled her eyes, and Gavin grinned at her. If they'd still been on the *Ceridwen's Cauldron*, she'd have put the hand right back where it had accidentally landed, daring him to move it again. This, however, was not the place to play games.

"That's so impressive." Wenyan really did sound impressed and interested. If he'd never been off his home station before, it made sense that he had an intense fascination with all things Not From Here.

Their little caravan resumed walking, Wenyan and Rhiannon in the lead. The corridors were just wide enough for the two side by side. A third abreast would be dodging fronds and tripping into circularly curved portal frames.

"May I make a suggestion?" Wenyan asked, voice tremulous like a student in a class. "Maybe you'll want to introduce yourself just as *Queen Ceridwen*, not Queen-Commander? There's a military connotation in my language that might upset certain parties."

That was interesting hedging. Rhiannon shrugged. What did it matter? The "Commander" title was more about personality and organization as far as Dyfed was concerned. Her position wouldn't change just because the name did. It was only a translation issue, not a request for her to alter her methods. And, really, she was Queen, after all.

I may have cheated the Test and picked up an unorthodox Hive, but no one can deny my status now.

Victor took his place as close behind her right hand as he could, displacing Gavin to her left-side shadow. Rhiannon wasn't surprised. Someone had mentioned *military* and implied that she may be in danger.

Victor had a history of dedication to her physical service—starting with the instance of his Devotion in a pool of his own blood after taking a bullet for her.

She wanted to learn more about their guide. "Do you get a lot of visitors here?"

Wenyan nodded, artful hair not moving a centimeter. "I love meeting people from other places. It helps me appreciate what I have even more. And, like I said, you're my age. Do you know how many foreigners we meet who are our age? All my friends are station born."

We could be friends. Rhiannon smiled shyly and reached up to twirl a lock of hair in her fingers. Her rubber-coated hands encountered only air. Oh, right. She'd pulled it all back to stay out of her way in the gravity-less docking accordion… and also to look more intimidating underneath her crown. Powerful women pulled their hair back, unlike teenagers who let it fall free.

Wenyan continued, excessively casual. "We could be friends too. Not just coworkers."

"Yes!" Rhiannon pounced on the agreement, not casual at all. "I'd like that. *We'd* like that."

It was always better to have friends. Hadn't the ladies at Cleopatra's proven that on John Wayne? Wasn't it the point of Hives in general? And Wenyan would be a good friend to have. He was knowledgeable and curious, interesting and interested. *And quite good-looking.* She pressed her lips together, half embarrassed at the thought and half hoping nobody picked up on it.

Nodding emphatically in her peripheral vision, Gavin agreed. "I was raised on multiple stations and planets," he said. *"Those friends thou hast…"* Gavin trailed off as if the rest of his quote were obvious.

Victor slapped at Gavin's shoulder, rubber snapping against rubber.

"And here we are." Wenyan brought them to a stop and slid open a section of plaster wall into a hidden pocket.

Where the rest of the station had unexpected sectioning and offset door placement, this wall opened onto a shiny, but very normal, living area. Glossy laminate planks covered the floor, topped by a tan sectional couch and two uncushioned bar stools that weren't bolted down. No one here was worried about losing gravity.

The leftmost wall had a white screen on it with a shelf underneath. The back wall held framed calligraphic art, and the rightmost a collection of family photos next to a counter with a hotplate.

There were no plants.

Wenyan rapped on the wall where they'd come in. "I'll be back in two mornings to escort you to the conference. Until then, you're free to call on me for help settling in or comparing our station to your home or anything. Okay? Okay."

Rhiannon wanted to reach out and touch him. Just to shake hands, even. His skin called to hers. But she shook off the urge and gave him a regal nod instead. "How do we contact you?"

He gestured to the white wall. "Right! You see the screen here. You synch your arm band to it, and it'll show you everything you need."

Slowly, Gavin said, "We don't have arm bands like you do."

Wenyan shrugged. "I'm sure whatever you do have will work fine. We like smaller things here." He put on a face that was clearly mimicking something, but Rhiannon had no idea what. "*Smaller is safer*," he recited.

"Ah." Gavin didn't sound convinced.

Thankfully, they had Mel. "I've worked with this technology before."

"Wonderful!" said Wenyan. "So I'll see you in two days if not before." He gave a little wave and a smaller bow. *Delightful!*

Rhiannon forgot about settling in. She forgot about cajoling Alan's nervous worries away and looking after her other Devoted. Her mind focused on one thing: she hoped to meet Wenyan again soon.

Chapter Four

Do PRobs Pray to Electric Deities?

Yin He Yuan (Garden Station),
Rhiannon's Hive's flat

Later that same night, Mel moved his memory chips, old badge, and second-favorite knife into a dresser beside a bed with a Marilyn Monroe comforter. The American icon made him nostalgic for the Star Rangers and his anachronistic ex-boss. The other two beds in the room—Alan's and Victor's—had embroidered bedspreads, but Mel hadn't minded being the odd one out. Not in this case.

Alan peeked up from rummaging in a desk drawer and brandished a sphere. It was small and dense like a baseball on Mel's sensors, and its discovery led to Mel's roommates to playing the most physical game of catch he'd ever witnessed off an outdoor diamond. Who knew tossing a ball around could involve so much *tackling?* The grunting and rolling took the young men across the floor and over the now-rumpled bedspreads.

They were *indoors* and sure to break something that didn't belong to them. Mel stretched an arm out as if he could catch the ball when it next flew by, but Victor tackled Alan into Mel's forelegs and the resultant screech convinced him that simple avoidance was the right choice.

Mel left the tussling boys alone in favor of joining whoever was in the main room.

He emerged into perfect calm and sensible economy of motion. Rhiannon and Gavin shared the couch and appeared to be reciting poetry. The back-and-forth of metered verse paused when Mel stopped in the doorway.

He could turn back around. Instead of bothering their entertainment, he could deal with the rambunctious childishness in the room he'd vacated. *Are they more aggressive in their playtimes because they're younger than I am, because they're boys, or because they're human?* Mel had no good frame of reference.

"Come sit with us," Rhiannon said. She beckoned to the area beside the couch, plenty of space for Mel to comfortably lower himself to seated height. If he compacted his limbs.

"I wouldn't want to interrupt." Mel stretched and retracted his twenty-four fingers, low and out of his Queen's sight. In the kitchen area, Luciano snorted; apparently, he'd been of the same mind and had gotten out of the way. Mel hadn't even noticed he was there until he'd made the slight noise.

Gavin waved a dismissive arm, billowy sleeve swaying. "We're practicing our delivery for the upcoming poetry contests we won't attend." His heartbeat and respiration stayed even. So, not upset about missing some poetic rite of passage.

Mel took up the indicated space, still a bit taller than his Hive mates.

Rhiannon restarted her declaiming in a whispery voice that sounded like magic and brushed across his metal skin though he sat well behind her mouth. "*Cw ddeuynt, lletgynt, llid anoeth,*" she began.

He cross-referenced the word with the partial database he'd brought from the *Cauldron* for assimilation and found it was from the middle of a medieval poem written by a court poet. America had never had court poets. This merited further study.

Alan dashed into the room, hunched over his tablet, with Victor close behind.

Victor stumbled into a tall chair. "I feel a bit twinge-y. Hey, Luciano, can I get you to look at my shoulder?" Victor rotated his previously damaged shoulder in its socket, almost as well as Mel could rotate his own. It was an impressive range of motion.

The shoulder might have been aggravated by the birthday party they'd held for Victor en route to Garden Station. Mel's gift to him had been more fighting lessons. (Alan's, interestingly, had been a burning oak stick he'd brought from home, putting its smoky flavor in the air. Rhiannon had explained that this was meant to make the place seem like a real oak grove because Victor's patron god was Lleu Llaw Gyffes, whose worship included the making of oak fires.)

Or the foolishly overactive game of catch with Alan could have knocked the shoulder out of alignment.

"What's the point?" Luciano stood behind Victor anyway, placing one hand on the front of the affected joint and the other on Victor's elbow. He moved the arm from the lower position upwards, flexing his high fingers and feeling for movement. "The Americans fixed you to perfection, and they're right. You don't need the stress ball anymore." Pronouncement made, he curled up in a bar chair, feet on the seat.

Victor drew the ball from his pocket and threw it in the air like a graduation cap, but put it back after catching it. "I think I'll hold onto this all the same."

Like Mel held onto his memory chips? He hadn't even been able to leave them behind on the ship, in case of a repeat of John Wayne Station. If he had to leave in a hurry, he couldn't bear to abandon this proof of all his lives.

Her lives, until now.

"Still," Victor mused, "Happy birthday to me."

On the couch, Gavin laughed and began a chorus of "Happy Birthday." And why not? Yes, Victor's birthday was weeks over, but if the others wanted to sing, then Mel would too. He pitched his voice a bit higher than the smooth basso he'd affected until now. That tone hadn't fit his body. The excessive deepness had been all wrong, and he hoped this new baritone would resonate better.

Besides, the Hive didn't need another bass. Alan proved this when he added a coda to the tune, finishing with a deep flourish all the way down to the bottom of his range. "Happy birthday to yoooou."

The last note was sharp, but Mel was probably the only one to hear it.

Gavin said, "We should start a men's chorus."

"Yes!" Alan was the first to agree. His lips quirked on the left and the muscles around his eyes relaxed. His heart rate increased slightly, and he bounced in place. Conclusion: genuine interest.

"Count me out," said Victor.

"And me," said Luciano.

Alan's heart slowed to a more standard tempo. "What about you, Mel?"

"Of course." How could he say no to anything? He'd never sought out interpersonal involvement but knew he had to cement the bonds with his Hive mates. That was what Dyfed Hives were about.

Top five things Mel liked about being Devoted to Queen-Commander Ceridwen:

- Being alive
- Retaining his memories
- Friendly shipmates who treated him like a person
- Teaching (e.g., Victor about martial arts and strategy)
- Learning about his adopted culture (in this case, music)

Gavin offered, "If you need singing lessons..."

"And I can chime in on ukulele," said Rhiannon, "if this isn't a boys-only club." Her voice faded at the end of the sentence, and the human Devoted took that as a sign to pile on in a massive cuddle that buried her at the bottom. "Oof!"

Mel focused his sensors to make sure the Queen-Commander wasn't actually crushed. Her breathing was faster and more labored, but she laughed and petted whoever her hands could reach.

"Of course we want you with us, in any way you're willing to be," said Gavin.

Mel stayed out of the pile. Queen-Commander Ceridwen wouldn't bear well under the weight of an armor-plated PRob.

"While you four are singing, what about the rest of us?" asked Victor. "I guess that's just you and me, Luciano."

"We could do logic puzzles for fun and maybe get to a competitive level?"

Mel hadn't seen Victor alone since they'd left John Wayne. He was always training with Mel or Gavin, eating with whoever was in the dining room, or offering to help Luciano with the piloting vectors.

"Sounds great," said Victor. But his mouth and pulse rate both stayed flat.

"You know what else is a good idea?" asked Rhiannon. "Getting off of me."

A chorus of *sorrys* and grunts echoed through the common room as the Devoted detached themselves from their Queen.

Free of the smothering, Rhiannon's voice emerged less muffled when she spoke. "Quick check: Mel, has anyone approached our ship?"

The change of subject wasn't subtle but it didn't have to be. The Queen-Commander was among her friends and most trusted Hive mates. If Mel understood correctly, they were each meant to be an extension of a single unit. He was probably doing it wrong, too used to being on his own.

What he wasn't certain of in Dyfed Hive dynamics, however, he could offset with obedience. *Devotion, in the American PRob style.* He sent out pings to all his systems, felt the return echoes all the way down to his deepest drive casing. "No, my lady. The ship is untouched."

Her temperature spiked up on his thermal scanners. He'd bet it was a byproduct of overstimulated adrenals. "Are you sure?" she asked.

A little caution was to be encouraged, but it didn't belong on people so young. Rhiannon's pink eartips proved she knew her anxiety had gone too far.

Gavin slung an arm around her shoulders and squeezed her gently to his pliable body. No one ever wanted hugs from a robot like Mel. His thick skin had no give, no comfort to offer. He'd let the biological Hive members give the hugs. "You have to trust us to do our jobs," Gavin said.

Top four things Mel disliked about being Devoted to Queen-Commander Ceridwen's Hive:

- Leaving the American Space Rangers
- Being the oldest person on the ship (forty years from manufacturer's date, though only seven years from his latest coming to sentience)
- Being *The Weird One*: not a druid, not from the Dyfed system, schooled differently, synthetic
- Not solving crimes and saving lives every day

Mel cocked a headlamp and whirred to get Victor's attention. "Tell me more about this patron god idea." It had seemed an integral part of the real birthday party, but he hadn't found much definitive in the literature for self-study.

"Just, y'know, who you identify with and pray to, which god cares most about you personally, though you can call on all of them when you need. It's that kind of thing." Victor was both informative and very obviously unable to articulate the concept, all at once.

"How did you pick yours?"

"Well, I was born in Lleu's season. And something about him speaks to me. So I've built the relationship over time."

Mel's top arms flailed. "I want a patron god!"

"Or goddess," Victor amended.

Mel dipped his spherical head. "It'll help me fit in with the rest of you."

Victor narrowed his eyes. "That's not why you get a patron god. It has to mean something to you on a spiritual level, not a self-interested one."

Mel's right headlamp cocked. "Do you think I *have* a spiritual level?"

"Why wouldn't you?"

Why wouldn't I, indeed. These kids from Dyfed had a very different view of PRobs than anyone Mel had ever met.

"How about a god of engineers and cleverness and lawfulness?" Gavin said, settling back onto his half of the couch across from the Commander. "Mel's clever and engineered, *and* he used to be in law enforcement. Manawyddan would be perfect."

Mel flexed his headlamps. *Used to be.* "Hmmm." Nothing about that description had warmed his circuits. Including the masculine pronouns. He'd been a woman during his law enforcement days. Shouldn't the discussion reflect that?

"Perhaps," Luciano said, "instead of forcing yourself to fit the druidic panthecn, you don't want a patron god at all."

Perhaps. But he *did* want to bond with his Hive mates, which Luciano was refusing to do on this vector. All twenty-four of Mel's fingers splayed out with the tips curled inwards. He would do all the things that a Dyfed Devoted was supposed to do. He would not be swayed.

He'd been the American Space Rangers' best tracker, and he'd be a Dyfed Hive's best *something*. As soon as he figured out what.

"Of course we don't want to force him into anything," Rhiannon agreed with Luciano. "But we can lay out some options."

Victor twisted his mouth. "You already turned down my god, but maybe you should think about him some more. You're better than I am at the worshipful battle exhibitions."

Worship. How human must one be in order to worship a deity effectively?

Mel dipped his head. "I need a deity of machines."

"We'll start there." Gavin pulled out his tablet and leaned forwards. "What else do you need?"

Mel's perfect deity (working list):
- Of machines and for machines (possibly a sentient machine itself!)
- ~~Male~~ *gender neutral* female
- Likes lists
- Worship via... something Mel is good at (come back to this later)
- On friendly terms with the other Hive deities
- Special power: fixing machines, of course!

Alan compressed his lips and let them out on a pop that spiked in Mel's smallest microphone. "You could make up your own."

Mel wished he could access the *Cauldron*'s complete database, instead of the partial he'd brought along for study. A search for the most recent addition to the Dyfed pantheon offered up offshoots from the major names as well as tentative deletions and insertions that didn't appear to be actually taken as gods, yet had backgrounds and stories around them. "I don't need another reason to be weird."

Rhiannon stroked Mel's closest hand. "As Queen, I'm here to be your intercessor for the gods. You can take as long as you want to decide on a patron. Or never. It's up to you."

Alan opened his arms like he was giving a planet a hug. "It's about authenticity"—he shook the right hand—"versus validity." He shook the left.

Definition: authentic—of undisputed origin.

Definition: valid—having a sound basis in logic or fact.

"If your god works for you, then he's real, and everyone will respect that," Alan explained. "They might look at you funny when they don't recognize the name, but effectiveness is more important."

He presented it like an unassailable fact. But his hands were cooler on Mel's thermal sensors while his head was illness/anxiousness hot.

Mel felt his visor flash white. Making his own had even more room for error than picking an existing god or goddess... though it would let him choose those aspects that were most important to *himself*. "Is it allowed?"

"It's not *disallowed*," Alan said. "And it's been done before. Just not... recently."

By the time they left the Mandarin Station, Mel *would* have a deity of his own.

Chapter Five

Meanwhile, Back on Dyfed

Planet Dyfed, hiking trails

Olivia puffed as she hiked up the steep hill. After a century on nice flat spaceships, this wasn't what her creaky joints were used to. *"Let's start with the girlfriend!" What was I thinking?* She knew what she'd been thinking. She'd wanted to question the known associates of the doctor who'd held her captive and experimented on her, and the girlfriend was the most obvious one.

"We'll take break at the top of the hill," said Amanda, the girlfriend. "You'll want to experience the view."

If Olivia was going to discover where the other stolen Queens went, she needed information. And if she planned to expose the vile tormentors involved in the plot, she had to start with the tormentor she knew. Still... *When Paul found out Doctor Holly had a mother and a girlfriend, I should've gone with the mother. Milk and cookies and a sitting room, that'd be better than all this outdoor exercise.*

Paul was right behind her, of course. Probably thinking that he'd told her so. Her Hive weren't letting her meet a potential suspect alone—she didn't *want* to go anywhere alone, truth be told—and they had wanted to see Holly's mother first. Olivia's Devoted had figured the mother probably wasn't complicit. Which was exactly why Olivia had chosen to visit the girlfriend. Who turned out to be a hiking instructor. *Great.*

Olivia stumbled over a stick and could only be grateful there were a mere two people to witness her grace level.

Paul caught her. "Are you all right?" he whispered. Louder, "We can leave if this is too much."

"I'm fine." She scowled at him, feeling the lines around her mouth deepen. She'd scowled a lot lately: in her dreams, when she woke up and realized what time it was, when people asked her questions. "It's just this extra gravity." She shook off his arm.

"We could take a fruit juice break," Amanda offered.

"How very kind of you." Before going deeper into the questioning, she needed to create rapport: "So, what prompted you to start your own hiking business?"

Amanda took a deep breath through her nose, as though scenting the trail. "Who wouldn't want to spend time outdoors?" she asked. "Technically, I was supposed to be an accountant, but the world has plenty of accountants, and I'm a woman, so..."

As a woman herself, Olivia wasn't entirely sure what that meant. "So?" she prompted.

Amanda startled back, spine thumping into the tree behind her. "So I wasn't a Devoted or anything important like that. Nobody cared. Maybe it was different for your generation."

Very different. There were no hiking instructors in Olivia's generation because people didn't hike for leisure. They'd all learned together how to navigate this new world, or they'd died. From exposure, dehydration, or any number of causes. The first generation of terraforming children had lived in much harsher times. It made them hardy and determined. So that Olivia, among the first to be raised on this world—though born on Earth one hundred and fifty seven years ago—could keep up with her hiking. "Would you want to be a Devoted?"

Amanda laughed, but the sound was short. "No, no, not for me. My girlfriend, though. If she'd been male, she would have been Devoted." Her voice was quiet when she added, "At least we met in our thirties. I can believe those alternate versions of us would still have fallen in love after the Queen-Devoted honeymoon period."

A fantasy, of course. Even if they'd still met in their thirties, the Queen-Devoted stabilization period lasted *at least* ten years. Holly wouldn't necessarily have been ready for an out-of-Hive relationship, and it certainly couldn't have been serious unless the Hive was based locally and had needed to see Amanda—and liked her—over a long term.

Amanda was lucky her girlfriend hadn't been able to Devote. Or maybe she wasn't so lucky. After all, Holly's sins had brought her to Olivia's attention.

A loud inhalation behind her, and Olivia flicked a hand at waist level. *Wait*, it told Paul, *back off while I question my informant.*

"I met your girlfriend recently, you know." Olivia knew that Holly wasn't the true villain in the Queen torture. The neuroscientist hadn't *really* been in charge, and had kindly let Olivia go, but she was the only lead Olivia had.

"Are you a patient at her clinic?" Amanda busied herself with uncapping her flask. Olivia couldn't read her expression.

Olivia hummed, neither confirming nor denying. "She's a brilliant woman." It might even have been true. After all this time, Olivia still wasn't sure what exactly the experiments had been about.

But Olivia's noncommittal reply had tipped Amanda off. "Look, Holly is a bit of an agitator, but she's also brilliant, like you said." Amanda stowed her flask and turned away, back to the trail. "I know she's doing the right thing wherever she is, so don't go telling me anything else. You're wrong. Let's move out. Break is over."

Olivia readjusted her much tinier pack and followed with no fuss. She waited a few meters, until Amanda had a chance to raise her heart rate and feel the calm that comes over hikers while on the trail. "Holly helped me. She hid me from my enemies."

It had been a nightmare. Dizzying alarms and flashing lights. The orderlies who'd held her down and spiked needles into her brain ran to and fro, then jostled each other and fought to pack up the Queen cargo, the torture medicines, the medical devices. To get out.

Olivia's hands shook as she pulled at invisible straps. On a table, in a cell, it was all a trap. Her heart pounded, so loud in her ears that she couldn't hear the shrieking sirens that demanded evacuation. She opened her mouth to scream, to beg for release, but nothing came out. Only the bile on her tongue to fight her heart's gonging.

Sound whooshed back in as Holly appeared in front of her. The woman was all she could see. A large face and a white coat. Disembodied. Holly had seemed like the worst and most detached of the lot until she'd pulled Olivia aside and given her freedom. Freedom and a last needle prick to knock her out.

Olivia slapped at the site. *Get it out of me!* Her breath came shallow as she scratched the wound.

Needles and screaming. Crowds of herded Queens who'd lost their minds. Crying and alarm whoops.

"Your ladyship? Your ladyship!"

"My lady! Olivia!"

The sirens in her mind resolved into words. She wasn't *there* anymore. Not below ground and hopeless. No, she was on the surface. Hiking in the open air with Paul to protect her and a sweet-seeming young lady to guide her.

"Terribly sorry," said Olivia, "I must have missed you calling me. The gravity, you know." As excuses went, it needed some work. *I can't let myself get so easily disturbed.*

Paul hauled her close to his side and wouldn't let go. "You were screaming," he accused.

Her throat was raw, but she didn't remember making noise. Only choking on the attempt.

"I'm glad my Holly could help you," Amanda said. The younger woman reached out a compassionate hand, but let it drop before making contact with Olivia's still-shaking shoulders. "Whatever you escaped must have been awful."

Thank you, my dear. Not for the clumsy sympathy, but for getting back to the investigation. "I'd like to find her and thank her, but she's moved to another site." *Sirens and screaming.*

"If you know that, then you know she should be back soon."

"Do you have a way for me to get in touch? Perhaps through another mutual friend?"

Amanda tilted her head to the side, evaluating Olivia on some scale. She produced her tiny pad. "I've got a photo." She swiped the screen six times before turning the device. "Do you recognize anyone in this picture? It's from a work picnic a few years ago. One of these people recruited Holly onto her 'special project.'"

Five people posed outdoors beside a human-made lake. The clinic staff spanned multiple generations, and Olivia recognized two of the women. One was Holly, and the other was her own school friend Effie.

Effie! The aging woman could be in serious trouble if she'd come to these agitators' attention. Ffion Kendrick, the Permanent Undersecretary for the Department of Health and Well-Being, was not just an old friend but also high up enough in government to make a difference in the world. Which meant she was a prime target for anyone who wanted to influence or threaten her.

When Olivia had come to, finally free of captivity and 100 percent conscious again, she'd gone to Effie's office. Olivia had hoped they could investigate the Queen stealers together, but Effie was away on the periodic Earth tour of Wales.

Anyone could have gone with her as staff or ship's crew. Anyone could be plotting to attack her the way they'd done to Olivia.

Though Olivia had decided over a month ago not to bother her old friend, preferring to take over the investigation herself for the time being, she couldn't let this stand. She had to warn Effie of the danger!

And she could simultaneously check on the other people in the photo. "Can you send me a copy?" she asked Amanda.

"Of course."

Obviously Effie wasn't the mysterious mentor, but she might have insight into the other three picnic-goers. Olivia sipped the air between barely parted lips. *If only I could report these findings to someone I trusted!* But until her friend returned from Earth, there was nobody in government she could trust. The Queen stealers had been backed by some low-level officials, possibly including that Llewellyn weasel who Olivia had unknowingly foisted off on the new Commander Ceridwen, which left only Olivia herself for the investigation.

"Thank you for your time and cooperation," Olivia said.

Amanda bobbed her head. "I'm always happy to help Holly's friends."

Later that same night, Olivia sequestered herself in her bedroom in the rundown house which had been provided for her on her return to Dyfed. "I need to make a video message," she'd told her six Devoted. "Shoo!"

They'd shooed.

Alone, she waved at the camera, conscious of the peeling paint and crooked doorways behind her. The house was in a bedroom community for the capital city of Machynlleth, but a home that had gone unused for decades.

She'd remembered the area as a nice place to live, and leapt to claim it from the government's availability lists when they'd offered her free housing in return for her service. These days, though, the location seemed populated entirely by people her own age and young non-Hive families. She might have to move. Later. Right now, she was comfortable enough.

"Hi, Effie," she said to the camera. To her friend who would receive it in a few days with the rest of the mail packet. "I ran into someone today who knows you, and I thought I'd share this adorable photo she had."

Keeping Effie updated while maintaining a certain level of circumspection took time, effort, and five versions of the video. In the end perhaps she was *too* circumspect. How did you warn a friend about a potential danger without tipping off an assistant who might read her mail *and* be in on the plot?

No matter what Effie knew or could share, though, Olivia's old friend was still on Earth for the foreseeable future. Olivia was alone in her work to discover the parties responsible for kidnapping and experimenting on Queens.

So far she'd questioned a conspiracy member's known associate. What next?

She rejoined her Devoted in the house's sitting area. Four men were arranged on overstuffed couches. Paul's hands hovered over the coffee table-cum-space heater at the room's center, his blanket fallen low enough for Hideki to stick his feet under it. Mark's face was bathed in pad-screen light, and Alexander snored quietly beside him.

Olivia crossed the uneven carpet on bare feet, unlocking and relocking the front door to make sure it was really secured. "Where are Owen and Toan?"

Mark set his pad down on the table-heater with a clink that made her jump and woke Alexander. "They went to bed already. It's pretty late, Liv."

Her heart thudded against her skin, faster and faster, hard enough to shake her. She kept her back to the men lest they be able to see the overclocked throbbing in her chest. Her toes curled into the carpet, focusing on the scratchy texture to keep herself in the now. Breathing deep, willing her body to calm, she unlocked and relocked the windows. *No one is getting in here unless I allow it.*

It was a false security. Any determined villain could break the glass or force the walls. Could drag her down to—

Paul walked through her field of vision and took her shaking hands in his recently warmed ones. "You don't usually go barefoot," he observed as he tugged her towards the couch he'd vacated.

She let him arrange her under his abandoned blanket. Hideki twitched it down to cover even her pinkies, warming feet she didn't even know had gone cold until fire rushed into the skin. Had it been so long since she'd taken care of herself that she'd simply forgotten socks? Did she even still want to wear the confining garments?

"I need your help," she said, ignoring the clothing dilemma. Mark and Alexander leaned forwards on their couch, postures twinned, chins on palms connected to elbows atop knees.

Paul sank to the floor in front of her. "What can we do?" His voice was breathless. Maybe this was too much for him.

"I'm investigating what happened to me," she said. They knew that much, having helped her choose whom to question first. "But I don't know what to do next. How do I conduct an investigation?"

"Fingerprints!" Mark burst out, body surging off the couch before falling back onto it with a blush across his space-pale cheeks and nose. "I mean," he said, more quietly, "that's how you determine whether people are who they say they are—or are in the right place."

It sounded more like he'd been reading detective novels than actually knowing about the subject, and she was about to say so when Alexander backed him up. "Yes, fingerprints are key to discovering the identity secrets of your witnesses and enemies. You'll also need to ask a lot of questions. *Question everything*." His eyebrows rose and then rose again on the last two words, emphasizing his seriousness.

When Alexander got serious, she could trust his information. Rarely in their century together had he expressed a straightforward opinion. Usually, he'd say something more like "in seven out of ten studies, the majority of the results suggested that questioning might be the best course of action." He required a certain level of fact or probability before he'd state something this boldly.

Paul had his hands back in the heat, so his face was hidden. "Don't you need disguises?" he asked.

That was definitely taken more from spy movies than from reality, but she couldn't discount his suggestions without disrespecting his position in the brainstorming.

"Hideki?" She stroked the toes of her so-far silent Devoted. "Would you take notes please?"

This investigation would be good for her Hive. They would have a focus again, other than to simply survive retirement. They could exercise their creativity and research skills in pursuit of a worthy goal.

She'd get them all involved.

Chapter Six

It's Only Natural

Yin He Yuan (Garden Station),
Rhiannon's Hive's flat

That first evening, Rhiannon sprawled on the tan sectional in their flat's common room. Gavin lay beside her with his feet under her thighs and head hanging over the arm rest. Alan fiddled inside the drawer portion of the storage shelf underneath the wall screen. Rhiannon had no idea what he was looking for, but was sure that going through the original occupants' belongings was a breach of good manners.

Luciano sat in a tall chair, engrossed in his pad. Victor stood next to the other, shifting from foot to foot in a way that betrayed too much nervous energy for simply *sitting down*. "Let's get dinner," Victor said.

Alan slammed the drawer shut. "Yes! Food."

What is Wenyan doing for dinner tonight? She didn't ask that. "I wonder if there's anything in the kitchen area," Rhiannon said. Maybe the others would pick up the hint and go check.

"Or," Victor said, "we could go out." His restless shifting picked up speed.

"See the station," Alan chimed in.

"Not use someone else's supplies," Victor added.

Luciano looked up from his pad, brows wrinkled. "Where would we go?"

He made a good point. So far, they'd seen the docking area and these quarters. Without Mel, who was still in a bedroom, they'd never find their way to a cafeteria. They wouldn't even be able to find the airlock. *This station seems designed to confuse unwary travelers.* Rhiannon patted Gavin's knee beside her, indicating that he should extricate his limbs since it looked like they were going out.

Gavin didn't move. "We should ask Wenyan," he said.

Rhiannon's stomach swooped. Yes, he'd offered his guidance at any time, but what if they were bothering him? She wanted to see him again. She wasn't ready to see him again.

She tapped her lips with her finger, a tight tattoo.

"Yes, good," Alan said. "Obviously that's the right answer." His brusque voice made the words sound condescending, but he meant them in a more positive spirit than they came across.

Gavin, familiar with Alan's ways at this point, nodded acceptance of the praise.

Her four human Devoted aimed their faces at Rhiannon. Expectant.

"What?"

Gavin nudged her thigh with his sock-clad toes. "You should call him and ask."

Why me? Oh, yes. Because she was Queen and it was her duty to contact their guide in order to provide for her whole Hive.

Gavin continued, *"Let us have Ram's vetches on Aries!"*

Sometimes his declamations made no sense at all. Rhiannon poked his closer calf. But that was as much distraction from her responsibility as mild punishment. Under her crown, her forehead heated. What if she called him and said something brainless? What if he thought it was weird, and he'd only made the offer out of politeness? Because it was weird. Totally weird. They could go exploring without a local guide. Mel sort of knew the language.

None of those were good excuses in the face of her Hive's desires.

Rhiannon said, "I need to figure out what to wear first. Why don't you call?"

And that was the weakest excuse she'd ever given for anything. She tried not to look any of them in the eye after saying it, but caught Gavin's expression out of the corner of her vision. His mouth was pressed into a flat line with the place where dimples would be on a smiler replaced by—what should she call them—*disappointment dimples*? His eyes looked like they were tilting up because his brows had crumpled downwards. He opened his mouth and sucked in a breath, clearly to school her in something, but closed it again. Words unsaid.

If there were ever a face that called someone out on their ridiculous words, it was *his* face.

Alan was oblivious to all that. "What's wrong with what you've got on?" he asked. He'd never been much for fashion.

He was right, though. There was nothing special about her clothes... and nothing special about anything she could change into either.

Bobbing yet more energetically on his feet, Victor suggested. "Call first, then dress. That way, we'll be ready to go soonest. And if he's not there, you haven't lost any time."

Rhiannon's breath sped up. What could she say that would absolve her of this?

"Why don't you want to call?" Luciano stared down at his pad, the ultimate in non-confrontational posture. The position didn't muffle his voice.

She firmed her shoulders and beckoned for Alan to pass her the pad that he'd connected to the screen. "I'll call. I only wanted to dress first. It's not important."

Gavin pulled his feet out from under her and patted her on the wrist. His face was knowing—smirking and with eyelids at half-mast—like they were sharing a secret, but she wasn't sure what the secret might be. "I'll do it. You go freshen up."

Taking Alan's outstretched pad, Gavin tapped to a directory. His choices were mirrored on the flat's large wall screen. "Hmmmm." While the word *Directory* had been written in multiple languages, the names of the station residents appeared in Chinese characters. Gavin scrolled.

Rhiannon stood from the couch and stretched, slowly. She had nowhere to be now that she wasn't in charge of making the call. Arms overhead, then bending at the waist.

"That one!" Alan waved his arms in large arcs. "I have an email with that name on it."

Victor said, "Maybe we should ask Mel." Louder, he called out, "Hey! Mel!" Mel ambled in, four booted feet silent even on the wooden floors. Mel was a master of stealth. "Which of these people is our Wenyan?"

Mel cocked a headlamp and turned a medium-blue visor to the screen. "Fourth one."

"Hah!" Alan crowed. "Told you."

Gavin tapped on the name, accompanied by a warbling *blip*, and let the call connect on the station intranet.

In two blips, Rhiannon retreated to the little kitchen where she moved the hotplate first to the right a few centimeters. Then to the left.

In four blips, Wenyan's pinkened face filled the screen, his smooth nose the size of Gavin's head. Speakers filled the room with chattering people and clattering goods. Behind Wenyan's right ear, a yellow paper lantern lit the image. His left ear didn't fit in the picture.

"Hey," said Gavin, losing his regular articulation. "That is, hello. Ah, *shwmae*?"

Hovering behind Luciano's chair, out of the picture, Alan snarked. "Like the guy will speak Cymraeg."

Luciano came to Gavin's defense. "Second languages are hard. Maybe it's Gavin's default when he's speaking to someone who doesn't necessarily use English. Sometimes I say things in Italian when the rest of you use Cymraeg."

"Hello, and 您好," said Wenyan. *Nín hǎo.* She'd heard that before. "How can I help you this evening?"

"Right, so we wanted to eat dinner and hoped you had a recommendation." Gavin sounded almost as nervous as Rhiannon had felt about initiating this conversation. Maybe there was no good way for an outsider to feel comfortable in a new place, other than to push through until one wasn't an outsider anymore.

In reply, Wenyan listed an overwhelming selection of food styles and places, as one does when asked for such consultation. He came to the end of his recitation and asked, "Do you need me to tell you again?"

"If you're not too busy," said Gavin, "why don't you join us?" He speared Rhiannon with sly eyes. She busied herself with more nothingness behind the kitchen counter, knowing she hadn't fooled him at all.

Wenyan nodded, briefly flashing his wispily parted black hair onto the screen before his face returned. "I could pick up a few options with your conference speaker expense allowance. Some local goodies for you to eat in your room. You must be tired."

"That sounds perfect," Gavin chirped. "See you in a few?"

Wenyan performed the top-of-the-head maneuver again. "I look forward to seeing you and your Queen soon." His video transmission cut off.

And your Queen. Why did he mention Rhiannon specifically? It could have been because she was nominally in charge. That would make sense. But it could have been that he was *thinking* about her in the way she'd been purposely not thinking about him.

It could have been.

Yes yes yes. And no no no. She hadn't prepared for this.

Mel made a throat-clearing sound from his speakers, gathering the attention of all in the room. "Now that that's decided," he began.

Victor cut him off. "Have you already picked your patron god? I still think it ought to be Lleu so you can back me up in protecting Rhiannon. I'm not the best fighter in the Hive anymore."

That had been true since Mel had joined up, over a month ago. Possibly had been true since the beginning when Gavin had been Victor's teacher. Rhiannon tapped a finger against her bottom lip, a gesture she'd picked up since Victor and Alan had made her a crown. Since she couldn't run a hand through her hair anymore.

"So?" Mel asked.

"So you should take over as Rhiannon's bodyguard and strategy consultant."

It wasn't a bad idea. Mel did have more experience and interest in protection duties. They'd taken the American Space Ranger out of American space, but could they change him so fundamentally?

Mel synthesized the smoothest laugh Rhiannon had ever heard. "No, thank you. I'm law enforcement, not security."

Victor huffed. "You know you want to." But the edge of his mouth tilted up with relief. "You'd better at least be willing to step in when necessary. Rhiannon's safety is more important than—"

"Speaking of jobs…" Mel trailed off, then started again in a stronger voice, "If the rest of you don't mind, I'd like to try out being the Hive's bard. I did myself some research on your society's history, and lots of the old courts had bards and historians. Right now, ours doesn't."

Before, Mel was a brilliant American Space Ranger, and now he was trying to be a brilliant Dyfed Devoted. Was this really what he wanted? Or did he feel obligated to be the perfect Hive mate? She could only give him space and time to find out.

"Do we even need a bard?" Alan asked. And that was just not on. Hive members were meant to support each other, not demand justification. No one had asked if she needed a physicist when Alan joined her Hive!

Luciano muttered, "Technically, this Hive doesn't need anything." And that was definitely true. While most Hives came together in order to further some specialization, Rhiannon's had been utterly ad hoc: made entirely of people she knew personally and for the purpose of getting away from Dyfed before romances and friend groups were split asunder.

How far we've come.

"*Success depends on beauty,*" Gavin quoted from gods-knew-what. "I, for one, believe a bard would be welcome."

Victor slouched, obviously content that Mel wasn't taking over his place. Rhiannon realized that she was the only one who could see his smile.

Grumbling, Alan shoved his hands into his pockets. Wordless.

"We would be honored," Rhiannon said. As she'd told Luciano, Mel could try out whatever path he liked and see how it went.

Rap rap rap. A firm knocking came at their station-side door, causing a disturbing rattle in its wake.

"That must be Wenyan," Rhiannon said, utterly unnecessarily. Her face heated, and her heart knocked against her ribs like knuckles against a metal door just waiting to be opened. But she had another thing to offer Mel before this enticing, urgent outsider joined them for dinner. "If you want, I can give you my practice Tests. It might help you find a better fit than Bard."

Mel cocked a headlamp in acknowledgement. "I'll think about it. There's no way to be sure I won't game the Test accidentally, though."

How does he know what I did? Rhiannon's hands clenched and her spine froze straight, but her voice stayed even when she replied, "Fair enough." Offer complete, she left her Hive crowded together and stood in front of the door.

Even if he did know, he'd tied his fate to hers. Betrayal had no place in a Hive. Though her first passenger had blackmailed her, her rescuers had stolen from her, and Manawyddan could only guess what might happen on Garden Station, she could always trust her Devoted.

She paused to adjust her crown firmly before opening it. No reason to be less than composed when greeting a diplomat. The grooves where the gold-covered leaves rested on her skin felt raw. Great. She was probably showing off pink dents in her forehead just as the guy arrived. Not that it mattered what he thought of her appearance. Nothing romantic could happen between them, and she had Devoted who needed her attention. For instance, Mel was very vulnerable at the moment and could use personal guidance.

Behind her, Gavin said to Mel, "I can help you learn some of the things you need to be a bard."

"It's not just recording history?"

She heard the smirk in Gavin's voice. "How are you with poetry?"

Rhiannon opened the door and was greeted by legs topped with a pyramid of lacquered boxes.

"Hello," said a muffled voice from behind the boxes.

She giggled and pushed the door fully into its slot to make maximum room for the delivery-translator. Wenyan turned sideways and sidled past her, leaving a humid garlic cloud in his wake. She smelled something sweet and tangy, star anise and cinnamon, musky fish and sesame. The scents shouldn't have blended, but they did.

They didn't have a table for the bounty. Wenyan set his mound of goodies on the floor where they could all circle around it.

"Luciano," Rhiannon called. "Could you find us plates please?" Then she joined the mob on the floor. By the time he'd returned with plates, utensils, and cloth napkins, the boxes were open and steaming.

Bright orange-red strips nestled in a bed of wilted green leaves that sparkled with a pepper-dotted sauce. In another container, thin white onion strips knocked into peanuts and chilies and milky cubes of the tenderest tofu Rhiannon had ever seen.

Boxes upon boxes. Scattered among the wafting packages, still other boxes failed to send up nebulous vapory goodness.

Wenyan took a plate and a set of chopsticks from where Luciano had deposited them amongst the food. "With your permission?" he asked Rhiannon. He didn't wait for her reply before he plunged his sticks into a cold, steam-free box.

Family style, then. She took her own plate and chopsticks. As did the rest. As soon as Wenyan's first food had been plated—it looked like a simple iceberg salad—her Hive fell on the cuisine like the *cwn annwn*.

Rhiannon waited for a clear space, watching over her friends and curious which delicacies their local guide would choose. He dipped his chopsticks into another box with the perfect grace of someone whose fingers have always been longer than everyone else's. The digits were long and rectangular, like slender trees that somehow could bend at the joints to form other angles. He had short pink nails with a little more skin—rounded—peeking over the top. They were clearly strong, from the way they'd carried the oddly shaped containers. And flexible for delicate operations, evidenced by Wenyan's ability to eat salad with chopsticks. *Salad.*

He broke into her musings. "Let me teach you how to use them."

Pulling her gaze from his mesmerizing hands and up to his eyes took a willpower Rhiannon hadn't used in... She'd been exercising her willpower a lot in these foreign situations, even before leaving Dyfed. Before taking the Test.

She used her chopsticks to pluck a green vegetable spear, coated in soy and ginger, from one container, grateful that the action had seemed both simple and controlled. "We have Chinese food on Dyfed, y'know." Though, the salad was going to be nigh impossible. *How is he grasping the thin, dressing-slimy lettuce leaves?*

Wenyan accepted her rebuke with aplomb and changed the topic. "What else do you have on Dyfed?"

And so the telling of stories commenced. Victor spoke about the silver maple trees, Gavin about experimental theatre. This was part of what Rhiannon liked best about traveling with a huge group of friends. They all came together to create a familial atmosphere.

Rhiannon put something that smelled like chili and came in red, yellow, and purple onto her plate. This food was so colorful!

Gyah! Her tongue vibrated, and her eyes squinted as if to protect themselves from the heat. *Water!* Rhiannon sniffled as her sinuses objected to the sudden change in their situation. Through the tears in her vision, she could see that her Devoted looked at her worriedly, possibly wondering if she'd just been poisoned. "Spi—spicier than expected," she gasped out.

Mimicking her earlier words, Wenyan said, "We have spicy food in China, y'know."

Her Hive laughed—whether at her tear-streaming face or Wenyan's mocking. *Traitors, all of you.* Her stomach leapt up into her rib cage and her tear ducts worked a little harder, but the physical reaction from the spice masked her embarrassment. Lucky. Real Queens acted collected all the time. They didn't get embarrassed. So Rhiannon couldn't either. She had to be strong for her Hive.

And if that made her seem extra amazing to the good-looking local boy, that was just a bonus.

A bonus her Devoted could never encourage. Still in its first year, her unorthodox Hive was supposedly built around a romantic love flowing from Devoted to Queen. That bond would erode over time, leaving only familial affection to stitch them together, with Rhiannon free to take a lover (preferably from the Hive) after a decade or two.

So the films and books depicted it. She'd skipped the planet before taking any courses in how to be a Queen. Who knew what non-romanticized reality should be like?

In light of her obvious embarrassment, the stories resumed with a new tone. Now they were all about Rhiannon's brushes with unexpected events. She cursed her hot cheeks.

Victor started with, "How about that time Rhiannon performed in a brothel?"

The way Victor said that... it was phrased for maximum shock impact. She couldn't look at any of them. "I sang in a play," she tried to explain to Wenyan. "The only theatre around just *happened* to be connected to a combination brothel-casino."

Mel chimed in with his own details about her ability to charm an utterly confused audience. At least that made her sound competent.

When the tale came to an end, she was ready to move things along, maybe ask an innocuous question about the upcoming conference. Something that would take the focus off her and give her the chance to learn more about the station... and their station guide.

Gavin foiled that plan. "Tell us about the time you got kicked out of a casino."

Wenyan laughed, his breath sweetly vinegarish. "What?"

But there was no way Rhiannon planned to tell that tale. "What about a more serious story? Like when I blessed a room?" It would also give them a chance to discuss druidry, which she was sure Wenyan would find interesting.

"Awwwww," Gavin and Alan chorused in playful disappointment. They harmonized nicely.

Victor reached over the food mountain to shove at Gavin in retaliation. At least *someone* stood for his Queen's dignity. Though, Victor *had* cast the first stone. "Don't pay any attention to my lady Queen," he said to Wenyan. Those words negated any chance that he'd intended to protect her reputation. "She's a bit intense when it comes to taking care of us."

Murmured agreement rose from the rest of her Devoted.

Mel added, "Like protecting me from attackers with nothing but her voice."

Luciano said, "And finding me a suitable internship in a place where we didn't know anyone."

Before the rest could chime in, Wenyan asked, "So should I call you Princess Intense?" The way he said it, it rhymed.

Rhiannon's neck prickled and she took another bite of the spiced spiciness to hide her feelings. The heat on her cheeks came from the chilies, nothing more. She shouldn't let him call her anything but *your ladyship* or *Queen*

Ceridwen, but he fit in so well among her Devoted. And the informality warmed her intestines.

He'd made a special name for her, and it was hers alone. Maybe if the others had objected, she could make herself give that up. But they hadn't. Everyone was getting along.

She swallowed a procrastinatory mouthful and gave him a small nod, pleased when he grinned back.

Dinner progressed for nearly an hour and devolved into discussions of future plans and her Hive's guilty feelings over living in what was clearly someone's flat. "It would be one thing if these were visitor quarters," Luciano said, summing up their general attitude, "but we seem to have displaced a family from their home."

Wenyan waved away their concerns with his long, perfectly rectangular fingers. "Nah. The residents are getting to stay with their friends. This is like a birthday present."

Naturally, Rhiannon didn't believe this, and she doubted her Devoted did either. But it was clear that Wenyan would not allow them to move out—nor would they have anywhere else to go—so they let his little lie pass.

Besides, with birthdays having been mentioned, she could talk about the nature that had been missing from Victor's party. "All the plants on this station are gorgeous," Rhiannon said.

Gavin added, "We can't help but notice the chrysanthemums."

The station's chrysanthemums *were* beautiful, but the real point was the amount of foliage strewn across metal and plastic. Its velvet touch comforted when a traveler brushed a hand across it, and its fresh scent kept the station feeling almost like a real planet. Whereas she'd held Victor's birthday celebration in their plant room en route, she could have held a ceremony anywhere in this place.

And even our plant room was lacking.

She'd asked Victor at the time, "How do you like the party?"

And he'd replied too fast. Too automatic. "It's great," he'd said. "You're great." *More sincere.* "But there are no trees."

And once they'd started down that road, he'd realized just how little nature was on the ship, how little he'd seen in the months since leaving Dyfed. "By the gods, we had to burn an oak stick for a few seconds, and then stop so we didn't use it up. We're not connected to the planet or the stars. So what are we connected to?"

She'd patted his shoulder, skin sticking on nervous sweat as she tried to slide it downward. "We have each other." It had sounded so trite. "We have the stars and our ship, owned by generations before us."

This was why so few Dyfed-born could be spacefarers. Only those who were already a little crazy could handle it. Their society didn't belong in space.

Victor's eyes flitted everywhere, not seeming to fix on any one thing. "None of that is *real*."

Rhiannon had tapped a finger against her lips. *I'm very real, thank you so much.*

"Actually," said Wenyan, listing into Rhiannon's side to pull her back to the present, "you have yet to see the best parts. I can take you to the gardens."

Rhiannon wanted to push her shoulder into him for firmer contact, but that would be weird. *He's so warm!* His leaning could easily be an accident of too much food. And his touch was light. If she returned the gesture, it would be obviously intentional.

Victor bounced from legs-crossed to kneeling with a *thunk* noise that made her wince. "There are *gardens*?"

Wenyan turned to look directly at Rhiannon. "I could show you around, if you like." His ginger breath washed over her face, and she inhaled a second time. The closeness, the offer to take her out, it all sounded so much like a date. With Wenyan's being outside their Hive system, he could be curious and creative and beautiful... and acceptable for Rhiannon to date without causing a hierarchical upheaval. Her heart pumped blood directly to her warming ears.

Of course, that wasn't what was happening. He *had* to ask her first because she was in charge. And it wouldn't be just the two of them on this garden excursion; it would be the whole Hive. All men who were, supposedly, in love with her for the first few years of their Devotion. She still had obligations. It didn't matter that her Devoted had come to her less traditionally than they might have.

In the background, Gavin and Victor started up a childish chant of "Can we? Can we? Can we?"

Alan pointed out, "We have another day before the conference starts."

If they thought she hadn't replied because she didn't want to see the garden, they were mistaken. But by the cauldron, she wanted it to be a date. "Is that where the 'silver river' is?" she asked. "The *Yin He*?"

Her accent was undoubtedly atrocious, but he didn't have to laugh. Rhiannon could feel her lips forming the universe's most childish pout, but she couldn't seem to make them stop. "No, no," he gasped. "I'm not laughing at *you*." It sure seemed that way. "*Yin He*." He gestured to Mel in between giggles.

Mel's visor darkened, not appreciating the laughter any more than Rhiannon, then. "Silver River, yes."

Wenyan shook his head from side to side, his hair unmoving and his heaving lungs finally under control. "Technically, it means that, yes. And we pipe much water through the station. But it also means 'Milky Way.' It's a poetic way of saying we are part of the galaxy's great garden when we live here."

Rhiannon *did* want to experience this galaxy-class garden. "We'll see you in the morning then?" It was both acceptance and dismissal, and maybe a bit of annoyance with the still-unapologized-for laughter.

Wenyan took it in the spirit, and he stood. The air around Rhiannon's nose and mouth cleared. It was cooler, calmer, and much subtler in its food scents. "Thank you for inviting me for dinner. Feel free to leave the boxes, and I will send someone for them tomorrow."

Rhiannon inclined her head. He looked taller from her seated position on the floor. Longer, even next to Gavin.

"I'll show you out," Gavin said, standing as well. The two men were halfway to the door when Gavin spoke again in a low whisper that she could barely hear. Rhiannon leaned backwards in order to get a better wavelength.

"She's not a fun-hating kind of intense, you know, just a little hesitant about new people. And she likes you. I can tell."

Don't tell him that! She ducked her head to hide behind her hair, but again the crown held it out of the way. Weeks, and she still wasn't used to its heavy weight.

In the same low hush, Wenyan asked, "How can you tell?" Did he sound more hopeful than curious? She would be too self-centered if she believed it. And it was impossible to be sure of subtle tonal gradations in his accent, so different from her own.

"It's in the little things," Gavin said. "If you look for it, you'll see it."

Rhiannon did not turn to see if they were looking at her. *I don't want to hear any more of this.* She leaned forwards to pluck a cold broccoli floret with her chopsticks.

The door swished open and rattled closed again before she unfocused on the food's remains. She hid her smile in a chunk of pineapple. She was seeing Wenyan again in the morning!

Interlude 1

Good Morning, Machynlleth

Dyfed, News Station 3

A blond woman sits behind a gleaming wooden desk. Her hair is cut at a knife-slash down to her chin. She wears enough makeup to enhance her features on camera. Beside her, a man in flowing white robes runs lazy fingers over a goblet-shaped trophy.

She says, "Good morning. This is Early Machynlleth News. I'm your host, Gretchen Wyn." She pauses as her name appears at the bottom of the screen.

"Today, I'm honored to have laureled bard Marcus ap Calabro with me here at News Station 3. Yesterday, he announced he would not participate in this year's worldwide poetry contest. Here at Early Machynlleth News, we're excited to find out more. Marcus, thank you for joining me."

The man's fingers stop moving on the trophy. "I'm pleased to be here." He sounds unsure.

"Let's jump right in to the major question." The woman smiles into the camera, sharp. "Your detractors accuse you of fear of failure. Why haven't you shared any work you've produced recently?"

He ducks his head. "Well, Gretchen…"

Chapter Seven

Another Day, Another Inoculation

The Llyr's Llambo, in the "fleet" of Devoted and Queenless ships over Dyfed

It was only supposed to be two weeks. When Holly had left Dyfed for the backup research site, she was only supposed to be gone for *two weeks.* Holly's mentor, Ffion "Effie" Kendrick, had given the warning to evacuate the raided facility under the old Senedd, and swore the furor would pass.

Two weeks, she'd said, and Holly could call home again, could invite Amanda to come join her at the research station, or could just *go home.* So far, it had already been six.

Six weeks alone, unable to tell her beloved what had happened or that she was safe.

Amanda was probably leading a hike right now. A tour group that wanted to walk on barely processed dirt and touch the rough bark of an uncultivated tree. At the top of a hill, Amanda would have them experience a world that was half city and half alien wilderness. To one side, city bubbles and spires. To the other, shifting wasteland sands.

Holly hoped that was what Amanda was up to, at least. Sharing her passion for the not-quite-frontiersy outdoors and growing a business built on heart dreams. She hoped Amanda wasn't *too* worried about Holly's absence. Didn't miss her conversation or her warm kisses *too* much or *too* often. Just enough. Just every now and then when she saw a flower she wanted to tell Holly about, or when she made dinner for two, or when she was alone in bed at night.

True, Holly had only spent two weeks at the rundown research lab. As she'd been promised, and as she'd told Amanda would be the case. But then the Devoted ships had arrived. One by one. Two by three. They'd moved into a loose formation around Dyfed's surface, and Holly's time filled with ships full of crazed men whose Queens were locked up in Holly's own cells.

"Another day, another inoculation," said Holly's med tech assistant. He wasn't as clever as he wanted to be.

For today's inoculations, she'd come across to a ship with bizarre plush carpeting, in the company of one med tech and two guards.

The guards wrangled a Devoted with a long grey plait down his back and a wizened, wrinkled face like a decaying nectarine. They pulled his arms at strange angles, making his body seem more like a cartoonish putty-doll than a person. He smelled like rotting meat, probably because he hadn't bathed since his Queen went missing.

Holly set her medical kit on the carpeted ground and produced a sterile syringe. She filled it with the Devotion vaccine that she'd invented herself—*send me a form rejection, will you, Neuroscientist Research Association?*— and tapped it to dispel any air bubbles. "Put him on the floor, please," she directed the guards.

He thrashed against the guards' firm grip until they pressed his thighs and triceps into the carpet. He bared fuzzy teeth as tear tracks ran through the oily dirt on his cheeks. Tears of pain or depression, she couldn't know.

As a child, Holly had known she'd be a doctor someday, but she'd never thought she'd have unwilling patients and ages-old equipment. Her shining dreams had included running her own lab where they got the really difficult cases. The brain cases.

She still had that, she supposed, in a roundabout way. Yes, she did research, but it was illegal and forced her to harm others on the quest to cure all of society. Yes, she had her own lab, but it was staffed by less-trained technicians and outfitted by an underground organization's meager budget.

If only the Senedd (and the Neuroscientist Research Association whose form rejection had made her heart ache) believed a woman could have that level of analytical brain! She'd never have joined the rebel cause otherwise.

Her med tech swabbed the injection site with iodine, and Holly slid the needle under the subject's skin. The Devoted man seized up, going stiff, but the guards waited. They knew the procedure.

A few moments later, his limbs all tried to contract, and he spewed spit and unbrushed breath all over the fabric beneath him. In those first moments when the drug took hold, it was possible for former Devoted to break bones or bruise their own organs, and Holly was not in the business of damaging perfectly capable citizens.

She was in this to free the Devoted from their Hives' tyrannies. More important, her efforts would make space in those lofty power structures for those not lucky enough to be the chosen 0.25 percent: women who didn't have the temperament to be Queens, bad test takers, non-gender-binary persons, anyone whose interests changed sometime after secondary school ended.

Why should the majority make sacrifices so that the special few could create impressive things? Had she not proven that a non-Queen, non-Devoted could pit herself against the best brain specialists the planet offered... and win?

"All right," she directed. "You can let him go."

The freed man slumped in on himself and twitched. Twitched like his nerves were being scalpel-scraped. Holly pursed her mouth on the unspoken order to make him more comfortable. She would've liked to give him some painkillers and a blanket, but she didn't have enough for everyone and his mind was beyond caring at this point.

"Ships sensors say there's another one two rooms over," said a guard.

Holly nodded and closed up her kit. "Let's go."

All these Devoted, riding around in spaceships and coming when Ffion Kendrick called in their Queens' names, they were proof that the government had created its own contagion. So many, however, were proof of something else. Something she couldn't blame on the status quo, like recognition or the right to practice medicine as an unDevoted (and good luck Devoting if you were female).

Holly had a problem with the sheer *number* of Devoted coming from the depths of space. And the problem was that she didn't have enough corresponding Queens locked up and experimented on. She'd been with this rebellion since the beginning. She'd experimented on the Queens on Dyfed, beneath the Old Senedd, and she'd taken in more since leaving the planet for the backup site. Even if those Queens had exceptionally large Hives, Holly should have worked on a few hundred patients. Maximum a thousand.

So who did all these Devotion-mad men belong to?

She didn't know. And that meant not *every* stolen Queen had gone through her labs.

Holly followed her guards into private quarters where a middle-aged man with crow's feet and red hair slept under a dark blue coverlet.

"I already sedated him!" chirped the med tech. "Pad identification says his name's Brysen Bristow."

The inoculations didn't necessarily react well with the sedatives they had on hand, but this would certainly make the work go faster. She put her case on Bristow's study table with a clank and slipped a syringe from its package. "Iodine," she ordered.

If some stolen Queens had gone to other facilities, that could mean that the resistance had another pet neuroscientist. And what was the good of multiple scientists, unless you needed a spare? Holly wasn't going to be anyone's spare. If someone out there planned to make her a scapegoat, they'd watch their plans fall apart.

She needed to make herself indispensable.

Behind her, the guards whispered to each other. "Why's it even matter if we clean the skin first? It's not like these guys are getting up any time soon."

The other guard replied, in full agreement, "Yeah, if we got rid of all the Devoted completely, there'd be more space for the rest of us."

"Because we're not here to harm *them*," Holly said, "but to *elevate* everyone else."

The med tech swabbed the vein—blue and pulsing—and Holly injected Bristow with her vaccine.

"First," she said, "do no harm. Then, push and fight and work until you get to the top." She repacked her case. It was time to take her own advice. She wasn't going to let whoever sent these extra Devoted set her up for failure. Not when she had temporary control of the entire operation theater.

She rested her pad atop the now-closed inoculations case and called the staff/lab ship. She reached the med tech in charge of vaccine fabrication. "Nakamura, I need you to reorganize the next shifts of medical and security volunteers. We'll need to add hours and change things around so that our people are the ones in charge of ship navigation."

Nakamura's dark brown eyes, so like Holly's beloved Amanda's, widened and narrowed in comically fast succession. "The admin staff can handle that, can't they?"

But the admin people weren't under Holly's control and she didn't trust them. "Not just our ship, but all the ships. I know you can figure this out, Nakamura. You're a galaxy-class project manager." It was true. Nakamura had a Commander's talent.

Dyfed's loss there was Holly's gain.

"Thank you, ma'am. I'll have the new schedule drawn up before you return."

And then Holly would be too important for the rebel government to throw to the judiciary committees. If they wanted to get rid of her, they'd have to break her control over the fleet first. Much easier to choose a different conspirator to wash their hands of.

Chapter Eight

Suzhou Style

Yin He Yuan (Garden Station),
The Scholar's Garden

Rhiannon knew this was a *true* garden from the moment she passed through the metal lattice guarding the entrance to the station's serene heart. Her Queenly confidence turned to awe when she stepped inside. If she'd thought the airlock and the corridors were as nature-filled as a space station could get, she'd just been proven wrong. It was like being on a planet.

The garden smelled spicy, like cardamom, and running water pounded a hidden grotto with a rushing that might belong to a small waterfall. The entryway was laid out like the airlock, with only a single doorway to show off a few plants against a far wall, which had a window onto a second yard, which had a door, and so on. The place seemed huge, as if it continued on forever, with trees—she could smell pine on the light breeze—and yard after yard after yard.

High overhead, gold branches formed a mesh that complemented the blue-lit ceiling. The artful metal seemed natural, organic, for all that it was obviously worked instead of grown.

Gardeners dodged the Hive to clear away the last of the cultivated chrysanthemums, and Wenyan led Rhiannon through warrens of plum trees and willow vines that brushed down to the stone paths. Peering through the weeping fronds led to more glimpses of wintry white-and-pink blossoms. Her eyes couldn't chose where to rest among the conflicting textures of bark and plaster, wood and overhead gold, stone and petal.

Deeper Wenyan led, and deeper she and her Hive followed. Through hidden doorways and over raised platforms, they trusted his sense of direction. And always, always, a leaf or bamboo stalk or twining vine would encroach on the path. None of the vegetation moved in Wenyan's wake, his expert steps keeping him clear of nature's grasp.

Rhiannon brushed a plum blossom with a finger, its softness contrasting with the crisp air.

Wenyan paused inside a small pavilion atop a giant lake. She'd never seen a lake on a space station before; admittedly, she'd only been to two.

Craggy monoliths with shadowy holes punched through them stretched from the lake's interior up to the garden's metal-lattice ceiling. Above her head in the pavilion, flying buttresses held up the roof while dragonfish bit at their edges. Rhiannon smoothed a palm over lacquered wooden supports and grinned when she felt the edges of a power outlet. *Of course they blend the new with the traditional.*

She sneaked a look at Wenyan's calm features. Did he find peace here at the end of each day? But the question sounded bizarre, so she contented herself with watching the ease of his posture and the pleased way his eyes closed.

"Listen to the mountains," he said.

Rhiannon sucked her bottom lip inwards and raised her eyebrows, heart speeding as she realized she couldn't follow the instruction. She was already messing this up. *Thank goodness he can't see my confusion.* On this, the Hive's first morning on the station, Rhiannon had woken early to check with Mel about the *Cauldron*'s still-untouched status, then put on her best red tunic over black leggings. Armored in the most enticing outfit she had, she'd greeted Wenyan at her door with something resembling Queenly confidence. A confidence she was quickly losing in the face of his quiet knowledgeability and impossible requests.

Her Devoted crammed onto the platform, breaking the peaceful companionship.

"That is a lot of water," said Luciano. The lake spanned from the pavilion to a hall and went around a corner. Its dark green reflected the pavilion's winging edges and the garden's lace lattice ceiling right back at the viewer.

"More than you know," said Wenyan, turning tour guide. "Underneath the topmost layer, we keep the water tanks for the whole station. Our heart is made of flowing water."

It probably meant the station wouldn't be interested in stealing the *Cauldron*'s provisions, at least. That was good news because Rhiannon hadn't prepared for that eventuality. She *should* have asked Mel to add extra protections around the water and oxygen tanks before they'd left the ship in the dock. Much as she liked Wenyan, she knew better than to trust a foreign station's administrators. She'd been through that epic betrayal before.

"I could stay forever," said Victor. "In this garden, on this station. It's like we belong here."

Alan squinted at the lake. "Why is it green?"

"So the algae doesn't get into the drinking supply," said Wenyan. "It helps with the carbon in the air and also turns the rocks jade green, but it is not safe to drink or wash. Not for us. Koi and goldfish are hibernating beneath our feet."

Because it was *winter on the space station*.

The longer Rhiannon spent on Yin He Yuan—the more piney, spicy, clear air she breathed in this garden—the more she liked it. The whole place was soothing.

"It's so much like home," breathed Victor, echoing her thoughts. "Everything is alive!"

"Excuse me." Alan was frowning. "Why can't I access the station intranet? And what is *that*?" *That,* said oh-so-disgustedly, was a potted miniature landscape. It had a tree and a cup of water from which blossomed a broken shard of Swiss-cheese rock.

"Communication doesn't flow between the garden and the station. Here, we are peaceful and meditative." Wenyan pointed at the metal lattice ceiling. "All is contained in a Faraday cage."

That was really clever. Rhiannon leaned over the pavilion's railing to get a straight-on look at the cage. The artisans who'd crafted the mesh to look like branches had even added in bark-like striations, only visible at her current angle. That was *art*. "The mesh is so decorative. I never would have guessed." A screeching hawk flew through her field of vision, and Rhiannon shrank back into the pavilion.

Wenyan rubbed his shoulder against hers. "Personnel brought pets when they came to our station. Somewhere, there is a cat shaved to look like a tiny lion. If you are lucky, we'll see him."

Of course. Cats that looked like tiny lions. Why not?

"Come, we must experience the walkways." Wenyan led them out of the pavilion and across a tiny bridge over the green water.

On the other side of the small lake, half-hidden by the porous rock monoliths, a man in a practical jumpsuit stood in barky mulch and petted a blue chrysanthemum. Rhiannon longed to join him in his communion with nature.

Her time would come to loop her bare arms around tree branches and nuzzle her cheeks into dew-soft petals. For now, she would take her guided tour and feel the buzz of untapped life energy in the air. She pushed up her tunic's red sleeves in anticipation.

Thudding footsteps shook the small bridge. Rhiannon squeezed close to the handrail as two gardeners and three grey-uniformed locals rushed past.

"Where are they going?" she asked Wenyan.

He didn't answer before the five runners stilled in a ring around the man reverently stroking the chrysanthemum. A gardener pulled him backwards onto the stone path, and the other four loomed around them.

"No," said the gardener, making an X with her arms. "No touch. Bié pèng tā." She thumped her forearms together again, emphasizing the X. "You understand?"

Interesting that the gardener spoke English to the transgressor. Did everyone know some of the language?

Two grey-clad guards grabbed the nature lover's arms and hauled him backwards. His arms rotated in his shoulder sockets. After weeks observing Victor's therapy sessions, Rhiannon would bet the angle was excruciating.

She whispered, "What are they *doing*?" It looked a lot like when the security force at Cleopatra's Palace had tossed a sexual harasser out of their casino, but in this case the culprit was alone. No one around to torment.

She tugged her shirtsleeves back down and twisted her fingers in the cuffs. Not long after she'd seen that frontiersman blacklisted, she'd been thrown out of the casino as well. What unwritten law might she run afoul of here?

"They'll deport him from the station," Wenyan whispered back, loud enough for the Hive to hear but quiet enough not to echo to the enforcers. "We do not touch the plants." His voice held a note of scandalized inevitability.

But the sentiment was less obvious to Rhiannon and her Hive than to their local guide.

Alan gasped, overplaying his horror. "But how do you connect to the nature?"

Wenyan's perfectly sculpted eyebrows scrunched together, the individual hairs sticking up and down in confused directions. "We watch and experience." His voice tilted up at the end, half question and half request for confirmation. "No one can *touch*." It was as though he'd been stymied by the very idea.

Explanatory, Gavin used his practice teaching Mel about the ways of Dyfed to extend that education to their newest friend. "Our people experience nature by twining ourselves with it," he said.

Rhiannon shifted to observe her least Dyfed-friendly Devoted. *Does he really believe that?* Gavin had lived off-planet, away from plants, for so long. He'd been the most desperate never to go home again, happy with his devices and the metal ship. Of all her Devoted, she wouldn't expect him to take the strange hands-off custom so personally.

Yet he did. Gavin's shoulders hunched forwards, his fingers tore at his belt, and his teaching expression was marred by a tension line running down his forehead. Even the "Anywhere But Dyfed" Gavin seemed horrified to see a nature communer manhandled.

Rhiannon bit her lip, letting the sting draw adrenaline to the surface. It might get her in trouble. Might get her kicked off with the culprit before Alan could attend or give a presentation. But she had to show solidarity with the stranger. "We should stand up for him," she said.

Wenyan's head shook so fast, his gelled hair moved slightly over his ears. "He knew the rules."

Rhiannon's fingers twitched and her heart sped. She wanted to muss that hair further, feel it against her skin. It was an utterly inappropriate moment, and she could only sag with relief when Mel interrupted her untimely thoughts.

"Actually, no," said Mel. "He's here for the conference, like us. And probably is ignorant of the prohibitions, like us. He's an astrophysicist from Earth. Singapore."

Rhiannon, Wenyan, and the rest of the Hive all squinted into the distance as if they could tell by the transgressor's features whether he was local or foreign. As if they could verify Mel's information with their eyes. As if Mel would steer them wrong.

Wenyan scratched his ear. "Are you sure?"

"His information was in the registration packet," said Mel. "I can call up the relevant biography on a tablet if you have one."

Right. Rhiannon firmed her shoulders and took a firm step forward. She trusted Mel's information and had to stop this travesty before it went further. Ignorance—when no damage had been done—ought to be a defense. And no Dyfed native could fault someone for contacting vegetative life.

A hand on her elbow brought her to a stop. Wenyan's hand. He shouldn't be touching her. She was Queen and inviolate and so righteous in her cause, but the warmth from his fingers seeped through her shirt. It was somehow calming to have his guidance. His care for her actions.

She caught Victor frowning at Wenyan, just the same. Ever her protector.

The two guards hauled their quarry to the bridge. She *had* to speak out. When they passed, she'd make her move. Victor and Mel would back her physically if need be.

As they approached, a frowning guard said, "This is your first and only warning. We will let this pass for now."

That was fair. The guards had the right to demand visitors comply with local law and custom. But to avoid contact with plants? Garden Station and its inhabitants were so like Dyfed's, yet still so different. On entering, Rhiannon had felt at home in this garden, but now she had to wonder: could she belong here?

In a few seconds, the guards were forgotten and Wenyan led their group through two—*rooms? yards? enclaves?*—distinct spaces until they stood on a floor made of pebbles. Overhead, willow branches dripped to caress the stony ground. To the left, carved gingko panels told a story Rhiannon expected Wenyan to explain in a moment, but the bumpy ground made no sense at all. "Why isn't it smooth?" There, that sounded less confrontational than "your ground is messy."

"It's for texture and contemplation," said Wenyan. "Take off your shoes."

Rhiannon looked to her Devoted. Their faces sported the same lack of enthusiasm she felt. Not only was it a strange request, but it was less safe... especially if the ground were uneven. In an emergency, if they needed to rush to the spacesuits, they'd be slowed down (and the fit would be hampered by the unexpected lack of sole height).

"Off, off!" urged Wenyan.

There was no way to turn him down, and Rhiannon was already too short for most standard-size spacesuits anyway. What was another inch? She bent and tugged off her boots.

Upside down, she saw her Devoted do the same.

"Now, concentrate on the sensation of stones against your feet. Where do they stand on edge? Where are they flat? All are worn, so you won't be hurt."

It didn't hurt, no, but the rocks pushed into Rhiannon's skin like pens and rulers strewn around a friend's bedroom floor for ultimate tripping and stepping on. She would not call it pleasant. This was her least favorite part of the garden so far. To minimize the effect, she stood as still as she could, letting her Devoted walk around to their hearts' contents. They couldn't go too far. The textured area was only a few square meters.

A shared glance with Mel proved that someone else wasn't getting much out of this experience either.

Wenyan's voice in her ear was closer than she expected, and the warmth of his breath tingled all the way down her spine. "How do you like it?"

Rhiannon opened her mouth to come up with some reply when the air hissed around them. A containment breach so far interior?

Wenyan grabbed her shoulders and pulled her into his arms, muscles tight and chest practically suffocating. She couldn't think, couldn't breathe. No one touched her like this. No one was supposed to. No one wanted to.

She gasped, trying to take in air through his leather cardigan and warm pectorals. Was this an assassination attempt? She wasn't important enough to assassinate! Was it a romantic gesture? Dear Ceridwen, let it be romantic.

Wailing alarms bleated their warnings.

Rhiannon couldn't see anything other than Wenyan's navy blue shoulder.

Between alarm howls, Alan said, "What"—*bleat*—"going"—*"bleat"*—"hap?" *Bleat.*

A rush of air over her neck, unprotected by Wenyan's embrace. A solid *thack-thwunk* that shook the ground. The heave of Wenyan's heart and lungs against her cheek.

Ringing silence.

Wenyan disentangled them. "My apologies." He stepped back, letting her have her own space, but not so far back she couldn't reach out and touch him. "It is safe now."

Rhiannon's focus was all *shandivang*. She was hot and cold. The air had changed from chilled breeze to unmoving nothingness. Her feet still ached from the smoothly spikey pebbles, and a glance up proved the Faraday cage still laced the air overhead. That glance up also filled her with vertigo and she listed to the side.

Other than the ground and the sky, she'd lost her sense of perspective. The garden had been blotted out by walls. She could reach out her arms straight at 180 degrees and touch metal sheets on both sides. Two people would be cozy—she and Wenyan would be cozy—and four would be cramped. "Where are we?" she asked. Though the answer was obvious. She was still in the garden; she just couldn't see it. "How do we get out?"

"It is a safety measure," said Wenyan, voice gentle. He continued to give her the chance to come to her own conclusions and comforts, choosing to lean against a metal wall rather than into her space. She could have used the distraction, really. "In case of an air leak, cells slam down from above. The central garden is so intricate that the life-pod cells here must be small to avoid damaging the architecture or the plants. Further out, the rooms are larger."

Rhiannon's breath came faster. Her toes dug into the empty spaces between pebble spikes. "Air leak!" Her stomach pushed at her skin and blood pounded in her ears. "We need to get to the emergency spacesuits."

Wenyan laughed. "This is nothing. It is normal, just an experiment. Come sit with me."

He was delusional. "Emergency spacesuits," she said again. The pounding in her ears could have been her pulse. Or it could have been her Devoted banging on the other side of the wall. They could be trying to get to her. They could be in their vacuum-sealed death throes.

She splayed her hands against the metal prison. Trapped! Everything was hot and confusing. Her vision turned grey like the walls around her.

"Shhhhh." Wenyan's hand on her shoulder was yet more heat. She wanted to shake him off and strip her tunic till it all made coolly rational sense.

He reeled her in till his chest cradled her back, and she let him. Sagging into his strength. What could she do on her own? Shouldn't she listen to her guide?

"My Devoted..." She couldn't finish the thought.

"They're fine. In compartments the same as this one. We have only to wait until the emergency is over and normalcy is restored." He pulled her along until she felt his back hit the wall with a *thunk* that vibrated into her bones. They slid down to sit on the bumpy floor, and he placed her beside him, pliant and limp.

Rhiannon flopped back against the supportive imprisonment. The coolness felt good, seeping through her clothes. Her crown sang out, striking metal on metal. She dropped her head to hang forwards, keeping the leaves from driving into her brain.

"This happens a lot, does it?" she asked, getting her wits back. She'd overreacted. She could see that. Wenyan was far too calm for someone actively worried about thick, air-impervious walls slamming down around him, locking him in a two-person cage. Too calm, unless he'd grown used to it.

"Just breathe. We have air in here." He stroked the top of her curved spine with gentle fingers, almost tentative.

And she wanted to tell him it was all right. That she gave him permission to touch her, that he could use more pressure, that she didn't want to be alone. "How long will we be here?" She didn't use the word *trapped*.

"Not long. This is standard procedure." He readjusted to sit in front of her, ducking his gelled head until they were on the same plane.

"What caused it?"

His hair was probably crunchy with all that product, no matter how shiny it looked. "This was just an experiment."

The factual delivery dragged her from her contemplation of his hair. Her eyes narrowed. "How do you know that if you can't get in touch with the outside world?"

He took her hands in his. Her fingers fit, protected, within them. They felt as long and warm as she'd dreamed. "It's what we offer to the homeland. Zero-g experimentation." He tossed his head—the hair shook slightly, but returned to its native position—and his eyes sparkled with pride. "It makes the station valuable and important. We all work together to make our home a better place to live."

He made it sound like a whole station of Devoted, all brilliant in their pursuit of scientific advancement. She gripped him where they were joined, keeping him with her and not with some invisible Queen. "So my Devoted are fine, then, in their own little cells." Obviously, Mel would survive sudden exposure, but the rest... Though even Mel could be crushed by a falling wall.

Her heart pounded. Wenyan stroked along the backs of her hands. "With the experiments comes danger, but we're safe here, in the heart of the garden." He was so close. Their fingers grasping together, their knees almost touching, their faces close enough to share breath. He was a water droplet, and if she touched him, their boundaries would combine into something bigger and stronger. "It's my heart," he whispered, as though he also felt the intimate solemnity.

She leaned closer, and he came to her.

Lips touched lips. Rhiannon's world narrowed to the sensation, as if all the nerves in her body were busy feeling the hot-cold prickle of sensitive skin. His soft beige-pink lips had tiny lines that felt like scratchy gifts along her mouth.

He pulled back, blushing.

"Oh," she said. Which was the stupidest thing she'd ever said in her life, but she'd never kissed anyone before and hadn't expected this wellspring of mind-numbing feeling. She was eager to muss his hair, but she couldn't do that yet. Not when all her concentration focused on his mouth.

Wenyan didn't seem to mind. He only grinned at her and gently nipped the side of her lips before putting his together with hers again.

By the time the walls rose—*crisis averted!*—Rhiannon firmly held her beau's hands and knew she wore the most besotted smile.

The ceiling rumbled and cold air blew over their former nest. The wind shot straight through her and tossed her knot-woven hair briefly into her neck.

After a struggle with his sleeves, Wenyan stripped off his leather cardigan and offered it to her in two hands. It was still warm, and when she wrapped herself up in it, it felt like the coziest hug. He took her hands again and raised them to press against his chest, where she could feel his heart beating.

"Rhiannon!" Luciano's voice intruded into her romantic dream. He was so distraught that he forgot to call her *my lady* in a public place.

She snatched her hands back. Luciano couldn't see her engaged in such practices. None of them could. Not until she'd told her Hive of her romantic intentions and received their permission... permission which tended not to come to young Queens for *years*. Oh, she was mostly sure that Gavin would be all for it, but the rest of them?

"My lady!" Alan ran into her at full tilt and would have bowled her over if Luciano hadn't steadied them both from the other side.

She returned all their affection with hugs and snuggling and the laying on of hands. *They're alive! They're fine!* Her Devoted huddled altogether, and there was no space for the beautiful man who had shared his home's personal memories. Luciano kissed Rhiannon on the cheek, and it was nothing like her exchange with Wenyan. *That* had been quiet and sexy and wonderful, whereas Luciano was relief and brotherly affection.

Wenyan, left out of all this familial buffeting frowned at her, perhaps accusatorily. Those lips that had so recently been on hers should never do anything but smile in her direction, even if his blank eyes were so compellingly dark.

Her heart thudded once, hidden in the mass of bodies and in Alan's hyperventilation. *He has no idea why I pulled away.* Wenyan had to think his advances were unwanted, that she didn't value him, that she wanted to hide their budding relationship from her love-tagged Devoted. She had to tell him that she respected him and wanted him and would proclaim "he kissed me!" to anyone who asked. He couldn't go on thinking that she didn't care for him.

...after she'd put the question to her Hive.

"My lady." Mel sounded less relieved and more like he needed her attention.

"Yes?" Rhiannon's voice was muffled by Victor's near chokehold that pressed her between his body and Gavin's.

"We need to look into this incident." *You could take the American Space Ranger out of the law enforcement world, but you couldn't take the investigative tendencies out of the former Ranger.* "I find it suspicious that there are no reports of deaths or injuries."

Gavin shrugged and it jostled Rhiannon's shoulder so she bit him. He squirmed away, but not very far. "Looks like these safety cells really work."

"By the gods," said Victor, "you're upset that nobody is hurt?" Victor was usually on Mel's side in any disagreement. This schism could be a sign that he was branching out and feeling more self-confident. She leaned into him, and he leaned back, muscles pressing together in solidarity.

Mel's visor darkened. "There's no outward sign of it, but that's rare in something like this. Someone should at least be complaining about hitting their head when the alarms went off."

"Maybe in *American* space," Alan scoffed.

That was enough! They didn't need to be weighing Mel down just because they didn't want to think about potential dangers. She wouldn't have her Hive so fractured nor so willfully ignorant. "Break it down for me. Are we safe now?"

"Well, we might be." That didn't sound very good. "It looks like we are." *That*, however, sounded fine. Mel might simply be a bit paranoid, hunting for a case to solve. "But the Americans would be looking into something like this."

Alan bristled, shaking the whole mass of hugging Devoted. The whole mass except for Mel. "We aren't Americans though. We're Dyfed-born Welsh. It's different."

"Speak for yourself," said Luciano, but there was no heat in it. Were friendship and Hive bonds trumping his differences at last?

Victor said, "Maybe we're more like the Chinese than the Americans." With all the nature and the poetry around them, it seemed likely.

"Maybe," said Mel, letting his friend placate him.

Rhiannon was floating, held up only by her loving Devoted. Fear had deserted her until all that remained was pleasure and companionship. Sure, Wenyan left at some point in the middle of Mel's argument, but she had her Hive and she'd see Wenyan tomorrow when he escorted them to the conference. Then she could explain she needed her Hive's permission for things like kissing and hand-holding, and everything could go back to the way it had been when he'd given her his cardigan.

"For both our peace of mind," Alan asked Mel, "would you map the emergency spacesuit locations in each room we enter?"

Mel dipped his lamps and cocked his head to the side in the quintessential gesture for *thinking now.* "The manifest I downloaded on arrival shows that most rooms don't have them," he said.

What?! Her eyes flitted to all the corners that *could* have suits in them, but apparently didn't. "No suits at all?"

Mel made it worse. "Our quarters don't have any."

The locals may be willing to live on the edge, an experimental accident away from vacuum death, but Rhiannon was not. "We'll have to count on our own." Even if that meant carrying them around everywhere they went, sweating under the rubbery weights and looking very foolish.

Maybe just sometimes, then.

Chapter Nine

Queens and Questions

Planet Dyfed, a Queens-only event

Olivia smoothed her yellow silk dress and twitched the hem away from her shoes. Crisp air cleared her nose as clattering shoes and humming skimmers fogged her other senses.

All around her, Queens in beaded gowns and bright colors climbed the stone steps to a private, Queens-only event. *They're so young!* But that made the most sense. Older Queens wouldn't need the community or the guidance that these sorts of things were meant to foster.

If any other attendees had a single Devoted yet, she'd be surprised.

Olivia stood where the stairs met the sidewalk, flanked by two Devoted, neither of whom could join her inside. Her heart yawned wide, desperate to fill itself with their presence, and she pretended to lose her balance so she could clench at Paul's space-pale hand.

"You know you hate crowds," Paul reminded.

"It's dangerous to go out alone. You've already been captured once," Mark pled.

Night air hissed between her teeth, but she felt cool and strong like a Queen should be. Like she had always been. They were both right, but she had to press on. She freed Paul from her clutching fingers.

A whole *event* full of Queens. It was the perfect place for a determined Queen stealer to snatch more than one prey-child.

Though, the conspirators hadn't taken *her* from an event like this. They'd simply approached her and made an appointment! When she'd shown up at a now-defunct government building, they'd locked her up and turned her into an experimental subject.

How *did* her nemeses pick the Queens? Did *everyone* make an official appointment? She knew so much about the Queen stealing, but not the important parts: who, why, or how to stop it.

Olivia's heart fluttered and her eyes closed on sleepless grit between the lids. This wasn't a government building. Nobody was going to take her from here. So long as she didn't leave with anyone other than her own Devoted, she'd be safe.

She swayed into Paul and Mark, lightheaded. She shivered in the evening cold. She could still smell the panic and excrement from the prison cells that had neighbored hers.

"Let's go home, Liv," Mark said.

No! She was stronger than this, stronger than fear and memory. She could go into a perfectly safe situation and learn more about the stealers. People who needed information about Queens would go where Queens were. The young ladies inside must have heard rumors or acquired information Olivia had not. These events aimed themselves at the youngest and newest Tested.

And new Queens gossiped. *I can only hope they'll share that gossip with me, older and more official-looking than they may be comfortable with.*

She would do as Alexander had proposed and question everyone who looked suspicious and write down everything. (She hadn't needed to follow Paul's suggestion of disguises in this instance. She was already a Queen. She belonged at this kind of function. Aside from being significantly older than the average attendee.)

Olivia gathered her skirt, silk cool between her fingers, and ascended to the large doors, swinging open under a marble arch.

"Ah! Queen Ceridwen!" a male voice called out. *That's not my title anymore.* She'd passed on the moniker along with the ship to Queen-Commander Rhiannon Jones.

Olivia recognized the man in a tickling sort of way. His face was familiar, but not well-known. "Hello," she said. "If you'll excuse me." He had a hawk nose and appeared to know her from her space-Queen days. She couldn't wonder about him now.

She stepped past him and into a different world.

The crowded ballroom was larger than the house she'd rented, with ceilings that rose at least three stories high. Across from the entry, red curtains framed the snacks table. Off to the left, blue curtains rose to the tall ceilings supported by archways and topped by a curved roof. The plaster was painted in pale greens and creams, with rope-like carvings limned in gold that seemed to radiate out from the chandeliers. The room smelled of heavy perfumes—amber, jasmine, sickly cherry—and cups of sweet punch.

It was warm, humid almost, as swarms of young women swept from one side of the wood floor to the other. Their chattering was a high-pitched reverberation in her ear, reminiscent of the time her geological sampling tool had stopped working on a planet with a very heavy atmosphere. Valiantly, the device whirred and whined and shook in her hands.

Her hands were shaking now. *It's just from the memory of broken machinery. It has nothing to do with being in a crowd, by myself.* Olivia wasn't sure anyone would believe that, least of all herself. She ran the back of her hand discreetly over her heated forehead, unsurprised that it came away clammy.

All around, ladies showed off their dresses or frowned in an attempt to look severe. Every exterior door was an archway crafted to simulate tree branches. Druidic symbols covered the paneled walls.

Olivia pushed through crowds, thick air, and taffeta to stand at the punch bowl. It was the perfect base from which to question everyone.

And for the first thirty minutes, it worked beautifully. She relaxed beside the bowl, sipping her own drink and engaging girls in small talk which quickly turned to, "Have you heard about the missing Queens?"

Sadly, this question consistently received the answer, "Oh, wow, no. Tell me all about it!"

After those thirty minutes, however, her anonymity and unobtrusive questioning were forcibly changed. Word had gotten around the ballroom that there was a veteran Queen by the punch. Soon Queens converged on Olivia's location.

Their faces were round and almost unfinished, high blooms of pink on their cheeks—that could have been natural—and wide smiles on their faces as they surrounded and drowned her. Olivia reminded herself that they were youths rather than the first alien encounter.

Each wanted to meet her and ask any number of questions not related to Olivia's investigation.

"What's being a Queen really like?" asked a tiny girl who didn't even look old enough to take the Test. Well, what did Olivia know about people's ages? Under the age of seventy, they all looked the same to her.

"How do I pick my Devoted?" another asked.

Aha! Olivia had an answer for that. "Look to the freshly Tested. These new Devoted are the closest in interest and experience to you."

The girls arrayed around her nodded wisely and sipped the sugary red liquid in their cups.

"There's this boy..." started one young woman. And another echoed with, "There's this girl..."

Those questions were dangerous, so she simply poured punch for the dear things and commiserated over the difficulties of Queenly romance. She'd never cared for it herself. Olivia had her Hive, and that was enough. She'd never wanted to change the dynamic with any of her men, and she hadn't had the opportunity to find someone outside the structure... besides, she was so old and set in her ways that if she did find someone, it'd be very difficult to integrate them.

Before she'd been a Queen, she'd dated around, but she'd been happy to give it up if it meant gaining a permanent tribe. She'd never had a steady thing until then. Hives appealed far more than dating, but that was a personal foible.

"I feel like an imposter all the time. Does that go away?"

That question could have made Olivia cry. These poor girls. "You're all so lucky to be Queens at this point in history. Our system is so well established, and there are resources like this event to help you. At your university, you can lean on counselors for support and ask for guidance. You'll all do fine." She beamed at them as best her trembling lips could support.

This went on for two hours before Olivia "accidentally" spilled red punch down her yellow dress—*cold, so cold, and the color of fresh-cut blood*—and excused herself to change at home.

She pressed a gel strip onto every punch cup for her fingerprint collection.

Olivia had followed her Hive's detective advice perfectly. She'd asked questions, taken down notes, "disguised" herself as a Queen, and acquired fingerprints. But what did she *do* with the fingerprints?

Not even Alexander had a resolution for that problem. Nor Paul, Owen, Mark, Hideki, or Toan. She made sure to include them all in her brainstorming. They needed something to do, to focus on, or else they'd collapse in worrying over her.

But in the end, it became clear that they had no close connections to whom she could trust the fingerprints. She'd have to use a more distant acquaintance.

So long as she didn't explain why she needed the Queens' identities checked, it would be fine.

Which was how she ended up sharing her cup collection with Dylan Pughe, a man in the security division with a reputation for discretion. She didn't give him her name. She didn't tell him whose prints these were nor where she'd collected them.

Pughe sent her the results within a few hours. Every single set confirmed that the Queens she'd met were exactly who they said they were.

Her long night had been an investigative dead end.

Chapter Ten

Keeping Secrets

Yin He Yuan (Garden Station),
Rhiannon's Hive's flat

Alan knew exactly the reason why choral practice was going badly that evening. "You know," he said, trying to sound conversational, "choral practice goes better when we actually sing."

"Just give us a moment," Gavin said. He'd taken yet another break to go off on a long and complicated monologue to Mel that boiled down to "don't worry about sounding good; worry about being friends with us."

"He'll get better if you give him time to observe instead of stopping every three seconds to explain that chorus is about working together." Alan paused, head tilting as he thought about it. "And what's *wrong* with technical perfection anyway? Good job, Mel. Keep it up."

Considering the acoustics of the space, Mel was amazing on the sounding good front. A giant room with a single couch and some stools, a wood floor? It was like their quarters were designed for maximal echo. Even if they'd decided to practice in the bathroom, it wouldn't have gone much better. That room was smaller, but still all tile and hard edges.

Still Mel's impossibly smooth tenor tones hit every note of the Welsh national anthem with enviable skill. *Wasn't Mel a bass during Victor's birthday party?* Next time Alan paid attention, the robot would have worked his way up to soprano.

"Do *not* keep it up." Gavin launched into yet another description of tone and melding, which Alan tuned out.

If they were going to chatter and argue instead of singing, Alan had better things to do, starting with checking his messages. He pulled out his pad and immediately wished he hadn't.

There was a new message all right, and it was from Professor Cantor. Again. Who knew there'd come a time when he avoided messages from his favorite professor?

Six months ago, he'd have delighted in a message from the professor. Cantor was the only person at the university who treated Alan like a valuable team member instead of an unfortunate ant who needed coddling. Because of his Queen-free status. At the rigorous graduate level, all researchers were expected to have Queens, and the Queens did all the advocacy.

Alan was too young, ascended too early to the university to have a Queen at the same time as he needed lab access. No one had purposely looked down on him for it; after all, he *was* so young. But their involuntary expectations had meant marginalization at every turn. He couldn't get a research grant because "there's a Hive that needs it more."

He couldn't worm his way onto an exciting team because "we already have enough Devoted physicists."

Then there'd been Professor Cantor.

Cantor had tenure, knew all the most interesting projects, and was an oddity himself. Somehow without being Devoted, he had ascended to great academic heights. Not just of knowledge, but also of making connections and acquiring funding. Alan didn't know exactly how he'd managed it, but Cantor was unfailingly willing to share his bounty with star pupil Alan Jones.

Now Alan was dodging his messages.

Alan skimmed the words, not wanting to think too deeply about whatever Cantor's message said. If he happened to miss an important detail, it was only because he'd read too quickly, not because he was a bad physicist (or a bad Devoted, since his Hive wanted nothing to do with the things Cantor represented... like home and authority).

The gist was that Cantor had arrived on Garden Station and wanted to meet.

The pad was heavy in his sweat-slick hands. Screen light made his eyes water. *What?* He leaned away from the device, protecting his eyes, and jabbed a finger at the delete button. How had Cantor even known he was here?

Message gone. There, safe. He tossed the pad onto the couch, hoping it would get stuck between the cushions and the back, never to be seen again. He'd have to keep an eye out for Cantor whenever he left their quarters, but the man would stand out. An old Welsh guy among the Chinese population? Alan could avoid him.

It'd be a bit harder to hide his Hive mates, but he could do it. Alan was a genius. He knew it; Cantor knew it; the gods knew it.

And if, somehow, the professor did find him, he could simply turn down the offer to join whatever Dyfed-based project Cantor championed. No need to worry his Hive mates by telling them about the messages. They'd rather have him out here than send him home, or go home with him.

It wouldn't be so bad. He could disappoint his mentor while impressing upon him the necessity of keeping quiet about Rhiannon's Hive. Cantor would respect a Queen's needs, wouldn't he?

Though Professor Cantor had always been unorthodox. He could as easily choose to share Rhiannon's secrets as keep them. Cantor's mysterious, non-Hive-based connections made him an outsider in a way that Alan used to appreciate. Now all he wanted to do was protect his Queen.

Gavin was petting Mel's metal, the same way Alan petted his computers when they weren't listening to him and it was either that or tear them apart and hope nothing went awry when he put them back together. "Don't worry about the note," he said, "worry about the tone." Which was rubbish advice from Alan's standpoint, and *he* understood what Gavin was trying to say.

Mel, of course, was lost, but gamely made a warbling noise that wouldn't have been out of place in a vulture's nest.

Gavin sighed, and Alan ducked into his room (shared with Victor and Mel) to grab some cables. The snaky mess combined his own equipment with stuff he'd found in a dinged-up dresser beneath some pens and belts. White plastic insulation flopped next to blue connectors and clear-coated wires.

Who puts their cables in the same dresser as their belts? What if the owners accidentally decided to use one as the other?

That wasn't a bad idea, actually, and Alan snatched up a few studded belts too. He could use the buckles for connectors if nothing else.

He laid the whole cache on the common room floor and linked the obvious ones end to end, plugging one into his spare pad. Power came from back in the bedroom where Victor whined at him in the dim light shining through a lacquered panel supposed to simulate a window.

Not everything matched up with everything else, but it could be an experiment in wired/wireless recording.

"No more," Alan said when he was done, interrupting Gavin's blathering. "You're just confusing him."

All four of Mel's arms turned into akimbo triangles. *Great, I've managed to annoy the most even-tempered Devoted.* "I'm making progress," he said. "Gavin thinks so."

Gavin nodded, forcefully enough that his head might fall off. If that wasn't a case of "protesting too much," Alan would throw away his miniature tensor jet.

"Look," Alan said. "Let's make a recording. It'll help you to hear the differences in sound and tone."

Gavin played with the ends of his belt loops, not making eye contact. "We'll get more done if we just keep practicing. It takes time to record and then to listen…"

Alan could have shaken him. *Like we're getting any practicing done* now? "As a favor to me then?" he asked, brilliantly refraining from throwing his hands in the air and calling on Manawyddan to save him from fools and well-meaning idiots. "I need help with my sound and human perception experiment."

Mel nudged his shoulder into Gavin's in a way that was probably supposed to be gentle but made the slouching boy sprawl forwards before he caught himself. "We *are* supposed to support our Hive mates in need."

Gavin frowned and mumbled, *"For both our reputations."*

Which meant absolutely nothing as far as Alan could see, but the body language spoke Gavin's defeat, which meant it screamed Alan's victory. "Good," he said. "Sing for me."

As he checked the wave forms on his spare pad, Alan very much did not think about the deleted message on his regular pad. He'd be here with his Hive mates, doing Hive-y things, and *nothing* would get in the way of that.

Chapter Eleven

Tripping Into Courtship

Yin He Yuan (Garden Station),
Rhiannon's Hive's flat

Nothing was getting in Rhiannon's Hive's way today.

Not the other scientists—Alan would be utterly brilliant and impress everyone.

Not misunderstandings—she'd explain things to Wenyan, and their potential love would triumph.

Not scary vacuum-edged damage—Mel had mapped out all the rooms with emergency spacesuits in them and uploaded those maps to everyone's pads.

Rhiannon had woken early, put on her second-best tunic—a dark blue perfect for looking serious—and taken up her spot on the tan couch in the main room. She'd be there if her Hive needed her. She'd be ready when Wenyan arrived.

Until either of those things happened, she would read a trashy prose novel about a Queen who breaks up her Hive in order to be with her house-painter lover. When she'd chosen the literature months ago, she hadn't had a potential lover of her own.

Maybe I should switch over to some optimistic epic poetry with aliens in it? While that always cheered her, it took a bit more mental effort to read epic poems than it did trashy novels. And she needed all the spare brain power she could get when her Devoted counted on her mental alacrity.

Victor appeared from his bedroom, wearing the same black trousers and grey tunic that he did every day. His messy brown hair clumped around his ears and he mumbled a long morning greeting to Rhiannon that might have been "good morning, my lady" and might have been "the marmosets duel with tea services at noon."

He proceeded to trip over the cables that had appeared on the wooden floor sometime in the night. He caught himself, boots squeaking on the wax polish, and glared—at her, at the cables, at whoever had put them there—before heading to the tiny kitchen to perform some arcane ritual which would hopefully wake him up.

Alan arrived from his room next, stepping neatly over the cables. This astonished Rhiannon so much that she didn't initially notice the arms waving over his head, too focused on his toes until: "Ceridwen give me strength! Manawyddan lend me your clever eyes!" His shirtless shoulders heaved, and his sides jiggled over the waist of his trousers.

He stalked towards Rhiannon, and it was all she could do to stay firm and *not* to shrink into the couch back as if that would help her stay far away from the madman. "Have you seen it?" he accused.

She didn't answer, and he strode right into her seat cushion, then over her to check behind the couch.

"Sorry, my lady," Gavin chirped. His sleeves flowed like water with his *good morning* wave, and his red-blond hair was tied back with a green ribbon. That man was more of a morning person than the rest had proven, though it didn't stop him from stumbling when he reached the mysterious cables. He caught himself easily, stepping hard on his second pace into the room. "We're looking for a rogue belt."

Alan, behind her, threw up his arms above his head. "It's been stolen!"

Rhiannon didn't laugh. "That's a job for Mel, then."

Alan glared at her, round hazel eyes turning oval.

"Oh!" Rhiannon called when Luciano appeared in the doorway. "Look out for—"

But he'd already tripped over the black snakes on the floor, this time directly into Rhiannon's lap. His nose was buried between her knees and his right hand flew out and gripped her hip to support himself.

She sucked in a gasping breath. Waiting for her heart rate to ratchet. Waiting for her cheeks to go hot. They didn't.

The positioning, the way it had happened, it all should have been charged with unresolved sexual tension—or the desire for there to be some. That was how Hives formed. They came together around one charismatic woman, and every Devoted was supposed to have romantic feelings for her. Erotic feelings. And those feelings were supposed to go on for years, decades, until the Hive stabilized.

Oh, yes, her Hive had been unconventional from the start, but two of the Devotions had been as typical as any Dyfed had seen. Alan's… and Luciano's.

Luciano pulled back to kneel in front of her on the floor. He wasn't blushing either. Their eyes met as he laughed.

She blew the held-breath back out and shrugged at her own silliness. It wasn't awkward at all. They were Hive, already established in the course of months instead of years. They didn't have sparks or a charge or whatever anyone wanted to call it anymore. So much had happened; any innocent infatuation between them—from before they'd been kidnapped, stolen from, or mutually disappointing—had been too changed and damaged to last.

Rhiannon batted her eyelashes at Luciano teasingly, and he only laughed harder.

"They're for an experiment." Alan excused Luciano's unfortunate fall. *We ought to forgive him then.* After all, Alan's experiments were what made their Hive so sought after. "But it's over."

Victor's voice sounded like grinding bicycle gears when he said, "Let me help you put them away."

"Or he could get ready to go," Mel said. He coiled the unnecessary wires around two of his hands in an infinity symbol made of rubber and metal.

Alan yelped and dashed back to the room he shared with Victor and Mel.

Gavin and Luciano moseyed into the kitchen, which left only Victor at loose ends. "Come sit by me," Rhiannon said to Victor. *This is my chance to provide for my Hive's mental well-being.* She waited until he was situated and couldn't escape, then pushed a pad into his hands. Weighing him down. "Help me with my poetry recitation, would you?" It wasn't a request. "Gwyn used to rate my storytelling and diction skills back home," she said. "You're my last link to her, you know."

The corners of Victor's mouth tightened, pulling his lips extra wide and flat. Blank. Pushing off the couch, Victor stalked back towards his room, but ran into Alan coming out.

A-ha! There is no escape for you. Rhiannon's mental voice sounded like a melodrama villain—maybe Penelope's lead suitor from the Cleopatra's Palace version of *The Odyssey*—and she resisted the urge to rub her palms together.

Victor bypassed her on the return, heading for the exit, and Rhiannon's eyes widened. *Would he really abandon Alan on his presentation day?*

A brusque knock rattled the pocket door in its frame, and cut off Victor's escape yet again. It also foiled Rhiannon's plan to get him to think about Gwyn and acknowledge her lack in his life. Victor couldn't leave, but Rhiannon couldn't concentrate on anything other than the conference once Wenyan entered and brought official Mandarin business with him.

"Good morning, everyone," he said as he came into their space. Wenyan was friendly and awake, but impersonal. "We have quite the schedule today, and it starts with breakfast."

In the kitchen, Gavin and Luciano cheered.

Wenyan waved to them in reply. He proceeded to bubble over Alan ("Everyone is so excited about your presentation"), to admire Gavin's outfit ("You are such a brave revelation"), and even to effusively thank Victor ("So fast with how you opened the door"). Rhiannon couldn't help admiring how wonderful he was with all of her Devoted.

Nor noticing he'd all but snubbed her.

Still, she needed to talk with him before he said anything to the others about their kiss the day before. A sweat droplet tangled in her crown. What if she couldn't get to him before everyone learned she'd been kissing out of order?

Mmm, that kiss. His lips had been so soft, yet so textured on hers, like an extra-fine corduroy that Gwyn had once made an outfit from.

"Yes, now." Wenyan clapped his hands to get them all moving. "It is time for us to go. Let's eat!" He didn't even look at her as he shepherded the others out the door. First Victor, then Mel (who got a brief exchange in a language Rhiannon didn't speak). Why wouldn't he even acknowledge her? Sure, she needed to explain her behavior, but shouldn't he be curious? Wouldn't he want to know?

Luciano left, then Alan. And still Wenyan wouldn't so much as look at her! She could burst out with the truth right that second. *I want to kiss you again, but I can't until I talk with my Hive about it. They have to approve you before we do anything, so be sure to stay quiet about yesterday.*

Of course, yelling that—to Wenyan, to the stars, to the whole station through the open door—would also mean yelling it to her Hive, which rather defeated the purpose.

At the door, Gavin looked at her over Wenyan's shoulder and frowned. His head pulled back to give him something of a double chin. He shook his head and told Wenyan pointedly, "You drink the lees of Lombard's vinegar."

Rhiannon was eighty percent sure that was a putdown of some kind, and 40 percent sure that Gavin had been coming to her defense.

Which meant that Wenyan had 100 percent no clue what it meant. He bobbed his head, gelled hair swaying and screaming at her to touch it, and chivvied her Devoted down the corridor. If she didn't hurry up, they'd leave her behind to miss Alan's presentation.

It took twenty minutes to walk from Rhiannon's Hive's flat to the conference room, set up with keynote speakers and breakfast. Twenty minutes of Rhiannon's Hive keeping Alan calm and asking questions about people they passed. Twenty minutes of torture, wondering if Wenyan would let slip yesterday's secret whilst he ignored her.

Finally, the halls opened up on a conference room that was surprisingly like every other conference room she'd ever experienced. Even on this station filled with nature and life, the room seemed dull and soulless. *The better for concentrating on attendees' speeches.*

Two long tables near the door held up platters of toast and eggs, fish and rice, tea and tea and coffee and more tea. Her eyes skipped over the small groups chatting with plates in hands and the lone bamboo shoot on a dirt bed.

Her Devoted picked at the buffet options. Gavin already had a towering plate.

Wenyan would leave them to their breakfasting devices soon, and she'd lose track of him. She had to get him somewhere secluded *immediately*, but where?

Luciano at the coffee carafe—*coffee? Really?*—pointed a finger towards a wall. She squinted, and the closer inspection showed her it was one of those zigzag walls so common to Garden Station. It looked like a full-length, off-white sheet of plaster, but it was really two such sheets. The wall in front truncated a few feet from making a corner, which meant *something* hid behind.

This station really didn't like doors.

How did Luciano know this was here? And why had he pointed it out to her? It didn't matter; she was taking her chance. The rest of her Hive was engrossed in the table's offerings, freeing her to wrap her fingers around Wenyan's wrist unnoticed.

Rhiannon tugged him in the hidden cove's direction. Impolite it may have been, but sometimes a person needed to be impolite to get what she wanted. Her grip was strong enough to intimate insistence, but they both knew he could break it if he wanted to... and was willing to deny a visiting dignitary.

The double wall hid a service door, and Rhiannon pulled Wenyan into a closet tight with shelves and solvents and bleach and mops and rags and ballpoint pens (but no paper). The shelves dented her shoulder blades.

"What do you want?" Wenyan hissed. It was so different from his comforting tones in the garden.

"I'm sorry about yesterday. Not the kissing. I could never be sorry about the kissing, but about the pulling away." She dropped his wrist, palms slippery.

"Fine. Yes. I understand." He rattled off his acceptance without looking in her eyes. "No hard feelings. So let me go, please."

But he didn't open the door, even though she wasn't holding his wrist anymore.

She wished she could run a hand through her hair. It would be calming, and maybe he'd feel the urge to run his own hands through it. "It's different on Dyfed. There's more that needs to be done before... It's just different. For everybody, but especially for Queens."

While normal people could experience love and dating however they wanted, Queens had to wait until their Hives were sufficiently stable, then they needed permissions, and *then* the courtship had to be undertaken with the utmost formality. Would someone from a society that didn't have Queens respect that? Would Wenyan even want to try?

His face was more open now, lips parted and eyes focused. So she explained about Hive culture, and he nodded in all the right places, asked sensible questions. She finished with "I don't want to upset Alan on his big day," which sounded more like an excuse than anything else she'd said so far. The foolish weight of it tasted like sulfur on her tongue. Or maybe that was the cleaning chemicals in the cupbcard.

"I don't want to upset him either." Wenyan took her hand, the same one she'd used to drag him into the closet, and pressed it against his beating heart. Impossibly, it brought them closer together in the cramped space. She shivered. "But I'd like to stay with you. Even if it's difficult."

Yes. What did she say to that? Wenyan was proving himself to be the perfect man; he was interested in all her cultural mores, excited to be with her, and so very warm against her side. This was a natural breaking point in their conversation. She'd said what she needed to say, and they should return to the others, but she wanted to keep Wenyan's eyes on her just a little longer. "I was never meant to be Queen," she confessed. She'd never said it out loud. "I chose it myself by practicing for the Test, over and over until I got what I wanted."

He stepped even closer, until their joined hands covered both his heart and hers. "And do you want me?" His breath smelled like mint leaves, so much like home.

"You know what else I want? I want to kiss you again." So she did. He kissed her back, like she'd been afraid he wouldn't. And it was all gentle pressure and shared breath and quiet flying.

What is the ideal kissing technique? She was probably doing it wrong. Their mouths parted and came together again, and Rhiannon had to admit that kissing was kind of boring. Move here, move there. Repeat.

Her heart hammered, and not for good, sexy reasons. If she didn't break off this kiss before she lost all interest in it, Wenyan was going to know. Worse, if he was too caught up to notice her disinterest, she wouldn't know how to introduce the topic later.

She pulled back. "Does this mean we can date in secret?"

His mouth was shiny pink from her efforts. "I'd rather be an official couple with you, the kind where everybody coos over how cute we are together. We could be seen, and nobody would find it odd or wrong."

Rhiannon stood on tiptoe to brush their lips together again for that. *An official couple*. The idea was so comforting that she felt her heart rate slow. "If you really want to be serious, and you're interested, my culture has a sort of courtship ritual."

How best to explain it? In the old days on Earth, people had simply dated, but she knew from films and books that Dyfed had grown a custom all its own. "There are three phases and three gifts," she said. "The first phase is nature-based. Gifts are usually plants that the couple can watch grow together."

He nipped her ear and whispered into it, "Garden Station has an extensive plant library." His breath drove scampering love-claws across her skin.

"The second phase is for the gods because they must be involved in any relationship."

Wenyan pulled back to look at her, and she regretted the deep bags under his eyes. Had they been her fault? "Will it matter that my gods are different from yours?"

She shook her head no. "The third phase is personal; it's all about showing you know someone and getting to know them better. Here." She leaned against the bleachy-smelling shelves to wend a hand to her belt. Once her pad was free, she had him tap at the screen and show her how to send him a message from it. Which she did. "Now I've given you a personal gift. It's a recording of basic Welsh lessons because I know you're into languages."

Technically, she'd made the tutorial for the prostitutes on John Wayne, but it was still something she'd created herself and which she knew he'd like.

A screeching noise heralded the start of the keynote speeches before he could even open the message.

They fixed their outfits—her tunic straightened, his layers all falling appropriately—and went back to join Alan on his big day. Wenyan's hair was a mismatched mess, and Rhiannon took great pleasure in admiring it while the opening speeches droned on.

She looked forward to mussing it again.

Chapter Twelve

Working for the Revolution

The "fleet" over Dyfed,
Holly's staff ship bedroom

Holly had a plan for her day. Wake up, drink coffee and eat a protein bar, admire a picture of Amanda while wondering what her girlfriend was up to that morning, and schedule her inoculation plan for the day.

Because, of course, there were yet more Devoted to inoculate. As soon as that task was done, she could break radio silence to call her mentor... and then she could call home. Amanda had to be worried, seven weeks into Holly's two week absence.

Holly messaged her team of inoculation pros from her pad. They'd meet at the airlock tunnel in ten minutes. Her door chimed, but she ignored it. If anyone needed her, they'd flash her on her pad. Or they were already waiting for her at the airlock tunnel. She added a note for her med tech, a reminder to bring extra iodine.

I wonder what Amanda is up to this morning? At this time, Amanda would be puttering about their old farmhouse, bought when it was crumbling because no one wanted to live that far out from a city. Amanda and Holly had given up their central apartment to be closer to the wilds that Amanda loved—spare and inhospitable as they could sometimes be, far off the routes of emergency vehicles—and where Holly had space to build her own private lab.

It had taken them twenty years to get the house just as they liked it, with reinforced windows that stood up to sandy windstorms, a cozy kitchen with secondhand gadgets that they modified in their spare time, and a horribly impractical flower garden that Amanda loved and Holly thought a waste of energy and resources.

Holly bought bulbs and tarped over the garden during storm season all the same. The nurturing foolishness of the garden was everything that Holly loved about Amanda, the best trait they brought out in each other: fighting to forge their own lives against a system that pushed and molded and forced them to go another way.

What did it matter that they lived almost in the untamed areas? Should they move back to the city and be unhappy just because people—and the tax assessors— would make their lives easier? Should Amanda have stayed in her accounting office job instead of showing hikers to new places on their home planet? Should Holly have been happy as a family doctor when all she'd ever wanted was to do neuroscientific research?

So many people would say "yes" to all those questions. Holly and Amanda said no. *Together.*

Holly smoothed her bed and tucked the corners under at perfect 30-degree angles. Burgundy satin, ridiculously opulent for a research vessel. If she'd been the decorator, she wouldn't have chosen the sheets, but if they had to be there, at least they were her favorite color. And very different from the choppy stone floors in her Dyfed farmhouse.

She'd probably lost her planetside job at this point, but that wasn't as important as the revolution. By the time Holly returned home, victorious with the rest of the rebels, she'd leave her generic physician's position behind and trade up. Nobody could deny her talent for neuroscientific research now. *Take that, Neuroscientist Research Association!*

The only snag was that more Devoted ships kept showing up. Whenever it looked like she was halfway through, more arrived. It had to be at least 10 percent of the whole Devoted population now. At this rate, someone on Dyfed would notice the goings-on in their local space before Holly had finished her inoculations.

The Dyfed Space Defense Force could blow them into so much revolutionary space debris.

Her door chimed again, then slid open without her permission.

Holly whirled on the interloper. "What do you want?" The words came out before she recognized her visitor.

Short. Redheaded. Pursed lips redder than her hair. Holly had seen the woman before, a minor functionary whose name she hadn't bothered to learn.

"What do *I* want?" The redhead seethed like a rabies patient. "I want to do my job." Siân Edwards, that was her name. Holly remembered now. The woman was in charge of... ah, navigation. Which Holly had taken over as insurance against being made a redundant scapegoat. *Too bad, Edwards. I'm not giving it back.*

"So do it. I'm not stopping you. And I have places to be, so..." Holly made a shooing motion with her free hand, the other hefting her inoculations kit.

The annoying woman darted between Holly and the door. *Persistent—I could like her if this weren't so frustrating.* "You're only here to look after the Devotion puppets. Navigation and fleet tracking are mine, so stay out of them."

"In that case, no. My department is taking them over." Holly refused to lose her position as well as her (dwindling) patience. She was keeping her power and her dominion over the navigation systems.

"I won't have anything to do. My team won't have anything to do. Should we use the extra time to take naps?" Siân's wide, intense eyes were going crimson at the sclera. The red infiltrated from the edges, spindly veins reaching out to her irises.

"There's plenty to do in a rebel space fleet. Unless you're just allergic to work," Holly mused. She knew her musing voice would frustrate the former navigation supervisor. Much as Holly enjoyed spending time with some of the ex-military guards, she wasn't here to make friends.

"What?" The woman's nose scrunched up. It was almost cute.

"Allergies? Your eyes. The red can be a stress reaction." Holly shrugged. "Or glaucoma. I don't particularly care, but you might."

"What?"

"Now get out."

The confused expression turned into a challenging frown. "No."

Holly gave another shrug and walked into the woman's shoulder on her way to the door. They knocked together with minor impact, and Holly knew neither would have even a bruise. Soon enough, everyone would take Holly seriously and then she could give all the navigation problems back over to this admin. She'd be free to do science, live with Amanda, and be *happy* in the new world order.

"This conversation *will* continue," said the functionary, still in Holly's bedroom.

"Mm-hmm." Holly left her there. Time to go inoculate.

⟍ Interlude 2 ⟍

Morning Gossip

Dyfed, News Station 3

A blond woman of indeterminate age leans forwards across her gleaming wooden desk. Her posture invites viewers to engage with her, wherever they are. Beside her, picture-within-picture, a flower crown and a golden circlet form the shape of a double helix. It's impressive photo manipulation work.

"Good morning. This is Early Machynlleth News. I'm your host, Gretchen Wyn. In medical news today, two great Hives have united to combat the bone density epidemic affecting our remaining first-wave settlers."

Wyn's tongue wets her lips. "In a shocking move, they have sealed their temporary alliance in the bedroom rather than in the laboratory. The two involved Queens declared their intentions to court each other in an effort to share power." Wyn takes a long, dramatic pause. "Of course, neither has ever managed a relationship longer than two months, and everyone knows that romances between Queens are exceptionally volatile."

This is not standard fare for Early Machynlleth News, usually torn between hard-hitting political-scientific journalism and puff pieces such as how best to scramble an egg. Wyn has to take what rumor-mongering enjoyment she can while she may. And her viewers take it with her.

"Viewers may remember the amorous excesses of Queen..."

Chapter Thirteen

Road to Nowhere

Yin He Yuan (Garden Station),
corridor outside the conference area

Rhiannon didn't like leaving Alan by himself in the conference room. Oh, her Devoted had the right to ask for privacy. And he may have been correct that the Hive could only be a bored distraction. But now he was all alone, surrounded by strangers.

Cut off from reinforcements.

Rhiannon shivered in the winter-cold corridor, empty except for the rest of her Devoted. They stood on a short, red-laminated bridge that separated one side of the hallway from the other. It would have taken three steps to cross.

Now that she'd come to an agreement with Wenyan—*we're officially dating!*—her nervous system had calmed. Her skin cooled and her muscles ached with released tension.

Tension that was creeping back with clenched fingers and tightening shoulders. *We shouldn't have left him. Let's go back in.* But she forced her white-wisp breaths to slow and kept the words to herself. Instead she reassured everyone in the hallway

"He's got Wenyan with him, and he loves physics."

Mel tilted his headlamps. "Is Wenyan joining the Hive too?"

Rhiannon's heartrate rocketed. "What? Ack! No!" She swallowed hard, the saliva going down thick and painful. *Can he tell that's how our relationship feelings are going?*

Her outburst caught the attention of her other Devoted. Victor, Gavin, and Luciano all stepped closer to the not-argument. Which meant Rhiannon couldn't hide the topic. Her palms went damp. *They could find out.* It was far too soon for that.

Mel's visor flashed a confused blue-white-blue. "You like him, and he clearly admires you." His voice fried up on the end to make the statement sound almost like a question.

Too close. Too close. Bran's beard, he's way too close. "What makes you say I like him?" Rhiannon had to look away from them all, making eye contact with the floor. *Though it's true.*

Victor slouched against a post at the bridge's edge. "*I* like him." Was Victor really agitating to add a new Devoted? "If Wenyan joins us, we'll be linked to this station with its culture that's more like Dyfed than any of us expected to find." Yes, yes he was.

Gavin clasped one of Mel's arms and cleared his throat, gearing up for another of his teaching moments he'd been so enjoying sharing with the newest Devoted. "Devotion isn't just about our Queen liking someone who happens to be male," he said. "To be a potential Devoted requires many characteristics."

Luciano chimed in, "For instance, there's the propensity for Devotion, which we determine through the Test." His white teeth made a smiling arc on his bronze skin.

Gavin quickly recovered from the surprise of Luciano's interjection. "Or creative academic smarts that would be nurtured by an entire group of like-minded thinkers to bounce ideas," he added.

The way our Hive's specialty keeps bouncing around, we're an unlikely match for anyone! When they'd formed their unorthodox Hive, they'd filled out an application to inherit the *Ceridwen's Cauldron* from the previous group. On that application, they'd said they planned to be an explorer Hive, not that they knew what that meant. And not that an explorer Hive needed three Creative Technologists.

Since then, they'd gained a martial strategist and a semi-decided bard while losing their agricultural expert. *If Hives are meant to further the works of their members, what does my Hive stand for?*

"Also," Luciano said, "Devotion requires a romantic interest in the Queen." His even wider smile made her feel guilty for doubting his need for a Hive just like this one, a Hive happy to take someone with his interests and background. Watching him tag team with Gavin proved Luciano's deep understanding of the culture all of them claimed as their own now.

Mel snorted, a funny sound through a robotic speaker. "I'm pretty sure Wenyan's feelings are romantic."

Rhiannon tittered. *Please stop noticing things like that.* She had to move. Her feet itched from standing still, so she clomped on heavy boots for the three steps across the bridge and into the connecting corridor.

The sound didn't drown out the conversation that came with her.

Victor sighed. "Gods, just think. We could have someone on our side to make sure we stayed here."

"Is that how Hives come together, then? The Elder Dylan writes about the relationship of Devoted to Queen as a romance. So, an orgy would—"

Rhiannon's very teeth shook. *Manawyddan's mousetrap!* She whirled, eyes so wide the balls went dry. *"No no no no.* There are no orgies. No actual sex is involved."

Mel crabbed backwards on his four insect-like legs, and Rhiannon regretted the outburst. It was a valid question from a newbie, she supposed. All-inclusive orgies made as much sense as having no romantic contact with the Devoted at all when the intent was not to play favorites. The choice could as easily have been "all" as "nothing," if you weren't from Dyfed. If you didn't already know how it worked. How it had worked for generations.

"We could *stay* here. Don't you get that?" Victor was still stuck on adding Wenyan.

Gavin's lecture continued. "The underlying romantic tension stabilizes the Hive, the same way a ball pulled in multiple directions by attached strings will float perfectly in the air."

And his alter ego in Devotion studies, AKA Luciano, picked up the thread: "Forcing erotic energy into the romantic structure would destroy the balance." His dramatic words made him seem even more like a Gavin-extension.

Does he really feel that way? Of course he did. Luciano and Alan had been her two traditional Devoted. She couldn't let them down. They couldn't know about her interest in Wenyan.

As they walked deeper into the station's heart, the halls became more crowded with impractical dressers in heeled shoes and tight skirts and so many layers they'd never be able to move inside a spacesuit. They huddled closer to one another, keeping the conversation alive.

"Usually, Hives wait about ten years before bringing up the idea of their Queen being..." Gavin trailed off and made a hand gesture that was undoubtedly meant to indicate "sexually/romantically active" but looked more like "drying dishes."

"Then again," Luciano said as he winked at Rhiannon, and she shook her head fondly in return, "our Hive has been through so much, so fast, that we may not wait the minimum ten years."

Does he suspect my feelings for Wenyan?

"Americans probably don't learn Dyfed history," Gavin continued, "but your people must know of England's Queen Elizabeth I." They'd reached more a populated section of the station between the conference and their borrowed flat. Women in bright-patterned mini-dresses and men in enough layers not to need jackets against the wintry cold rushed along, all busy on their way to somewhere. "*She* was completely celibate—the sources say—but kept her rings of spies and agitators in line through their personal loyalty to their queen."

Victor grunted when a local's elbow caught him in the chest on his way past. "Mel is our people now, Gavin."

"He knows what I mean," Gavin said.

Now walking at Rhiannon's right hand, Mel's visor flashed white. "If it doesn't actually matter, why are there no female Devoted?"

Behind them, Luciano balked. "There can't be!"

"Shhh," admonished a local, gone as quickly as his or her etiquette lecture had been administered.

Gavin's voice came close in Rhiannon's left ear. "Women don't feel the same sort of desperate pleasure in hoping for a romantic crumb from a Queen."

"Which means they can't be part of the stabilizing tension," Luciano piped from further back.

Mel drew his next words out slowly, like he didn't believe they could possibly be true. Like he didn't understand even after this strange teaching moment. "So, a Devoted has to be male to Devote. I Devoted. But I was a woman when we met."

Rhiannon linked her hand through one of Mel's arms. He needed the soothing, she could tell. *You belong with us, and don't let anyone tell you differently.* "What you were prior to Devotion didn't matter. It's what you are in your Devoted heart."

Mel cocked his arm to better accommodate her, as a good Devoted should. "What about Gwyn?"

Rhiannon heard a quick inhalation behind them, which had to be Victor, but he said nothing.

Rhiannon answered the question instead of worrying about her best friend's ex-boyfriend. "Gwyn didn't Devote. She was more... Hive-adjacent."

Mel shook his spherical head. "So, do Queens date at all?"

Only bad ones like me. "Only with the blessing of their whole Hive."

"Will you have a lover someday?"

Rhiannon felt the heat creeping across her face. *That's an uncomfortable question.* "Ah, well—"

A harsh ping came through Mel's speaker grille, cutting off any answer Rhiannon might have made. The tone bounced off the vine-covered walls, drew frowns from the locals streaming past, and echoed in Rhiannon's ears like a school bell come too early on Test day.

"What the—" Victor's incredulous voice got as far as asking before Mel answered the question. "One of my proximity sensors at the *Ceridwen's Cauldron* has gone offline."

Rhiannon's breath caught and her blood went silent in her veins. No. No no no. *Not again.* All around her, locals pushed into her Devoted to get on their way. Overrunning her Hive and trampling their hopes and calm.

Mel's speaker pinged again. *A second sensor or the same one?* The sound restarted her blood and Rhiannon dashed forwards.

Her boots thumped on laminate bridges and thwacked on stone. They reverberated on springy wood as Mel called out directions behind her.

She twisted out of locals' ways, the people mere blurs of color. Colorful obstructions.

Someone yelled something, probably "No running in the halls," but Rhiannon didn't speak the language and she didn't care to. Not if these people were stealing her ship or her engine or even something as insignificant as her duvet cover.

She approached the airlock's bamboo-marked turns with her oath-bound men fast behind her. The crowds had thinned to nothing. Just the winter air and Rhiannon and her Devoted.

Without the chrysanthemums still in place, the path to vacuum space was bare. Stripped tree branches posed beside partial walls.

Walls made her blind until she could take each turn. Anything might hide behind them: someone to bump into. Someone who planned to take her down.

I will not be overpowered. My Devoted stand with me, and we are strong.

That would mean nothing if an entire security force waited to prevent her from defending her rights. Her ship. Her freedom.

Finally, they arrived at the stone marker that separated the airlock from the Garden Station. A silver sheet wall kept her from going any farther, but Rhiannon had seen that wall raise and lower. On its other side, there would be image screens with trees.

Would there also be work crews ferrying over whatever they liked from the *Ceridwen's Cauldron*?

"Open it up," Rhiannon ordered.

Mel and Gavin surged forwards to opposite ends of the wall, hunting for an access panel.

Rhiannon wished Alan were with them. In the light of this potential betrayal, she wanted to keep her Hive close together.

Long moments passed. Victor joined Mel on his side of the door, and Luciano grasped Rhiannon's shoulder, but she shook him off. This wasn't right. Her heartrate ratcheted higher, punching at her ribs. *Anything could be happening behind this wall. And I can't stop it. Even though I'm* right here.

Rhiannon pounded her fists against the steel door. It barely vibrated under her desperate force, a dull gong that thudded in her ears. Her hands turned red from pinky knuckle to wrist. The heat of it burned.

She couldn't even get to the docking spoke, much less out to her ship. Not if she'd gotten stuck inside the station. *Why did I trust them?*

A buzzing in her ears played counterpoint to the basso thwacks of fist to metal.

The buzz resolved into Luciano's voice. "My lady. My lady, please."

It was the "please" that got her attention, and she slumped against the wall to better listen. "Yes?" Without her hand striking it, the metal made no sound. Its cold surface sucked the heat from her forehead.

"This man is asking you to stop hitting the airlock door, my lady."

Rhiannon sniffed some suddenly loose snot back into her nose before she turned to present her most composed self. "I would like to see my ship please."

"No, sorry." The local man was old, with a venerable lined face and stooped posture. "Maintenance."

All her muscles tensed in a full-body twitch. *Can't they even come up with a good lie?* She could fight for her safety and her people. Rhiannon bared her teeth in a smile analogue. "That's *my* ship out there," she explained. "I need to get to it."

"No, sorry. Maintenance," the man repeated.

"You don't have the right!" Her voice rose to a shout, and her red-pink hands rose up with it, still clenched.

The man cringed back from her, back hunching further.

Oh.

Oh.

Oh.

She'd scared him.

"No, *sorry*," he repeated. "Maintenance."

Luciano's hand covered her fist on one side, and Gavin's did on the other. Together, they brought her into a warm cocoon of Devoted and Queen that wouldn't intimidate a helpful passerby.

Her breath hitched. She could still fight her way out to her ship, but she wasn't sure anymore. There was reasonable doubt now. She'd scared someone trying to help her and who didn't even speak her language. What kind of person was she?

One who'd been cut off from her ship, among other things.

⟍ Chapter Fourteen ⟋

What is Natural?

Yin He Yuan (Garden Station),
The Scholar's Garden

All Mel's psychology modules suggested the Hive would prefer to avoid the gardens. As they were a scene of recent trauma. But here they all were, except Alan. Seeking to find serenity in the gardens—the gardens!—in the wake of Rhiannon's minor meltdown.

Mel needed Dyfed psychology modules. The American ones weren't working.

"There are no spacesuits in this area," Mel said. His Hive mates had asked to be informed whenever they entered a new section, and by his TBD patron god, he was going to inform them.

"Thank you," said Rhiannon. Gavin, Victor, and Luciano muttered their gratitude as well.

Mel dipped out of the way to let a pair of local women pass. One brushed against Mel's upper left arm as she squeezed by. Her drapey thigh-length cotton shirt—deep purple, painted with pink and silver flowers, belted over harem pants that draped as well—tickled his sensors. Her friend followed, more sedate in a blue and yellow polka-dotted *qipao* like the woman at the conference had worn.

"I wish our ship were more like this garden," said Gavin.

The whole Hive nodded, and Mel moved his spherical head up and down, even as his shoulders rocked side to side. Why would they want a ship like this garden? Not only was it difficult to navigate (with pointlessly labyrinthine walkways and constantly obstructed doorways), but the Faraday cage gave him a headache.

"Let's do it," Victor said.

"Do what?" Mel let his voice come up so high on the question that it might've risen to alto levels. He'd been testing out the tenor ranges this past week, up from baritone the week before. His voice still wasn't right. Unnaturally smooth, sporting a cross between a Welsh lilt and a Texan drawl. There was something wrong with it.

Victor's hair flopped everywhere with his giddiness. His feet slid around on the textured floor in a way that made Mel want to correct his stance. "It can be our project while Alan does his thing."

A quick glance at the alert faces around him, and Mel knew. The rest of them understood Victor's implied subject. Mel didn't. Well, he'd figure it out from visual and contextual clues. Preferably before the others saw how uncomfortable he was.

"It'll be like bringing nature and home with us everywhere we go," said Victor.

"A skill learned *far from home*." Gavin's intonation matched with a quote from the classic song *Far From Home,* first performed in the musical adaptation of *Goodwin's Road* in an off-Broadway performance in 2048. Mel had never cared for fantasy musicals.

Luciano bounced on his toes, crinkles forming at the corners of his eyes. "We'll need to learn more about scholar's gardens. Isn't there a gardener around here? Wenyan dismissed last time's, I believe."

Mel tapped his fingers against his opposite arms. They couldn't possibly still be on about making the *Ceridwen's Cauldron* more like this station. Could they?

"Maybe that could be my superpower!" Victor said with a small laugh. The supposedly joyful sound took a forced huff from his lungs. "Usually, I say I wish I could see through walls—would've been handy in the airlock—but this kind of gardening…"

Gavin hummed. "For my superpower, I'd want to fly. And we all know Mel's a shapeshifter."

Luciano quirked an eyebrow. "Flying a spaceship isn't enough for you? I'd want to see the future."

If Mel wanted to bond with his Hive mates, he needed to chime in. And he understood this much better than the gardening obsession. "I would like to read minds."

There was a silent beat. *Is there something wrong with mind reading?*

Victor furrowed his forehead. "But you're a shapeshifter."

"So?" It was Rhiannon who stood up for him. Rhiannon for always, who saved Mel from enemies who wanted to kill him and from friends who didn't realize the damage they might do. "He can still want something else. I, for instance, have a Queen's power, but that doesn't mean I won't want a superpower too. Mine would be teleportation."

Mel nodded his head, backing his Queen with human-style gestures, though they moved his metal spine in unfamiliar ways. "And I bet Wenyan would want to speak all languages."

Beside Luciano, Commander Ceridwen sighed. Her face was pink and her eyes were fever bright. Her cheeks somehow had a softer cast to them, like she'd relaxed the muscles, but they couldn't be lax because a small smile played over her lips.

Oh. Wenyan.

Luciano's heels bounced off the floor stones with a smart *clack*. "I'm going to find a gardener."

Rhiannon hummed her acknowledgement, but her voice still shook. "Why don't I step outside and ask Wenyan to come translate? The rest of Alan's program is in English today, so he'll be fine on his own."

Then it was just Mel, Victor, and Gavin among the flowering vines and strangely shaped vestibules.

And the locals, of course. A gaggle of teens, just younger than the Hive, flocked by. Boys shoved each other, blows glancing off the jewel-toned layered clothing. Girls posed and giggled, resplendent in both the draping fashion and a progression of ever shorter mini-dresses, and all in bright patterns. Dots, animals, abstracts, florals, the colors mixed in gradations that even Mel's advanced sensors couldn't distinguish.

His own vest, the only clothing item he bothered to wear, was drab in comparison. He was another blandly colored man, grey and blue from headlamps to shoe-shod leg spikes. As a disguise, it was perfect.

He widened his stance until his left legs were partially in the dirt. *Men take up more space,* he reminded himself. *It's supposed to make me feel more powerful and in control.* Bamboo leaves poked his underbelly where the new leg position brought him closer to the ground. They couldn't get through his armor plating, but they were certainly attempting it.

Gavin didn't notice the group passing through on the way to the Hall of Lace Gingko (if Mel was reading the stone-carved sign correctly). He was too busy leaning over a miniature landscape, a shallow dish with a twiggy tree hanging over a mouse-sized bench beside a puddle of water.

Maybe Mel could acquire some bright buttons and brooches for his vest. Add a bit of color. Now that he wasn't a Ranger anymore, his old badge never decorated the outside. Not that he'd ever flashed it around like that. Usually kept it in a pocket. That's what pockets were for.

Victor bounded off, footsteps merging with the younger teens', but an auditory check turned him up beside Luciano, both their heartbeats fast. "How much water do you need for bamboo?" Victor asked.

He got a garbled, "Ah, umm, *lah*" in response. The gardener likely didn't speak any English, and Victor had no other languages. Otherwise he'd have practiced them with Mel. Wouldn't he?

A pressure on Mel's arm, and he didn't spin around to shake it off. "My lady," he said to acknowledge his Queen.

"Wenyan is on his way." Her arms jerked with minute tremors, and her smile was so broad another Devoted was going to notice something had pleased her. They'd see her flushed face and realize that she and Wenyan didn't have a standard visitor-translator relationship.

Right now she needed someone to hide her secret romance. And Mel knew his place. This was the one vector he understood unequivocally: be whatever your Queen needs.

In the most affronted tenor cadence he could copy from a famous operatic diva, he proclaimed, "I could translate equally well." Though it had been proven he couldn't. The attention was on him, not his Queen, and that was the important part.

Gavin clapped him on a lower shoulder. "That's rough, man. Don't let it *rend your very heartstrings*."

Mel didn't have heartstrings. But his inability to speak with the locals rankled all the same. He could read and write the language just fine. His processors ran hot, racing to create a grammar for the station topolect. He *ought* to be able to translate. It was a skill he sold to his Queen.

Another deficiency for the list. American, synthetic, no heartstrings...

...lacking connection to nature. He trailed his Hive through the impractical walls and scattered trees. They were all together except for Alan, with Wenyan on the way. Each and every Devoted tried to converse with the gardener. They touched the plants, getting their fingerprints all over everything in an action dangerously close to what that other visitor had been warned against. And for what?

Oh, Mel would go along with their plans, but he couldn't feel the way they did about nature. As a Dyfed Hive member, he was flawed. Broken. And as a Devoted, he appreciated his Queen—gave her fealty and called her *my lady*—but he didn't desperately need her. If the others lived like she was the air they breathed, Mel was the PRob who could survive in vacuum.

Maybe he couldn't connect because he wasn't really male. He tried, but it was just plain wrong.

Reasons Melissa wants to go back to being female:

- Because she is
- Because she prefers to be referred to as "she"
- Because she doesn't grasp why it matters to Dyfed that Devoted be male

Melissa had pretended long enough. The logic was clear. She was Melissa. She was a woman. If she had to, she'd play the game for her Hive's sake, but only for a little while. She'd know the truth. And she could tell Queen-Commander Ceridwen once the Hive had departed from this station and Melissa could be sure her status wouldn't destabilize anything.

She narrowed her legs' positions, ringing her shoes back onto the path and protecting her body from bamboo—or weaponized—incursions.

In space's long, dark expanse, they'd have time to discuss how best to position her gender for Dyfed's arbiters. Melissa was already so out of step with traditional Devoted, another difference couldn't possibly matter.

"Maybe we really do belong here," said Gavin, spinning around in a circle with arms out and eyes closed. Soaking in the garden, like the plaque over his head (and that he couldn't read) encouraged him to do.

Melissa hoped again he was wrong. She understood this place even less than she understood Dyfed's poetry and music. Why was nobody investigating the lockdown events of the past day? The American Space Rangers would have been questioning the scientists about sabotage. Perhaps Rhiannon would let her investigate, if it wouldn't cause an international incident.

"We'll fill our ship with green growing things," said Victor. As if the plant room on the ship didn't provide enough for a voyage.

Luciano, ever practical, said, "We should go back and take measurements."

At last! A task she could help with. She'd measured the entirety of the *Ceridwen's Cauldron* on her first day, the better to know her new home. "Done." She kept her tone a husky tenor. No need to give away her reclaimed gender with her voice box.

Victor bounced over, popping up and down across the cameras in her array. "Are there any significant features we should plan around?"

Melissa's visor flashed white, but she kept her shoulders still until she deliberately shrugged them all at once. A tiny motion made longer by synchronicity. "We'll find out what's significant and what isn't as we learn how best we can reshape our home."

What constituted a salient detail when turning a serviceable ship into a floating garden? Melissa's ignorance made her yet more of an outsider among these people who gave her everything. All the acceptance she'd ever wanted, and somehow she still failed them.

As Gavin might have reminded her: "to err is human." But she wasn't.

Chapter Fifteen

Windows to the Soul

Yin He Yuan (Garden Station),
the conference room

Alan wished he hadn't sent his Hive mates away, if only so he'd have someone to complain to. It was way too hot in the conference room. Sweat dribbled beneath his arms and made his tunic sticky. *Why do people always turn up the heat in winter until it's at midsummer levels? I did not layer enough for this.*

If only he were wearing a qipao like the local female scientists! He might look pudgy and weird trying to squeeze into one of those sleeveless tubes with floral embroidery, but they were *sleeveless* tubes with floral embroidery.

The conference room wanted to be beautiful and inspiring, but it didn't have anything special. A podium off to the side looked like every podium in the history of podiums. The ceiling was striped with dark beams that looked like wood (but probably weren't), and a long table at the front of the room had that "professional" white tablecloth draped over it (meaning it probably was a bunch of cheaper, smaller tables shoved together).

Five men and women sat at the panelists' table waiting to begin. Behind them, the tiny locker Mel had pointed out stored six spacesuits. Six! For a whole conference.

"Hello, Alan." Professor Cantor slipped into the twill chair beside his and poured two water glasses.

And *that* was why he'd told his Hive mates to visit the garden and check on the ship. Alan flicked his eyes in Cantor's direction, a polite passing familiarity. He flicked them away again. They couldn't know Cantor was here and wanted to talk with him.

Either they'd be mad at Alan for bringing them to the Dyfed establishment's attention, or they'd give everything up in order to give him the chance to hear what Cantor had to say. Either way, Alan would be left to stew in a pool of guilt.

His cheeks tightened as he maintained a fake smile. *Nothing wrong here, professor. Just your regular old protégé attending a conference. Alone. On his way somewhere else.* Would Cantor believe Alan had amnesia and *that* was the reason he'd been avoiding the man's messages?

"Hello, professor." Alan squirmed in his "ergonomic" chair, clearly intended for some species not yet discovered by humanity, and looked out the tiny window at the nothingness of space.

"I was excited to see your name on the program. Congratulations on getting your miniaturized Alcubierre drive to work."

"Thank you," Alan muttered. Cantor had timed this perfectly. He couldn't leave his seat so close to the start of a fresh talk, and he didn't want to cause a scene. He was cornered.

"I know how much you like to keep busy, so let me tell you about this interesting new project. It's a missile defense grid, and you're going to want to look at the maths."

Out the window, two Chinese scientists were setting up some sort of array. He'd seen their demonstration listed on the agenda, something about classical mechanics, showing that Hamiltonian orbits could be achieved around an object the size of a bowling ball when in space and far enough from a large planetary body. They weren't half as intriguing as the innocent little pad Cantor slid in front of Alan's water glass. It sat there, mocking him. *Where's your scientific curiosity?* the pad demanded.

"All right!" Alan threw up his hands and snatched the device, scrolling through pages of diagrams that meant little and stopping on long lists of equations to make sure he was satisfied with the conclusions.

Beside him, Cantor hummed happily. Outside, the two Chinese scientists did their thing. All around them, physicists paused to check what the yelling was about, then resumed chattering away in their native tongues and making sweeping declarations in their shared mathematics.

Alan's eyebrows rose and fell and pulled together as if trying to form a perfect rectangle. He hadn't wanted to entertain Cantor at all. He'd intended to turn him down flat. But... the professor was right. The project was intriguing. And he'd already found three places for obvious improvements.

"I don't believe you're letting Naam work on this," Alan said. In all three cases of inefficiency, Naam was the culprit.

"Only because I don't have you." Cantor smiled. "Yet."

Alan put the pad down. "I'll think about it," he said.

It was a lie. He was done thinking. No matter how exciting the project might be, he couldn't go back to Dyfed. Not with his Hive. They had to avoid scrutiny. And maybe some Devoted could leave their Queens, but Alan wasn't that kind. He wasn't even going to tell the others about this conversation.

Alan drew listless infinity symbols in the condensation on his water glass. Maybe someday they could go home and he could meet up with Cantor. Maybe at his year's end, he'd be more interested in this particular application of physics than in staying with Rhiannon, Luciano, Victor, Mel, and Gavin. (In no preference order, except for Rhiannon. She came first, always.)

But he doubted it. Much as he liked Cantor's company, much as he wanted to be on this missile defense project, the Hive was more important.

"Keep the pad," Cantor said.

As if Alan could keep himself from poring over it in his spare time. And making notes where Naam (and others) had gone wrong, wrong, wrong.

Cantor knew him so well.

"Good morning, everyone," said a panelist, getting the room's attention. "We are ready to begin. I would like to start by introducing—"

A flash lit the room, coming from the window where the two scientists had been setting up *something*. Alan blinked, spots forming in his vision even after the light had gone back to black.

Creak-crunch!

The wall around the window splintered and air hissed near it. A flame erupted at the panelists' table and died out just as quickly as the room's oxygen fled.

Scarf-wrapped men shrieked.

Qipao-wearing women ran for the doors.

The hole in the wall widened.

An alarm wailed.

Alan dashed for the spacesuit locker, dodging other attendees in various stages of panic. The lacquer-look plastic door tore off in his hand, and he jumped feet first into the suit he found. A little tight, but serviceable.

Zipped in and hooded, he grabbed the repair kit from the closet floor and headed straight for the leak. Behind him, scuffling overwhelmed the panicked screaming as physicists and administrators fought over the remaining five suits.

Alan didn't have time for their foolishness. He was going to fix that wall before the cracks blew out the window.

The repair kit had a tube of resin, an insulated patch the size of his fist, and two aspirin. It would do.

A splash of not-black flickered in the window, and Alan looked away from his bounty. Only for a moment. Outside, the two scientists floated in zero-g, no purpose to their movements. They weren't trying to get in or to repair their device. They just floated.

Are they...?

Alan couldn't worry about the outdoor strangers. They were on their own. At present, they wouldn't fit through the crack in the wall, so he couldn't bring them in. And, Manawyddan help him, he'd make sure they'd never fit.

After pushing the insulated material into the widest part of the hole, Alan tried to open the resin tube. The cap was stuck.

If he removed his helmet-hood, he could bite off the top.

He could also asphyxiate and/or have his blood boil off when the wall inevitably blew out and took him with it. His breathing sped to dangerous quickness, proving he could asphyxiate even inside the suit.

No, let's not do that then. *I'd rather not turn into a prune.*

Alan threw the tube to the floor and stomped on it, smashing the cap into red plastic particles that someone would later have to clean out of the floorboards. Freed, the resin flowed easily, pushing into the smaller cracks and sealing up the edges where it met the fabric patch.

He smoothed his hands over his work, feeling for tugs where the air wanted to vacate the room. None. The place was airtight once again.

Alan unzipped his suit. The room felt cool on his panic-heated skin, sweat starting to evaporate outside the rubber container.

"It's all right," he said.

No one listened, still panicking. Alan didn't even care.

He slumped against the wall a few feet from his patch job and let himself trickle down it like mud until he sat on the floor, head balanced on his knees. People were screaming, though the alarms had quieted.

"Here." Cantor appeared in front of him like a dream bearing a glass of water.

Alan opened the emergency repair kit again and took out those two aspirin. Now he knew what they were for: the sanity of the poor guy who made the repair. "Thanks." He washed the drugs down with a sip of water, then gulped the rest. His skin inside the suit was sticky and sweltering, cooling rapidly now that he'd freed the fasteners so his body heat had somewhere to go.

"That was quick work." Cantor refilled the glass with a sealed bottle from the table, making a weight in Alan's hand that bound him in place.

It was nice to be appreciated. "I've been working on my emergency response skills."

Cantor pointed at the fix. "Very impressive."

Alan followed his gesture and couldn't help tracing the crack with his eyes, up the wall and to the window sill and then out the window where the two bodies still floated. Unclaimed and insensate. All he could think to say was, "I've never seen a dead body before."

The sweat cooling on his skin made him shiver.

"No, no." A conference organizer came over with a blanket and stood in front of Alan, blocking his view of the outside. "No dead bodies here. But let us go to a more stable room."

Warm blanket clutched to his shoulders, Alan was hurried away with the rest of the attendees. But he knew it for a lie. Death was death was death.

Thank the gods his Hive hadn't been here. In the aftermath, however, all he wanted was to be with them again. To touch them and see them and breathe the same, safe air.

He wanted his Queen.

⟋⟍ Chapter Sixteen ⟋⟍

Gilded Cage

Yin He Yuan (Garden Station),
The Scholar's Garden

Rhiannon was watching the garden entrance when it happened. She'd been listening to her Devoted discuss the merits of various flowering plants and shivering in the light snow sprinkle that supposedly mirrored Beijing's.

Then the walls came down, one whooshing so close to her nose that she might have lost some skin if it were a little closer. They clanged into the pebbled floor around her with finality.

The snow stopped.

The ringing of metal on stone faded.

She was alone, alone in a tiny cell that discouraged lying flat on the ground and stretching. All she could see was metal and metal and metal and metal and a sliver of metal-latticed sky. Everything was quiet loneliness. She clenched her hands against her thighs and tried to find a place to look that wasn't the vile, never-ending metal. Her knees shook from the vibrations... or maybe from the sudden adrenaline.

Ah. She squatted on the uncomfortable pebbled ground and pulled out her pad. So long as she concentrated on little things, she would keep her mind clear until the walls lifted and everything was safe once again. Her breathing tried to speed—*oncoming hyperventilation, eh?*—but she clicked out a rhythm with her nails on the stones and inhaled to the timing. *Inhale, two, three. Exhale, two, three.*

She worked her way up to a count of eight before she stopped tapping.

This had seemed much less daunting when Wenyan was with her last time.

Gods, Wenyan had been on his way to meet them. Her hands clenched again, rumpling her tunic hem. Were the corridors safe for him? He'd said the central garden was the safest place to be, and he hadn't been in it. She reached behind her head and pulled a lock of hair out of her practical Queenly braid-weave so that she could twirl it around her finger. Around and around and around. What would she do if Wenyan had been hurt? What if he needed her? He'd never have been in the corridors if she hadn't called him to join her.

No! She had to think of her Hive first. She would keep her Devoted safe and together as best she could, and Wenyan... Wenyan wasn't hers to worry about it. She had to remember that, before even worse circumstances made it devastatingly clear.

Before she'd determined whether he was part of a plot to steal valuables from her ship. She needed to see him. Needed to ask!

She was already falling back into the trap. *Breathe in, Rhiannon. In, two, three, four. Out, two, three, four.*

If the gardens were the safest place, then the person she had to worry about most was Alan. He'd been in a whole different section of the station, nowhere near her tiny cell. What if she contacted him, but he didn't answer? She took a deep inhale—*one, two, three*—firmed her shoulders and her mouth. No matter how she dreaded the potential outcome, she had a responsibility.

A few taps, and she called Alan.

Nothing happened.

She waited a few moments, expecting to see his face on her pad screen. Perhaps a little worse for the wear. But no.

Nothing.

The connection wasn't even catching on his end.

Her vision blurred and her hands rose to her head, grasping her crown on both sides as if she might pull it off and throw it away, cast off the worry and the care. But Alan had given her this crown, and she would not take his gift lightly.

She *thunk*ed her head against a metal wall, letting the gold leaves dig into her skull. Penance. It gave her a beautiful view of the latticework ceiling.

Oh! The Faraday cage. No wonder she couldn't communicate with Alan. He was outside of it and she was inside. The "serene" inner garden had lost its serenity as far as Rhiannon was concerned, but at least she could let herself believe there were perfectly sensible reasons for why Alan didn't answer when she called.

Within the cage, though, she should be able to contact the rest of her Devoted. Their pads' interactions didn't depend on anything other than the space between them. The thick metal doors might get in the way, but Rhiannon doubted it. Only one way to find out.

She started with Luciano because she still felt guilty for the way she'd let him stew in his own despair when they went hypoxic the first time. "Hey, Luciano," she said when his face filled her screen. With his digital presence in her cell, she could affect the nonchalance that would comfort him. *Ceridwen as my witness, it's good to have company.* "Whatcha up to?"

"Oh, you know how it is." He strove to match her tone, but his intense brown eyes were crusted with telltale overflow. "We're having a grand time. This is the perfect moment for some spontaneous prayer."

"Who is 'we'?"

Luciano panned his pad to show off Mel behind him, four legs crooked upwards to make him the same height as a kneeling penitent.

"Are you two all right while I check on the others?" Rhiannon didn't want to keep Luciano on the channel when she contacted the others. Panic could spread outrageously fast, so she'd keep all her Devoted separate from each other until they were sure to support rather than undermine. This was the single advantage of being apart.

Rhiannon cut the connection and tapped her pad again. *Who taught Mel how to pray?* She hoped her newest Devoted had chosen an attentive deity for the experiment.

With a scraping rumble, the metal walls came free of their stony confines.

As soon as the imprisonment reached a yard high, Rhiannon was tackled to the ground. Her attacking limpet smelled of sugary lime, and that meant Gavin had been snacking during his captivity. Her face mashed against the stones, and her breasts smushed against the bumps, but she couldn't stop the smile that broke out.

When another of her Devoted piled on, pressing her even less comfortably into the rugged walkway, she exercised her Queenly prerogative. "Everybody up," she ordered.

They hopped to their feet, just like they were supposed to. Five hands—from four men—reached down. She accepted the closest two and let the remaining three "help" on her elbows and forearms. She understood their need to touch. She wasn't letting them go any time yet either. "Huddle close," she said, giving them the only command they wanted to hear. "We won't split up again."

Victor's face in her nape mumbled, "Not ever."

Rhiannon rearranged their formation to put herself against Mel's chest, the best orientation for mutual grasping among all four of her present Devoted.

"Rhiannon!" It was Wenyan's voice. And calling her by that name was a sure sign that he'd forgotten all decorum in his need to find her. "*Rhiannon!*"

She peeked out from between Gavin's and Luciano's arms, and had a perfect view when he skidded over the bridge and around the corner and right into a planting of banana leaves. His hair was at all angles, his jacket unbuttoned. He looked soft and needy and worried, and she wanted nothing more than to fall into him and never come out.

But she had her Devoted. With Wenyan here, there was only one man missing from her Garden Station life. And he had to be more important than the love interest she couldn't quite trust yet. By Ceridwen, they needed time alone! She couldn't ask her questions surrounded by her Devoted, and Wenyan with his silken lips...

She was Queen. She had a duty, and her love life was not part of it.

Rhiannon looped her hands around Gavin's and Luciano's elbows, forcing them into a walk. "We should go." Her Hive arrayed around her, ready for anything.

But Wenyan stood before them and shook his head emphatically. "No, no. You must stay here. This is the safest place on the station."

No. Alan wasn't here, and she couldn't contact him from within the Faraday cage. Moreover, the garden had turned into a scary trap 100 percent of the times she'd been in it. She might never return to it again. Logic may have told her that it was a safe place, but her heart felt otherwise.

"I have a right to choose my own traps," she told the obstructor.

"All right." Wenyan stepped gracefully to the side. He smoothed his hair down and no longer looked upset. If she was healthy, then all was right with his world, apparently. *Doesn't he have anyone else to care for?* "May I recommend the marketplace level? It's the next safest area with the most doors."

The garden and the marketplace. The station's metaphorical heart and the area with the largest population at any given time. *Manawyddan's mousetrap!* Garden Station was *designed* for this type of thing. The architects had figured out how to minimize the loss of life when something went wrong. Instead of trying to cut down on emergencies, they'd mitigated the damage from them.

Rhiannon wasn't sure if that was clever planning or a pessimistic way to avoid worrying about human lives. It was a miracle Wenyan had survived long enough to meet her. Well, she could look after him now.

Rhiannon gripped Wenyan's hand as she passed him. "You'll stay with us of course."

His hand rested in hers, but where she kept her fingers tense and strong, his were relaxed and warm. Just like his kisses had been. Wenyan said, "I know a place we can have some soothing tea."

She hoped she'd be able to drink it with Alan still missing. Gods knew she needed it.

Her cheeks heated with more guilt than embarrassment. How could she think of tea and kisses when she had Alan to worry about?

The moment they passed out of the central garden, Rhiannon freed her arms and elbows from her Devoted and her secret dating partner. She tapped and tapped at her pad, trying and trying to contact her absent man. Now the calls and pings all connected, but no animated face filled her screen. No messages said *totally fine, busy with physics* to make her roll fond eyes. Why wasn't he answering?

Her calves clenched, shortening her strides.

She left a recording. "Meet us at the market when you get this."

Chapter Seventeen

Video Mail From Earth

Planet Dyfed, Olivia's bedroom

Olivia twitched in the silent dark.

Where were the guards? Why was it so silent? She choked on a cry. *Don't let them notice me.* Her chest hurt with the pressure—blood or fear—but she couldn't open her mouth. If she did, they'd know. They'd see her. They'd bring her to the experimental room.

Her ears felt muffled. That was why she couldn't hear. Had she been moved? She squinted into the blackness. Was that a dead body in the next cell?

Her hands trembled, but she shifted out of her bed. She had to know, even though dread pressed cold against her ribs.

Her bedframe creaked, old steel bending at the joins. The duvet over her legs weighed her down with soft cotton. Soft cotton, not scratchy wool. *Not wool!* She shot up in her bed, sweating and gasping, and remembered.

She was in a house outside Machynlleth. She'd escaped her confinement. Her Devoted were nearby if she needed them.

She didn't need them, though. Not enough to wake them from sound sleep.

Sleep would evade her like a hellhound on a misty hill for the rest of the night, she knew with the weight of experience. She threw off her covers and padded across the ropey floor mats. On the beaten-up dresser across the room, her pad blinked. Its little light flashed pink, illuminating a half meter of ragged plaster wall and dented furniture.

The blinking came from a delivered message. She turned down the volume and sank onto the bed's edge before hitting play.

Ffion Kendrick's face filled her pad screen, casting friendly shadows onto the walls. Olivia imagined that the light would make an Olivia-shaped shadow directly behind her, maybe good enough to fool anyone watching the house about her position. As if anyone would be watching the house at this time of night. *You're getting paranoid in your old age.*

"Hi-hi!" Effie chirped, looking directly into the camera. Her pointer finger touched her grinning chin's point, the other digits curved under. It looked like she was chucking herself under the chin. Olivia recognized the posture, not something that Effie had always done but Olivia's own mannerism since her university days.

"I was so excited to get your message. It's been way too long since we've seen each other. Of course you'd pick a time while I'm out of town."

As if another planet counted as "out of town." Well, it did, but it was more than that.

"Hmmm, news from Earth. Oh! Would you believe that someone threw me a retirement party? Apparently this goodwill tour is my farewell trip. 'A gift for decades of service.'" Effie's eyes drooped like she was *so* unimpressed with the person who'd said that. "I'm not having any of that. *Hells, no*. I've been quietly in charge for forever, and I'm going to stay quietly in charge. If that means I need to change who I'm in charge of..."

Olivia couldn't imagine anyone making Effie retire. Then again she couldn't imagine herself locked up in a prison for Queens. *Be careful, Effie. There are people out there who can hurt you in ways you don't expect.* This message wasn't helping Olivia's investigation, only making her more nervous about her old friend.

"Do I look old enough for retirement?" Effie's mouth was an offended purse. "What are you up to, Livliv? We can do something together when I come home!"

The rest of the message included pictures from Effie's frustrating Not a Retirement party.

Effie had clearly missed the subtle hints Olivia had thrown into her original video, which meant she couldn't help sleuth into who had taken and tortured the Queens.

Everything rested on Olivia's gravity-weak and sleepless shoulders.

Chapter Eighteen

Hide and Seek

Yin He Yuan (Garden Station),
Street Food Alley (in "The Marketplace")

As soon as Alan spotted his Queen loitering at the entrance to the marketplace, he dashed forwards and wrapped her in his arms. She clasped him back tightly, biceps expressing what her slack face hadn't.

He reached for Luciano, Gavin, Victor, and even prickly Mel (who returned the hug with unyielding limbs). Wenyan patted him on the back before Alan had the chance to grab him too, preempting the relief of contact. That was fine. Alan didn't have strong feelings about the translator's safety.

Other people might do grief better than I do. Alan was self-aware enough to see the symptoms in himself and his Hive, though.

"Come," said Wenyan. They followed him down the market's narrow rows. There was no place for the otherwise ever-present plants. Just stall after stall after stall. Hot and sticky with people's sweat and peppery-oystery foodstuffs.

As they threaded through the permanent food carts, everyone they passed, *everyone*, was eating and drinking and celebrating life. Laughing over alcohol, sharing plates of bite-sized morsels, telling happy stories. Their smiles ran together into a giant euphoria, and it was so wrong.

Had they already forgotten the dead scientists? Did they even know?

Those empty bodies floating through space could be anyone's friend or neighbor.

"When will the funeral be for the scientists who lost their lives today?" Alan demanded from Wenyan.

"We don't want to be out of place," said Rhiannon, smoothing his abruptnesses, "but we would like to attend and honor the dead." She was a good Queen. Alan reached out and squeezed her hand, pleased to feel it warm and vital in his. She was here, alive, at his side. He was not alone.

Wenyan shook his head, scarves and beads *clack*ing and *thunk*ing with the motion. "There will be no funeral here. We ship the ashes to the families on Earth."

Gavin slid his own hand on top of Alan's, joining him to the tactile Hive-pile. "Don't the people who live *here* know and miss them? Those scientists must have had friends, jobs."

Unhappy downward lines spread from Alan's nose to meet the edges of his horrified smile. Did they even have names? Alan hadn't heard anyone refer to them as anything other than "the scientists."

"They were acceptable losses," said Wenyan with a shrug that jostled his click-clacking scarf beads again. *Acceptable losses!* "Will you eat?"

People had *died*, for the good of Wenyan's own home station as well as for science, and he wanted to *eat*. "I'm not hungry," said Alan.

"Me neither." The words overlapped from Gavin, Luciano, and Victor all.

Mel's visor was a dark royal blue. "I don't eat," he said.

Wenyan's please-the-tourists smile didn't fade. "How about some bracing tea?"

Nobody objected to that, so they stopped beside a tea stand. Soon enough, each Hive member had a hand-warmer radiating away the deathshock. Even Mel, which just went to show how useless the drinks were. The PRob certainly couldn't imbibe. They smelled like sweetness and yeast.

"Tell us about this marketplace," said Rhiannon over her steaming drink as they ambled forwards. "What kind of stalls do you have?"

She was clearly trying to distract them all from being upset. Which: *thank you, my lady.* A person couldn't wallow in grief nonstop. The Hive needed a break.

Also, they needed Wenyan to talk about nice, light things because he was infuriating on topics of his own.

"Our market is the best in all of space!" His smile as he enthused about his home was not nearly as offensive as his earlier ones. "We have absolutely everything, all sorts of variety and interesting people. For instance, do you need clothes or charms or food?"

They passed a stall with water tanks, blackened so that nobody could see what was inside. A woman called out to Wenyan from inside the stall. He laughed and waved. "Hello, Mrs. Li."

He explained to the Hive, "Mrs. Li and her daughters are always here. I buy my snails from them often."

Buying things. Today was not a day for *buying* and *consuming*. Alan jabbed his finger at each of his Hive mates. "Remember we only have money to buy because the station is paying *my* speaker fees." Which wasn't what he wanted to say at all. He just wanted to hug them again and be sure they were there.

This was why he didn't have friends.

"When do the Lis go home?" Rhiannon asked Wenyan, ignoring Alan's outburst.

"Never! I think they live in their stall."

Alan expected Wenyan to wink or to laugh but he didn't. He was serious. The family *lived in a market stall*.

"They're part of what makes this such a great place to live." Wenyan was so *sincere*.

Mel ran an idle hand across the black-water tanks as he passed them and cocked a headlamp. "Overcrowding is such a problem?"

"I don't have a room or apartment either," said Wenyan with a shrug. "I've got a stairwell underneath a restaurant, right next to their cleaning supplies. The people who own it let me press my clothes with theirs."

Overhead, lanterns and cables vied for space, heating and lighting and appropriating power as needed. Nothing here had enough space. Nothing was where it belonged.

Mel's voice was concerned. "The restaurant areas are more prone to venting."

Alan hadn't checked the stats himself, but he believed his Hive mate. He hoped the residents whose quarters the

Hive was borrowing had a better temporary place than Wenyan. He didn't think Rhiannon would have accepted the rooms if she'd known the rarity.

"Yes." Wenyan nodded, beads clicking again. "My little spot is in an area more likely to vent air to the outside than your borrowed apartment, but that's a small price to experience the awesomeness that is Garden Station." He flung his right arm out and into a stall they passed, too pressed by crowds on the left to do the same there. "It's the best place to live in the universe."

"No one is safe here!" Alan blurted. He wanted to cuddle his Hive mates close to his chest and spirit them away. Could he carry them all and run?

Wenyan's brow crinkled. "Everyone who lives here knows the risks. You should look in the shops, experience the station. Then you will understand."

Alan dashed into the stall nearest him, just to get away from the platitudes and the strangeness. Immediately, the owner or shop worker or whatever came over and tried to make a sale. Gods. Alan couldn't even understand what this shop sold. It was purple and round and might be a food. Or a technological marvel.

"I don't understand," he said, grimacing his closest approximation to a smile because he wasn't mad at this unfortunate person. This person was just trying to live his life and do his job and thought Alan looked like a good prospect because Alan had led him on by appearing in his shop!

He wanted to go home. Or at least somewhere less crowded. Somewhere he could think.

Gods, he didn't want to think.

Gavin nudged Alan's shoulder. "Hey."

"Hey."

"I think he wants you to buy the thing."

Alan laughed, a high-pitched giggle that surprised him, and whispered, "What do you think it is?"

Gavin's eyes went comically wide and he waved his arms in a warding motion in front of his chest. The shopkeeper narrowed his expression shooed them both out of the stall.

Alan was still laughing, and wow, did it feel good.

Out of the corner of his tearing eyes, Alan spotted Cantor marching towards them. The professor's shoulders led him at a serious incline, hips maybe a foot behind. His coat's upper arms flapped and swiped at passersby. His mouth slashed brown-pink across his pale face.

Alan's lips parted, and he sucked in air that he couldn't find. As though it had leaked out his hastily repaired hull hole. There was no way he could avoid Cantor, not without the rest of his Hive knowing what was going on.

To admit his presence, or to let him corner us all?

Alan leaned in and whispered in Gavin's ear. "Ummm, you see the man behind you?"

Gavin's look let Alan know how silly that question was.

"No, no," he hissed. "Don't turn around! Then he'll know you know he's there." Though Gavin was about to know he was there either way. All he could do was confess. "He's a professor of mine from university on Dyfed and he followed me out here to offer me a job. At home."

Gavin shook his head, a confused dog with a fly on its nose. "But we're not going home."

"I know! That's the point!" Alan lowered his voice again. "I've been avoiding him as best I can, but..."

The nausea tightening his stomach since the early afternoon took on a new dimension. It was like when he'd eaten too much at a festival before getting on a Ferris wheel whose compartments had the heat pumped all the way up. His torso made boiling noises.

"So we need to run away?" Gavin started humming a song that Alan didn't recognize, probably from some musical about running away from attackers or problems or people who sang songs apropos of nothing.

Alan nodded.

"Right." Gavin turned away to whisper something in Victor's ear beside him.

Victor in turn grabbed Luciano's hand and did his own whispering.

Gavin tugged Alan past two stalls with what might have been artisanal pillows and ducked behind a display of fried and battered cockroaches the size of computer monitors. Their golden legs pointed and kinked almost like Mel's, but much creepier.

They were probably really lobster. Either way, Alan wasn't going to eat them.

Either way they obscured everyone's faces beautifully.

"I think he's passed us," Luciano said.

"I don't hear his footsteps," agreed Mel, now flattened along the ground in front of them all, hiding behind the table rather than behind the deep-fried things with legs.

All this reassurance didn't keep Alan's heart from drumming like an overenthusiastic kid in band class.

"How do you know what his footsteps sound like?" Gavin asked.

"His boots," said Mel, which wasn't enough explanation as far as Alan was concerned.

"By the gods!" Victor's eyes roamed everywhere, not settling on anything. "We've lost Rhiannon."

"What?!" Alan couldn't tell who'd said it.

Mel pushed up from the floor and lengthened his spine till he stood tall and normal and looked less like the food on a stick. "She'll be fine. You'll note that Wenyan isn't here anymore either."

Wenyan. He was too local. Like the rest, he didn't care about the dead physicists who just floated in a pool of nothing. *Acceptable losses,* he'd called them. "Hmmph."

"Also," Mel could obviously tell that Wenyan's presence wasn't enough to comfort the rest, "I can track them via the station's internal sensors. Right now, they're approaching a row labeled 'children's hands' on the map."

"I hope that's a metaphor," said Luciano.

"There's a map?" Victor.

"Hey, we *successfully evaded the pursuit of—*"

Alan had no interest in hearing the rest of Gavin's unattributable quote, but he appreciated the sentiment. His stomach unclenched and he grinned, feeling smile lines extending farther and farther across his face. Cantor hadn't found them, they'd survived shopping with Wenyan, and everyone was safe and happy. "Should we buy one of these, do you think?" He refrained from poking the closest insect-on-a-stick in case that obligated him to purchase it.

Victor was already pestering Mel to check the map for him. "Do they have any plants for sale? A nursery row, maybe?"

Alan stayed in the middle of the pack as Mel led them where Victor wanted to go. Every now and then, he'd reach out and touch a Hive mate to prove they were really there. Sick of the intermittent touching, Gavin grabbed Alan's poking fingers on the next pass, and tucked Alan's hand safely into the crook of his arm.

On his opposite side, Mel did the same.

The group turned right after a stall that smelled like scrambled eggs smothered in stinky cheeses. The walkways expanded in lush greens. No steam here, but pine spikes and dripping catkins from the awnings.

"Plants, ahoy!" Gavin pointed down the aisle, and it was plants and plants all the way into the distance.

Victor nodded his head decisively. "What do we need?"

Gavin's eyebrows quirked and his mouth trembled, probably holding in a laugh. Victor was unprepared for his own plant-finding excursion. "I liked the bamboo," he offered.

As if called by the siren promise of customers, a man melted out of a forest that Alan had thought belonged to the stall beside it, but appeared to be a business in and of itself. He wore multiple clothing layers in browns and greens, but all his scarves and bracelets had been painted bright orange. They couldn't miss him. The man stopped directly before them, forcing the Hive to halt or to rudely part around him.

"How can I help you today?" the man asked in American-accented English. English!

Luciano replied to Gavin's last words, apparently not ready to engage with the newcomer just yet. "It should do well on Dyfed too, if we ever return."

Gavin growled in a manner reminiscent of something Alan had heard from Mel, back when he'd been Melissa on John Wayne Station. "Don't even suggest it."

The man spread his arms, bright orange bracelets jangling against each other. Nobody was getting around this sales guy without working for it. "We have some lovely cacti, freshly imported and full of water. Good for space travelers."

That got Victor's attention. "How can you stand living in space, surrounded by all this nothingness?" They were never going to escape from the salesperson's clutches now that Victor had engaged.

"It is not nothing!" the shop's proprietor insisted, arms raising to wave his orange bracelets all around them. "The universe is full of stars and spirit. The dust... ah, particles?"

"Atoms?" Alan suggested.

The proprietor nodded his thanks. "Yes, the *atoms* are present in space just like on a planet."

Luciano murmured, "It's full as an egg."

"But it's not safe," Victor protested.

"Hah. Is all nature safe?" The proprietor herded Victor towards his copse of trees, strong smell of evergreen cutting through the lingering cheese and humanity that hovered in the air around them. "Here on Garden Station, we live at the intersection between livable and unlivable nature.

If you don't love the inhospitable openness of space, then why are you here?"

And then they were in a clearing. A clearing inside a tiny group of trees inside a stall inside a marketplace inside a space station inside of vacuum. Like a bizarre collection of Russian dolls.

"Wow," said Victor.

Gavin's shoulders pulled low, dragging Alan's arm along with them. "I guess the stars are as natural as a tree."

The proprietor speared Gavin with a look of polite disbelief edging into unprofessional. "No one planted the stars."

"Whoa," said Victor.

Alan wormed his limb to freedom.

"I'd like to buy that little tree, please," said Gavin, pointing to a miniature pot.

The proprietor abandoned Victor and led Gavin towards an entire table of little trees that Alan hadn't noticed before. "Can I sell you a star too?"

Luciano snorted, taking Gavin's place at Alan's side. "We're not *that* provincial."

The proprietor pretended not to hear.

Alan shrugged, seating his elbow more firmly against Luciano's. "Can't be mad that he wants to make a large sale."

Victor joined Gavin as if pulled by an invisible string to be nearer the proprietor. "What are you going to do with the tree?"

"It's for our Queen." Gavin's ear tips went red, and he shook his hair forwards to hide them. "I want to shape it into something like a silver maple for her, to remind her of home."

Alan couldn't resist. "Awww, is it a courtship gift?" On Dyfed, courtship was makership, and came with three major gifts—one of nature, one with godly meanings, and one that was extremely personal. Of course, if Gavin truly planned to court Rhiannon, he'd have to wait a few years for the Hive to settle and then ask permission from all the Devoted to do it.

Victor chimed in, ruffling Gavin's now-hopeless hair. "That's a really sweet first courtship present."

"No! Just... I really liked those miniature landscapes. And she's our Queen." *The man doth protest too much.* "Besides, she's off with that boy."

Whoa. "What boy?"

Luciano echoed Alan's confusion.

"You mean you didn't notice?" Mel's headlamps spun once. *Is that the synthetic equivalent of rolling eyes?* Yes, it was! That was rude!

"Amazing," Victor was talking to the proprietor again, "you commune with space the way our people do with living trees and grass and water."

The man gestured to the trees all around them, shaking his arms to make the bracelets twinkle. Such a salesperson. "They're all made of the same things."

Gavin cleared his throat, reclaiming the proprietor's attention. "How much does this cost?"

Alan wanted the comfort of his Queen and her unwavering declaration that she'd never send the Hive's stability reeling, especially not for a stolen moment with some foreign male. "Can we find Rhiannon now?"

Alan was done with this claustrophobic not-forest. Done with the market. Done with everything. He could feel the frustrated ridge lines forming on his forehead— and heard his mother's voice warning in memory that he'd get wrinkles if he made that expression too often—and his eyebrows pulling together.

What if she was in trouble, and he was here in some nameless shop, unable to help her? He could save conference attendees, but not his own Queen!

He'd only just reunited with her, and already she was gone.

Chapter Nineteen

A Request You Can't Refuse

Yin He Yuan (Garden Station),
Street Food Alley (in "The Marketplace")

Rhiannon fell behind the Hive while her Devoted looked through the goods on display at the market. She loved them and enjoyed the distractions made by brightly lit fried foods and heavily embroidered duvets. Watching over them as they moved through the market filled her with satisfaction, even more than her purchase of a calligraphic painting simple in its blacks and greys. Alan—*not dead!*—glowed under the lantern lights.

Hidden by the crowds and her Devoted's inattention, Rhiannon angled her body to stand close to Wenyan.

He grasped her hand. She imagined she could feel his supportive strength through the combining warmth of their palms. Her fingers were still cold. "How're you feeling?" he asked.

She wanted to say she was feeling fine, happy to be out with her Devoted in this interesting place. She wanted to say she felt in love, and to let her heart flutter as she gazed into her secret boyfriend's face. She wanted to feel anything—hunger, cold, joy. All she had was weariness. Nothingness.

People were *dead*. And she'd used up all her energy worrying when she hadn't known whether one of those corpses was her own Alan.

She'd been so close to them. Could've sent help to them if she'd broken the station's rules and let Mel check on the ship outside.

She shrugged.

A puff of white ginger-y steam scalded her cheek and was gone before Wenyan could pull her out of its way. Rhiannon squeezed his hand in hers and rested the cooler side of her head on his shoulder. Their walk slowed to an amble, undoubtedly frustrating the patrons dashing through the market to the stalls they needed.

"After a few months living here, we'll find your favorite street food vendor," said Wenyan. His words rolled over her, a gentle massage made up of inanity and future plans. "This place could use your facility with administration and your rebelliousness, *Princess Intense*." He paused on the nickname, and continued in the wake of her silence. "Those of us who are *born* here, we don't always have the same skill sets as the ones who get sent for a tour."

It was premature in their relationship to be talking about forever together, wasn't it? But it sounded lovely. She could disappear into Garden Station's obscure scheduling details and never come out. Wenyan would be right there with her.

She liked him. It wouldn't be a hardship to stay here with him and create a new life. *Did I agree to stay here at some point, or was that implicit in becoming an official couple?* They could make it work somehow, and she could make the station safer for everyone on it by importing in Dyfed's reverence for life. Now she knew exactly what the local administrators had been up to outside, and it had nothing to do with stealing from her ship.

She wasn't sure she ought to be relieved.

They'd fallen far enough behind that she couldn't see her Devoted anymore. She sucked in a breath, and it stilled above her solar plexus. Where? How? *Alan!*

Wenyan's thumb smoothed circles over her knuckles. His voice faded into her consciousness again, "...suppose I'll have to trade for officially defined quarters so you will have all the space you need..."

Rhiannon allowed herself to be distracted. He was so sweet, and her Devoted were just fine wherever they were.

"*Esgusodwch fi.*"

Rhiannon straightened and looked for the speaker on instinct, not curiosity. When someone said *Excuse me* in her native Cymraeg, she needed to learn what had gone wrong.

Off to her left, by yet another snail vendor, waved a middle aged man in a tunic with tight, long cuffs that couldn't get in his way. His simple dress and obvious waving singled him out as her attention-seeker. Against a backdrop of colorful saleswomen in their crammed booths, he looked *foreign* to this station.

He looked like her, not Wenyan.

By transitivity, that made *her* foreign too, no matter how at home the nature and the poetry and the good-looking man at her side made her feel. This older gentleman with his neat tunic and polite Cymraeg stirred something inside her stomach, and it wasn't the food she hadn't eaten with her tea.

"Can I help you?" she asked. He looked familiar.

"As I'm sure Alan has told you—"

That was where she'd seen him before. "The university!"

He gave her a flat, unimpressed look at the interruption and Rhiannon's hands turned damp with embarrassed sweat. She surreptitiously slipped her hotter one out of Wenyan's grip in order to rub it dry on her trousers. "Yes, we met the day you came to make your offer."

She remembered. Rhiannon inclined her head in as Queenly a manner as she knew how. It was the best way to indicate both that she was listening and that she was Queen, and thus in charge of this exchange. She hoped her gold circlet crown glinted in the yellow-orange lantern light.

She would not stand for Dyfed citizens ignoring her status. After John Wayne Station, she'd learned it was dangerous to let *anyone* dismiss her Queenliness. She let Wenyan get away with it because he was a special case.

Alan's professorial mentor was not a special case, however. He bowed in his shadowy alcove, dark and light playing over his greying hair. "Your ladyship, both my university and my grant bestowers, together in my person, request your presence." He'd taken note of her unsubtle posturing. *Good.* "Alan's help will be instrumental in our current endeavors."

What is it about formal requests that makes everyone sound like Gavin performing a dramatic recitation of an unknown quotation? Her lips quirked up, and she leaned forwards, her weight redistributing to her toes from her heavy heels. "What would interest my Hive, should we acquiesce to your request?" Even she wasn't spared the ridiculous formality. The verbal sparring was a relief, made up of silly solemnity and familiar needs. There was no death, no worry, only the petition of a Dyfed citizen to a Dyfed Queen.

The supplicant straightened. "I know Alan is interested in the project in question."

Rhiannon's brows flew up as her eyelids pushed down. Her head drew back on her neck, and she felt her face arrange into the perfect embodiment of disbelieving condescension. "He hasn't mentioned it to me." It was as much her duty to protect him from those who would use him as it was her responsibility to give him amazing opportunities like presentations at physics symposia.

"We spoke this afternoon."

It could have been true. Alan wouldn't have had the time to tell her about something that happened during the conference. He *might* have, yes, but not necessarily. Unless... had Alan been in contact with his mentor all this time? What secrets had he shared? Her unorthodox Hive couldn't stand up to a concerned official's scrutiny.

"We will, of course, compensate your ladyship and her Hive for derailing your plans." His posture changed from a petitioner's bowed head to a crooked slouch, weight balanced on a hip. "It used to be so inexpensive to use Alan on projects, but now I need to barter with his Queen. Ah, how times change." The words could have been frustrated, but they came out fond and pleased.

This man *did* appear to hold Alan dear to his heart, and if it was true that Alan was interested.... She'd made too many mistakes in the past when keeping her Hive away from their planet. Luciano had almost defected back home, after all. And these days her Devoted chattered happily about the plants and the seasons. She couldn't avoid Dyfed anymore. Not and be the good, careful Queen who looked after her Hive's interests. Maybe they didn't need to go home, but they needed to acknowledge their souls' roots.

"I was happy to see him find someone worthy of his Devotion," said the professor with thinly veiled flattery.

It was her duty to her Devoted to give Alan this opportunity. They'd all be glad to see their homes again, with Gavin the only possible exception. So long as it was just a visit, Gavin would go along and appreciate the chance to see his family. She no longer had a culturally weird female Hive member since Gwyn had stayed behind on John Wayne and since Mel had shapeshifted with his Devotion.

I bet we can *stand up to administrative inquiry these days. We're as standard a Hive as anyone else.* Her limbs loosened, and Rhiannon let her arms swing saucily as she walked closer to Cantor's shadow and the briny-smelling tanks. *At least, we look that way, even if our formation was irregular.* The smirk on her face couldn't be helped. Not when there was a possibility she could parley this request into safety for her Hive back on their home planet. The possibility of *options*.

A throat cleared behind her. "Are you going to perform the introduction?" asked Wenyan.

Not yet, my dear. You'll have to wait. Rhiannon was thriving before this representative of her heart's culture and society. She would not give up the feeling of content competency… nor her superior position in the upcoming bargaining. "We left for a reason, you know."

Cantor nodded. "I had assumed so, your ladyship, when finding your Hive proved difficult."

Curious. Their tracks had been clear to anyone caring to look. She put it from her mind and worked with his words rather than her own impressions. "You couldn't find us because we needed space. My Hive is more unorthodox than you perhaps realize."

Her pulse whooshed in her ears, but it seemed to be transporting cool confidence instead of hot nerves. Everything—her Hive's future and ability to ever go home—hinged on this moment, on this man's desire for Alan's company.

If she gave him too much information, he could use it to destroy her Hive. If she didn't give him any, then she'd be just as destroyed when they returned to Dyfed. She'd been over this many times in her head when the Hive had left Dyfed—the threat of jail or reassignment hanging over them. She'd been over it again with Llewellyn when he'd blackmailed them as soon as he'd discovered their little quirks.

"What can I say to convince you to bring Alan onto my project?"

The stakes were so high Rhiannon didn't even feel them anymore. Her breath came shallow, but her heart beat slow and easy. "Those reasons we left still stand, and I won't have my Devoted getting into trouble for following me out here." They would not be re-Tested nor thrown into some hard-labor prison. "If you can guarantee our ability to live our lives as we will, then you have room for negotiation."

She speared him with her focus, the Princess *Intense* proof. "We will not be split up. We will not change designations. We will not yield." She heard herself echoing the lyrics to Alan's favorite national song, and it seemed appropriate in context.

Onward! 'tis the country needs us / He is bravest, he who leads us. / Welshmen never yield.

"I can do all of that," said Cantor. "I'll vouch for you to the highest office and make sure all your paperwork is in perfect order."

It seemed too easy.

"May I also offer a significant commission if you'll accept my presence on your ship?" He affected the face of a man blushing, but no color rose to his cheeks that she could see in the sickly yellowed darkness. "I didn't make return trip arrangements."

She nodded. "We would be pleased to escort you. After I check with Alan, of course."

"Of course."

It still seemed too easy.

Wenyan asked, "Are you also here for the conference?"

Wenyan, who made plans for her permanent residency. Wenyan, who she'd kissed and given a courting gift. Wenyan, who thought Garden Station was the best place in the known universe and would never want to leave it.

Alan's professor introduced himself ("Professor Maximilian Cantor") and engaged Wenyan in a lively discussion about the keynote speaker that morning. Wenyan was smiling and nodding, and when Rhiannon clung tightly to his arm, he seemed content to lean into her muscles and continue his conversation. His heart stayed steady against the hand she put on his back. His smile never faded.

He didn't pull away, but it was only a matter of time.

This was the death knell for their relationship. Their time, so brief and so fraught with misunderstanding, would be cut short. She couldn't stay here, not and do what she must for her Hive. She was leaving in two days when the conference ended and Professor Cantor's passage home began.

She couldn't even feel bad about it. Not right now.

She'd faced Cantor, a symbol of the Dyfed authorities and she'd *won*! She'd behaved as a Queen should and made the best deal possible for her Hive. Between her accomplishments here and the day's earlier adrenaline, there was no room in her body for missing a man who stood inside her embrace. Yet.

World News Tonight

Dyfed, News Station 3

Behind a pitted desk made of dark igneous slabs sits a blond woman. Behind her, downlights illuminate a blank wall that post-production magic can turn into any image. She smacks her lips twice before the camera light comes on. The deep brown furniture imbues her with seriousness.

"Good evening. This is World News Tonight. I'm your host, Gretchen Wyn, standing in for your regular host Huw Dalmia.

"We have unexpected ships coming home." She gestures to the wall behind her, which she trusts will make sense after the boffins get done with it. "Our colleagues on the space station have this footage to share. Preliminary research tells us these arrivals are friendly ships, returning from myriad long-range expeditions to foreign territories and unknown stars."

She looks into the camera, smiling her welcome through penciled and painted lips. "We here at World

News Tonight would like to be the first to welcome home our recently returned cousins. To that end—"

The camera operator makes the cut motion with a palm's edge across his neck. Wyn isn't to say they've managed to contact an approaching ship. They haven't. They've encountered radio silence. Maybe the ships' communications arrays aren't working or they're sleeping for the night.

Strange.

Chapter Twenty

Between This World and the Next

Yin He Yuan (Garden Station),
Rhiannon's Hive's flat

Rhiannon lit the candle she'd bought at the market before returning to the flat and leaving Wenyan at her door. Her pockets held small cloth bags of salt and sugar, quickly made before her Devoted had returned to the flat. She knew the location of everything inanimate in this room. The two chairs lurked against the walls. The only living beings were the six Hive members—Rhiannon, Luciano, Alan, Victor, Gavin, and Mel—and it was late, very late.

"We gather to honor the cycle of life, death, and rebirth," she began.

A Dyfed druid's relationship with death and life and nature was not like an American's nor Garden Station's. Seeing Cantor, hearing his Dyfed accent, had reminded her of what made her people great. Her Hive surrounded her in grief.

Years ago, Rhiannon had attended her mother's death ritual. She hadn't seen one since. But it was her right as Queen, and what her people needed. Even if she didn't know what she was doing. This wasn't about her. It was about the two Chinese scientists, about Alan who had seen them die, and about grief and joy at losing brilliant minds to the primordial cosmos.

They would get through this ritual together, and in closure's calm she'd inform her Devoted about returning to Dyfed with Cantor.

She stood in the center of a circle, shape distorted only by how far back Luciano sat. He steepled his palms in front of him and closed his eyes. *His ways are not our own. It matters not whether he listens to the specifics only so long as he grieves.*

Starting with the things she had done before, she produced a bowl and had Victor pour a pitcher of water into it. Smoke filled her nostrils, burnt and bitter. She wished she'd sniffed the candle before choosing it. Too late now. "The cells in our bodies die and renew every day. They die so that we can live. In a way, we are all dying all the time."

Luciano nodded in the shadows. At least she was getting the organic science right.

For twenty minutes she guided her Hive through the ritual. From her pockets she produced the sachets, three of salt and three of sugar. She chose salt for her own offering. Opening her pouch, she said, "Here is salt, which I return to the primordial pool." With as much ceremony as she could muster—this was for her Devoted, after all, to help them compartmentalize the day's tragedy—she poured the grains into the bowl of blessed water and stirred them with a finger. Once it dissolved, she gestured for Alan to go next.

Each member poured a sachet into the blessed water. Even Luciano, though he was quick to retreat into the corner, far away from the ritual.

She wanted to ask whether the words meant anything to Mel, having only just started learning about Dyfed-style druidry, but it wasn't the time. "These elements symbolize the limited resources of the universe. The carbon in our dead friends' bodies will be recycled into a new friend, here among the land, the sea, the sky."

Victor asked, "Are you redefining 'sky' to include *space*?" She should have known he'd be a stickler for the *land, sea, and sky* aspects framing all rituals.

Rhiannon drew a shaky breath and blew out the candle, plunging the room into darkness. "How much closer could you get to the starry sky than on a spaceship?"

"That... makes a surprising amount of sense if the finite matter we're made of is everywhere."

"Scream and cry for the dead," she ordered her Hive, letting them know that this was the time to feel their grief and make it real.

A collective wail went up. It had no musicality, no sense of time. A raw sound of shared pain, it went on and on. Mel's voice warbled, an unending addition to the noisy gestalt never broken by need for breath.

Tears pricked Rhiannon's eyes, and she knew they weren't just from the candle smoke.

Over the maelstrom of distress, she spoke the names of the dead. "Yasmin Keyi and Lu Zhi, we thank you for your contributions to the universe."

Alan's lamentations grew higher and louder. Gavin maintained an even moan, which Mel matched. And Victor sobbed, "I loved her," by which Rhiannon assumed he did not mean Scientist Keyi.

Mel swiveled his head to put his speaking grate at Gavin's ear. "Am I doing this right?" he asked. He'd probably meant to be appropriately quiet, but it took some volume to be heard over Alan.

Gavin nodded. "You're doing fine."

She couldn't hear Luciano at all.

This whole ritual had turned into a mess. No one seemed to be grieving except for Alan and Victor, and Alan was taking a disturbing turn while Victor seemed to be mourning his expired romance rather than the dead scientists.

She relit the candle, still in her grip. The small flame heated her face and brought her mourning Devoted back into view. "Gavin, lights," she ordered. "Mel, bring those chairs back over please." Alan took another breath, and she cut him off. "The rest of you, sit."

Alan's mouth clicked closed.

"What is it?" Victor asked.

Rhiannon tugged her sleeves down but kept her hands at her sides and her face impassive. "When the conference ends tomorrow evening, we return to Dyfed."

"No!" Victor exploded, nearly as loud as Alan's lamentations.

Rhiannon raised her eyebrows. "It's not up for discussion," she said. "Alan's mentor, Professor Cantor, has requested our attendance, and I have agreed."

Gavin tilted his head down to look up at her through red-blond lashes. "So, if Alan doesn't want to go..."

"I know you're not trying to undermine my authority." She held his gaze until he blushed and looked away. "Although if Alan would like to comment, I will listen."

Crinkles formed at the corners of Alan's eyes. Quietly, whether because of his tired throat or because Victor and Gavin were so obviously against it, he said, "I would like to work on this project." He cleared his throat twice and gestured with his whole arm to point at Luciano where he'd retreated to a corner during the death ritual. "If Luciano wants to be my mathematics buddy, we could involve more Hive members."

Luciano puffed out his chest like an adder. "I'd like that."

Thank you, Ceridwen. Rhiannon hadn't liked the idea of Alan's splitting off on his own. The project would be good for his career, but she needed to keep him integrated with the Hive. Initially she'd hoped to send Gavin into the wolf's maw with him, but it looked like Gavin was taking his Anywhere But Dyfed stance again. Luciano, however, could use the prestige and appreciation as well as the chance to spend time with a Hive mate in a Dyfed-approved environment.

"No," said Victor again, calmer this time but no less vehement. He pulled at his tunic's hem until she worried he might rip it. "What was the point of leaving if we go back?"

Gavin slashed his arms across his chest, sleeves fluttering in their wake. "Weren't we expanding away from our origin point forever like the universe after the Big Bang?" Hands now by his sides, he picked up the end of his belt loop and tore at it violently. "Ever since my mother made me go back to her home planet... I didn't fight her on it then, and look how that turned out. I can *only be happy away from those weighted rocks.*"

Luciano's hands rose up to shield his eyes, and Rhiannon thought he might cry. But then they came down to reveal a flat mouth with no betraying trembles at all. "I thought the point of leaving was to be together to do what we liked. If we go back, we'll still be together, and this sounds like something Alan would like to do." His eyebrows pulled in. "The only *real* reason you didn't want to go back was because your girl—"

"As Luciano says, I've made sure we'll still be together." She had to interrupt him. She couldn't make Victor face his truth, not laid out starkly like that. He had abandoned his world and his family to be with Gwyn, and then Gwyn had left him; he needed handling. "This is the best thing for us. Not just because it will please Alan and bring us much-needed cash. This is good because Professor Cantor has foolishly agreed to sponsor our whole Hive, even though he doesn't know anything about us."

She reached out her hands in supplication to all of them, no longer trying to play the hard, all-knowing Commander, but the gentle Queen who wanted them to *understand.* "We'll be free from danger, all the things they think we've done wrong. We'll be a legitimate Hive."

Whether imprisonment, forced sundering of her hive, reassignment from Devoted to drudge, or exile from home and family—whatever punishment the Senedd might mete out would, of course, fall most heavily on her, but those other punishments could still happen. However, Cantor's sponsorship would make them look good, a more traditional-seeming Hive.

After her negotiations, with amnesty for whatever forms they'd failed to observe, fear of reprisals would be long gone. "No more Llewellyns," she said.

"I still don't want to go back," Victor grumbled, but his voice was a mumble.

"I like it," said Luciano.

"Me too." Alan.

Mel said, "I am eager to see your ol' homestead."

Gavin sighed. "You know how I feel." But he watched Victor's reaction rather than hers.

"That's a majority, then," she said. "Not that it matters." They could protest all they wanted, but they'd tasked her to be a strong Queen, and she would do what they needed rather than what they claimed was best.

Rhiannon fed her Hive their last unwelcome information. "Mel, you'll have to be on your best Dyfed behavior for the duration of the trip." They needed Cantor's approval until he'd tidied their records. Mel was their strangest outlier—synthetic, American, formerly female. "Professor Cantor has engaged us as his transportation home."

Chapter Twenty-One

Captor Café

Planet Dyfed,
café in the Machynlleth Covered Market

This had been Olivia's favorite chocolate shop, once upon a time. Before she'd met the rude man who'd scheduled her Queen-napping, she'd considered this little café her reward for coming down planetside.

Now she hated the crowds bustling down the ripe alley outside the shop and the other crowds who crammed the counter inside. Anyone could be hiding in the anonymous crush. Her stomach flipped and swooped, fighting her most recent meal and trying to escape via esophagus, whenever a stranger came too close.

Her appointment-abductor from months before, Jay Rogers, seemed to lurk around every corner, waiting to capture her again. Not that she'd seen him yet.

It was the worst of all worlds: his possible presence made her ready to run, and his lack of presence meant she couldn't follow him and discover whom he worked for.

Her Devoted Paul set a hot chocolate in front of her on the white table. It clattered on the thin metal, but she didn't jump up, only gripped her chair with tendon-taut fingers. It was *Paul*. He was here with her, protecting her from the mob. Hideki, beside her, held her arm, but lightly.

"Thanks." She took a sip. It tasted bitter and smelled like sour milk. She swallowed it down like it was still her favorite drink in the city. "And thanks for coming."

"Of course!" Both Devoted leapt to reassure her, voices overlapping.

Paul had shown his commitment to his "detectives wear disguises" idea by darkening his space-pale, blue-veined skin with a cosmetic tanner that made him seem orange and alien. As he'd sipped chocolate from early morning to midmorning, he'd needed to reapply lip bronzer five times. Hideki wore clothes in the American fashion—thick and practical trousers with a blouse tucked in rather than a tunic. Olivia herself had gone all out: wig, hat, glasses, Hawaiian muumuu with giant palm fronds and ruffles all over.

Her Queen event hadn't led to actionable information, but it had made her realize that she already knew *something*. She had the abductors' modus operandi. She also knew where an operative had picked up a Queen before: here, where Jay Rogers had nabbed *her*.

He had to come back.

A chair scraped the dusty floor at the neighboring table, and Olivia whipped her head to make sure it wasn't a serious threat. Her spine buzzed and the left side of her mouth pulled down. Just a patron getting up.

She took another sip of the bitter liquid in her cup. *Didn't they put sugar in this?* She kept her eyes on the noise-making patron in case he was less harmless than he appeared.

The stranger stalked to the now-empty ordering area. "I want to speak to the manager," he demanded of the woman behind the counter.

The woman in question was middle-aged and slender with center-parted black hair and a bright green apron over her tunic. "What can I do for you?" she asked.

The patron leaned across the counter, looking aggressive and dangerous in all the worst ways. "I said I wanted the *manager*. Man-a-ger." He drew the word out.

Olivia nudged Paul and Hideki, hoping they'd understand she wanted them ready to defend the hapless woman.

The shop woman cocked a hip against the pastry display, bringing her closer to the irate customer as well as to the metal tongs that Olivia could see but the angry man couldn't. "I *am* the manager. What can I do for you? Should I remake your chocolate?" Her voice came even and conciliatory, for all that she was smaller and facing potential violence.

The patron rocketed backward, no longer in contact with the counter. He stood straight as a stick instead of looming forwards. "Oh! You're a *Queen*." He breathed out the final word and dipped his head with reverence.

Which... sensible if the woman *were* a Queen, but individual shops tended to be owned by individual people. Queens were far too important and busy for small business ownership, embroiled in cultivation of ventures and administration of progressive work for the entire planet.

The woman rolled her eyes. "No, I'm no *Queen*." She bit the word, and Olivia shrunk down into her seat before straightening from her craven cower.

A snort from the patron. His anger may have been derailed, but his overall terrible personhood had not. "You own a chain," he countered. "Obviously you aren't any good at it."

The woman—owner, non-Queen owner of a whole *chain*—turned her back on the fool, tangling her hands in clean towels that apparently needed folding into perfect thirds. "I am good at it, actually. I have a twenty-store empire that my mother and I built." She slammed a towel onto the back bar. The slap rang as far as Olivia's table and flattened the linen. "I don't appreciate your insinuation that only Queens can run prosperous global companies. They get more help than other women, but that doesn't mean the rest of us can't do the same."

Olivia drew a quick breath. She understood the horrible, rude patron's surprise. The entire Hive system was premised upon nurturing outstanding talent. While a non-Hive person might do well enough, they should not be able to thrive on the same scale.

Olivia's drink sloshed in her stomach. She didn't want to have anything in common with this lout and his vile behaviors.

The patron slashed his hands down ineffectually, slicing through air. "You can't even make a decent cup of chocolate!" he yelled before he stormed out.

The owner muttered, "And no thank you for your business."

Olivia snorted, shoulders loosening with the brute's leaving. She knew he was in the wrong here, and was pleased that the owner had come out the winner in their exchange, but she couldn't quite understand why the exchange bothered her. She swallowed down nausea as she realized: *If society's best are part of Hives, and if women can only join Hives as Queens, where are the exceptional female non-Queens?* The scientists and artists, the inventors and businesswomen. They had no Queens to advocate for them, no fellow Devoted as compatriots, no special training to help them triumph on grand scale.

Olivia's own blindness stole her breath. *How have I missed this?* Going forwards, she'd be careful to recognize her own female-but-not-a-Queen prejudices. To start, she'd acknowledge the owner of this establishment. "Well done with that man," she called out.

"Thank you." The owner continued towel folding, but looked up to grace Olivia with a smile. "We get someone like that at least once a week. I'm used to it."

Olivia frowned. The woman shouldn't *have* to be used to it.

Her pad vibrated against her leg, distracting her from the conversation. She pulled it out. A text message from Llewellyn—*the man who caused all that government interest!*—saying he wanted to catch up and chat about the *Ceridwen's Cauldron.*

Now that she thought of it, was he the familiar stranger she'd seen on the steps to the Queenly networking event?

Shoppers bunched together outside the café window, backs to Olivia and eyes trained on a projection screen deeper into the market. She couldn't hear the music or dialogue over the rumble of patrons' voices or through the flimsy window, but she'd seen the film before. *The Ninth Devotee,* about a frustrated janitor who bombed the Test but was Devoted material underneath it all. The film had won an award, odd for a romantic comedy.

She couldn't get distracted by a film, not during a stakeout! She tore her gaze from the unfolding drama and back to her pad. Llewellyn's message waited, and she typed out a suggestion to meet up. In the process of checking her calendar to find a useful date, she saw *him.*

Her pad fell from slack hands to smack on the table.

He passed by the café's glass at a busy man's pace, attention devoted to his destination somewhere ahead of him. His white-and-black beard, tonsured hair, and slew of moles hadn't been there back when he'd approached her, but there was no mistaking him.

Jay Rogers.

Fingers nearly numb, she finished out her reply to Llewellyn. <<*I'll get back to you about a suitable time.*>>

She had him!

Blood rushed back into Olivia's extremities and she rocketed out of her chair. "Come on!" she called to her lollygagging Devoted. "We have him!"

Olivia dashed on rubber legs, dodging blurs of shopping bags and humanity, desperate to catch her prey... and to run him off. Rogers towered over a young woman in front of a shop. The woman's long blond hair tangled in her green apron strings, and she gestured like a symphony conductor.

A meter away, he saw Olivia barreling towards him. Rogers slapped the young woman's arms out of his path and ran.

Olivia couldn't hear his footfalls over the market's hubbub. She'd lose him if she didn't speed up. But first: "Are you all right?" she asked the girl, probably a Queen.

"Who are you?" the girl demanded. "That was my best customer!"

Olivia's lungs seared her throat with each forced breath through too small a pipe. *A shopkeeper?* The woman wasn't a real clue, then, and Rogers was escaping.

Olivia patted her on the arm. "Terribly sorry."

She took off again. Stumbled in the gravity as her feet pounded on the stone market floors. Outdoor grasses were a sweet relief on her shins and knee joints.

She ran and ran and ran. Past people and into road skimmers' paths. Her Devoted called out to her and she waved an arm over her head. She was fine. She wasn't letting Rogers get away.

Stone and grass, dirt and concrete. Onward, she pressed. Her chest heaved and her thighs shook.

The landscape ahead of her coalesced into a sparkling outdoor park with a human-made lake and plenty of maples for cover. Rogers had led her into a crowded, if idyllic, scene, all the better to evade her. Now she was all alone. She'd left behind the two Devoted who should have been close enough to trip her heels.

Olivia had chased her quarry into exactly the sort of crowd she'd been avoiding all her life, but she could *not* lose him. Not when Rogers was her best lead in solving the Queen-capture mystery.

There! She spotted a tonsured man running next to the water's edge. His form shimmered and wove into and out of reality, thanks to bonfires tended by the hordes present for their renewal ritual. She knew the druids had to prepare, but fires at midafternoon were ridiculous.

She breathed through her mouth to get enough air as she ran after him. It tasted like wood smoke. Half ash and half barbeque.

Yes! Catching up, she reached out, hoping to grasp the edge of his tunic. Instead she bumped against a priestess dipping crystals into a bowl of water. The water spilled across Olivia's arm, a welcome cool against exertion-hot skin.

"Sorry!" she called, dodging around the woman and chasing the growing distance.

"Blessed be," the woman yelled after her. But her voice was annoyed, as though she had to say the words because this was a holy day and not because she actually meant them.

Olivia's generation hadn't been brought up into these druidic trappings like the younger sort had. Over a hundred years, and now Dyfed's children took ancient myths as facts they learned in school. Who would tell them no? The older generation had either died or been the ones to put that education in place.

Olivia preferred the secularity of space.

Her right leg cramped, and Olivia paused, hunched. When she stood to survey the area, she'd lost her quarry.

Someone grabbed her arm, just above the elbow. Her intestines went cold, froze. The hand was too tight.

The last time she'd been forcibly held, the guards had strapped her to a table. All struggling got her was more bruises, more straps, more treatment like a rowdy dog in a kennel. Her chest compressed, breath came too quickly when she inhaled to scream.

Not again!

Chapter Twenty-Two

It Ain't Over

Yin He Yuan (Garden Station),
Rhiannon's Hive's flat

Rhiannon and her Hive would depart for Dyfed in a few hours, and she hadn't told Wenyan yet. Alan was off at the last conference event, and after that: leaving. Victor and Luciano had gone out on final excursions.

She, Mel, and Gavin were the only ones still in their common room.

Rhiannon had to tell Wenyan, couldn't just go without warning and let him find out when he next dropped by their quarters only to find the regular residents.

She had to break up with him. That was the real problem.

She let her head tip back to *thunk* against the tan sectional. She didn't want to leave him. He'd been so kind, so warm. *So kissable.*

"How's the poem going?" Gavin asked Mel, breaking the depressed silence. Unless it was a poem of despair, this couldn't be a suitable atmosphere for the neophyte bard.

"I'm on the hunt for the best 'bravery' rhyme," said Mel.

The last time Gavin had asked Mel about his poem, Rhiannon learned he was working on a commemoration of both Alan's hull repair and the deaths of the brave Chinese scientists working to expand the frontiers of knowledge.

Where Alan had been selfless and life-affirming, Wenyan's attitude mirrored Garden Station's. He didn't seem to care about the dead. Hadn't even known their names! And on a station this size, that should have been impossible. "I can't believe he would be so callous." All conversations led her back to Wenyan.

"This poetry thing's no harder than aiming a rifle," said Mel. "Takes some practice is all, but I'll get to marksman fast enough. It'd go better though, if people didn't keep distracting me while I was writing."

A quiet *clang* told her that Gavin had kicked Mel. Not that it could do any good, physically. Her dramatic Devoted appeared beside her on the couch and hugged her close. She let herself melt into his lanky embrace, heat pricking her eyelids.

Leaving Wenyan behind felt like the end of an era.

Eventually Gavin pulled back, dashed off into his shared room, and returned with a shallow platter in his hands. The platter held a tiny tree on the side, shaped like a silver maple and painted into the appropriate colors for spring on Dyfed. Underneath it, a crumble of rocks created a stone path between mossy parks and wires shaped into a small bicycle. It was the place their Hive had come together and their plans cemented.

It had been late afternoon on Test Day, the wide streets still mostly empty. Whistling breezes echoed in the middle of civilization, usually unheard outside the groves. Rhiannon had gone to the park to meet Gwyn, basking in her status as Queen and Commander as well as in the sunlight. She'd been so excited to share her news with her best friend. *I fooled the Test! I don't have to be a Perceiver, and I'm getting Queen training instead.*

When she'd arrived underneath the silver maple where Gwyn waited, the other woman hadn't been alone. Victor pounced the moment she drew close.

"You want Gwyn to be happy, right?" he'd demanded beneath that tree on that sunny day.

And she *had* wanted Gwyn to be happy. Gwyn, who'd offered unconditional friendship when Rhiannon had forgotten how to interact with other children. So she'd gone along with Victor's conversation and introduced herself to the third person beneath the tree, a runner-thin, flamboyant dresser with reddish blonde hair, a mischievous grin, and an exceedingly sharp nose surrounded by an outdoor-person's freckles.

He took her offered hand bent over it like a Shakespearean actor. "Gavin. It's an honor to meet you." He looked up at her through pale, playful eyelashes, still bent over her hand. "My lady."

Rhiannon remembered thinking, *he's a ham, but a delightful one*, and being disappointed that she couldn't do anything about his charm for another few decades. It was Queenship's downside: no relationships that might damage your Hive's dynamic.

In the end, Gwyn was the one who'd made the request, and Rhiannon remembered the quaver in her best friend's voice. She'd never denied Gwyn anything, and so Rhiannon had given in when Victor asked her to join their Hive as a Queen.

Then Gavin had pointed skyward through the leaves, his many sleeves inching up towards his head, and explained about the ship. The *Ceridwen's Cauldron*, with its beautifully alliterative name, the perfect opportunity to provide for the skill-crossed lovers and to get practical experience. He'd been struck by her sensibility and wanted to join her Hive, but didn't trust the Devotion system.

None of them had been perfect candidates for Devotion. Nor for Queenship, in truth.

Rhiannon in the now ran a finger over the spikey treetop in the miniature landscape. It was beautiful, and it reminded her of everything she missed: the reality of ever-present nature, her father, a whole society of people who understood her life. "It's wonderful." She meant it. "Did you do this yourself?"

Gavin deposited the miniature landscape in her lap and shrugged. "Luciano suggested the maple, and it went from there?"

She ran her hands over the air around the trees and rocks, not wanting to touch any of it. The slightest vibration might tip the bicycle, and this treasure was not hers to accidentally destroy. "Thank you for letting me see it."

Gavin shook his head and his fingers tore at his belt loops. "No. Well, yes. But, it's for you. I made it for you. It's a present." He trained his eyes on the fraying belt in his hands. "An apology for the scene I made last night. Sort of because I thought you'd like it." He looked up through his lashes. "You *do* like it?"

He hadn't said a single thing in his weird, declaiming tone for their whole conversation. As though he knew she was too delicate to handle it just then. Or because this was all too important for a nuance to go uncaught.

She gave him her best smile—all the top teeth, kind eyes, excited forward lean. "I adore it! Will you take care of it and get it onto the *Cauldron* for me?" She dared to slide both hands under the platter and lift it up in offering back to Gavin. "Right now, I have to see a man about some truth."

Smiling, he relieved her of her burden, and she flowed to standing. Wenyan needed to know, and she needed to find that tree root of strength in her soul to let him know she liked him, but she was leaving. She could keep the part about their long-term unsuitability—and her perceptions of his behavior—to herself. This breakup conversation was based on unfortunate circumstances, not on blame.

"Maybe," Gavin paused in the doorway, still weighed down by his slice of Dyfed. "Maybe Wenyan has a heart like ours, but has learned to hide it because he has to live here. He may thrive elsewhere."

Yes! He could come with us! Wenyan could leave this horrid place behind and go where she and her Dyfed-born Devoted went. Garden Station was pretty with its flowers and its markets, but she didn't belong here. And if Gavin was right, Wenyan didn't either. It was her decision to make, and Gavin already approved of freeing Wenyan from this place and its skewed ethics. She could ask him to Devote and give up his love for now. Maybe forever.

Her heart swooped to her stomach at the thought of losing his affection, and she measured her breathing until the organ resumed its normal location. *In, two, three, four. Out, two, three, four.* Besides, she wouldn't be *losing* him, just transmuting his attentions from romance into... unresolved romance that she could not in good conscience encourage or return.

She freed her pad from where it had fallen into the couch cushions and used shaking fingers to tap out a message to meet in the central garden. They had a history there, their first kiss. So, even though terrible events occurred with alarming frequency whilst in that place, it seemed the right location to remind him that their mutual attachment was born in trees and rocks and strength. If she was lucky, he'd agree to join her Hive on its journey. But one thing was clear:

With or without him, she was leaving.

Her boot heels thudded from the corridor to the stone ground inside the garden's entryway. The cardamom-spiced air whistled in her nose as she sped through the first yard, past the metal lattices, around a plum grove, and into the pavilion on the lake.

Wenyan waited for her on a lacquered bench. The late afternoon's dimming lights reflected on the water to enhance his smile. "Princess Intense." The name was greeting, a teasing, a declaration of affection. He stood and crossed to her in the romantic dusk, hand rising to cup her cheek as he leaned in. His leather cardigan creaked and rustled with the motion and his fingers made individual lines on her skin. Each an intimate mystery.

She shivered under his touch, seared all the way to the bone. Her mouth parted, just a little, just enough to draw in breath and life and—

No! She couldn't do this. Not until she'd said what she came to say. It wasn't fair to accept his kisses when he might not want to share them once he knew. She stepped back, out of his caress yet still angled towards him as if he could draw her back in via special gravity.

His hand dropped, fingers brushing hers as they returned to his side. "You've not informed your Hive of our association yet," he said. Surmising a problem, but the wrong one.

"No." She tugged her sleeves down, letting them warm her where his missing fingers could not. The soft wool felt scratchy in comparison with his gentle touch. "I'm not sure if I should either." His handsome head cocked to the side like Mel's did when confused. *I'm not doing this well.*

Rhiannon sucked in a cold, piney breath. She needed to come out and say it. No more hesitation. "I'm leaving," she said. *Wait! No! That's not what I mean.* It sounded worse stated baldly like that. She winced. "That is, the conference is over and the station is closing soon."

"You could stay," he said. "We will find a place to live, together. It will be wonderful for the glory of our Garden Station... and for us."

She shook her head, wishing her hair could move from its confines, but between her crown and braided weave, it held fast. A golden leaf caught and pulled, and her scalp tightened with the discomfort. She'd have liked to readjust the placement. But this wasn't the time. "*You* could come with *us*." She had commitments, commitments embodied by this very accessory.

"If you can't mention me, will it not be worse to spring me upon them?" He sat back upon his bench and crossed his arms, shoulders twisting till he looked out over the water rather than into her face. His profile was as beautiful as the rest of him with a rounded nose tip softening that triangular plane. His lips were a brown greater-than sign, parting to build up his arguments. "And should I leave the best place in the universe? Your situation comes with no guarantees. Your ways are strange to me, and your friend group unstable."

Her face heated. They wanted to be together. It should be easy!

He rested an elbow on the pavilion railing and stretched his other arm out to her, palm up. "Stay with me. I beg you. We will live a marvelous life together. Here on Garden Station."

"I can't." She wanted to grab his trembling fingers in her own, wanted to fix this situation by giving him everything he asked for. A hawk screeched overhead and she flinched, eyes darting to the ground as if there might be a carved inscription describing how to bring a swift and painless end to a short-lived romance. "Even if *I* could find work and a small place to live, what would my Devoted do here? I have a responsibility to my people. They depend on me." In the end all she had was logic and duty and the heat on her neck that was probably wreaking havoc with the wintry temperature controls.

Both his hands slammed onto the railing. "Then stay without the Hive!" The whole pavilion hummed like a tuning fork. His shoulders vibrated, and the hems of his layered shirts and jackets swayed. His leg muscles clenched under his trousers. "If you are no real Queen, then they will survive without you!"

Rhiannon gasped and stepped back, away from him. Cold winter air dried her widened eyes and she blinked hard. Blinked again and again until normal service returned. She couldn't focus on Wenyan anymore, so close and yet so far. Instead she cast her gaze all around them.

Nature stretched out in all directions, glimpses through windows, vast and unknowable. As it expanded, her skin shrank until it was too small to hold her inside, and yet it did. Compressing her into a more compact version of herself.

She licked her lips with a dry tongue. *How could he!* "I told you that in confidence," she said. He'd thrown it back at her, barely a day later. She might not have started her path as a true Queen, but she'd come to fill all the roles a Queen would. She loved her Devoted and looked after them, she guided their lives, she interceded on their behalf both to the gods and with humans in authority.

She looked out over the water, hearing the waterfall she knew existed around some contrived corner. If she'd done as the Senedd expected, taken her Test like a good little citizen, she'd never have been Queen. But she'd flouted the rules and become herself, flown upwards into the sun on a ship of her own. She was a wild weed, small and strong. Nobody would stomp her out. Not the Senedd, not Cantor, not Llewellyn, and not her short-lived boyfriend from a station full of domesticated flowers either.

"I *am* Queen," she said. She speared him with laser eyes, even as her shoulders loosened. She'd been working like a Queen all this time, and embracing her power felt so, so good. "I could never abandon my Devoted." *They* were worth so much more than a budding romance among the plum blossoms.

He still had his back to her, looking out over green water. "I refuse to believe you can just leave me like this." He slumped down as though his support-strut legs had buckled under too high gravity. "Please don't leave me like this." Bowed, he was a heaving curve. His spine rose like a rankled cat's, then deflated to miserable child's, with each breath.

Rhiannon tiptoed one step closer, then another. She smoothed a palm over his bumpy vertebrae. His leather cardigan caught at her skin, causing the motion to go in fits, but it served its purpose. He eased under it. Wenyan straightened from the unnatural curve and into a normal teenager's slouch.

His forehead rested on his hands' heels, attached to elbows resting on his knees; layers of flesh and clothing and wintry breeze obscured his mouth. She barely heard his final plea. "The others are acceptable losses. Think about what you're giving up here. With me."

The wind whipped his words across as he spoke them and pushed them through Rhiannon's ears. Spiking into her brain. Freezing her insides like a retro-futuristic cryogenics chamber. *Acceptable losses.* Those were the same words he'd used to describe the two dead scientists, Yasmin Keyi and Lu Zhi, may their names be forever celebrated and mourned.

Wenyan's hunched form seemed more petulant now than romantically miserable—a childish slant to his chin tilt.

This pavilion, handmade by talented artisans, was beauty and grace. Its dark lacquered wood recalled centuries of elegance, and the latticework trim proved the undying talents of generations of craftspeople. No mention had been made of them on her brief tour. Were its makers as dead and forgotten as the scientists'?

Rhiannon bit her lip and stood, pulling her conciliatory fingers into her tunic sleeves. She really didn't belong here... and Wenyan really did.

"Thank you," she said. *Thank you for showing me this new world even if it is not for me; thank you for teaching me about romantic love, for not wanting only my body and my status.* She dropped a kiss to the top of his head, smelling coconut and plastic in the poking strands. *Thank you for making it so clear that I need to leave.*

He craned his head to look at her, boyish smile taking over his features. "You're staying?"

She smiled back, unable to stop herself, but it was a softer smile. Her chest clenched with the fondness one feels for a friend's younger sibling or for an unrealistic film that has ended. "I need to see my Devoted."

"We'll meet again after you finish with your Hive," he said. "I'll share my home with you until we can find a better place for the two of us. Together." He was lit from within by innocent happiness, and he clearly did not understand.

She left him in the pavilion, surrounded by moldy green water and walls that could slam down out of the sky at any moment.

Rhiannon collected her Hive—Cantor was on his way— from their quarters and urged them onto the *Ceridwen's Cauldron*. No time to waste. She wanted to be gone as soon as Cantor finished up. Considering that Alan had been with the Devoted instead of hobnobbing with the scientists, she wasn't the only one who felt that way. *In fact...* She tossed her bag onto her crimson duvet and sent the professor a message to that effect.

She headed for the kitchen. She didn't want to be alone. Not today.

Her ship's corridors smelled musty, like they'd been gone for more than a few days, but the mustiness smelled of home: mint and lamb and Alan's apple-scented body wash, Luciano's sweaty morning runs, decades of Cymric ownership by the previous Queen Ceridwen.

She ran a hand over every blue arrow painted on the walls and bulkheads, proof that the Dyfed-raised preferred to mark their way rather than to drown in a vastness of switchbacks and warrens. "Hello, old friend," she whispered to a panel that sprang free of the wall when her fingers brushed over it. A not-quite-brokenness that had been so frustrating mere weeks ago, now only proved that the *Ceridwen's Cauldron* was hers. Hers to know, hers to love, hers to call home.

The kitchen was less musty when she reached it. Victor lounged on the long table's bench across from Alan, tossing his therapy ball up in the air and catching it again, fending off Gavin's lazy attempts to snatch it from its arcs. Luciano made a sandwich, which necessitated toasting bread and filling the eating area with yeasty sweetness.

When Gavin saw her, he paused his swiping at the ball, voluminous sleeves coming to rest at his sides. "How'd it go?"

Rhiannon barked a laugh. It went fine, so why was her heart bouncing against her ribs? Why was she dragging in deep breaths only to feel like the air was too thin, like it had been once before when their ship had run out of air and they'd been "rescued" by John Wayne Station? She laughed again, trying to reassure him but catching the words against the giggling gasps.

Victor swung up from his sprawl and stood to peer into her visage, like an old man in a comedy who has to squint to tell his grandchildren apart when they're up to mischief. His expression made her laugh harder. "Are you all right?"

She let him escort her to the table, leaning heavily on his healed shoulder and slapping a free hand against his pecs to make him laugh too. "What if he was the perfect love of my life?" Gods wouldn't that be a nightmare: the perfect partner for her being so cavalier about life and Devotion. She wheezed another giggle, glad to be free of that burden. "I'm lucky. I *never* have to be involved with anyone again."

Her laughter calmed as she buried her gasping mouth in Victor's upper arm. She'd never wanted to get close to someone romantically before. Wenyan had been the first. Wenyan had been the *only* interest she'd ever had, and she'd given him up for what? Duty and responsibility? What were those compared to love and happiness? "What if he cries over me? I've made him miserable, and it's all my fa—ault." Her voice hitched in the middle of the last word, but it didn't matter.

"What exactly is going on here?" Victor asked. His confusion vibrated through her teeth and into her jawbone.

Gavin replied for her. "She broke up with her boyfriend this afternoon."

"Boyfriend?!"

Luciano said, "How did you not know this?" The toasty bread smell came closer until he sat on Rhiannon's opposite side. He laid his hand over hers, clenched on the tabletop. "People's emotions are their own. You couldn't protect him from liking you, and you can't make him happy that you left. But that's his problem, not yours. You did the right thing for you."

She nodded into Victor's side, knowing that Luciano could see her and take heart that she'd understood his words.

"We need a rule about important life events," said Victor. "Gods! It's like I'm destined not to know anything until it's too late. We need to keep each other informed about stuff like this."

Good. He wasn't angry at her. That was nice. Rhiannon's head floated to lean more gently on him, not pressing into him like she could burrow through from one side to the other anymore.

"*This could be a marvelous undertaking,*" said Gavin. "*Unlike those years gone by in which you served the state of Venice with...*" He paused, either having forgotten the line or realizing it was irrelevant to the context. Rhiannon had never heard Gavin stutter on a quote before, and she couldn't help him with whatever bizarre thing he was going for. "Dating is now an option for Rhiannon, and we should support her in it."

"I think I liked it," she confessed into Victor's grey tunic. Her breath dampened the fabric and spread their combined warmth to her nose. "But I'm not sure about anything more than kissing... or even the kissing, really."

Gavin found a piece of Rhiannon's head to pat, between crown and Devoted-pillow. "You don't have to do anything you don't want to do," he said. "And if anyone tried to make you—"

Luciano finished the sentence, mumbling around his sandwich. "We'd make them regret it."

Mel made a throat-clearing sound from his speakers, gathering the attention of all in the room. "I suppose now is as good a time as any."

Rhiannon raised her head from Victor's shoulder. Luciano came to the table. They were all close and ready to listen.

Mel crossed all his arms over his chest, then uncrossed the top two as though showing he had the same number of limbs as anybody else, so long as nobody looked lower. "I know the rest of you have gods and goddesses of your own, and you were kind enough to help me consider my options. So I wanted you to know."

Victor interrupted Mel's meanderings. "Are you picking my god-patron? You're so good with the warrior stuff. Lleu would be pleased to have you."

Rhiannon's stomach turned to impenetrable brick. This was *Mel's* moment, not Victor's. She glared at her lanky Devoted and tried to gentle her voice for the one who needed reassurance most. "Don't let anyone talk you into anything you don't want," she told Mel. She'd protect him from that if she needed to.

Mel curled and uncurled the fingers on his two free hands. Eight fingers, four thumbs. "It's unconventional. That's what I get from the discussion we had a few days ago."

Giggling, Victor interrupted again. "You're already unconventional, Mel, being a shapeshifter and all."

"*Here is rhyme, not empty of reason,*" said Gavin. Always with the quoting! But Rhiannon understood this time. And agreed with Gavin and Victor both.

"Shapeshifter?" Mel scoffed. "I don't know about that. I'm Mel. M3L-15-A. Always been Mel, always will be."

That was a willful refusal to admit the obvious.

Mel's visor flashed dark blue, and his crossed arms came apart to rest on his hips. The position was more open, more comfortable, even if robotic bodies didn't feel physical discomfort the way human ones did. No matter what Mel believed, or how much he wanted to talk about his new patron god, this interpersonal camaraderie was good for him. *What was it like when he used to work alone?*

Thankfully, Alan pointed this out for her so that Rhiannon didn't need to find a supportive and polite way to say so. "Oh, come on. You used to be female, now you're not. That's classic shapeshifting right there."

Lest Mel be afraid that shapeshifting could be construed as a bad thing, Rhiannon added, "Our culture has a strong history of shapeshifters and magicians. You make our Hive more robust simply by being."

Mel's fingers drummed and clicked against his legs and his spherical head ducked down till the visor looked at the floor.

Alan wagged his finger at all the Hive mates. "Let the man tell us what he wants to tell us!" As if he hadn't done the interrupting this time. Rhiannon stifled a laugh.

Head coming up, Mel started again. "Right. Gods, all of you have 'em. And now I do too."

Luciano sucked in a breath, but didn't say anything.

"And, ah." The drumming from Mel's fingers intensified. "I wanted to make my own."

"Yes!" Alan burst out. His arm pumped the air and his body rocked forwards with the movement.

Nobody moved.

Alan pulled his arms back in after a pause too long to seem natural—the action screamed sheepishness—and cleared his throat.

Her Hive was working out! Mel's assimilation continued past friendships and into cultural norms. Rhiannon's shoulders settled further in their sockets and she felt larger, more able to encompass multitudes.

Mel's headlamps swiveled in a full circle once. "I call her Saberhawen, the goddess of machines."

There was only one proper response to that. "Congratulations on finding your goddess," said Rhiannon. The new deity's name was correctly shaped too, with a – *wen* ending suggesting femininity and possible magical connotations.

The others all offered their congratulations too. They stood to swarm their Hive mate, slapping him—and each other—on shoulders and backs. Rhiannon laid hands on each of them in turn.

Except Luciano. He stayed in his chair and stared at his balled fists. "Is this just to blend in with the others?" he asked.

Oh, Luciano. You try so hard to hold onto your identity. Rhiannon tried to run a hand through her hair, but the crown stopped her. Symbol of her responsibility, not just to Mel, who clearly had made a conscious choice, but to Luciano, who was looking out for Mel's interests as best he could. Every time that Luciano tried to blend, the effort chipped away at the heart of who he was, but it wasn't the same here. His worry was, hopefully, misplaced.

"I think we can respect Mel's choices," she said, trying to sound reasonable rather than pushy, "and be here for him as he discovers whether it was the right one." She walked a fine line between showing Luciano that they would all let Mel change his mind, and remaining positive in the face of Mel's happy news.

This should be a celebratory occasion. People didn't choose—or create!—goddesses every day.

Victor's hair flopped everywhere with his enthusiasm. "Congratulations, Mel," he said again, dragging the conversation back to where it belonged. "I knew you'd find the right patron for you.

So much had changed on Garden Station. Mel had a goddess now, and Rhiannon had learned that dating was an option. Though, she still loved her Hive more than anything. How could she ever have considered giving them up for some boy?

How could the Senedd's Test ever have wanted her to be something other than a Queen-Commander?

Over the quieting congratulations, she acknowledged Victor's earlier request for ongoing information sharing. "We'll make sure to discuss important things over dinners from now on." Then she couldn't hide a boy again. Alan couldn't hide his emails anymore.

Were the others hiding anything?

◣ Chapter Twenty-Three ◢

Renewal

Planet Dyfed, a park by the Senedd

Olivia froze against the iron grip on her arm. All sensation stopped. She gasped for air, but invisible bands constricted her lungs. She couldn't move, couldn't think. *Captured!*

She'd been a fool to chase her abductor. Now she was all alone. Alone in a sea of uncaring strangers. He'd grab her and take her and shut her away in the darkness forever. Spots formed in front of her eyes, obstructing the lake view. She might never see the lake again. The sun. Her freedom.

No! She would not be taken. Not while she had strength and breath.

Olivia forced as deep a breath as she could, full of bonfire smoke. She opened her mouth, and—

A voice droned in her ear, "We are love and we love everything. Ancestors, trees, and stones. Animals, sun, and sky."

It was not Rogers' voice. She'd know *that* anywhere.

Olivia drew a real breath; it filled her chest all the way down to her lowest ribs. She wasn't captured. She was safe.

Liquid lapped at her trousers. Her toes were cold, squishy. The sensations were proof! She wasn't in the lab. She was outside. In the midsummer breeze, with her feet in a lake where she'd been led by a stranger. *Not Rogers.*

The guiding hand clutched claws into her triceps. She'd have bruises.

At least she'd be free to admire them in her own home. "Excuse me." She peeled back the druid's fingers. "*Ask* next time."

If she remembered correctly, magicians could only work with consent or else their evil act would come back to them threefold. She couldn't wish the druid every forced breath, each fear-pained heartbeat, that he'd forced on her. But she hoped he understood just how badly he'd erred.

The man's face formed a slack, horrified board. He'd realized the situation's gravity.

She swung her head from side to side like a bull elephant. She'd lost her quarry. She'd been so close, almost touching distance, and when would she see Rogers next? He'd never go back to the market. Not if he was smart.

So long as she remained the pursuer, she wanted to find him.

"Argh!" She would have hit something if there had been anything nearby to hit, other than citizens tending bonfires and meditating.

Olivia blew out a long breath and firmed her jaw. So she'd missed *this* chance. She had an entire park's worth of possible witnesses to question. She started with a group tending a cooking fire rather than a sacred flame. "Excuse me. Did you happen to see a man running past here?" She described Rogers as best she could and played up her sweet-little-old-Queen angle with batted eyelashes and a higher-pitched voice. *I'm totally harmless; trust me with your Rogers-related secrets.*

She could go after the villain when she had more information and all her Devoted in her defense.

The cooking group didn't know anything. In fact, she'd *startled* them, so they weren't very forthcoming.

Olivia worked her way down the lake's coastline, avoiding the people having sacred sex. If Rogers was hiding in those combinations, he'd get away completely free.

Eventually, she stumbled across a crew of four crystal blessers who recognized Olivia's description of the man she was chasing.

"I saw the guy you mean," said the youngest druid. "He ran through here. Rude."

A woman to Olivia's left grunted, pulling a dripping crystal necklace from a pool of sacred liquid. "Yeah, he works for the government."

"Didn't even leave a crystal, just knocked over my water bowl," the first druid complained.

A man in white robes spoke up from the other side of the working area. "No, he works for a *foreign* government and is posted to Dyfed for a while." When the woman who had said Rogers simply worked for "the government" clucked, the man defended himself: "I met his ambassadorial buddies at a networking event."

Curious. Olivia smiled enough that her lip wrinkles smoothed out. "Where was that?"

"The Old Senedd building," said the robed man. "Did you hear they've spruced up some of the old meeting halls? Gorgeous flower arrangements."

"Thank you." The fourth crystal blesser glared at her companions. "Now can we get back to work? The ritual starts soon."

The robed man shook his head, fabric twitching with the movement. "What?" he asked.

"The flower arrangements," repeated the fourth crystal blesser. "I do all the contracts for that building."

So this woman had access to the place where Queens had languished. Before or after the evacuation? "Neat," Olivia said.

The woman placed her crystals down on a velvet tray, willing to give the complimentary Olivia some of her attention. "Own my own shop and everything."

Olivia widened her eyes while she smiled, maintaining both eye contact and the illusion that she cared about this nameless woman's business. "Congratulations. You know, you're the second successful small business owner I've met this month."

The florist snorted. "Including the guy you're chasing, right?"

"No," said the second druid, "she's looking for the government official."

"A *foreign* government official," the robed man qualified.

The florist just rolled her eyes. "I saw the guy she meant. He's got a dry cleaning shop down the block from my place. He's always calling high profile Queens with overdue bills. Aiyah. Let me tell you about the big Queens who never settle debts on time."

Olivia cut off *that* story before it could start. "Do you have any names you can share?" She included all four of the crystal blessers in the question.

"Aaaah..." All of them made filler noises.

Olivia supposed a name had been too much to expect. They would only be aliases anyway. "Thanks so much for your time."

After that she met a few other groups who had seen Rogers. Any who recognized him had the same muddled set of stories to tell. By the afternoon's end, she was sure that he changed false identities like shirts, had access to money and/or diplomats and/or government buildings, and that those diplomats might be accomplices.

That was a heck of a lot of accomplices... unnamed accomplices. Official accomplices.

Taking that a step further, the organization that had abducted, incarcerated, and experimented on the Queens was larger than she'd originally thought. It was huge and powerful and had facilities everywhere. It was impossible to pin down and appeared to involve a number of middle- and high-level officials.

The weight of it struck her. This was no simple plot, no single man she could hunt down and turn in to the authorities. She was powerless against such a force.

Olivia gasped under the enormity, scorching her throat on the smoke from midsummer bonfires. All these citizens celebrating renewal, and their ends were coming so fast. So close.

Her heart labored, and her toes tingled without the necessary blood. Up to her knees, prickles stabbed. She left the park on increasingly unsteady legs and ducked into an alleyway, needing to be free of the crowds and the smoke. In the overcast alley, she could breathe. The shadowed air was cooler. Quieter. She slid down a wall to sit on the uneven ground.

Shadowed air. More like a shadow government!

The villain in this piece was too big for her to take on alone. A single woman armed with a little information couldn't stop a bureaucratic machine. She needed accomplices to help gum up its works. She could see three pinch points in the plot so far: snatching the Queens, performing the experiments, and working in the government buildings.

Olivia couldn't do much about the first two, but she thought she might get help in closing the buildings down... and making sure other Queens knew what was happening to their sisters. If one good thing had come of being captured and experimented upon, it was that she had connected to some very active political dissenters.

A few taps on her pad, and she looked into Amanda's face. The maybe-not-so-mad scientist's girlfriend was indoors and hopefully alone. "Do you have a network for warning people about terrible things the government is doing?"

It would be a risk, using someone friendly to the shadow government to end the horrors, but Amanda was the only political agitator Olivia knew.

The younger woman laughed, bright and happy. "Sorry, no. Nothing outside the usual."

Olivia's shoulders drooped.

"But we're holding a rally next month. If you have something worth saying, you're welcome to come say it."

A month was a long time, but better than never. "I'll be there."

⟍⟍ Interlude 4 ⫽⫽

Early Machynlleth News

Dyfed, News Station 3

A blond woman sits behind a wooden desk. Beside her, picture-within-picture, a spaceship looms over Dyfed3— also known as Nuova. It's giant by comparison, only made larger by its anti-Hawking-radiation cooling container.

"Good morning. This is Early Machynlleth News. I'm your host, Gretchen Wyn. Today we have more on the silent ships converging on Dyfed space. We have identified them all, and each carries a complete Hive as its crew complement. As of a few moments ago, fifty ships passed Dyfed3—known as Nuova by its inhabitants—on their lumbering progress to Dyfed. We go now to Dyfed Space Defense Force Commander Bendigeidfran. Commander, are you there?"

An aging lady in a blue and grey DSDF uniform fills the picture-within-picture that used to belong to a spaceship. "Good morning."

"Good morning," says the host. "What can you tell us about these ships approaching our home?"

"Well," says the DSDF Commander, "I tried to get one to stop today. Talked to it on every normal channel we've got. It kept on going, and I didn't want to fire on our own, so I don't have any real news for you."

Gretchen Wyn makes a production of frowning. Her professional makeup obscures all but the deepest lines, and it somehow doesn't look theatrical on the station monitors. "What are Defense Force's next steps?"

The Commander accepts a pad from a subordinate and reads it, interview forgotten, before looking back up. "Those ships are coming home unless we stop them, and the fleet has mobilization orders."

Wyn nods, a concerned furrow between her brows. "Thank you for that information, Commander."

"Always a pleasure," says the lady before her connection cuts out, and only Wyn remains.

"Only time will tell what these Hives want." She swallows hard. "In other news, three scientific Hives have worked together..."

Chapter Twenty-Four

Familiar Not-Friends

The Ceridwen's Cauldron,
kitchen/cafeteria – 1 month later

Approximately a month after leaving Garden Station, Rhiannon watched Gavin and Mel, bent over their pads at the kitchen's trencher table.

Side by side, her two Devoted tracked data across their screens with their eyes. Blue visor versus blue orbs. Their fingers—metal and flesh—tapped screens, paused for long periods, tapped again, paused. Mel and Gavin had spent considerable time together on the journey, with Gavin volunteering to help the newest Devoted learn about Dyfed customs. Was it a helpful spirit or a need to establish himself above his former boss that spurred Gavin's commitment to his Hive mate?

She snacked on roasted nuts as she observed them, nibbling on almost meaty protein in absent fascination. "How's the poem going?" she asked.

Mel's four shoulders rose and fell in their joint sockets. "I'm still getting all the information down."

Also in the room, like a spider waiting in its web or a snake curled up and cute in the sun, Cantor rested his elbow patches where the steel table's long lines met a bright orange runner that Luciano had picked up on John Wayne.

Rhiannon didn't know why he was there. He didn't have a pad, wasn't talking nor staring. If he simply didn't want to be alone, wouldn't he have gone to the engine room where Alan was on shift? It was like he was judging them. Silent and surreptitious. Carefully not making contact in case they were wild animals ready to pounce.

They weren't.

"Like a background document or outline?" Gavin checked on his sometimes-student.

When Mel had decided to be the Hive's bard and historian, citing the old courts in Wales, Rhiannon had been skeptical. What did she need a historian for? She was still skeptical, but it appeared to be good for Mel, who had learned much about Dyfed while asking relevant questions.

It did not, however, mean he understood poetry.

Mel's headlamps twitched away from Cantor, an obvious flinch intended to tell Gavin that he didn't want to say *something* in front of the audience. "What are *you* working on?" he deflected.

"A paean unto the goddess Rhiannon," Gavin said. Rhiannon was pretty sure he meant the actual goddess and not herself. "An ode to death and rebirth, in the style of a Shakespearean sonnet."

That sounded very... English.

Which was a terrible thing to say, especially since the poem was, without doubt, full of Cymric symbols and druidic meaning. Rhiannon held her tongue and focused her gaze on the calligraphic painting she'd hung on the partial wall between the kitchen and dining areas. The painting didn't add color to the room, but it imparted a homey flavor and reminded her of the good parts of Garden Station.

"I'm working with our narrow escape from John Wayne Station." Mel apparently felt more comfortable in the wake of Gavin's sharing. "Once I finish writing up the report, I'll break it into random lines of 'blank verse.'"

Ack. No. In many ways, that was a far more Dyfed style of poem, one about informative facts rather than flowery language or special structures. However, a *bit* of lyricism and metaphor made a poem more... poetic.

"Ah, Mel." Rhiannon was unable to help herself from chiming in. "If that's how you plan to write it, why make a poem at all? Wouldn't the report be enough?" Reports still had value and counted for Mel's new "historian" role, even if they would not add to the body of *literature*.

Mel cocked a lamp onto the table in front of Rhiannon's nut bowl. "You do poetry as well?"

We all do poetry.

"Here's a thing you'll learn about the Dyfed-raised," she started. Rhiannon drummed her fingers on her lips and darted a glance to Cantor, who was no longer feigning disinterest. Well, then. Whatever she said next would be part of her record, would influence the professor's defense of her and her Hive. "We *have* to do poetry. For instance, it's been exactly half a year since the Test, and our entire planet is now embroiled in the annual poetry contest. It celebrates living complete lives, and school kids are required to enter. Even though they don't have those lives yet."

"All right then." Mel was metal-faced and blank, but his words came out slow, then faster, and Rhiannon knew he was sifting through her words. "If bardic-ness isn't just easy documentation, how would you approach this poem?"

Gavin looked at Mel through his lashes, coy and leading. "Let's start with getting the idea. First, you pray to your gods."

"Why?"

Cantor spoke up. "For *awen*."

Mel's visor flashed white, and Rhiannon got spots in her vision from looking right at it.

Gavin answered the unasked question. "*Awen* is our word for divine inspiration." Well, it was more complicated than that, but the definition would do for poor Mel. "Perhaps, if you already know your topic, you don't need any. But it can only help you with refining what will make your report into a poem. The gods hear your prayers and help you to create."

"Why?" Mel cocked a headlamp like an adorable puppy's ear.

Gavin opened his mouth and closed it again, head tilting to mirror Mel's confused posture. "Because you ask, I suppose. Your goddess of machines"—Rhiannon sucked in a noisy breath, but Cantor didn't so much as blink—"needs you as much as you need her. Often, people pray to Ceridwen for inspiration because she's classically the brewer of *awen*."

She could see Gavin's own ideas about the gods and creativity and Dyfed's culture clearing. As though his thoughts and beliefs had been a murky bucket of well liquid before, and Mel's questions were the Hydrolyze that created pure water. Pure clarity.

"Once you've thought about whatever the gods have given you, you make it real in the world. At the right time."

"And the right time is opposite The Test in your calendar?"

Mel's voice came out with extra Ameri-Texan drawl. Rhiannon laughed as she answered, "You *can* hold onto a poem from earlier in the year. You don't have to make it the same month as the contest. The magic of making should never be rushed."

Over the speakers, Luciano's voice crackled from the pilot house. "I thought you all might want to know that we're here-ish." The shipwide shut off again.

"Exactly." Gavin nodded in agreement, ignoring the interruption from above. "I'm working on this poem now because it's ready for its birth, not because we're going to be home in time for a contest entry."

"I must say, Queen-Commander, I'm impressed with your Devoted's talent in language arts and teaching." Everyone fell silent before Cantor's words. Mel's visor flashed white again. "May I ask what he does on the ship for you?"

Rhiannon tugged at her sleeves, then let them fall how they would, refusing to tidy her appearance for her visitor.

Why can't you ask Gavin yourself, and why no curiosity about Mel? The way Gavin pulled his shoulders low indicated he felt the same. "Gavin Reynolds is an engineer actually, my Handsman. He's multitalented."

Cantor's elbow patches came off the table at that, and his eyebrows flew up. "Handsman? But he's such an expert on poetry and philosophy!" As if Rhiannon's Hive members weren't talented enough to be both. As if they *had* to specialize just because everyone else did. But his surprise was short lived and he was quick to take advantage. "I've been meaning to ask about a small problem—"

Rhiannon cut him off. "Not during poetry time."

Mel drummed his fingers on the table, then put down his pad and steepled all four of his hands into a pyramid. He asked Gavin, "Is this a good position for a prayer to Saberhawen?"

Rhiannon tried not to smile. "She's your goddess. You would know best what she might like."

"Does it focus your mind?" asked Gavin. A leading question if there was one.

Mel's visor deepened through middle blue to royal, then lightened to the color of an Earth summer sky. "No," he said. Decisive.

Rhiannon's heart skipped. It was beautiful to watch someone find himself and his own path to spirituality.

Gavin abandoned his place at Mel's side and bowed deeply, squatting with one leg in front like he was stretching a hamstring. "My lady." Rhiannon put down her pad and extended a hand in benediction, and he touched his forehead to the back of it. "If you would permit me..."

He ran out of words there. Between that and the continued bowing, she could tell he was working himself up for something.

Her pulse picked up, and his forehead heated on her skin.

He straightened and revealed his own pad clutched in his grip. Quietly he said, "You can give it back if you don't like it." If he weren't holding the pad with whitening fingers, she'd expect him to tear his belt edges the way he had when giving her the cunning miniature landscape.

"I'm sure I'll love it," she said. Her voice was low and as soothing as she could make it. Quiet too, so the crowd of Mel and Cantor couldn't hear easily. "But I can't accept if you don't tell me what it is."

Gavin ducked his head and looked up at her through long lashes. With a deep breath, he thrust out the pad on stick-straight arms. "Will you take the poem I wrote?" His blue eyes were outlandishly large. "It's about the goddess Rhiannon, and I used you as a model, so I thought you might like it." He rushed through the words as though, now that he'd broached the delicate subject, he had to get all the information out at once so that it could do the least damage. "Unless"—he gasped for air, even as he repeated himself needlessly—"you don't like it."

"I'm honored," she said and reached to take the pad. Their fingers brushed.

Luciano bounced in on shoes polished to extra high gloss. "Are you giving Queen-Commander Ceridwen a gift of the gods?" His teasing voice broke Gavin's crisis of confidence.

"Nothing of the sort, my good man," Gavin called back with all his usual actor's diction. "It is a perfectly decorous gift for so lovely a Queen."

But Luciano was right. This could be a gift related to the gods, coming after a gift related to nature, both crafted by the gift giver's own creative hand. If Gavin felt like infusing romantic meaning, he could give her a third gift—something personal to them—to fully declare his courtship intent. So soon after her first romance... but this felt different from Wenyan, calmer. *He certainly knows what sorts of gifts I'd like, which is ideal in a partner.*

Her lips parted involuntarily and she sucked in a breath. *What would the others say?*

"Thank you, Gavin." She called his attention back to her. "Would you share this with my pad so that I may have my own copy?" How did these gifts turn her so crazy formal?

She shook her head, air blowing out through her nose. Rhiannon would take the poem in the spirit it was meant.

And she could break any remaining tension by taking the focus from her vulnerable Devoted and onto her newly arrived one. "How goes the pilot house?" Rhiannon asked Luciano.

"You will be amazed." The young man bobbed over to her side. "I've got us parked because the view out the window is a little strange." His tiny mouth twitched like he was repressing a smile—or getting tickled by invisible fingers—so she wasn't too worried.

"Do tell."

Luciano slid onto the bench right next to her and pushed his pad onto the orange runner. "Everything was going smooth as oil"—he'd clearly been practicing what he wanted to say—"when I caught sight of this spaceship scramble."

He tapped the pad with a flourish worthy of Gavin. The image on screen was a local map-chart. Dyfed dead ahead but distantly out of reach, space station currently off to its right, and a jumble of dots in between the *Ceridwen's Cauldron* and her objective. Each dot signified a ship, labeled with a name. If she wanted to get home, she'd have to detour around the mess, and they'd undoubtedly seen her by now.

He was right to call it a scramble. The dots on screen had no recognizable pattern in their formation. Up and down, upside down and perpendicular to each other.

One dot on the cluster's edge caught her attention. She could only read its label because it was in a blank zone. Its nearest neighbor was a cluster of seven ships whose names overlapped each other on Luciano's map.

"Oh! There's the *Llyr's Llambo*." Rhiannon bit her lip. "I wonder if they ever got their Queen back."

Mel, Gavin, and Luciano made vaguely considering noises.

"I hope so. *To live without the center of one's universe is to live with a gaping hunger*," Gavin declaimed.

"Ah, excuse me," said Cantor. "But may I ask...?" He didn't actually ask, just trailed off and raised an expectant eyebrow at Rhiannon.

So she explained about the unfortunate Devoted whose Queen had been stolen and who had briefly kidnapped Rhiannon's Hive in their separation madness. She left out the parts about *why and how* she'd been blackmailed into engaging with the *Llyr's Llambo* crew and that she'd affected their escape mostly by suborning someone else's Devoted.

Cantor stood from his place at the end of the table to study the pad over Rhiannon's shoulder. He loomed like an owl in her peripheral vision. "And do you believe all these ships are missing their Queens?"

The thought hadn't occurred to her. Though it would explain the disorganized mess of dots.

"I need to see this myself," Cantor said. He demanded of Luciano, "Is there a porthole in your pilot house?"

Rhiannon shrugged, the movement forcing Cantor to step back from his hover. "Let's all go."

...Which was how she ended up climbing the ladder into the pilot house while Cantor, Mel, Luciano, and Gavin waited on the command room's floor below. There wasn't much room in the little capsule, every surface covered in switches and lights and readouts. If Luciano hadn't been so talented with translating theory to practice—reading the manual to flying a ship—her Hive would never have escaped from Dyfed space to begin with. She'd crammed in here with him before, but for the moment the little haven was all hers.

Out the tiny window, ships floated against the standard "space" backdrop. All in all, what she got was: *hey, there are some ships out there and, like most spaceships, they're suspended in the black-and-pinprick of space.*

She snorted ruefully. She couldn't say that to the others. Cantor expected some deep thought. But she'd seen more ships in one place at John Wayne Station, where colonists and supply vessels constantly came and went. She'd seen larger ships when she'd taken possession of the *Ceridwen's Cauldron*; these all appeared newer than her own ship, but not significantly more important. She'd just have to fake it.

Her boot soles clanged as she descended the ladder rungs. Rhiannon jerked her chin upwards. "Who's next?"

Gavin swarmed up the ladder.

"Well?" asked Cantor.

Rhiannon put on a serious frown, pushing her lips into a formation that would surely give her concerned mouth wrinkles. "I'm new to being a starship's Commander, but I've never seen so many ships in this context." As she said the words, she realized they were true. *Oh, this could be bad.* Her fingers clenched on air. "At a station or just before a major event, yes, but there's nothing special about to happen on Dyfed, and those ships are converging on the planet anyway. They're not aimed at the station either, which could explain why they're so untidy."

Cantor hummed, then left to take his turn looking out their tiny window—as though it were more useful than the map Luciano had curated. In moments he descended and demanded that Luciano move the ship so that he could get a better line of communication. "I don't want my message going through all those potentially dangerous ships."

Luciano looked to Rhiannon. She nodded. He squeezed past Mel, coming off the ladder on his way to the controls.

Rhiannon busied herself with looking as tense as Cantor obviously felt, but it was hard to drum up concern about a few Dyfed ships hovering in Dyfed space. Oh, she cared that nothing horrible had befallen any of them, but in an abstract way. Even for the *Llyr's Llambo*. She felt for them, for their Queenlessness, but they'd incarcerated her and shot Victor. Her sympathy could only go so far.

Luciano called down that he'd cleared them of the ships' concentrated area and that Cantor could make his call in the clear.

A woman's voice filled the *Ceridwen's Cauldron*'s command room. "Please authenticate."

Cantor tensed, as if only realizing then that he would be surrounded by strange teenagers about to overhear all his passcodes. *Too bad.* Rhiannon settled her shoulders more firmly and crossed her arms over her solar plexus. She wasn't leaving. This was *her* ship, and her guest was working from *her* information.

After five call-and-response certifications and two long strings of alphanumeric nonsense, a warm male voice— clearly not a recording this time—exclaimed, "Max!"

"Hello, Dylan," said Professor Cantor.

"Why are we audio-only?" Cantor's contact didn't demand visual confirmation, but asked why he couldn't get it. Very civilized and polite. Rhiannon approved.

"In case of danger." Cantor's reply left much to be desired, and the snort he got in reply proved that Rhiannon wasn't the only one to think so. "Burn these codes after today. I have witnesses."

Dylan sucked a breath. "And yet you still—" He cut himself off. "What's the emergency?"

Rhiannon was curious to hear the answer to that as well. She adjusted her stance to place all her weight on her back foot. Off to her left, Mel slipped a leg out of a shoe and tattooed the spike into the floor with a quiet *plink plink plink.*

"Have you heard of all this Queen stealing?"

That's what Cantor wanted to talk about.

"Rumors, rumors, but nothing concrete. Paranoia." Dylan paused. "There's this particular Queen... do you know an Olivia Jones? She's been asking questions."

Rhiannon felt her eyebrows fly up to meet her crown. *Olivia Jones?* The woman who had bequeathed the *Ceridwen's Cauldron* to Rhiannon and her Devoted had been Queen Olivia Jones. The name was common enough, and could belong to a slew of people. For instance, Rhiannon's own last name—and Alan's—was *Jones,* but no relation to the old Queen.

Still... how many involved Queens named Olivia Jones could there be?

"It's not paranoia," said Cantor. "I have companions to testify. I also have a converging space fleet that we think may be composed of Queenless Hives."

Rhiannon tapped an annoyed finger against her stretched lips. She'd never said that and didn't appreciate Cantor's using her as backup for his—admittedly interesting—theory.

A clacking noise came over her ship's speakers. "Now that I have probable cause, I can send out a DSDF ship to take a look." The man on the ground paused. "I thought you were out of the game."

Cantor shook his head, though his friend couldn't see it. "One last field op, Max. You know how these things go. These crews have to be crazy. I'd recommend shutting them down until we know more. Of course, it's up to you."

What?! Not only was that infringing on Hive autonomy, but *anyone can* do *that?*

"Will it take?"

"As far as I can tell, they're all government-issued ships from the last few decades. Your override codes will be enough." That explained why Cantor wanted to eyeball the ships, then. Not for their arrangement but to determine their provenance.

Rhiannon tapped a finger to her lips. She didn't like the idea that someone could stop her *Cauldron* at a press of a button. She liked even less that the anonymous person could control every ship ever built on her planet.

She pulled out her pad and was pleased to see they'd drifted close enough to the planet that she could connect with a communication station intended for receiving and transmitting long-distance packets. She sorted through directories, knowing that Queen Olivia had been living in Rhiannon's own district. Though she might have moved.

She hadn't.

An entry for Queen Olivia Jones had a picture of the woman much as Rhiannon remembered her—short white hair over leathery lined skin, like a pale elephant kept too long in a cave. Rhiannon pinged her predecessor, the former Queen Ceridwen, but received no answer.

She left a brief message asking for details about the missing Queens and explaining that she'd run into a Queenless Hive after performing the courier job for Llewellyn, which Queen Olivia had kindly secured for her Hive's first assignment. It was close enough to the truth.

Cantor said goodbye to his contact, then sniffed loudly to get everyone's attention. "As the government's representative on the scene, I need to go over to those ships and report back on what's going on." He nodded, encouraging Rhiannon and her Devoted to mirror his action. She would not be so foolish. "To that end, I'll be using your ship and connection tube. I expect all of your cooperation."

Rhiannon sucked in her cheeks. His speech smacked of Llewellyn's take over.

"You could ask," said Gavin.

Cantor's forehead wrinkled as though he hadn't expected opposition. Maybe he was simply as socially awkward as Alan, and he needed someone to point out the inappropriateness of his words?

"If your buddy'"—she purposely used informal language to remind him he had no official authority over her—"has shut down all the ships in this area, how are we still moving?"

"Ah!" Cantor pointed a finger at the ceiling. "This ship is older than all the rest. It shouldn't have the long-distance fail-safe."

"My lady," said Luciano with emphasis on her title, "we will go wherever *you* lead."

She smirked. No way Cantor could have missed that.

"As the man says, my lady," agreed Mel with a thumb jerk in Luciano's direction. *Oh, Mel.* They'd all been trying so hard to make Mel seem utterly normal to the visitor, and now this.

"Well," said Cantor, "I need you to fly us over to one of the ships so I can determine the situation. Since you're already familiar with the *Llyr's Llambo*, we may begin there." A sop if she'd ever heard one. "There may be fighting. You'll send a Devoted with me."

Rhiannon's heart slowed and her vision came clearer than it had been before. She stared directly into the professor's eyes and informed him of her plans. "I will be leading the expedition to gather intelligence, and we shall begin with a small ship, not the *Llambo*. Mel," she addressed her Devoted without breaking her stare with Cantor, "would you be so kind as to clear a ship with your special skills?"

Mel's old ship used to run completely without life support, she knew. What was the good of a Devoted who didn't need to breathe if you didn't utilize him in deep space?

"Of course, my lady."

There were a *lot* of "my lady"s going around. They needed her to stand up to Cantor and put him in his place.

The professor's hands made useless shapes in the air as he tried to figure out where he'd gone wrong. Rhiannon didn't give him the chance to recover and take up the argument for power again. She looked away from him and waved an imperious hand, causing Mel to crowd into Cantor's side and edge him towards the door.

"You are welcome to join me and my personal guard," Rhiannon told him, the picture of magnanimity and control. "After Mel determines it is safe. We'll meet in the airlock once Luciano acquires the necessary sedatives from the medical bay."

Whatever was out there, *whoever* was out there, Rhiannon's Hive had the skills to deal with it. And if they didn't have the skills, they at least had the responsibility. If not her, then who would find out what had happened to these floating crews?

Chapter Twenty-Five

Amalgamated Hive, Inc.

The Ceridwen's Cauldron, *airlock*

Rhiannon had one leg in her red spacesuit when Victor entered the airlock, Cantor right behind him. She tightened the muscles in her standing leg so she wouldn't fall over. *This already looks awkward enough.*

With the human component of the boarding party on location, she toggled the shipwide communicator. "Hey, everybody." Her own voice echoed in her ears, coming through the speakers and doubling in the microphone. "Victor, Mel, and I are heading over to a floating ship. Until we return, Luciano is in charge, so pester him if you have questions." She cut off the broadcast. "That'll do."

Cantor rummaged among the suits and came out with Gavin's favorite black one. "Where *is* Mel?"

Mel answered for her, voice piping in through Rhiannon's pad on the ground beside her red-suited foot. The space onesies required both hands, so putting the pad down had made sense. "I'm opening the ship's airlock now," Mel reported.

Rhiannon had chosen the smallest ship in hopes of minimizing any potential resistance. If all the people out there were as violently upset as the *Llyr's Llambo* crew had been, Rhiannon wanted to keep their numbers as even as possible.

She shimmied the thick red rubber over her hips. "So, ah, this may be a weird question."

Cantor, already suited up, but with his face hood still off, gave her his wide-eyed attention. "You can trust me," he said.

Could she really trust anyone other than herself?

Mel interrupted. "Sleeping gas deployed."

Victor slouched, perhaps in response to those words or else to get his suit over his shoulders. "Gods, it's so much better to be prepared than to poison people."

Rhiannon hoped Cantor wouldn't ask what that was about. She distracted him with her own question, the one she hoped wasn't too weird. "Are we using the spacesuits right?" Every time she left the ship, her heart raced. She envisioned an incorrectly fastened hood, crackled paint flaking off and taking the rest of the suit with it, holes spontaneously forming because she'd done something wrong.

She tried not to think about it until going outside. But she went outside pretty often.

Cantor stepped backwards, raised his arm to check his own suit's fit. "They look good, seem to fit you...." He trailed off, undoubtedly letting his imagination mirror her usual worries, but he broke into a boyish grin that reminded her of Alan when he got excited. "You're probably too young to remember when these were a popular style."

That was as positive a spin on her ignorance of spacesuit usage as any.

Mel cleared his faux throat. "The corridor right next to the airlock looks good. Y'all can deploy the accordion."

"Think of these suits like really thin condoms." Cantor's ear tips went pink. "You need layers of protection if you're going to trust it. That's why you also have the accordion tunnel."

Rhiannon pulled her hood over her head and took a deep breath. *In, out, in*. Good, the air flowed cleanly so far. Through his flimsy plastic face "plate," Cantor's mouth moved, but Rhiannon heard nothing. If the suits held a communication system, she still hadn't found it. *My protective layers are suits of indeterminate age and an accordion tunnel that hadn't even matched up on Garden Station. Great.*

At her arm's downward slash, Victor tapped the console next to the airlock door. Air whooshed past her and into the airlock. In Rhiannon's hands, her pad flashed a message from Mel: *Accordion secured.*

Victor repeated the procedure on the second door and the accordion tube stretched in front of them. At the far end, Mel waved his four arms.

Faster than "usual," whether because of recent practice or because the whole operation felt a lot less safe now that she *knew* it was, Rhiannon reached the other ship's airlock. Cycle, cycle, just like on their own ship.

She, Victor, and Cantor slipped out of their suits and followed Mel into the corridor. The "fresh" air hung heavy with garbage-sweet sweat.

Rhiannon braved the walkway, open panels making the walls into porcupine prickle. She pushed at the first panel door she reached, and it closed with a *snick*.

Wait, wait. She held her arm at a right angle to make her entourage wait as well.

The door stayed closed.

Which meant that all these maintenance access doors had opened without anyone's trying to put them back in place. Had they all popped at once? Or had a physically unbalanced individual wheeled down the corridor without a care for proper arrangement? Either way, something had gone wrong. Rhiannon knew that Cantor's theory was "no Queens anywhere," but the *Llyr's Llambo*'s involvement didn't prove enough for her.

In many ways, the hall reminded her of her own ship: walls painted with sporadic maps and the occasional open access point. But where the *Ceridwen's Cauldron* had a few panels that opened whenever an unlucky Hive member walked too close and triggered the mechanism, this ship had many.

Rhiannon lowered her arm and let the group walk again. "Keep an eye out for a Queen."

"Or," said Cantor, quick to jump in, "whoever took over in the power vacuum."

She tapped her finger to her lips. Even if he was right, that this was a Queenless ship... "That's not how it was the last time we ran into a ship like that."

He shook his head like a disappointed parent. But he *wasn't* her parent. "That was only one experience, and early on."

Rhiannon felt vindicated when they reached the ship's command room without spying any potential Queen analogues. They'd passed two sleeping bodies—whose pulses Mel had somehow checked from a distance with thermal cameras—and both had been male. Male and scruffy, dirty and ragged.

As expected, the command room was empty save for a large viewing screen, currently dark. Ascending the ladder to the pilot's cage, they found a lone Devoted slumped in his chair. Perfect. They could wake up this single man for Cantor's interviewing, and also grab any relevant data from the computers at hand.

"Mel." Rhiannon called down to her Devoted.

Clanging metal on metal, Mel retrieved the pilot and laid him on the command room's floor. He pulled a vial from his vest and injected something into the supine man's carotid.

Dark brown eyes shot open. The man's gaze darted to the ceiling, to sphere-headed Mel, to the three onlookers, to his ladder. He sucked in a breath, too short and too shallow. He gasped for another, looked at Mel again. Mel's headlamps cocked, and the newly wakened man screamed.

It was a brief scream. He dragged in a sip of air, and tried again. "Aaa"—breath—"aaa!"

Rhiannon fell back, even as Cantor stepped forwards and waved his arms to get the pilot's attention. "Excuse me," he said politely.

The supine man thrashed against Mel's hands on his shoulders, getting his legs up into the air like riding an invisible bicycle. Victor surged into the fray and pinned the legs, but the man's spine still twitched and bucked for freedom.

If he was Queen-separation crazy, this wouldn't do them any good. If he was scared of waking up to a stranger's holding him down, maybe he could be soothed.

"Aaaaaa!"

Rhiannon sidled around Cantor and dropped to her knees by the poor man's head. "Hello," she said, voice modulated and gentle. "I'm Queen-Commander Ceridwen, and nothing is going to happen to you." She dared to put a hand against his sleeve in hopes that a compassionate human touch might calm him.

His screams *did* ease to whimpers, but the bucking continued and his eyes didn't focus. He was too far gone to respond to anything more than her tone of voice.

Victor at the man's feet asked, "May I?"

Letting Victor take a turn certainly couldn't hurt.

He kept his voice low as he talked about the quality of nature and how space was all around us. But the poor pilot kept on twitching and moaning.

"Victor." She spoke his name like a warning.

Her lanky Devoted sprawled across their squirming captive's thighs, keeping the man in place while freeing his own hands to reach for his pad. Victor passed the little rectangle up to Rhiannon and retook his position at the ankles. On the screen, a copse of silver maples sported yellow leaves on chocolate stick branches.

Rhiannon brought the image up to the trapped man's face. Tears leaked out of his eyes, gazing at the screen before him.

"Let the image focus him," said Victor. "It's the focus people need to find the magic in themselves. With the spirit all around us, *in space*, we don't need the actual trees to commune with nature. See?"

Rhiannon wasn't sure *she* quite followed Victor's logic, but then she'd never been very druidic to begin with. The man underneath her shook and shivered, and she changed the picture on the screen to a plum blossom, white and furled tight.

Still he squirmed and cried. The water in her captive's eyes had to be precluding any sort of clear vision, so she knew he wasn't looking at Victor's pictures.

But he'd responded to her gentle touch, to her tone of voice, to the images of home and nature. He was aware on some level. "Mel, switch with me."

At the nameless man's head, she petted his hair and soothed him with the whispers and cadences that she might use on a scared kitten. Somewhere between pushing his black locks off his heated forehead and telling him how brave he was, the man's twisting stopped and he relaxed into the floor.

He'd had his Queen ripped away, his sanity dragged out of him by space and distance. It was a miracle that she could soothe him. It was unfortunate.

Because that meant Rhiannon could fix him, could take away his pain if not restore his sense of self. It was, perhaps, the worst knowledge she'd ever been given.

Because that old adage was true: *just because I can, doesn't mean I should.*

He whimpered. "So alone..."

She couldn't let him continue like this. *Whether or not I should, I can't abandon this man to his circumstances.* "You'll never be alone again." She leaned over him, mouth against the ear her fingers stroked.

In the moment, she knew all the problems with what she was about to do, and she didn't care. This man needed her help, and Cantor needed his information. If anyone asked Rhiannon later, she'd tell them it was an instinct.

"Now, say the words with me." She whispered and he followed along in a croak: "My sword and my service, my body and my blood, my agency and my anima. These all belong to you, so I swear." His voice cracked and he shuddered in her grasp.

In her peripheral vision, Victor's fingers tightened on her new man. Long and white and so tense. Well, she was Queen. That meant she didn't need to consult her Devoted before adding to their number. It *was* considered good manners under normal circumstances, though.

"I accept your sword and service. Your body and blood are mine to direct. Your agency and anima are my agency and anima, now and forever more. Call on me in times of trouble, as I will call on you, but always you will be my first defense."

These were not normal circumstances. *Have any of my Devotions been "normal"?* Official business complete, she told her other Devoted, "You can let him go."

Mel's hands released her newest Hive member. "By Saberhawen," he whispered.

Victor followed suit more slowly.

Off to the side, Cantor sputtered. "You... you can't just..."

Rhiannon paid them no mind. Her energy was all for the man in her arms.

"It's not the same," he whispered. He curled into a tight ball, like a kidney bean, with his feverish cheek on her knee and his legs on the opposite side as if he could encompass her and still stay so small. "Can't feel you like I felt Sandy. Can't feel San at all. Is she dead?" Bright hot tears seared her knee through the fabric. "She's got to be dead."

"Shhh." Whatever the state of the man's previous Queen, he was Rhiannon's now, and she would safeguard his well-being as best she could. "Shh, I'm here. I'll protect you like Victor and Mel protect me." As if called by their names, her longer-tenured Devoted came to stroke her newest's legs, a far cry from their imprisonment moments before. "We're all together."

She favored Mel and Victor with a regal nod. Good, they'd accepted this poor, broken man into the Hive. That would help him acclimate. But merely acclimating to her Hive wouldn't put him fully back together. He needed to feel secure, which meant getting planetside and eliminating the Queen-stealing danger. For there was no doubt now that his Queen had gone missing.

She had to act as if he was permanently hers because there was no guarantee that she could give him back to his Sandy later. If the other Queen could even be found.

"I'm Queen-Commander Rhiannon," she introduced herself, still stroking his hair. Gentling him. "What's your name?"

"Eka Johnson," he croaked. *Good, he's tracking conversations, not just automatic quotations.*

"Can you answer a few questions for me?" If she was going to make this strange Devotion worth all the Hive-dysphoria her newest was going to battle, then she was going to get all the information Cantor could possibly need.

"Yes," Eka whispered. He grasped her hands and used them to lever himself up to kneeling so they could look directly into each other's eyes. More strongly, he repeated, "Yes."

"Wonderful!" Cantor's voice was overloud in the hushed aftermath of the crazed crying, and all three of Rhiannon's Devoted whirled to put themselves between her and the threat, facing the professor.

Mel and Victor immediately relaxed, shoulders softening and hands resuming their stroking. But her newest continued to tremble with tension, head swinging to keep Cantor in the center of his visual field. Because, apparently, Cantor was an idiot about how to treat the traumatized.

Or expected her to keep all of her Devoted emotionally balanced, even the one she'd just acquired.

"Get back," hissed her new Devoted when Cantor was within arm's length of the huddle. "No closer to my Queen."

"Why don't you go back to your corner and question him from there?" Rhiannon suggested to Cantor. "We're safe. He's not going to hurt you or me."

Eka subsided, leaning back into her touch, but his ribs still trembled with readiness to spring. She kept a calming hand on his back as he related the whole of his tale. It started much like what she'd heard on the *Llyr's Llambo*: someone had recalled his Queen and never returned her, then promised to give her back if his Hive were in a certain place at a certain time.

There the story diverged. *This* ship's crew waited and waited for their lady's return until they received a message from the vile Queen stealers to return to Dyfed if they wanted their Queen to live. By that point only Eka had the wherewithal to do any piloting, but he didn't remember the other ships around them, which meant he'd lost the thread of awareness sometime before Mel's sleeping drugs had knocked him out.

"What should we do about the rest of the Devoted on this ship?" Rhiannon asked. She hoped Mel or Victor or even Cantor would have a strong opinion. Having received the information she'd needed from her newest Devoted, she wished she could return him to his un-Devoted state. What would she do with him? How would he integrate with the others? Could they even *like* each other outside the haze of exhaustion and necessity? This Devotion had been a survival tactic rather than a true choice, and that was a foundation for resentment, like when she took on Mel.

She'd got lucky with Mel.

"You must save them all, my lady!" Eka's eyes were so round she could see the white ring around his dark brown irises. In his desperation, he took his wary gaze off Cantor so he could prostrate himself before his Queen. "Please. Don't leave them like they have been."

He *would* know whether it was truly untenable.

"Someone has to pilot these ships before they run into each other," Cantor said. "I'd be happier if your crew could handle it alone, but if you must accept a pilot on each ship..."

A pilot on each ship. That was a lot of pilots.

Mel made a throat clearing sound from his speaker grate. "We can't keep them all asleep forever."

Which meant she'd end up taking all the crew because doubtless each pilot would beg for the sanity of his previous Hive mates. "Can you stay here and pilot this ship for me?" she asked her new Devoted. "Even if I leave?"

Eka gripped her hands with urgent fingers until Victor moved to knock him away lest bruises form. Where could she put any other new Devoted if each clung to her like this? But he let her go and smoothed over the abused skin. "As you command me, my lady."

That was something, at least. One thing was clear: if she took on more Devoted, she'd have to get a larger ship, a flagship that could hold them all, preferably with a large room in which they could all see her for themselves and be reassured as to her safety.

"Though," Eka said, "I'm not usually the pilot."

Rhiannon was here, the Queen on the scene. She was responsible for her own Hive, which included this new man and all his worries. Which included his previous Hive and all their needs.

She couldn't think of herself as Rhiannon, neophyte Queen of an unconventional Hive. Not if she was going to give the support she'd bound herself to provide. She had to be an important Queen of something very big that required her to be strong.

She'd prepared for this since the first time she decided to game the Test. She was Queen. She was Commander.

"All right, Mel," she said. "Wake up the next one."

Welcome to my amalgamated Hive.

Interlude 5

News From Space

Dyfed, News Station 3

A blond woman sits behind a wooden desk. Her mouth is a thin line and the production department has painted her eyes to look bright for the camera.

"Good morning. This is Early Machynlleth News. I'm your host, Gretchen Wyn." The pad in Wyn's hands shakes, and she drops it to her desk with a clatter. "The loose group of Hive ships approaching Dyfed has now taken on an organized fleet formation. Our contact, Commander Bendigeidfran, assures News Station 3 that the Dyfed Space Defense Force is doing everything in its power to protect our homes and that there's no cause for worry."

"Despite this reassurance," Wyn continues, "riots have broken out across Machynlleth. Until this panic dies down, we here at Early Machynlleth News suggest that viewers remain indoors and conduct their business remotely."

She gestures off to her right shoulder and a picture box pops onto the monitors. In the grainy footage, men dressed as historic Queens throw rocks through store windows that tinkle and crumble. Everything is cast in grey, and smoke billows out from a storefront.

The picture changes to a bunch of ships in space. "Commander Bendigeidfran also revealed that the Dyfed Space Defense Force earlier fired a warning shot into the middle of this converging fleet. She says this is standard procedure and does not mean anyone should worry about *escalation* or *retaliation*." Gretchen Wyn says the words with extra emphasis, which guarantees her viewers will certainly worry about exactly those things.

Chapter Twenty-Six

A Fake Queen, a Real Girl

The "fleet's" tiniest ship

Melissa was no longer the Hive's newest Devoted. She liked it that way. It made her less remarkable.

Still remarkable for her provenance. Her American-ness. But not for being newest. Given the way these fresh Devoted had come to her Queen, she might not even be the *most* strange anymore.

Her insides seemed to speed up and cool down with the knowledge. More efficient.

The command deck vibrated under her shoes as a newer Devoted moved the small ship closer to the *Ceridwen's Cauldron* under Queen-Commander Ceridwen's orders. Melissa stretched out her sensors, pinging and pinging in hopes of connecting to the *Cauldron's* network. It had become her home, and she preferred to be in contact with her Hive's other early Devoted and with that particular ship's databases.

She felt the external ping before it chimed through to the room's screen. It shivered her substructure. An outsider attempting contact.

The communication chime sounded. Victor darted to stand between Queen Rhiannon and the screen. The ten new Devoted alternately screamed and flattened themselves against any available surface. Professor Cantor, arbiter for the status quo, stepped backwards and out of potential picture areas. Melissa kept a camera on him in case he had something nefarious planned. *By Saberhawen*—how she adored swearing that oath!—*she would keep him honest.*

"Hello?" A young girl's face filled the little screen. She was perhaps younger than Queen-Commander Rhiannon. Her face was rounder, cheekbones invisible under fat that had yet to melt away. Mouth too big for her head, making her look friendly and innocent when she flashed white teeth. Her doe eyes squinted, as if collapsing under pressure. As if she hadn't slept enough for a young teen girl. "I'm Que—een Chloe." Her voice shifted on *Queen*.

"Hello," said Rhiannon, neutral and calm. *Isn't she at all curious?* "Queen-Commander Ceridwen." Odd that the other Queen hadn't used a ship designation in formal introductions.

"Your ship moved," said the girl. It was almost an accusation, but her excited hair bounce said otherwise. "It's the only one that did, other than mine."

A voice in the background said, "Confirmed, my lady." A male voice.

Devoted! And a Queen. What made this ship so different from the insensible ones in the so-called fleet?

This was not the question Melissa's Queen asked. "Why would any of the others move?"

Chloe's eyes slid all the way to her left, as though thinking or scrutinizing Rhiannon's face on another screen. "The shot?" Her voice fried up at the end, intimating what a moron she thought adult-esque Rhiannon was. Melissa dipped her head to hide her lightening visor color. She'd seen Rhiannon treat adults to teenage contempt many times, but never had Melissa seen anyone try it on the Commander. "It didn't get you, right?"

Of course, Rhiannon wasn't ruffled. *Because she is Queen or because she's used to these interactions?* "What shot?"

"I'm *not* crazy." Chloe's image jumped on the screen as she thumped her hand down next to the camera. "Nor are the Devoted guys."

A few older men, much older, old enough to be her father, ducked into the picture. A bearded man waved.

That was a clear mismatch. "I'm surprised any Queens are still in control of their ships," said Melissa. *Tell me what makes your ship different.*

Chloe squirmed, turning her head into profile and showing off a down-twisted side of her mouth. "Well, ah, actually…"

Melissa was about to try her favorite "intimidate the suspect" tactic: crackled growling with question repetition, but her Queen-Commander waved a languid hand that demanded silence from others on her ship. "If it makes you feel better," Rhiannon said, "I just illegally stole another Queen's Devoted."

Melissa's visor flashed white. Victor and Cantor gasped. The Devoted along the walls didn't react at all. Overloaded.

Through the command room's speakers, Chloe laughed. Too high-pitched, too breathy. Hyperventilating. Masculine forearms entered the picture frame, forming a boat-neck collar and effectively calming her. "My dad's Queen's been teaching me. She wants me to take over someday, I think. Ugh." She rolled her eyes.

Off screen, a man's voice said, "She's holding us together until we can find our lady."

Chloe laughed, though the sound hitched on a sob towards the end. "I told her I didn't want to learn."

Rhiannon's eyebrows flew up to meet her circlet crown. *Good thing this Queen had been teaching her anyway.* "You don't want to be a Queen?"

On a sub-channel, Melissa finally got a ping back from the *Ceridwen's Cauldron*. "I'm getting a message from Alan. He's asking if we're all right after the Dyfed Space Defense Force fired in our direction."

"Doesn't mean I can't."

Quiet enough that only Melissa could hear him for sure, Cantor breathed, "How are they not all crazy?"

"I've managed to take the Devoted on this ship for my own. I don't know whether it's permanent, but it's giving me control of this fleet." Rhiannon looked directly at the screen, making eye contact with Chloe's image. Serious. Queen to Queen. "If people are shooting at us, I'd like to have as much control as possible. But I can't get to every ship in a timely manner. Can you help?"

Chloe's lips screwed into a bird beak. She blew out a long breath, then said, "Yes, I'll help you. I want my mother back."

The owner of the calming forearms jerked backwards, taking his little Queen a few inches with him. "But, my lady!"

"Your *mother*?" asked Rhiannon.

True, the girl hadn't mentioned that relationship before. Melissa's research suggested that Queenship didn't tend to run in families, but it wasn't unheard of.

"Not *really* my mother, not biologically, but she's always been here. And Dad and the guys need her."

Rhiannon nodded. In a slow, low voice, she said, "Thank you for your aid. Having more women will make all the difference."

"*Pob lwc.*" *Good luck.* Chloe cut her connection, ostensibly to find and take command of whichever ship was closest to hers. Or possibly to argue with her sort-of Devoted about it.

With the number of ships floating around Dyfed, a second Queen wouldn't make for particularly rapid change, but there didn't seem to be too much rush. Unless the Space Force fired in earnestness next time.

Their cause needed more women. Melissa was a woman. It seemed like a match. Except for the way she'd been hiding her nature, her status, her very self from Cantor and everyone. She wished she could have discussed it with Rhiannon before taking a strong stance.

Melissa said, "I volunteer." Melissa's headlamps rotated all the way around, using up extra energy.

Cantor gasped, loud and horrified. His face elongated, mouth long and open, eyes showing their whites. "Can you possibly pretend to be a woman? You look..." His mouth clicked closed, no polite way to possibly finish that sentence.

Melissa had to admit, Cantor's was the weirdest anti-synthetic prejudice she'd ever encountered. In fact, it might not even be anti-synthetic. Just anti-woman? These Dyfed people were sometimes too far beyond her psychological experience. Her visor flashed white.

Victor banged on her back at his shoulder level, about the height of her lower arm pair. "Our Mel is a shapeshifter." He had a smile on his face, and a sparkle in his eyes that meant he was... proud? Of her?

He wouldn't be if he knew. She hadn't been a shapeshifter at all, but rather a woman pretending to be a man. Still, if that was how this culture understood her, then she could make her case in terms they would appreciate.

"You don't have to change who you are just because we need women." Rhiannon's brows furrowed and she tapped her lips. Signs of worry and frustration if Melissa's catalogue could be trusted. Conclusion: Rhiannon didn't believe Melissa wanted to be female, only helpful. Given how obsessed with usefulness she'd been while trying to find her place in the Hive, it was a fair assessment. But wrong.

"Being male was an interesting experiment, but I'm done with it. Changing now can help with the Queen shortage. Perfect timing." Her circuits all chanted "let me let me let me" in a language no one could know.

"I won't have it!" Professor Cantor waved his arms. "Devoted are male. They have to be. Our whole Hive system hinges on it."

Melissa splayed all her twenty-four digits, then curled them in again. She'd been breaking the law for a while in that case. If in good faith. "I *can* still be your Devoted after *shapeshifting*"—she used their word—"to female, can't I?" If yes, then it wasn't the unassailable truth Cantor made it out to be. He wasn't the ultimate authority over her, not really. Rhiannon was.

"Of course," said Rhiannon. "I've always thought that requirement was foolish. And you were male when you did the Devoting."

The acceptance was warmth pouring in through hidden seams in her welding. *I get to stay!* While she knew Rhiannon had a female Hive member—or Hive-adjacent friend—previously, but that wasn't the same as having a *Devoted*.

"You're one of *us*," said Victor. "We wouldn't get rid of you."

Cantor gasped again, but his heartbeat had remained steady for the past few exchanges. He was faking his horror. "What if he tries to steal your other Devoted away?"

Melissa's visor flashed white and she stilled her body to statue. "She." Cantor didn't get to take this away from her. Not with her Queen and her Hive mate in full support.

The newer Devoted, who'd been silently watching this interplay, laughed. Melissa chose to believe that meant they were supporting her—their Hive mate—against Cantor, and not astounded by the idea that she might be a Queenly contender.

Rhiannon scoffed, her skull pulled back on her neck stalk far enough to distort the skin beneath her chin.

"If they could leave me, for her or for anyone, I don't want them."

This was the second time Rhiannon had stood up for her to someone in power. Devoting to Rhiannon may have been the best non-choice Melissa had ever made.

"But—"

Rhiannon didn't let Cantor finish, addressing Melissa instead. "You'll start at the other end of the fleet; I'm going to take the largest ship next. We need a flagship and a place to put all my new Devoted." As though it had all been decided.

Just like that Melissa was a woman again. A woman with a mission given by her boss. "May I pick up some plants from the *Cauldron*? In case these people are space crazy, I can't give Victor's nature spiel." She could do this. She could be Rhiannon's most useful Devoted, just like she'd been a stellar American Space Ranger.

Victor narrowed his eyes and *slouched* at her. "It makes so much sense! Look—"

"Another time," said Melissa. She welcomed his teachings... when people weren't shooting at them.

"We don't have many," Rhiannon told her, fingers tapping at her lips again.

"This close to a planet, we can restock." She flexed her four insectoid knees, jaunty and happy and ready to spring into action the moment her Queen dismissed her. "I'll see you back at HQ when the job is done." Melissa tipped an imaginary hat, the way her old Space Ranger chief had loved to tip his anachronistic Stetson.

"HQ?" demanded Professor Cantor.

Rhiannon raised her eyebrows at him. "The large flagship we're about to take over, obviously." Thanks to Saberhawen that Melissa's Queen was operating on all the same assumptions and frequencies. They were a perfect match. "Go."

Dismissed, Melissa leapt towards the command room's door, jumping over all the new Devoted to reach her destination faster. First the airlock, then a spacewalk to the *Ceridwen's Cauldron* for potted plants that she'd have to bundle up against vacuum. Once those errands were done, she was off to pick up some Devoted followers of her own.

It might be a relief to be a woman again, but what did she know about being a Queen?

⟍ Chapter Twenty-Seven ⟋

A Series of Unfortunate Deductions

Planet Dyfed,
café in the Machynlleth Covered Market

Surrounded by three Devoted, Olivia felt safe enough to sip her tea and await her prey's arrival. Her prey being Nancy Driscoll, the shopkeeper who'd argued with Rogers prior to his running off and losing Olivia in the renewal ritual.

Olivia buried her nose in the steam of her morning's peppermint infusion. She hadn't originally intended to return to the market and track down Rogers' last known contact. The pair's argument had seemed the standard shopkeeper-and-irate-customer kind, and Olivia had felt safe to forget about the woman.

Safe like Effie isn't right now, surrounded by conspirators. But Olivia couldn't do anything about that, so she shook off the worry as best she could. Instead she would concentrate on the problem at hand.

So here she was, weeks after witnessing Driscoll's altercation with Rogers, working on information she'd received from Dylan Pughe. (Because of course Olivia had fingerprinted the shopkeeper.) Pughe *did* say that the blurry photo of the woman's uniform helped more with the identification than the fingerprints.

Buttonhole cameras were useful! If low-tech. However had her Devoted—Owen, really—come up with that idea? It didn't matter; it had worked.

Before the crowds arrived, before most of the shops opened, everything was quiet and calm and smelled gloriously of chocolate-infused roasting beans. "Is Driscoll's shop open yet?" Paul asked, seated beside her with a black coffee, unadulterated by milk or sugar. Strange man.

The shop was the thing that had brought Olivia back. Pughe's information said that Driscoll was a *pharmacist*. She could've been making Holly's drugs. Even if she wasn't, a pharmacist involved with medical experimenters was suspicious.

"Not according to the time," Owen said. His highly milky tea sat on the table, but he stood behind Olivia's chair, ready and alert.

"You're the only one obsessive enough to care about *that*," said Mark (holding a vanilla-flavored drinking chocolate).

Olivia tuned out the ensuing bickering in favor of checking her messages. *Nothing from Effie.* Just like the day before and the day before that. No matter what subtle information Olivia shared, she couldn't make Effie reply. She was still alone on her investigative quest.

Instead she had an advertisement for hull-cleaning robots, two requests for advice from young Queens she'd met at the networking event, and something from Rhiannon Jones. *That's Queen-Commander Ceridwen!*

Olivia read Ceridwen's message, pleased to see that the young Queen-Commander was making use of her ship and her connections.

Ceridwen's message was brief, but intriguing. In it, the young Queen posited that the missing Queens might belong to the ships in orbit, since Ceridwen recognized one from the courier job Llewellyn had requested (and which Queen Olivia had so kindly secured for the Hive's first assignment).

Apparently, Llewellyn *had* put the Hive in a spot of trouble. Olivia could read the annoyance in the words. Ceridwen didn't *quite* blame Olivia for whatever Llewellyn caused, but it was a close thing.

Olivia dashed off a reply, telling Ceridwen the barest details about the shadow government's detainment and experiments. She made sure to mention how helpful Holly had been. Maybe the young Queen could suborn the scientist. If needed.

"Shop's open," Owen said. "According to its posted hours, anyway."

That was good enough for Olivia. "Let's go." She left her tea on the table, still steaming. She had questions for this pharmacist, and she intended to get answers.

She stomped ahead of her three Devoted, flanked by the men and the empty walkways. Yes, mornings were definitely the best time for visiting the market. At the shop's door, she turned the old-fashioned handle, twined vines cast in resin.

The molded leaves pushed points into her hand, resisting. The door didn't click or open.

Olivia pushed down harder on the handle. Pulled up. Out. She rattled the door in its frame, not caring if the shaking displaced any product on the interior shelves. If the shopkeeper wanted to have a neatly arranged store, she ought to open it on time.

Paul put a hand on Olivia's shoulder, but she shivered until he let it slide off. She yanked on the handle again and was immediately pulled back. Warm arms caught her and kept her from her objective.

Olivia twisted in the grasp. She thrashed and kicked. She wouldn't be taken!

Tears pricked her unseeing eyes. Where were her Devoted? Why weren't they helping? They would never betray her. So they must be restrained. Dead? She redoubled her efforts, grunts pouring out with every strike against her captor.

"Shh, shh." The murmur in her ear was utterly unlike anything the guards had ever said when carting her off to another "doctor's appointment".

Mark's voice. *Oh.*

Olivia went limp in his arms, signaling her willingness to stop fighting. "Sorry," she said.

Mark set her on her feet, but kept her in his embrace. "No harm done." His arms were already bruising. How could he forgive her so easily?

If only she could have harmed her captors! But those days were over.

Paul joined the clutch, arms around both of them and hands shaking. "The harm was to *my* heart," he teased Mark. His words were breathless, not quite enough air for levity.

Olivia gripped his closest cold fingers. "We'll all be fine," she said. "I'll make sure of it."

Placated, Paul released her and Mark. Hands steadier, he picked the pharmacist's door lock, using Olivia and Mark to shield his activity from view.

She was in a public place in Machynlleth, she reminded herself, fighting down the tremors from the chill his absence left. Everything was normal here. Safe.

Except for what lay visible when the door swung open: the dead body on the floor, blond hair strewn all around it.

Mark led her away, petting her like a feral cat, while the others called the police. Olivia didn't even get to ask Driscoll her questions. She had no clues left. None.

⟍ Chapter Twenty-Eight ⟋

The Nature of Nature

The "fleet", the Iâr Du

As Holly's favorite med tech might say, "Another day, another inoculation." This ship had already been cleared, but Holly needed a vacation from Siân Edwards, so she'd put together a team and revisited the *Iâr Du*.

Her med tech and two guards had immediately taken advantage of the work-free environment and flitted off to the well-appointed and utterly empty gym. She'd warned them to keep an eye out for post-inoculation Devoted, even though her recent patients didn't have strong observational skills.

During the few hours of calm on the empty ship, Holly plopped herself on the cozy captain's chair and sewed three to-be-stuffed animals. She'd made two lambs and a dog to herd them, floppy for now. They'd be easier to pack that way. When she made it down to Dyfed again, she'd plump them with wool and ask Amanda to paint on cute little eyes. Then she'd pass them out to children in hospital wards who needed a friend to cuddle.

There was a reason she'd been made a family doctor, even if it wasn't her preference. She cared for the children just as much as for her research topics. Research was leading the way forward to a better overall societal health, and children were the next wave of that society.

Pleased with her efforts, Holly returned to the airlock.

It wasn't empty.

A young woman with a *crown* over her frizzing hair stood at the front of a boarding party. Behind her, skinning out of their spacesuits, were a teenaged boy, a man Holly's age, and a guy she'd swear she already injected.

The group hadn't seen Holly yet.

Holly's teeth clenched. A functional Queen could undo all her work with these confused Devoted. Whoever this girl was, Holly would *not* let her destroy everything she'd worked for. The Devoted would stay separated from Queens and drugs and Senedd-approved influences.

Quietly as she could, she set down her inoculation kit, begging it not to clank on the slate-colored ground that was probably actual slate. She slipped a sterile syringe from its package and filled it with the Devotion vaccine. Tapped and squirted out any air bubbles.

Holly would only have one chance at this Queen. If she couldn't chemically separate the younger woman from her Devoted immediately, the men would take Holly down before she could try a second time.

The skinny young man wondered aloud, "How many people do you think are on this ship?" His Queen turned to look at him. Which put her back to Holly.

One chance.

Holly took it. She leapt from behind the suit lockers, syringe fisted over her head. She reached the Queen's side before any of the men could shout. Holly stabbed down into thick muscle—plenty of blood vessels in there—and plunged down. *Success!*

Screams filled her ears, not from the Queen, but from the man she'd probably inoculated before. He screamed and twitched and swatted ineffectual fists at her. Not a reaction she'd expected.

A calm alto ordered, "Hold her."

Holly found herself ensconced in the teenaged boy's embrace, arms restrained. Her syringe fell to the decking.

The Queen stayed calm. *She* didn't scream. No seizing or crying, no begging for her Devoted as their symbiotic presences abandoned her brain. No, the Queen came nose to nose with Holly and asked, "What did you inject me with?"

Holly was too shocked to lie. "It should have severed the connection between you and your Devoted. The virus in you can't survive it." But it obviously had.

This made the second immune Queen Holly had encountered, the first being the old woman back on Dyfed. The one who'd managed to call in the Department of Civic Protection and close down the facility under the Old Senedd while still a prisoner. Once was an outlier, but twice couldn't be a coincidence. Holly flopped in her captor's hold. Was her research faulty? Worse, would these kids take her to jail and overcome her revolution until it faded quietly into history never to be heard from again?

Unless this Queen had a newer drug. The government, then, not only knew about her and her rebel friends, but they could counteract her. The old man holding the screamer was here to take her into custody. This young Queen could not be turned because she had a different drug. Holly's life's work was meaningless.

The Queen tapped a finger against her lips, and Holly felt an echo of the finger strikes at their close distance. "What virus in me?"

Of course the woman didn't know. No one was supposed to know. But the man holding the screamer had a horrified, slack expression on his face that he hadn't bothered to hide.

He explained on Holly's behalf. "All Queens and Devoted, when they register their bond, are injected as part of a ceremony. It's not a *virus*. It helps strengthen the connection."

Holly hadn't heard of any new Devotion drugs from the Senedd, which meant this immunity came from within. Or that *some* Hives were natural. Holly couldn't fight nature.

"Interesting," said the Queen.

"We didn't do that," said the teen behind Holly, his breath teasing hot at her ear.

That made no sense whatsoever. "They didn't inject you?" she asked, squirming to see the boy's face.

He shrugged, jostling her shoulders. "We didn't register with a central office."

The older man was nodding. "That explains why I couldn't find Alan's paperwork."

"We didn't know we had to. Maybe that's the kind of thing that comes up in more advanced Queen training at university. " The Queen smirked at them all, clearly pleased. "And it looks like avoiding that was a *good* thing."

No, no, it really wasn't. Because it meant this girl's Hive had come together organically. Holly had no control over them. Nor any right to try. They'd chosen their path, and Holly wanted that for herself and her friends and her world. The *choice*.

The oldest man gasped. Overacting, if you asked Holly. "You're not a *real* Hive!" If he'd come onto the ship with that young Queen, shouldn't he know?

The Queen's smirk faded. "How so? We think and act as one."

Too bad Holly couldn't study *that* phenomenon, but the arms around her suggested a disinterest in her personal freedom. This Queen didn't seem like an imposter, and the two Devoted she'd brought along gave her all the deference Holly had observed in test subjects.

The Queen looked away from her interrogator and into the distance. Her hands clenched. "You can't punish these good Devoted. They can all be rehabilitated away from my influence. I'm responsible for tricking them into leaving our home space to experience the universe."

If that isn't stereotypical Queen behavior...

The arms around Holly tightened. "Please don't blame Queen-Commander Ceridwen." The youth's voice was too loud in her ear. "This was all my idea."

And if that *isn't stereotypical Devoted behavior...*

"Hush, Victor," said the girl, Queen-Commander Ceridwen.

The older man's brow wrinkled and he shook his head, but his words agreed with Holly's thoughts. "You're the real thing, as far as I can tell. If we hadn't run into this mad scientist, I'd never have known."

Who are you calling mad? Holly snarled at him like a truly mad animal might. Her warm prison jerked back, but so did the annoying old man, and that was worth it.

"Humphrey," said the Queen, "are you all right now?"

"Yes, my lady." The other Devoted's voice was gravelly, but that was to be expected from a man who'd been screaming only moments before. Holly hadn't noticed when the screams ceased. Too embroiled in worries over what made a Hive and whether her whole plan to break the virus had been worthwhile.

"Good. Let him go, please, professor. Humphrey, go find me a chair."

"Yes, my lady." Humphrey snapped out of the older man's hold and stalked off.

Said older man speared Holly with his gaze, and she scowled right back. No flinching. He was *nothing* to her. He was another symptom of the societal disease she'd fought for years. "We've learned your plan," he said, "and you're not going to get what you want."

They hadn't even known she was *here* a moment ago. Holly laughed until her abdominal walls ached with the contractions.

"How do you know what I want?" she asked. Because that was a really frustrating thing to be told: "I know what you want."

She didn't fight as Victor and Queen-Commander Ceridwen put her in Humphrey's chair and tied her up. They took her inoculations kit, but it was just one kit. A drop in the pool of medication her labs produced.

The older man made a condescending moue with his mouth. "Don't you want to Devote?"

"Maybe I did once." Her heart sped and sweat pooled at her collarbones. "Before I realized that the whole system was flawed. Because you're right, I can't Devote as things are, even if I want to."

"Don't you want to save lives?" Holly could hear the accusation in his tone. That she'd killed Queens and destroying lives—the Hives, the people who raided her facility—with her freedom fighting.

He didn't see all the lives already destroyed. The little girls who wanted to Devote. The asexuals who couldn't breed the right level of romantic interest for a first-year Devotion. The experts in their fields who never got funding because they had no Queen to agitate for them with the award committees.

Holly spat at his feet. "I'm saving the lives of all the smart girls who would never be Queens and still want to do something with their lives. How many do you think can make it to that lofty position? Ninety-nine point nine five percent of us are what? *Wasted*? Not able to Devote, not able to be Queens."

"Don't you want—"

"Stop!"

A beat of silence in Queen-Commander Ceridwen's wake.

"Just stop," the Queen said. "All you're doing is making her mad, and she'll never help you then."

"I don't need her help," said the interrogator. "She's already mad in the insane way."

"No she isn't," said the Queen.

"Oh really?" The man's eyebrows rose, and Holly's did as well. No Queen had ever suggested that Holly's cause was anything other than crazy talk.

"Really." Ceridwen's crown bounced when she poked the older man in the chest. "In fact, she's right."

"What?!" Holly's nemesis exclaimed. She wanted to laugh. His face was like an owl's with the beak open after a mouse has just escaped and it's unsure how that happened and what to do. The great predator bested.

"The Hive system is broken," said Queen-Commander Ceridwen. "You can't ignore that fact."

"No it isn't!"

But the Queen ignored him, and the teenaged Devoted nodded vehement agreement with his lady. "Yes, it is. My Hive had a woman when we started. Did you know that? And it didn't weaken us."

The older man sputtered.

"And my ship's doctor would love to train with *this* woman. His Test scores closed off surgery to him, and I know he'd rather do that than be a GP."

Just like Holly. She hadn't wanted to be a general practitioner either. She'd had to learn patience and bedside manner when all her skills lay in picking apart unconscious flesh and observing people who didn't know they were being observed.

"If his Test scores—"

The teen boy cut off Holly's interrogator. "No."

"The system is broken," the Queen repeated, "and this woman—"

"Holly!" piped in Holly. She wanted to be known by this first ever advocate Queen.

"—Holly is right," she finished without a pause. "That's why we left Dyfed in the first place."

"At least," offered the teenaged boy, "it doesn't work for everyone?"

All her life, Holly had been told she was wrong. Her Test results knew better than she did. She wasn't good enough to be a neurosurgeon. She couldn't be a Devoted. *All her life.* Until the rebels came. Ffion Kendrick recognized Holly's brilliance and begged her to help take down the status quo.

But this woman, this Queen-Commander Ceridwen was *part* of the status quo. She was a *Queen*. If Holly and the rebels brought down the system, Ceridwen would lose her edge over the mainstream population. Yet she saw the truth. Ceridwen agreed. Her very agreement validated Holly's arguments for the first time. In the game of Us versus Them, somehow Holly was part of this Queen's Us.

This was more than her mother or her girlfriend under-standing Holly's position. More than the rebels and their echo chamber of righteousness. A Queen was revered! A Queen had no reason to side with Holly other than to bow before a greater truth. When this Queen said "Holly is right," she was doing more than changing the face of inter-rogation, she was in a position to change the world.

"Besides," said Queen-Commander Ceridwen, "Queen Olivia vouched for this woman by name."

Holly's heart was three sizes too big for her ribcage. She could have floated away like it was a balloon. "You have to promise me," she said. *Probably not the right way to frame a request to a Queen used to respectful discourse and unquestioning obedience.* "Promise me you'll look out for everyone. For the rebels, for everyone who's been hurt. Be-fore I help you, you have to promise me."

Ceridwen's fingers dug into Holly's hand. Oh, they were holding hands. A Queen was holding Holly's hand. Not caring about the slick sweat that made the grip feel like nothing. Nothing and everything all at once. "I promise." Her brown eyes had a puppy's innocence combined with a project manager's sharpness. *Queen-Commander, indeed.* "I'll look out for the rebels, the trampled, and our whole society. No one deserves the cage that the Test has made for us."

Could Holly really trust this young woman to do the most good? The rebellion had been her support and her goal for so long, even if it hadn't been doing much for her lately. Even if Holly had taken over the navigational systems on all the ships because she worried they were setting her up as a convenient villain. But that could be paranoia.

"Let me work *with* you," said Queen-Commander Ceridwen, and Holly really believed the young woman cared.

She could stay silent and hope that the rebels completed their mission successfully, riding straight through this Queen and her unexpected presence. Or she could make sure Queen-Commander Ceridwen knew all the atrocities she fought against, and make sure the Queen's voice could be heard.

"We can start by recalling the resistance leaders before their particular plan is ready," said Holly.

"Resistance leaders?" the older man asked, but everyone ignored him.

The teenage boy untied Holly's hands and gave her a pad. Holly drew in a deep breath, looked one more time into Ceridwen's encouraging eyes, and sent the *all clear*.

Immediately, she found it hard to breathe. *I'm a double agent*. Air thinned. She gasped and gasped.

The pad disappeared from her grip, and the Queen's fingers reappeared in it. "Breathe with me," Ceridwen said. "Now count. In, two, three. Out, two, three."

The man who'd got the chair was asking in the background, "Who else has she been sticking with these needles?"

"Can it be undone?"

Ceridwen gripped Holly's hands tighter. "Focus on me. In, two, three."

Holly tipped forwards and rested her head against the crook of the Queen's neck. It was calming, comforting. Is this what Queens were for? She could use one at her doctor's office if she still had a job there. "The shadow government will be back soon," she whispered in the Queen's ear. "A few days, maybe."

"A *shadow government?!*" That was the older man who'd failed at interrogation.

Holly grinned into Ceridwen's tunic where no one could see it. That confused owl had no place in the new world that Holly and Ceridwen would build.

Ceridwen stroked Holly's back, gentle and calm. "Where did you get the drug you injected me with?"

"Made it. Got a lab." Holly's eyes closed. She was so warm now. Her heart slowed.

Ceridwen's voice came through as a mumble, reverberating in her chest cavity more than as sound waves on the air. "We'll have to change Melissa's mission from pseudo-Queen to detective. Someone pass me a pad."

Ceridwen and the rebellion would work together. Holly would finally get the recognition she needed. She'd never thought that would happen in her lifetime, but with a Queen on her side, she was much more likely to succeed.

She could start her own practice in her farmhouse with Amanda and bask in the ability to choose her own future. No one could tell her no.

Not because of her test scores. Her gender. Her other potential.

She could go home to a free world. *Finally.*

Chapter Twenty-Nine

Devoted Ducklings

A ship at the far end of the "fleet"

By Melissa's second boarding, she'd run out of plants to give away. To make up for it, she put a recording of her voice on the shipwide speakers and uploaded images of plants to all the tablets on the intra-network. *Complimentary gift for regaining your sanity.*

She'd love to say the idea came from an answered prayer to Saberhawen, but she'd forgotten to ask the new goddess for help. She'd do better in the future.

Her recording, modified with the harmonic she'd learned from pseudo-agent Ward, contained only a Devoted's oath. Constantly repeated, it should put thoughts of Devotion in these men's minds while the tone soothed them.

"I pledge you my Devotion."

The first ship had taken a while, but her new Devoted agreed her voice was what calmed them the most. *If you say so, boys.* They hadn't been happy to see her go, but she couldn't tarry. Turned right around and pushed herself out the airlock.

They might catch up. She might be gone again before it mattered. She had to get all these ships set to rights before the Space Defense Force fired again. For safety and because her Queen asked her to.

This whole weird feudal system was a mess.

Down a hallway covered with brick veneer, she called out through her speaker-grille. "Hello? Anybody home?" The words didn't matter, only that she was available.

And, lo! came a body.

A man on trembling legs and with too fast respiration gasped out, "Who are you?"

"I am Queen Melissa, and I've come for you." It sounded odd to call herself a Queen, but hearing her name again made her visor lighten with pleasure to sky blue.

The man's knees buckled and he knelt in front of her. "May I? Would you?" He hadn't even balked at her extra limbs or metal skin. *By Saberhawen, I love the acceptance from Dyfed.* Was this what happened when a planet had never known PRobs? When psychology focused on the identification instead of "fixing" abnormalities?

She put a hand on his closest shoulder, gripping front and back with her two thumbs.

"My sword and my service, my body and my blood, my agency and my anima—these all belong to you, so I swear." The words over the shipwide had primed him but good.

"I accept your sword and service. Your body and blood are mine to direct. Your agency and anima are my agency and anima, now and forever more. Call on me in times of trouble, as I will call on you, but always you will be my first defense." When Commander Ceridwen had spoken these words to Melissa, they'd marked a new epoch. "What's your name?" Melissa pulled her hand back and motioned her new Devoted to rise.

"Daffyd, my lady."

"Well, Daffyd, let's find your friends."

"As you command." He fell in step behind her as she marched off, a difficult task when she had four feet and he only two.

Three corridor junctions later, they came across two crewmen. One stared at his tablet screen like it held all the answers to his life's questions. A quick ping on the network showed he was viewing her uploaded plant images.

The second man leapt at her. "Interloper!"

Daffyd, behind her, scuffled forwards as though he would stand between her and danger.

He was too late. She caught the flying man and bundled him in three of her arms. As with Daffyd, she said, "I am Queen Melissa, and I've come for you."

Unlike with Daffyd, this man pounded on her breastplate, desperate to free himself. "No more," he said. "No more!"

She ran her fourth hand's fingers through his hair—as she'd seen Queen Rhiannon do on the smallest ship—and he quieted under her touch until all that remained of his motions were twitches and hitching sobs. Her metal fingers gleamed with his hair grease.

Daffyd was silent. The man with the tablet hadn't even noticed the commotion. Over the shipwide, her voice suggested, *"My life and my hands are yours for a year and a day."*

She put the newly docile man down on the ground, curled on his side. He was safe enough now, from himself and from her. She hadn't had this problem on the first ship she'd taken. With that crew, once they realized she was a Queen, rather than a Queen stealer, they'd been quick to suggest Devotion. (If they had enough brains to make their own choices. Otherwise, she'd just start them on the words, and they'd mumbled them out on automatic.)

They could always change their minds later. First, they needed minds to change.

Daffyd spoke to the man huddled at her feet. "Hey, J.J." Soothing, quiet. He joined J.J. on the floor.

A third body leapt out of a doorway. He didn't scream, had neatly brushed hair. He brandished a long needle, leading with it.

Melissa let the needle hit her armor plating—9 out of 10 impact rating and proven in the face of firearms. It broke on her metal hide. Its wielder now well inside her reach, she grabbed him as she'd done with J.J., but not nearly so comfortingly. No hair petting for this man.

She pulled a set of handcuffs from her vest pocket and locked her attacker's wrists together.

Her captive snarled at her. "I'm in control here." He fought the restraints, bringing bloody bruises to his skin. "Not you."

"Where's your lockup?" Melissa asked Daffyd. "Because that's where this man is going."

J.J. looked her over as if seeing her for the first time. His eyes widened on her backward, insectoid knees and he flinched from her visor's steady gaze. "You're not with *them*."

Odds were good that "them" did not include Queen-Commander Ceridwen's Hive, and was some third group Melissa had yet to encounter. Excepting the captive in her grip. "No."

"All right." J.J. readjusted his position. "I pledge you my Devotion. My life and my hands are yours for a year and a day. May we choose never to part."

"I accept your life and your hands, and pledge you my consideration and attention for a year and a day. May our partnership continue forever."

Daffyd and J.J. cajoled their shy friend in the corner into her service as well. The three of them escorted the needle fiend to the brig. Daffyd led, and the other two followed behind. Every time they came across another crewman they stopped and brought him into their makeshift Hive. And every time the new Devoted joined the procession at the end. They followed her like goslings.

The cells, when they reached them, looked like something that should be on a planet, not on a spaceship. The floor was cracking cement and the fourth-wall bars rusted.

The normal owners of this ship had a penchant for planetary veneers, Melissa surmised. The brick walls in the corridors, and now this. Well, in zero-g, heavy materials didn't cause problems. Then again, a designer first had to get the cement and brick into orbit, and that could be expensive. Melissa would never choose it. When she'd run a solo operation, she hadn't even bothered to pay for air.

All the while, the shipwide speakers rang out with her voice encouraging others to chime in. "*I pledge you my Devotion.*"

How did Rhiannon handle it? Even with all these people happy enough to have a synthetic Queen, Melissa wasn't cut out for this weirdness.

She'd almost finished sweeping the ship when she got a ping from Queen-Commander Ceridwen. Melissa connected, but it wasn't live.

Rhiannon's text message read:

The Queen stealers are here! They have horrible drugs that sever Devotion bonds. I need you to stop everything and find the drug lab. Plus track down all the staff you can. They won't be Devoted, so they'll be easy to find.

Well, that explained the man with the needle who'd attacked her. At his cell door, she asked, "You wanna tell me where your drug lab is?"

He spit at her, not even making contact, so she wouldn't have to worry about rust.

"Didn't think so." But it hadn't hurt to ask. He might've been the cooperative type. Asking questions could sometimes be like checking to make sure a door was unlocked.

Well, she'd been the best tracker in the American Space Rangers, and now she'd be the best tracker in Queen-Commander Ceridwen's Hive. No drug lab could evade her sensors; no person would go unaccounted. If she could find the lab ship, it ought to have records of all the staff she was looking for. If it didn't, it'd still be a good place to start.

"All right, boys," Melissa told her ducklings. "Let's find some spacesuits and a string to tie us together. We're going on a field trip."

"Out in space?" Dafyd had gone white and his finger-tips were a cooler color on her thermal sensors.

A few others looked down to their nature pics on their tabs. The rest looked to Melissa with obsessive expressions in their eyes. Over the shipwide, her voice said, *"My life and my hands are yours"*, and she planned to take full advantage of that vow.

For as long as they were in her service, they'd get to be a search and rescue team.

"You'll feel the stars on your skin," she said.

Her Devoted cheered out loud at the idea.

"But only through the suits," she said as she hustled her charges to the airlock area. "Don't take them off."

Yep. These guys were space crazy and she couldn't wait to turn them over to Queen-Commander Ceridwen. Or their original ruler.

Chapter Thirty

A Second Investigation

Planet Dyfed,
café in the Machynlleth Covered Market

Olivia's favorite café had closed for the night, so she didn't have a good excuse to loiter in that section of the market. However, she'd found a way to casually walk past the area.

On this trip to the market, Mark joined her, lured by the promise of closing-time prices on fresh vegetables. If they used the correct entrance, they'd have to pass the café and the equally closed pharmacy on their way to the remains of the food market.

He was becoming suspicious, and rightly so.

"This doesn't look like a vegetable cart," he said as they took just the wrong covered turn past a black-caverned souvenir shop with glinting spoons in the window.

She tugged Mark down the gold-lit turns, footsteps echoing in relative emptiness. Two parents with screaming adolescent children cut across the walkway.

"*They're* probably getting cut-price vegetables," Mark grumbled. "Instead of heading to a *crime scene*." Of course he knew. Her Hive members could predict each other almost perfectly.

Almost.

"In a moment." Olivia threaded her hand into the crook of his arm, letting his warm muscles hold her up while guiding him to her destination. "The dead shopkeeper, Nancy Driscoll, didn't make the news." That was all sorts of wrong. A local girl found dead in a locked shop after talking to a man who ran off pursued by a Queen. The woman's murder should have been a sensation. With Gretchen Wyn herself reporting.

Olivia had given up on solving the missing Queens mystery. She'd taken the investigation as far as she could and had to admit defeat. Even a Queen would fold under pressure from an entire shadow government.

"What's her body going to tell you?"

"Nothing." The woman was dead. She had no secrets that Olivia could divine. Olivia knew her limits, and Sherlock Holmes-esque deductions were beyond their extent.

If she couldn't fix the big picture, she could at least deal with a symptom. That meant solving Driscoll's murder.

The alleyway that housed the ex-pharmacist's shop was dark except for a tiny patch of light and liveliness at the entrance. None of the neighboring businesses had stayed open, either because of the hour or because of the tragedy. The stone floors seemed an abyssal mouth, as ready to eat a pedestrian as allow one to walk along. Three men and women, with lanterns to help them peer in the windows, were exactly where Olivia wanted to be.

Mark shivered and stopped, forcing Olivia to halt as well. "Maybe we should leave them alone."

Olivia pursed her lips, feeling the wrinkles forming over her mouth like pinstripes. "Or maybe we should ask them questions." She tugged him along, and he let himself be dragged forwards.

"We can't even sneak up on them."

Such a whiner. Had he always been like this? For over eighty years they'd been together... "Who needs to sneak?" She stepped harder on the cobblestones, her heels ringing out in the corridor. "Hello there." She waved her free arm high overhead.

A man with flour caked onto his hands snorted. "Another investigator?" His blue shirt was powdered with white streaks.

"Or someone with a morbid sense of curiosity," suggested the woman next to him.

Olivia shrugged, as if their opinions didn't matter. In reality, these were her only still-breathing leads, and she needed them. "How would I have heard about this if I weren't investigating?"

Mark asked the question she should have, "*Another* investigator?"

"Yeah," said the man wearing more flour than not. "There was someone here earlier."

"Hah! He wasn't investigating." The third member of the group, holding both lanterns, was even more cynical than the woman had been. "He wanted to hush it up."

"Told me not to report the incident to my insurance," the woman agreed. "Of course I did that as soon as he left."

Powder man brushed imaginary flour off his shoulders. "He said he was 'dealing with it.'"

These three had Olivia's own opinion about detectives other than herself, and their mistrust appeared well founded. Only villains covered up a murder instead of investigating it. "Did this investigator leave a way to get in touch with him?"

The woman nodded and pulled out a bulky pad with all sorts of protective add-ons. "Let me send it to you."

Olivia checked her own pad to make sure the transfer had gone through. She narrowed her eyes at the name on her screen. *Llewellyn! We never got together, and now he's shoving himself onto my case.* That was suspicious.

Or helpful.

She'd have to corner him and question him. About Driscoll's murder, about Rhiannon, about the secret bureaucracy. About what he was doing back on Dyfed.

"Did he mention where he's staying while he's in town?" Olivia asked.

The powder-coated man said, "He told me he was working out of the Old Senedd building."

Olivia's insides went cold, like she'd swallowed an ice cube and it froze all the tubes on its way down from throat to stomach. She wasn't going back there. Wasn't following a man down the stairs into darkness then hospital brightness that stung her eyes and stripped her body's secrets.

Her fingernails pricked her palms until the pain pulled her back to the present. No, she wasn't going back to the

Old Senedd, but there was a park near it. She'd been there weeks ago when chasing Rogers through that renewal ceremony. She could wait outside and catch her quarry when he came out.

"Thank you all for your help," Olivia said. She put on her best "friendly granny" voice to order them, "Go home, kids. You all could use some rest." Gods knew she'd take her own advice if she could.

Olivia tugged on Mark's arm and escorted him towards the market's exit. She had a faux investigator to catch.

"What about my vegetables?" asked Mark. He'd been planning a tagine for the Hive's dinner that night.

Olivia sighed, but steered him back along another passageway towards the produce sellers' section. "Of course." She could go after Llewellyn in the morning. For the moment, she wasn't ready to be alone, and her Devoted needed her to be as present as she could be.

First veggies, then home to cook them. Tomorrow: stakeout.

During dinner that night, Paul said, "I got a new wig today."

Hideki giggled into his vegetable tagine. "Will it make you as handsome as I am?"

Alexander, ever the equivocator, said, "He can only be as handsome as he is. Perhaps our Queen would like to comment."

While disguises had been Paul's idea first, the entire Hive had taken to them with enthusiasm. *Too much enthusiasm?* Olivia put down her fork and glanced askance at Paul's excessively animated face. "Why do you like disguises so much?" He'd never been the kind to use costumes before.

"Ah..." Paul had no answer.

All the sleuthing suggestions from her Hive—the disguises, the fingerprinting, the note taking—none of it had served any purpose. She hadn't even used the data!

Olivia bit her lip. Even she didn't know whether she was holding in a sob or a smile. "Do any of you"—she gestured to the table at large; not Alexander, Hideki, Mark, Owen, Paul, or Toan met her eyes—"know anything about conducting a detective investigation?"

Toan mumbled, "I read a couple of novels once."

Water filled Olivia's eyes. Laughter or helplessness? "Really?" Her voice was dry where her tear ducts weren't.

Hideki offered, "I wrote to a few enthusiast groups for tips. Anonymously."

"We were worried," Mark told his tagine.

Paul sighed, all energy from his wig acquisition gone. "We wanted to help you," he said. "You needed to keep busy and stay focused on something positive."

Her heart expanded, too big to hold all her love for them. She'd been so caught up in her investigation—and in her desire to keep her Devoted busy and focused as well—that she hadn't noticed the care they took with her.

Mark quietly added, "You have to admit you haven't been in a healthy frame of mind."

"Thank you," she said as the tears overflowed her eyes. She picked her fork back up and let them flavor her tagine. "From now on," she promised, "we'll only work in a positive direction. If anything goes horribly awry, we'll switch tacks until we make good, positive progress." Like she did when she gave up on fighting the shadow government in favor of attempting to solve Driscoll's related murder.

Her Devoted agreed to that plan with shouts of "yes!" and "no more wigs!"

After dinner, Olivia ensconced herself in her room to record another video message for Effie. If nothing else, she could comfort her friend over the long distance.

"I'm sorry to hear about the forced retirement party," Olivia started. She had to get her friend's mind off her intimate life troubles, so she followed it up with news from Dyfed.

"Things are scary here with these Hive ships coming. Did you hear about that? I hate to think the space Hives have really lost it. I mean, I was fine out there for decades. Maybe it's related to this conspiracy I've uncovered, but I guess I'll tell you about that when you get home.

"It's too bad you're so far away. We could fix this together, like we did those sorority pranksters in our twenties. Do you remember that, Effie? Those were the days, before this whole Hive system got out of hand and people like us could form friendships."

Olivia took the winding path down memory lane, reveling in pleasant days gone by where nothing could touch her and everything was a joke.

The sorority pranksters in question had been teens stealing a hard cider ration. Effie had been on the case, asking questions and telling people to come to her with any information. Olivia hadn't known her then and hadn't much cared about the cider or the teens, but when Effie had gotten confrontational with the culprits and the police came after the investigator instead of the thieves, well...

"You ran into my dorm room. You always said it was instinctive, but I think you knew I was there and that a Queen's support system would save you. Which, now that I think of it, was ridiculous. Your family would have kept you out of serious trouble.

"But I hid you under my bed anyway, and Queens were a new thing then, so the police didn't want to mess with me before any real precedent was set."

For weeks after, Effie had told the story at parties, growing ever more proficient in emulating Olivia's mannerisms and speech until anyone would think she was a Queen too.

Chapter Thirty-One

Lock In

The "fleet", Holly's staff ship

Melissa had it on good authority that the ship in front of her was the ship with the drug lab on it. Sensor arrays dripped from the hull wherever they wouldn't obscure the observation windows. The ship loomed in space, a spider at the center of its web, painted in reds and golds. Even from the outside, it looked like a drug dealers' home.

She floated silently towards it, towing thirty Devoted in spacesuits behind her. They were dust mote specks in comparison.

Things drug dealers liked (in Melissa's experience):

- Spending a lot of new money
- Making sure anyone looking could tell they were spending that new money like oxygen
- Convincing innocent people to go along with their schemes
- Creating new buyers
- Lying

That was the kind of drug dealer Melissa had brought in for the Rangers, at least. Statistics said most were inconspicuous, but she'd never cared about the inconspicuous kind. Her job was finding criminals who *hurt* others, not protecting people from their own desires.

Well, it *had* been her job. Her job now was to lock down this ship and find the drug lab Rhiannon said was here somewhere. Other than that, she was meant to be a Devoted herself. She'd signed herself up for historical documentation and attempting to write poems. Thank Saberhawen for Gavin's help.

Thank Saberhawen for Saberhawen.

No sentries watched over the observation windows, so Melissa's duckling chain went unnoticed as they swam through vacuum. At the main airlock, she interfaced with the ship and let her contingent enter without setting off alarms.

Inside the airlock, burgundy silk swathed the walls behind plastic covers. Ridiculous in a spaceship airlock, inefficient and wasteful of the square footage. Her Devoted slipped out of their bulky suits, underclothes dark with sweat patches, and they resumed their press onward, now in air instead of in space. Still unremarked.

Their luck ran out when they reached the ship's command room.

Staffed by ten fully alert rebels.

"What the—" said one woman, getting the attention of all Melissa's enemies.

Alarms whooped and lights flashed. Melissa's Devoted yelled and crashed through the doorway. In the bursting lights, Devoted met rebel. Hand to hand and scream to scream. From above, two pistol shots popped.

The fighting only got louder, as if to make up for the humans' muddied hearing.

Melissa's headlamps rotated two times, three, inspired by the panicked alarms, before she locked them down to stare straight ahead. She scuttled to the pilot house ladder and swarmed up. The next three pistol shots meant nothing to her armor plating, and she soon had the pilot tied up with the same rope she'd used to tow her Devoted from ship to ship.

She'd run out of handcuffs significantly earlier in the day.

That done, her thirty Devoted dealt with the ten rebels neatly. She sidestepped a threesome engaged in fisticuffs and jumped over an unconscious woman with a bloodied nose. She'd take care of their health in a moment. First she had to seal the ship so that no rebels could escape to make further trouble for Queen-Commander Rhiannon.

Melissa tapped at a console and—*Saberhawen, don't let anyone know I did this or else they'll assume I can and will interface with anything*—plugged herself into it for faster data exchange.

In femtoseconds, she'd locked the doors for the personal quarters, the play areas, and the work spaces while diverting command access entirely to her console. First order of business would be removing all staff from engineering and life sciences, since those groups could still wrest back their ship. They'd have to go to the ship's holding cells instead of staying comfortable in their own rooms. Bad luck they'd been on duty when she came, but she couldn't have them running free and she didn't think they'd be cooperative about taking themselves back to their own bunks.

Holding cells, where are you? Melissa sorted through databases and live updates. *Whoa.* The twenty holding cells were already full, each holding two more than their three-person legal limit.

Because the abducted Queens were in them.

If she'd still been an American Space Ranger, she'd have cleaned up the ship, gotten any straggling baddies into makeshift cells, and turned the problem into HQ to deal with. But there was no HQ here. She had no protocols.

Hey, Saberhawen. What's the use of having a goddess if you don't give me some suggestions every now and then?

The goddess of machines was, unsurprisingly, silent.

She could release the Queens for help with the remaining rebels (and hand her Devoted back over to their rightful rulers), but that could be dangerous. Melissa didn't know enough. About the ship, about the Queens, and about what her own Commander Ceridwen wanted.

Melissa unplugged, pleased that her Devoted had tamed the criminal element while she'd been busy. "First things first," she said. "We're going to lock these prisoners up in the adjoining meeting room, and then we're going to take back engineering."

Or did Saberhawen tell me to do one thing at a time? Serial processing as divine inspiration. Saberhawen, please guide me in choosing correctly which thing to do first.

This whole druidic goddess thing was too confusing to analyze.

Within three Earth-standard hours, Melissa and her Devoted had the drug-and-prison ship locked down. They'd cleared the populated areas, swept the corridors, and made sure to bring water and untampered food down to the Queens.

The Queens yelled and cursed at them. None of Melissa's Devoted had seen their own Queens, for which everyone was grateful.

Checking against the manifest, Melissa had one staff member unaccounted for. Siân Edwards. The logs suggested she would know the operations of the ship better than anyone else and that she was loyal to the cause. Edwards was the most dangerous potential saboteur in the crowd, and she was the only one missing.

It couldn't be coincidence.

"We're going on a hunt," she said to the four-man Devoted team with her. They'd sent two of their group off with the penultimate prisoner. "I'm sending you a picture of the missing woman. We should assume she's armed and highly dangerous. She won't come quietly, and she's your top priority."

"Of course, my lady." Daffyd had been at her side since she annexed him away from his chosen Hive. Now she had to let him go.

"Where exactly are we?" asked JJ. "What are we doing?"

Daffyd shushed him, and Melissa took that as a sign that the others would keep her most confused Devoted in line until such a time as she could release him from her service. *How is that going to work?* A problem for Rhiannon and the future.

"I'm also sending you some extra tree pictures," she said, pressing forwards with the mission. "*Use them* if you feel yourselves getting lightheaded." Who knew what good the pictures would do? These Dyfed-born had a nature obsession, but Melissa didn't have any idea how to cure it. Nor whether lightheadedness would be the first symptom of an oncoming case of space craze.

She did, however, know that humans found comfort in plans for worst-case scenarios. She needed to soothe her new Devoted's overtaxed brains *subconsciously*, the same way her designers had given her headlamps at ear-like locations and a speaker grille where a mouth might be. Because they couldn't cease functions just yet. Not until she'd completed her mission for Queen-Commander Ceridwen.

"Why would we need pictures of trees when we have you?" Trust Daffyd to come to the right conclusions.

"You're in charge," she told him. "I have to assign the others their mission scope in person." With Edwards on the loose, she couldn't chance putting out information on the shipwide, and there was no guarantee the Devoted would all check their tabs.

With that, she left the group to their hunt. Armed only with tree pictures and dubious loyalty links.

A life signs check showed that she had four other teams on various decks, and six men in the brig area. Closest to her current location was a team in engineering, so she chose that direction. As she passed more brick-veneered corridors, branching off the Mexican tiles and crushed glass insets of the main junction, she pinged her Queen.

Queen-Commander Ceridwen's image flashed into a tiny square behind Melissa's eye visor. A friendly ghost in her head. "What's your situation?"

Melissa sent her an image of the cleared corridor in blue and green tile. "I've shut down the drug lab and found all the Queens, but there's still one rebel missing. A Siân Edwards."

Rhiannon's smile was so broad that Melissa could have fit a whole six-fingered hand in the Queen-Commander's mouth. Now she was picturing that. If this sudden creativity were Saberhawen's way of punishing her for wavering belief, it was effective as punishment.

"Good work! Don't worry too much about Edwards," said Queen-Commander Ceridwen. "As I told Holly, my inside source, I plan to do what I can for the rebels' cause, though not the shadow government's."

Mel's shoulders all rotated in their sockets. She was glad nobody was in the corridor to see her unsettled. There was a shadow government? "Send me a packet about that, please." Mel was out of the loop, it seemed. "About Edwards, the kind of person who evades capture *could* be aiming for self-survival... or could be planning sabotage. What does your inside source think?"

Rhiannon leaned away from her tab, picture zooming out and voice going echoey as she got further from the mic pickup. "Hey, Holly. What can you tell me about Siân Edwards?"

An off-screen voice (*female, middle-aged, Dyfed-accented English but not a Cymraeg speaker, probably six feet tall*) replied, sardonic, "I hate her tremendously, and she's always undermining me?"

Melissa had made it to the engineering section. She could tell because the walls turned to golden tessellations made of mirrors and precious metals. A practical reason to have so much gold and mirror in engineering: in an emergency, they could strip the walls for parts.

Somehow, Melissa didn't think that had been the decorators' intent.

Rhiannon was still chatting with the "inside source." "Yeah, but is she dangerous?"

"Hah! She's ineffectual at best."

Melissa didn't believe that. Siân Edwards' absence was no mistake on her part. She'd evaded a thirty-man (and one ex-Ranger) sweep.

No rule said Melissa had to tell Rhiannon about continuing the hunt, and her Queen hadn't put a halt to it, just dismissed it as irrelevant. This was Melissa's turf right now, and she deemed finding Edwards as part of locking everything down. "What do you want me to do with the Queens?" she asked instead of prolonging the discussion and possibly being forbidden from her objective.

Queen-Commander Ceridwen tapped her lips with a finger. It made a loud *thwack-thwack-thwack* in the microphone. "If they're sane, you can let them out, but we don't have the ability to stopgap fix them the way we did their Devoted. If they're a mess, keep them where they are, but try to make them comfortable. Speaking of taking over their Devoted," she added slyly, "how do you like being a Queen?"

Melissa's response was automatic. Years of collaborating with marshals and local sheriffs had taught her the right words. "I prefer to work alone."

Rhiannon was silent.

Because those weren't the right words anymore. Melissa wasn't alone. She may not want to Queen for the Devoted on this ship, but she was part of a Hive. She worked alongside Gavin and Alan, Luciano and Victor, and (most important) Queen Rhiannon herself.

All of Melissa's fingers curled inwards, making her hands as small as she wished she could make herself. No wonder the masculine sprawl hadn't worked out. "Or to be yours," she hurriedly corrected. "I enjoy being yours. Can I still..."

Now that she was so strongly female again, would Rhiannon still accept Melissa as a Hive member? Melissa's wires carried a cold frisson from her four clenched hands into her chest cavity. Her gender swap made her useful here, but Melissa wasn't sure she could switch back. "Never mind," she said. "We'll talk about it when everything is over."

The cold progressed down her legs and into the spikes that passed for a PRob's toes.

Rhiannon stared into her camera, and the gaze would have bored into a human watching it. As it was, Melissa noted the strength in the posture. When she spoke, her voice was strong and slow, her heartbeat elevated. "You are sworn to me, Devoted Melissa. There is nothing to discuss."

The reprimand eased all the sparking tension in Melissa's coiled insides. Rhiannon's very severity showed how much she cared about holding onto Melissa's Devotion.

Of course, Queen-Commander Ceridwen could have been lying to achieve that exact effect, but teens and Queens *were* known for their possessive natures. It did help. "Thank you, my lady."

Melissa reached the door to the engine room proper, behind which six of her Devoted loitered. "Do you have any other tasks for me?"

"You are dismissed." Rhiannon cut the connection. A few seconds later, Melissa received an information packet labeled *Shadow Govt Stuff*.

Melissa entered the engine room already talking from her speaker grille. "All right, Devoted. Listen up." Her shoes clopped as she walked in, and she looked down at swirling patterns in the floor, almost like the composite on John Wayne Station had been, but stronger. Someone had put a marble floor in an engine room. Great for slipping on, heavy, and expensive.

Why not industrial carpet? The person who decorated this ship was madder than a space-exiled Devoted without a Queen.

Not her problem.

"Check your tabs for an image," she said to her six rapt Devoted. "We're looking for *this* woman…"

Chapter Thirty-Two

All Under Control

The Iâr Du, *auditorium HQ*

Holly was lounging on a pear-colored couch when the call came through.

When Queen-Commander Ceridwen passed her a pad, the young woman explained, "Your contact pinged the drug lab ship. We've forwarded the call to this pad for you."

Holly ran a speculative finger over the pad's top edge. Would she get keep the device after the call completed? *Now that I'm no longer under a communications blackout, I could chat with Amanda.*

Her boss' face filled the tiny screen. Ffion Kendrick had introduced Holly to the rebels and was also a permanent undersecretary in the Department of Health and Well-Being. Though Holly had known those facts, she hadn't realized the woman was also the usurpers' leader until now. *Higher up in the organization than I expected.*

"Well done on organizing the Devoted ships into a formation," Ffion said. "Very intimidating."

"Thank you." Holly didn't know what else to say. That she could only have done it with Queen-Commander Ceridwen's help? That she'd betrayed the rebellion, if not its cause?

She chose silence.

"Anything else I should know before I swoop in to save the day from these *vicious* Hives?" Ffion asked.

Holly shrugged, trying to look cool even as her legs jittered off-screen. "The Defense Force fired a warning shot a while ago."

"Good, good. I'll keep you posted." Ffion cut the connection.

Ceridwen took the pad back. *So much for keeping a private line.* "Are you sure about this?"

Holly blew out a breath that shook on the fall-cool air. "There's no going back now." No one for Holly to lean on if she wanted to get away from Ceridwen and her room full of Devotees. When the experimental Queens came out of recovery, if they started a campaign against Holly, would Ceridwen protect her? Or would the benefits of cooperation effectively disappear? "I trust you," she said, partially truth and partially an appeal to Ceridwen's Queen-responsible nature.

From the auditorium's opposite wall, Gavin reported, "Cantor gave me a channel to listen in."

"Let's do it," Ceridwen said to the room at large.

The giant screen lit. Its left half bore a statue-sized projection of Kendrick, the other half, a pair of men wearing ministerial garb.

"I'm Ffion Kendrick, and I'm here to save you."

Victor, the teen who'd once held Holly captive in his arms' hold, barked and flopped onto the couch beside her. "From what?" he huffed.

He wasn't the only wonderer. A Senedd representative asked Kendrick, "From what?"

Effie smiled, sweet and sharp. "That fleet in space can destroy our world. Let me take care of it."

Across the room, Gavin heckled. "C'mon, Victor, keep up. She's saving us from the threat our lady already neutralized."

"Shh," Queen-Commander Ceridwen shushed the by-play. "Let them negotiate for all the things Holly wants."

On screen, a Senedd man said, "Thank you."

But he'd spoken too soon. "For a price," Effie qualified.

Holly's smile warmed the muscles in her face. This was all going perfectly. According to plan and design. *And* she had a Queen on her side. "For freedom, equality, and peace for all marginalized peoples," Holly whispered, prompting her mentor.

The Senedd men frowned. "We'll have to decline your offer. We're doing fine with our Space Defense Force, thank you."

Effie *tsk*ed. "Come now, I'm one of you. A permanent undersecretary in the Department of Health and Well-Being." Her smile turned knifelike. "And if you make me into something more than that, I can give you safety."

"Why isn't she asking...?" But Holly already knew the answer. She'd been right with her earlier paranoia. Kendrick had never planned to topple the Hive hierarchy, only to claw over its supporters to reach its peak. If she did dismantle the system, it would only be to elevate herself in the Senedd. She would be the silent ruler of a whole planet, pacifying and manipulating anyone under her.

A whine built in Holly's throat. She gulped it down. She'd never expected *Ffion Kendrick* to betray the rebellion's ideals. She'd believed that when someone inevitably turned Holly into a scapegoat, Ffion would be the one to speak in her defense. Holly clenched her fingers in her lap, pads pushing too hard into the palms and turning everything a bloodless white.

Victor patted Holly's knee.

"No." Ceridwen readjusted her crown and screwed her mouth along with her courage. "I won't let her make our people give up freedoms for false security. *We'll* have to be the new rebellion." She snapped her fingers. "Gavin, get me a pad with a clean camera. I'm taking over this negotiation."

The Devoted-packed auditorium erupted into murmuring.

Cantor, patsy of the status quo, asked, "Is that really a good idea?"

A flurry of shushing greeted his suggestion. The Devoted liked his objections even less than Ceridwen's determination to confront the powerful.

The auditorium's door opened, though everyone they'd expected was already present. Ceridwen flopped to the deck and out sight as red-headed Siân stormed in.

"Holly!" Siân whirled in a circle, taking in the room full of Devoted in possession of their faculties. "What are you *doing*?"

Holly lounged back onto the couch, exuding the non-chalant calm of someone who is in the place she ought to be and doing all the things she ought to do. As though her heart wasn't breaking for her mentor, her people, her last vestiges of innocence. "I'm watching the negotiations."

"We're not ready."

"Of course we are." Holly gestured to the screen where Kendrick and the Senedd men were discussing the world's future. If they were at that stage, then they had to be ready. Unless Siân could turn back time. Holly let herself smile, infusing the expression with all the condescension she could muster. "I'm in charge of inoculations, and I say we are. You should really get out of here and back to the staff ship."

Five broad shouldered men hulked in Siân's direction, ready to help the small redhead do as Holly suggested.

"You're setting yourself up as supreme Queen?" Crimson lips made a horrified O. "I knew I couldn't trust you scientific types!"

Holly blinked. Hard. She supposed it could look that way to an outsider. If that outsider didn't know that Holly was throwing in with a sympathetic Queen against any other rebel's good judgment. *Do I deserve Siân Edwards's ire?*

"Scientists!" Siân spat. "More interested in facts than in people. I won't let you get away with this." With that oh-so-scintillating parting line, she ran out of the room.

The five menacing Devoted followed Edwards as far as the door, where they slowed and turned to their Queen as though she had a special gravity from which they could not escape. *Perhaps she does.* For Devoted who had already lost a Queen once, abandoning another had the potential to be unbearable.

Victor leaned over and whispered in Holly's ear. "Is she going to make trouble for us?"

Holly let her eyebrows jump up and down. "She's just a functionary. What could she do?"

The Devoted heard her assessment, as she'd intended. Relieved of their duty, they shrugged and returned to the seats from whence they'd come. Maybe it was foolish to let Edwards go, but Holly didn't want to harm these unfortunate men any more than she already had. Edwards really *was* unlikely to do anything other than stamp her ineffectual little feet.

Queen-Commander Ceridwen cleared her throat, silencing the room. She lifted a pad in her hand, finger poised to tap the surface and join the conversation on the main screen. "Wish me luck," she said.

Last week, Holly had been experimenting on this kind of woman. She'd injected most of the men in this room. And now Holly's best hope, the *resistance's* best hope, was a Queen.

Chapter Thirty-Three

The Great "I Am," part 1

The Iâr Du, *auditorium HQ*

The longer Rhiannon listened to this wheedling between the remaining Senedd and the cryptocracy-to-be,
the less she liked it. What was the point of any government
if it didn't work on the people's behalf? Rhiannon was losing her belief in politics.

"Gavin." She beckoned him closer with a crooked finger. "Are we close enough to my other ships for pad-to-pad
communication?"

He nodded, tight and controlled. Had she forced the
flamboyancy out of him? Gods, she hoped not.

Rhiannon clapped her hands to get the attention of the
people in her auditorium. *HQ*, as Mel had called it. Cantor
frowned at her, unhappy to have his attention distracted
from the spying screens. Hah, this outcome was probably
what he wanted: powerful people working without the
public's knowledge and ignoring the underlying problems.
The rest, however,—Holly, Victor, and twenty of her newest and dearest Devotees—gave her their rapt silence.

"We're going to give these bad guys something else to worry about."

Cantor tried to interrupt, but Victor elbowed him in the gut. It was a shame. She'd liked Cantor. He had Alan's interests at heart, and hadn't challenged her too much for control of the situation since she made it obvious he shouldn't. But he kept trying to prove that he knew better.

Maybe he did. It didn't matter. She was Queen here. Queen of a giant, amalgamated Hive. If she seemed unable to handle her responsibilities, the entire structure would crumble. That was one thing when she'd had a mere six Devoted, all outliers. But now she had so many more, some barely hanging onto their sanity after weeks or months or more.

"Tell the rest of our ships. We're sending our fleet to surround the returning officials." *Let's see them ignore that unsubtle threat.* One person had power here, and it wasn't the usurpers. At the moment, she had more ships than the Dyfed Space Defense Force, so it wasn't the Senedd either.

No, it was Rhiannon, Queen-Commander Ceridwen, presiding from her flagship, the *Iâr Du*. She patted her crown to make sure it—and the hairs that wanted to frizz over the top—were smoothly in place.

"Our ships are turning, my lady," reported a new Devoted. She thought his name might be Humphrey.

"Tell me when—"

"All in place," said Gavin. "I bet the shadowy fumblers are seeking to find the best safety."

"*What?*" she heard someone hiss.

While it pleased Rhiannon that Gavin's normal personality and speech mode had returned, she missed the coolly
competent Devoted who'd stood before her moments ago.

"Now, put me through to the conference," she said.

"No!" Cantor's outburst was smothered by four of
her Devoted dragging him to the back of the room. They
couldn't take him into the hall without losing their line
of sight to their new Queen, and she'd lay odds that was
the only reason they didn't remove him from her presence
entirely.

The ship was giant, requiring multiple lifts to travel between the levels. Her *Ceridwen's Cauldron* didn't have any
lifts at all.

The moment Gavin inserted her into the conversation
taking place between Kendrick and the Senedd, she started
as she meant to continue. By throwing them all off balance
and shaming them into doing what was right. "What is the
meaning of this?"

The two gentlemen speaking for the Senedd wrinkled
their already wrinkled brows at her. White-and-black hair-
lines receded further. "Who are *you*?" one asked. "We've
never worked together before." Not like they had with the
woman they'd been talking with so far. *Incestuous, the lot
of them.*

"I am Queen-Commander Ceridwen, not the first of
that name." As she spoke the words, she felt the shiver of
continuity linking her backwards to earlier Queens. She
remembered speaking similar words on John Wayne Station and bringing an entire mob to a halt in the face of her

identity. "With all the power my Hive gives me, with all the power the previous Ceridwens possessed, I will unmask your faithlessness and give your power back to my people."

"Yes, yes," said the shadow government woman. Her pink shirt brought a glow to her cheeks that made her look harmless and vital all at once. "But what do you want exactly and why are you on this channel?"

Rhiannon squashed the urge to pull her sleeves down over her fingers. These people didn't need to see her fidget, or come across as anything other than perfect. She had the control here, not they. "Did you think nobody would notice your talking points had nothing to do with your supporters' needs? Did you think you could keep them down forever?" Because Kendrick wasn't doing right by Holly or the other disenfranchised people in her movement. "I have surrounded your ship with my fleet." Now Rhiannon let herself smirk.

"That's nice, dear," said the woman. "Unless you plan to attack, however, they aren't doing you much good."

The men from the Senedd had a stronger, worse reaction. "That's *your* fleet? You will cease and desist at once, young lady."

An angry murmur spread across Rhiannon's HQ at the man's words. Their discontent hung in the air stronger than Rhiannon's fear that this was all about to go horribly wrong and end with her in jail. Or worse.

Despite the crown on her head and the words of self-affirmation, these adults were right. Rhiannon was young and had no power base, not like the real Ceridwen. She couldn't eat her enemies like the great black hen her flagship was named for or brew *awen*. Even her bargaining chip—the sort-of-Queenless fleet—had turned into a liability under her inexpert guidance. Her unwillingness to do damage with them made her ineffective against the usurpers, and their mere existence threatened her relations with the Senedd.

She had one remaining asset: the stolen Queens. But if she loosed those now-crazy Queens to prove the cryptocracy's corruption, the Senedd could counter by restoring the status quo. Save the Queens, heal them, and give them back to their waiting Devoted (preferably over Rhiannon's incarcerated body). Worse, having crazy Queens around would confuse the issues that the rebels needed to address. They didn't want Queens to be *special*, and there was little more special than a crazy person in distress.

She stubbed her toe into the hardwood flooring, waves of pain reverberating through her leg.

"Are you all right?" whispered Gavin from across the room, ensconced in his tablet-and-green-linen control room.

She waved a careless hand. He shouldn't worry about her. She had to provide for all her new Devoted. They wanted their full and complete lives back.

She had to provide for her core Devoted. They needed her protection from possible punishment thanks to their rule bending on leaving Dyfed earlier in the year. They didn't have the luxury of saying "oh, but I was crazy/brainwashed," like her new men.

She had to provide for all the voiceless and disenfranchised misfits from her planet. They needed the Hive system to change, to include their kind. Nobody else would speak for these... and she'd promised Holly.

Until she could find a way to push all these agendas at once, helping one could hurt the others.

The cool air piping across her face carried the mutterings of upset Devoted. Everything on this ship was so *adult*—the color scheme, the linen and wood textures, the occupants other than her initial Hive.

What she needed was to make herself seem more serious. What would get these strange adults to pay attention to her? She still wasn't willing to actually damage any of the ships, nor to loose the Queens. Which left magically aging and becoming older, more venerable, and better connected.

If only she were more like the Queen Ceridwen who'd come before her. That woman had friends everywhere, and a face that proved her longterm worth. But Queen Olivia Jones was busy.

Busy investigating what had happened to the missing Queens. The missing Queens that Rhiannon had neatly wrapped up in Melissa's care.

Oh.

Interlude 6

The Unsent Letter

From the shadow government's ship

The camera rocks, then resolves into Effie Kendrick. Everything about her is perfectly in place. Her clothes are smooth, her hair immaculate.

"Hello, Olivia," she says to the lens. "I know things are sticky right now, but I'm excited to see you again. Unfortunately, that won't be in person for a few more days. It looks like I'll be up here in space a while longer. Gods willing, we'll have enough food and air while we wait for the mess to disappear."

She looks sharply to the left, frown pulling down her eyes and making deep cracks in her camera-perfect makeup. Apparently, the recording microphone is too direction-sensitive to catch whatever has been said behind it. "So reposition us relative to the moving ship!" she snaps.

Her new smile for the camera looks forced, or maybe that's because it clashes with the entrenched frown lines. "Hey, Olivia, isn't the *Cauldron* your ship? What's it doing out here?"

Kendrick pushes out of her chair slowly, until only her stomach is in the camera's view. Her muted voice orders, "Look up who's in charge over there."

A palm slams down on the recording device, and it goes black.

Message unsent.

Chapter Thirty-Four

Llewellyn

Planet Dyfed, Professor Cantor's office

Olivia sat in a shaft of morning light. Professor Cantor had kindly offered her his office lock codes so she could conduct her interview with Llewellyn in a neutral location, and she already appreciated the peace and serenity. An entire wall of windows looked out onto a clearing between trees and the stonework of the building's other wing. His long desk was coated with pads and coffee mugs, quintessential professor décor, and his wall art included watercolor paintings of equations and buildings.

Llewellyn sat in the visitor's chair, also soaking in the early morning quiet.

She wondered if the office had hidden recording devices. *The real question is probably "how many?"*

"I'm glad we're finally meeting up," Llewellyn broke their silence.

While it was true that he'd tried to corner her before beginning Driscoll's murder investigation, she'd forced *this* meeting on him. Her brow wrinkled. "We know why we want to talk with you, but why do you want to talk with us?"

He didn't even blink at her use of the royal *we*, though few Queens used it these days. "Look," he said, "you remember when you helped me get off planet? Well, I came back." He leaned forwards and lowered his voice. Maybe he was worried about listening devices too. "My old buddies were going to use my name to keep themselves out of trouble and then get all the benefits I worked for."

"Such as your murder of Nancy Driscoll?" *If he wants to confess, I'm not going to stop him.*

"Yeah," he whispered. He leaned back and splayed his hands to the side. His brows screwed together. "Wait, no! What? Why would I do that? I'm swooping in to save the day, not to kill people!"

She rounded her shoulders. *Then what was he doing hushing up Driscoll's murder?* "Save the day from what?" she asked.

"From the ships in orbit, of course! Haven't you been watching the news?"

She had, in fact, been watching the news. A lot of reports about space psychosis that she'd never personally experienced, but that didn't mean the condition didn't exist. "We're pretty sure that's a job for the DSDF."

He blew out a breath through pursed lips. "Except that there's no real danger. It just *looks* bad."

He explained how the shadow government had collected space Queens as bait. When they recalled the ships to Dyfed, they could halt the "invasion" and set themselves up as saviors of the planet. "So while most of the officials are gone on the Earth goodwill tour, I'm going to ruin their plans by doing their part. But I don't have a 'save the day' look, you know, so I need you."

Queen Olivia Jones was nobody's figurehead. "Me? I don't even like you."

"You do like the planet, though. And you're also not associated with anyone who might want to kill me." He gave her a smarmy, salesperson smile. "What do you say?"

What he'd told her was more than she'd been able to piece together in the course of her investigations, and *she'd* been an abductee. He clearly didn't know that part, though, or else he wouldn't consider her safe. "How did you find out about all this?"

"Because I was one of them. Just high up enough to get burned."

"How big is the conspiracy?" She'd given up before because she couldn't fight the secret elites who steered the planet. Maybe she'd been wrong. Maybe he'd say the actual group was so small that she could take it down alone.

He laughed. "Huge! I don't know how big it is. But this is definitely the only way to stop its plans." At the unamused look on her face, mouth and eyes flat, he shrugged. "I reported to Ffion Kendrick, not that it'll mean anything to you. She's the snake's head. And also Permanent Undersecretary for the Department of Health and Well-Being, which should give you an idea of how deep the whole thing runs."

Olivia's muscles tensed, and the left side of her mouth pulled down. Her gaze slid away from Llewellyn to look out the window at the quiet and the trees and the serenity.

It's another cryptocratic trick. "Not the real Ffion Kendrick, though. Obviously." She brought her attention back to her informant.

Llewellyn's head tilted to the side and he scrunched up his nose like a confused kitten. "Of course the real Kendrick," he said.

No. Olivia wanted to shake off the very idea, but... his greed was an honest motivation. "Could you pick her out of a crowded photograph?"

He shrugged.

The picture on Olivia's pad was the one Amanda had given her, of Holly at a work picnic with four other people, including the doctor's unknown mentor. Llewellyn wouldn't actually know Effie, of course, though maybe he'd have met Holly. Holly could have used Effie's name to increase her networking cachet.

"That's her." He pointed at Effie. "That's Ffion Kendrick."

Olivia's fingers trembled and she dropped her pad onto a stack on Cantor's desk. He'd sounded sure, but it couldn't be true. Olivia's own friend, who she'd asked for help with the situation, had been the villain all along? *Effie* had locked Olivia in a scientist's dungeon and let Holly experiment on her?

"Are you sure?"

She could still feel the leather straps biting her shoulders when the orderlies tied her down. She still woke up stifling screams because the guards hadn't appreciated noise from the prisoners, the *things* in the cells.

"Yes, and she's coming for the planet," said Llewellyn. "Will you help me stop her?"

Olivia had to, didn't she? She had to save the Queens and protect Dyfed. Had to keep people invested in the Hive system. Had to discredit her friend. Or force her out. *Someone had the right idea with that retirement party.* Olivia picked her pad back up. "I know someone who can help."

"What? We don't need anyone else!"

But she was already making the call. Olivia knew her limitations, and if Llewellyn wanted her to be his Queenly comrade, then he needed to trust her when she foisted off part of the job. She couldn't protect the world from the orbiting ships; she was too far removed from that. But she knew people working on that problem already.

On Olivia's pad, a face with teenage roundness and a golden crown blinked onto the screen. "The woman who made that fleet," she told Rhiannon without preliminaries, "I *know* her."

Llewellyn made a choking noise, but she shushed him with a hand-wave too low to be seen on screen.

"Wonderful." Young Queen Ceridwen nodded. Her crown winked in her ship's light. "Then you deal with her."

"I'd be happy to," Olivia said. It was a lie. She didn't want any proof that her friend could have harmed all those people. Harmed *her.*

"Here are some talking points." Rhiannon's list of discussion topics were all about breaking down the Hive system in a variety of creative ways. *No, you foolish child.* She had to find a way to impress upon Rhiannon that *Hives* were still good ideas and that these particular problematic ones were outliers. Rhiannon wouldn't want to cut off 90 percent of the population from its support system for the sake of the other 10. Not the Queen-Commander that Olivia had met and who had cared more for her Devoted than herself, emphasizing the group above the few.

Olivia had been there when Hives began. She remembered what things were like before: disorganized and full of people who'd been stuck and miserable in their unsuitable jobs.

Effie was on her pad screen. Olivia's breath caught. It was true. Effie was really there.

Olivia's screen expanded to show two men looking confused. If they were from the Senedd, their aides could look up her identity.

Effie gave her a closed mouth smile that made a chevron pointing down. It was Olivia's own smile. They'd been friends so long... "Looks like we're having our chat sooner than we thought, Livliv."

Sweat made Olivia's hair oily and her pulse speed its efforts to break through the clammy skin. Had Effie used the nickname to make Olivia look childish before the Senedd or to create intimacy? The other woman always been better at this sort of posturing.

But we're friends.

Llewellyn made shooing motions at her. She'd been silent too long.

"Your people locked me up, Eff-girl." Olivia used the other woman's university-era moniker in retaliation. This wasn't what she was supposed to talk about. Rhiannon wanted her to discuss Hives; Llewellyn, the fleet. Still, she had to *know.* Effie couldn't be involved with the Queen stealing. Not really.

"I never told them to go for you," Effie said. "Then again, I never told them not to."

Her mouth was dry and she sipped at air between barely parted lips. *I worried about you!* Extra wrinkles formed between her brows as she held back the water in her eyes. She could envision the testing room where she'd been strapped to the table, Holly's shadow in the observation box above; Effie could have been there, a second shadow in Holly's box.

Olivia curved her body into a smaller shape, trying to escape the image. "You've changed."

"I've always wanted the same as you did." Effie pursed her lips till the skin above the top lip formed pinstripes. It had long been Olivia's favorite expression to express annoyance and anger. *So odd to see it on someone else.*

"The best for our people?" Olivia hoped. But she felt her own mouth making the same pinstriped purse.

The men from the Senedd finally joined the conversation, no longer stymied by the personal byplay. "Everyone wants that," one said. "It's how we—"

"The effortless power," Effie cut him off.

"You're no Queen, Effie. Not like me and the others you tried to harm." Olivia hunched over further, but in a grandmotherly way. She had to draw a very visible difference between herself (sweet and normal and wronged) and Effie's scary monster persona. Because if Effie was threatening and *not* a Queen, whereas Olivia was helpful and definitely a Queen, then could Hives be so bad?

This message was the exact opposite of the one Rhiannon and her rebellion asked Olivia to plant.

"You have such deep background in the Hive system." Effie's flattery meant nothing. Olivia was empty. Her heart had gone cold in the section stamped with Effie's name. "Why don't you take it over?"

A Senedd man waved his hands. "You can't offer a ministerial post to a nepotistic friend via video interview."

Olivia shook her head. She'd never wanted to go into politics. Her specialty was geological survey, not government systems. "So that my outdated opinions can cause trouble for Dyfed's youth?"

She hadn't wanted to play the game. But that didn't mean she couldn't imply Effie was also too old to lead in this modern age.

"Experienced, not outdated. The Senedd could use you." Effie's eyes were too wide and too earnest. Did she honestly believe Olivia would succumb to false praise?

The Senedd men's pink faces gleamed with sweat. "Do you even care what we think?"

Olivia felt like she was floating, looking down at her pad screen from the ceiling. Effie really had locked up Queens, or at least given the orders. And for what?

Olivia couldn't talk with Effie right now. Not after such betrayal. Her heart pounded. Maybe not ever.

She tapped her pad, sliding Rhiannon's image back up in the corner. The young Queen could deal with this.

It had been one thing for Olivia to throw herself at solvable symptoms like Driscoll's murder. She'd barely found the courage to use her connections to rail against the establishment. She'd let herself be led by others, which was not how a Queen should act. But now...

For the rebels here on Dyfed, she could remind people that Queens were *good* and not affiliated with the drama unfolding above. Olivia would go to a place she could do the most good here: this afternoon's rally.

Llewellyn bounced in his seat. She hoped she never saw him again.

Chapter Thirty-Five

Let's Try This Again

The Iâr Du, auditorium HQ

"Thank you all." Rhiannon segued into the conversation. Now that Queen Olivia had warmed up the Senedd men and Ffion Kendrick, she could slide in. "And special thanks to Queen Olivia for discovering more about everyone's needs and deeds."

Needs and deeds? Did it have to rhyme? Rhiannon's authority with this crowd was sketchy, and sounding silly couldn't possibly help. She tried to keep her ears from going too hot. Blushing would add to her youthful image.

If she hadn't been in the conference, she'd have heaved a sigh.

"Yes," said Queen Olivia. Her tired eyes perked as they looked to the left, presumably where Rhiannon had shown up on her own screen. "My thanks to you for involving me in this discussion, Queen-Commander Ceridwen. It was lovely to speak with you in real time, Effie. Gentlemen." She nodded to them all, regal and sure. "I'll leave you in Queen-Commander Ceridwen's care." The elder woman blinked off the large screen Rhiannon watched from her HQ alongside Holly, Victor, Gavin, Cantor, and twenty of her newest Devoted.

It was as good an endorsement as Rhiannon was going to get. With Olivia's backing—older, more venerable, connected even to the usurpers—they'd have to take her seriously. "As Queen Olivia was saying, she's a wonderful example of what a queen used to be when the system began a hundred years ago. She's a vital building block of our society. But even Queen Olivia chose to retire from captaining a spaceship and move on to something new."

The woman on the screen—Ffion Kendrick, and Rhiannon didn't have the nerve to try calling her "Effie" as Olivia had done—raised incredulous eyebrows. "I had my people look you up, little girl. You're a rogue."

Rhiannon's stomach hiccupped and she barely managed not to laugh out loud. "That's quite the statement coming from someone who's broken off from the legitimate government and is trying to blackmail it." She turned to present her profile to Effie and address the gentlemen: "Thankfully you have me here, and I've pulled the teeth out of her attempted coup."

Yes! Rhiannon could have thrown off her tunic and danced naked under the stars and the gods' watchful eyes. She'd managed to talk herself into exactly the right words, instead of stuttering into worse straits. Her heart beat a joyful tattoo and she was sure the smile stretching her cheeks betrayed her elation.

The Senedd gentlemen gave her the same look as she'd received from Kendrick. "We do not need the help of a child working outside the law."

"Hey!" three of Rhiannon's new Devoted protested at the same time.

The sound only caused the "adults" on her screen frown. "If we were so inclined," said a Senedd man, "we could incarcerate your whole Hive as soon as you set foot on our planet. We could strip you of your status and power, take away your Devoted. So hold your tongue, little girl."

Rhiannon felt her eyes widen and her brows tilt down, wrinkling her forehead. Her mouth did that lopsided thing and her chin tucked back to give her the near double chin that was an integral part of the *did you seriously just say that to me?* face. This time she did laugh. Sure, Holly had proven that *some* Devoted could be taken from *some* Queens, but *Holly* wasn't working with the man who had just attempted to threaten Rhiannon.

Holly had also *already* tried to bring an end to Rhiannon's Queenship and been unsuccessful.

"Do you know where my Hive has been? We left Dyfed months ago. We can go anywhere." To be forever separated from Dyfed—from the parks and the trees, from the grove where she'd danced with her mother, from the culture she cleaved to ever more strongly with every new place she visited...

She'd get by.

The Hive system, set in motion a century earlier, may have launched her to her current position, but no single person could take it away. She could go anywhere and take her staggering number of Devoted with her.

Through a gasping laugh that bent her forwards and made her crown glint in the light—as seen in her picture on the discussion screen—Rhiannon said, "That's fine. Thank you for your time."

Her statement only made the three negotiators press their lips and adjust their shoulders in consternation. Wow. And she'd wanted to *impress* these dehydrated juice bags.

Rhiannon waved a hand to Gavin, who cut her connection to the negotiators. "Turn them off completely," she ordered when Kendrick and the Senedd men remained in full display on the screen. "We don't need them."

Clutching his pad to his chest, Victor looked like a little boy, if a very tall one. "Are we really exiled?"

It would be nice to go home, even if living in exile wouldn't end her world.

Behind him, Cantor nodded, but Rhiannon smiled as softly as she could and shook her head. "I'd been hoping we could solve things amicably." She gestured to the now-dark screen. "That didn't happen, but it doesn't mean we're done fighting for our home."

No, because she had another plan. That she'd just made up. Her new backup plan was the kind she mocked whenever she saw it on film... though she had to admit that it had worked on her. Learning from Holly and all her Devoted, she understood now that *everyone* was an outlier, and that forcing people to take injections for co-dependency was horrifying.

She spread her arms to the sides, silencing the crowded room as all her twenty-two Devoted (plus Holly and Cantor) watched her movement with hungry, rapt stares. "We're going to bypass these secretive rulers," she said. She wasn't one of those power-mad adults. She was a Queen, one of the people. "We're going to tell the citizens of Dyfed what's really going on up here and let *them* decide what to do."

Picking up on her tone, her men cheered.

"Anyone who knows the communications channels," she said over the happy noises, "please coordinate with Gavin to find the best frequencies or methods or..." She trailed off before she betrayed too much unfamiliarity with equipment. "Gavin, wave your hand, please."

Cantor, unlike her Devoted, had not cheered. He stalked up to her, looming between her and her men, filling her vision with his chest. Unless she looked up. Then she could see his stubbled, blotchy face.

His voice low, almost threatening, he protested, "If you equate Hives with forced compliance and nonconsenting medical procedures, the entire system will be wiped out." His breath smelled of the egg powder omelets they'd eaten at breakfast.

She leaned back and straightened her spine, trying to be taller even if she couldn't match him. "Obviously I have a stake in the Hive system—"

"No matter what you do or think," he hissed, "your rebels will get a part of what they want, and *our* people will abolish the system completely. Do you really want to do that kind of damage? Hives are a part of who we are."

Rhiannon ducked out of his curved body-cage and watched her Devoted scurry around the auditorium. They stared into their pads and fussed at access points in the soothingly grey-blue walls. They yelled to each other underneath the pear-colored lights. Gavin set up his communications command station on a smooth wood table he'd pushed in front of a grey-green couch, and all the frenzied activities ended at his side.

These men were brilliant, or could be when they weren't busy going space- and Queen-crazy. Why did they need her, a teenaged girl who'd been completely inexperienced before leaving her planet? Even with the months and crises she *had* weathered, they only flocked to her because she had power... and she only had power because they flocked to her.

But that first Devoted, the sad pilot on her fleet's tiniest ship. He'd chosen her because he had no other choices.

Her Devoted—all of them, from first to the last, from Luciano to the ones whose names she still needed to learn—they deserved more. They deserved to pursue their own interests, to make their own choices. If they still chose her, then it would mean so much more.

"Would it be so bad if they abolished Hives?" she asked Cantor. "After all, the system wasn't perfect for me and mine." She was living proof that outliers existed: a false Queen, CreaTechs who already had girlfriends or who grew into tactical specialists instead, one woman and then another. They all came together and gelled wonderfully, no matter what the expectations should have been.

All that without the Senedd's Devotion virus.

"Besides," she said. "You said it yourself. Hives are a part of Dyfed society and culture. They can't go away completely after a century of entrenchment. Plus that Kendrick woman and her compatriots were undermining the system already, proving its flaws."

"You know nothing!" Cantor's voice rang out from where he stood too close to her, echoing off the blue walls and catching at the pinkish ears of her feverishly laboring Devoted. "It will be weakened or changed!" His shoulders heaved and he panted before bringing his tone to a reasonable level and suggesting in an exaggeratedly reasonable tone. "I have more contacts and know how to talk to people. Maybe you should let me take over on the planning and negotiating front. Let me take another crack at the conference."

The blank screen hovered at her back, conference abandoned. Given up on.

Given up on too early?

Rhiannon could do it. She could give Cantor her blessing, have Gavin link him up with Kendrick and the Senedd. He'd work hard to help all the Devoted in this room. He'd be sure to free those Queens who'd been trapped and forced to be test subjects. He'd help many of the people for whom she was responsible.

But he wouldn't make life better for the misfits. It would be decades before they attempted to rise again, if ever. The misfits were her people too, because she'd promised Holly and because she was one. The women who would make great Devoted. The men who wanted to be genius specialists without ever Devoting at all. The people who didn't like their Test results and had the drive to change their lives if only they had the chance.

Her shoulders loosened and she looked Cantor directly in his disrespectful eyes. "Hives and Tests don't work for a *lot* of people." If he wanted Queens to act Queenly, he should defer to her judgement. The system was broken, and he could not possibly try to deny it. Still, it would be better to appeal to his compassion than to assume he could break through all that ingrained conditioning. "What about Holly?"

A warm line at her side and slightly behind: Victor had pressed through the crowds to protect her from the looming man who wanted to take her command away. *My Devoted are the best.*

"Yes, what about Holly?" The neuroscientist wore a velvet cape wrapped around her shoulders to combat the ships chilled autumn simulated air. (Was everyone except Rhiannon simulating the seasons on their spaceships these days?)

Rhiannon had forgotten that the other woman had demanded to be present for the confrontation with Kendrick. There was a history there.

"What about Holly's people? And Holly's sacrifices?" The woman spoke about herself in third person, and Rhiannon couldn't tell whether that was a choice meant to mock Cantor's uncaring heart or to distance herself from her unethical actions in the name of freedom.

Cantor barked a laugh. "With your history? You'll be lucky to be exiled."

Yes, Holly would be lucky to survive unfettered. But her cause was bigger than her own actions, and Rhiannon would stand up for *that.*

"And if you"—Cantor jabbed a finger near Rhiannon's shoulder, sensible enough to refrain from actually touching her—"want to support this torture mistress, then I'll make you disappear. Into jail or death or a work gang, it won't matter to you."

Rhiannon's skin prickled where he wasn't making contact, and dread radiated out from the area. *Can he do that?* She didn't know, and that meant she had to take him seriously. Her mouth was dry; her tongue, bloated. "You will cease these threats at once," she said. Her voice was slow and even and rang in her own ears with more power than she'd thought she could muster. "Or I will have you removed."

A loud shuffling rose up as all Rhiannon's Devoted took a few steps towards her. On this ship, at least, she had the power to enforce her will. Victor's arm hovered in her peripheral vision, looking like it had sprung from her own body, ready to do her bidding as soon as she thought the word *go*.

Cantor spread his hands before him in the near-universal gesture for surrender. Victor's arm stayed where it was, and Rhiannon kept her gaze steady. Her Devoted stilled in place like a room full of mannequins.

Cantor broke the breathless silence and slouched over to a linen-covered chair in a corner.

Rhiannon leaned into Victor. Surreptitiously, she nudged the back of her head against his pectoral muscle, shifting her golden circlet into a more comfortable position. "Thank you all." Her voice carried to the blank screen, to where Gavin had resumed his seat and his new Hive mates brought him data, to Cantor's corner.

The inside of her nose tingled. With the cold air? With an unacknowledged desire to sniffle? Cantor had been a benevolent mentor type all this time, and now she'd threatened him with captivity. *It seems excessive.* She tugged on her tunic sleeves, warming her fingers.

Meters away from Cantor, Holly tightened her cape around her shoulders and glared at anyone who looked at her too long.

One of Rhiannon's new Devoted braved that tiger's frost. "Can I lend you another jacket, ma'am?"

"I can inject you again," she said, airy tone not disguising the threat.

Rhiannon's Devoted only laughed and slipped out of his jacket. He put it next to her. "In case you change your mind," he said before he walked away.

...clearly he knew about the inoculations, but not that Holly had personally been experimenting on Queens.

What if Cantor was right about what could and *should* be done? Holly was no sweet and benevolent goddess. Even if she did have a point.

No. No more changing her mind. Not until or unless new data was presented. She was the focal point for all these people, for all the space-based resistance now (even if Kendrick didn't know it), and she couldn't let herself become paralyzed.

She took three steps towards Gavin's control center couch, Victor a familiar presence at her side, when a voice came over the shipwide. It was female, deeper than Holly's, but higher than Rhiannon's. And it had a curious vibrato underlying its anger. "Hello, Holly, you dirty traitor." She said the words like a standard greeting, and it took Rhiannon a moment to register the insult.

Holly produced a pad from within her cape, and her reply also came over the shipwide. "Hello, Siân."

Ah. The unknown voice belonged to the woman who'd pestered Holly over being premature with the notification to Kendrick and who had left under the false impression that Holly lured all these Devoted to her own banner in order to... take over the world maybe? Rhiannon hadn't been entirely clear on Holly's theoretical motive. She didn't speak paranoid rebel conspirator, she supposed.

The one Holly had called Siân Edwards cackled gleefully, making the auditorium speakers clip. "You'll never take us down now." She paused, giving Holly time to reply. "Ask me how."

Holly sighed. "Do you really need me to feed your ego?"

"I'm cutting you off." Clearly, Edwards *didn't* need Holly to do the feeding and answered her own unasked question. "You can't turn the rest of us over to the Senedd."

Rhiannon's fingers went cold where they weren't tucked into her sleeves. That didn't sound good.

Holly's suddenly urgent hunch over her pad made Rhiannon think the other woman agreed. "What're you talking about?"

"I've cut up all your spacesuits," said Edwards in a singsong voice, "and I'm about to destroy your communications array."

Not good at all. Rhiannon called to her Devoted. "Get someone down to wherever that is!" *Manawyddan's mousetrap*, she didn't even know the array's *location* on her flagship. "Who's from this ship?"

"You'll never make these repairs, and nobody will know to come for you," Edwards said. Her voice rose, in pitch and in madness. "If the cause fails, it's all your fault, Holly. *All your fault.*" She laughed right up until the shipwide cut out with a screech.

The auditorium shook and rocked to the side. In two thudding heartbeats, Rhiannon sprawled on the steel-blue carpet with a Gavin-blanket shielding her from falling debris.

Victor had done the same once. Almost bled out in her service. Almost died. Almost lost an arm.

Scalding flotsam scored lines on her exposed skin. Her hands clenched on the scratchy carpet. Everything smelled of burning wire.

The weight across her back flattened her as though helpless to do anything else. "Gavin!" She heard the panic in her voice and didn't even try to tamp it. Was he alive? "Gavin!"

"Shhhh." She barely heard his voice over the pulse pounding in her ears and the muted screams from her largely traumatized Devoted. "Let things settle."

It could have been seconds or minutes before Gavin shifted off her with a groan, coming to kneel at her side. An inordinately long amount of time to wonder whether he was shedding his death cells onto the ground around her.

Freed, she shot up and matched his posture. Kneeling together, patella to patella. Wide dark brown eyes to wide blue eyes. Her fingers flitted all over him, head undamaged, face unscathed, arms unbroken, hair mussed, stomach... growling? Rhiannon caught the bubble of laughter before it exploded out of her like the communications array out of the *Iâr Du*. That way lay hysteria.

Gavin let her go over him three times before catching her hands. "I'm hale and whole and still yours," he said, shooting straight to the heart of her worry. "Are *you* all right?"

"My lady, my lady!" Melissa's voice came to her as if through water, and Rhiannon shook her head. Not through water, through cloth.

She pulled her pad from underneath her calves, the place it had clattered to the ground and gone forgotten in the wake of Gavin's possible sacrifice. "Melissa? Where are you?"

"Spacewalking close enough to you that we're using the tablet interface to communicate." Melissa cocked a wry headlamp, but her visor stayed that serious shade of medium blue. "I was hoping to catch my fugitive before you noticed her, but it looks like I'm a little late."

Spacewalking! Rhiannon clutched the pad tighter in her hands. Siân Edwards may have cut up the spacesuits, but Rhiannon had a PRob in her Hive. "Don't worry about that. You did good work getting here so fast." Praise was always important, especially for her least typical Devoted. "I need you to fix the communications array. Make it your first priority because if we don't get it working, those usurpers will have taken over before I can tell Dyfed's people they're not a threat."

Melissa bobbed her spherical head. "I've got this."

Rhiannon may not have been able to trust so many people in her past, but gods knew she could count on her

Devoted. Even the weird ones. *They're all weird ones.* "I know you do."

If the array was fixed, they had a chance to shut down the secret elite and to tell their story. She didn't know how good of a chance—*my voice against all those officials'?*—but a chance all the same. Without working communications to the planet, they had nothing.

Her heart pounded, pushing energetic blood-heat into her face. "Thank you, Melissa. You may have saved us after all."

Chapter Thirty-Six

No One Belongs

Planet Dyfed, rally in front of the Senedd

As far as Olivia could tell, she was the only Queen at the protest. She couldn't change what was happening in orbit or with the Queen stealers, but she could convince these marginalized people that their problem wasn't with the Hives. Their problem was a sickened system that excluded where it ought to embrace.

"You're up," someone told her as twilight fell.

Olivia ascended the steps in front of the Senedd building. A glorious golden light haloed the crowd in front of her.

"I am a Queen," she said. Angry muttering began. A person yelled muffled words that might have been "get off the podium." Olivia persevered. "But things were different in my day."

Was that really such an endorsement? Her old friends were villains, and she hadn't noticed. Her networks and friendships were crumbling. Was she a bad friend... or a bad citizen? Maybe Effie was right.

And still she had the nerve to try and change the minds of these people here.

"Hives started organically back then. No Testing or special training." At least Olivia still had her own Devoted, not that she'd told them where she was going tonight. And she'd lost track of Amanda long ago. They'd never have let her into a hostile crowd, but these people needed to stop associating Hives with evil and danger.

"The Tests were meant to be like bonsai," she said. "They honed nature. Now that system has grown into a wildflower garden whose stalks wither under organizational weed killer." She raised her arms overhead and punched at the sky. That was what people were supposed to do when making rabble-rousing speeches, right? "We must make it clear that we stand for more than the status quo!"

A weak cheer ran through the crowd.

This was all she could do. These minds were what she could affect. Maybe it was small scale, but Machynlleth was still a small place.

The news had begun to link the Hive ships and the evil doers. They pushed the idea that Hives could never be wonderful. And she needed to fix that. Affecting one mind could change a burgeoning nation. The Hive system had pushed Dyfed's progress, and she would not see it die.

She descended the steps and shook hands with rebels. This one wanted to ask what life was like before Testing. That one asked how she'd found her Devoted. Another complained that a Queen didn't belong at the protest.

She told them all they should feel lucky, that before the Test naturally Devoted people fell through the cracks. But she also agreed that organic Hives had a strength and verity that the manufactured ones did not.

Apparently, her own views were subversive too. A bit.

Olivia took a break in the dark of night. She sat on the side steps next to a quiet person scribbling on his pad. Stone slabs seeped cold through her trousers while she watched protestors milling and orating.

They were a cross-section of Dyfed society. Their clothes proclaimed them laborers and artisans, doctors and professors. Young and old huddled under homemade signs. Men and women and gender indeterminates joked and marched and chanted. Together.

The unity made her eyes tear up.

There were no other Queens. No Devoted. When did the Hives become so far removed from the rest of the population?

A pair of protestors, bundled in evening jackets and nearly invisible in the early evening darkness, walked past. The first, weighed down by her sign, sighed. "I need a better sign."

"Something lighter weight is only going to blow away," said her companion.

"No, I mean it needs a better slogan."

"Just use the poem," said the second.

They both stopped, only a few feet away from Olivia.

"We don't have a poem," the woman whispered. "How did we forget a *poem?*"

The man sitting at Olivia's side kicked at the step beneath him. "I'm working on it!"

A young woman with black curls and her own lighting crew approached them then. "May I interview you for the Late Edition news?" She wore a striped tunic dress and didn't appear nearly as cold as anyone else. "If you're the official poet of this political movement, you're real news."

The man dropped his head and mumbled, "I'm not an official anything."

The journalist shrugged and turned into her light, as held by a news station compatriot. "I'm live, here at the protest in front of the Senedd building, where we've learned that an official poem has yet to be determined. If you're excited by this latest political movement or you're still looking for a topic for tomorrow's national poetry contest, the Late Edition has a challenge for you."

The sign-holding woman stomped off after glaring at the reporter. "Every serious protest needs a poem. I'm going to write my own."

"Send us your best protest poems," the reporter exhorted her audience. "I'll read the top entries live on the air."

Olivia moved out of the young reporter's shadow, no interest in being recorded as the only Queen in attendance. She should really get home before it was too late. She'd have to watch the news, though. Last-minute protest poems couldn't be any good. *Could they?*

Chapter Thirty-Seven

Not a Telephone?

The Iâr Du, *communications array*

Melissa came in through the airlock, because it wasn't blown up. Dodging debris might have given her a straighter line, but it would have been a stupid thing to do. The American Space Rangers didn't accept stupid beings.

Finding the exploded section took no effort at all. The *Iâr Du*'s entire planet-facing side had a thermal reading of zero.

All around her, server lockers and cabinets were missing their fronts and sides. Blue-grey doors hung at angles or torn in half like vacuum-rated metal should not. A set of intact cabinets called to her, and she opened them only to find emptiness. Possibly these had popped with minimal resistance in the blast, leaving their insides to clear out like a thief on the lam.

Oh, wait. This one had a single wire in it making a lonely squiggle. She pulled the box off the wall and saw it had been attached with a series of anchor hooks. *Those* weren't instrumental to sending information between ship and planet. They weren't going to help her fix the array.

She had to fix it because her Queen had a plan that required working communications.

At least she'd finished hunting the now-dead Edwards who'd blown herself up when blowing out this area. That was something.

Via the internal system, she pinged Gavin. "What do you know about this piece of junk?" The communications room itself was half internal, half spacewalk, and the actual array for flashing packets over long distances was much larger on this ship than on their own *Ceridwen's Cauldron*, and had multiple external panels (not dishes—they looked like solar panels, perhaps).

Alan's face flashed behind her visor. He'd somehow joined the same channel. Well, the *Ceridwen's Cauldron* was close enough to pick up the transmission, and Alan might have been monitoring the area to see what he could do from a distance. "Can you plug yourself in?" he asked.

Gavin's face joined Alan's behind her visor, but on the other side. His long hair flew everywhere as he shook his head. So vehement. "Just because they do that in films, doesn't mean she's compatible with everything."

He'd used her correct pronouns, even though she'd only switched over a few days before. Her circuits warmed against the heatlessness of space. Her Hive mates' ability to flow with the "shapeshifter's" designations was like nothing she'd experienced in other cultures.

Alan's arms waved above his head and he called on Manawyddan for patience. "Which of us knows more about these things?" he said.

Gavin glared. "Which of us is better at fixing real-life equipment?"

"Which of us—"

And so on. Their competition stood in the way of her repairs. Why were they even fighting? They'd never acted like this before in her presence. Which meant the tech details weren't the problem. There was a root cause that she needed to hunt down and delete if she wanted to get anything done.

Surely it wasn't returning to their home planet. That was a moot point. They were already in Dyfed space. Alan wanted to be there for the physics project. Gavin missed so many things about his home society... such as people who understood his poetry. They were in violent agreement on the main points, if not the details, and she didn't have time for their squabbling.

She reminded, "It was our Queen's decision to come to this planet."

They were silent for a moment before Gavin yelled, "I know that!"

Ah, defensiveness. She'd found the root. Now to excise it.

"Then why have you been mad at me?" asked Alan.

"Because I didn't want to."

"If you think I could stop our lady once she's decided something—"

"No, no." Gavin's voice was calmer now. "Of course not."

That would have to do. Melissa broke in. "Do either of you know how to run a diagnostic on this system?"

Gavin's head tilted down and he looked up through his lashes. Bashfulness incarnate. "Alan is better with sound equipment."

"Thanks." Alan's crooked smile quirked to the left. "You're pretty good yourself."

She didn't have time for polite admiration either. "Gentlemen!"

"What do you see?" Alan asked, finally getting to the repairs. "Maybe we can use some of my earlier experiments with wired and wireless sound recording."

She described the room so far, then walked out past where the hull had once been. "Outside, there's a dish-shaped set of panels with a stubby spike in the middle."

"Broken antenna," Alan diagnosed. "I know you couldn't plug in—"

Gavin whispered, "Rude."

In a perfectly equanimical tone, Alan replied to his male Hive mate. "I'd smack you if we were on the same ship." The tone was at odds with the words, and Melissa knew enough about sarcasm and Dyfed's drier interactions to feel relief that she hadn't broken up the Hive by demanding they work together. "Can you use a leg spike to stand in for the broken antenna?"

It would require her to stay outside the ship. *Not much in the breached room to work with anyway.* She pulled a wired console as far to the spaceward wall as it'd go, slipped off a shoe, and drove her reverse-jointed leg spike into the dish's center. The antenna's remains splintered off into space. A panel cracked ominously, but didn't shatter.

Her armor-plated skin shivered and resonated, and behind her visor, she caught ping after ping after packet transmission. Music and talking and movies.

"Good news is I'm receiving some transmissions from the planet. Bad news is there's still no way to get our own sound waves sent out."

"We're working on that," Gavin said.

Alan's eyes were flat discs. "No, we aren't."

Gavin's shoulders slumped and he gave an unimpressed look to his own camera. "I thought we weren't arguing anymore." Singsong.

Shaking his head, Alan spread his hands. Eyebrows rising. "There's nothing more I know how to do. We don't have schematics for the system, and it's not like the one on our ship or the stuff we were borrowing on Garden Station."

Gavin huffed. "So what was the point of hooking Melissa into the thing?"

"Optimism." His face was a long oval as he spoke the word, and Melissa projected an image of her human avatar laughing riotously onto their tablets, hair everywhere and teeth flashing madly.

"Onward into the breach, then," said Gavin.

Melissa, trapped on the outside with a leg stuck in the dish, growled. Platitudes from Shakespeare misquoted wouldn't fix anything.

"We'll just have to be creative. Melissa, how do you usually call on Saberhawen for her aid?"

When they wrote poems together, whenever Melissa needed to do something bardic or druidic, Gavin suggested she call on Saberhawen to provide *awen*. Melissa had never successfully figured out how to request and receive that *divine inspiration*.

He was right, though. She was out of sensible, secular answers. The only thing she had left to try was her completely manufactured faith.

Well, her body was manufactured too.

"Thanks, Gavin, Alan," she said. "I need to end our chat now."

"Of course," they replied. As though worshipping one's goddess obviously needed privacy.

Melissa chose to try singing her prayer this time. She'd never done that before. In the exposed room, she couldn't sing aloud, but her internal audio mixers could create waveforms. A digital rendition of a paean to the goddess of machines.

If any deity would understand it, it would be Saberhawen. And if any deity knew how to fix a broken machine when all the spare parts had blown out when the hull did, that would also be Saberhawen.

Melissa pushed her soundless song into the cosmos. She transmitted it on the shortwave frequencies that could only reach a few kilometers. She vibrated the dish beneath her leg spike to offer the song to any compatible receiver that happened to be listening. The feedback made her body shake, rasping the plates of her armor together.

It was a song only a sentient machine could hear and understand. A plea for help, sent into the stars.

The shaking between her armor plates stopped, though her skin still resonated with the sound waves. *Must have worked out an air bubble from the initial welding.* She felt larger somehow, connected to the dish and the ship and the stars. Saberhawen might be listening, or she might not, but either way, Melissa had a communications connection to the nothingness beyond.

A communications connection. She'd been so foolish. Yes, it was still true that she couldn't fix the array permanently, but she could clearly receive and transmit. While the others couldn't purposely send across long distances, they *could* speak to *her*, and *she* could do the data exchange. She could take visual input from the internal sensors, sound from any combination of microphones, and package it up. If Rhiannon wanted to speak in real time instead of packets, Melissa could do that too.

From her place in the center of the dish, unfolding into space, she had the ultimate control over all talk. Why, she could pick up any number of transmissions from the planet below. Here was one about a poetry contest. Here was another with dueling opinions about the fleet in orbit. Nobody on that second program knew anything other than a few ships' registries.

Things Dyfed should really know about what was going on in their local space (and didn't):

- Yeah, there were a whole bunch of ships, but they were harmless and crewed by near crazy Devoted whose Queens had been stolen

- One ship belonged to the Queen stealers, and they were conducting experiments

- Those experiments presupposed that Queens and Devoted were injected with a virus that bonded them together on registration (which had been proven mostly true)

- The newest ship in town belonged to a would-be shadow government who controlled the Queen stealers and knew how to break Devotion bonds

- *That* cryptocracy was made up of the Senedd's high-powered undersecretaries who had all been on Earth while their malicious-looking "crazy fleet" arrived

- Most of the rebels (who had thrown in with the Queen stealers) didn't know about the elitist coup and only wanted to live their lives freely at whichever level of society their interests and talents could get them into... without the Test

- Oh, and Queen-Commander Ceridwen (AKA Melissa's own Rhiannon) was in control of the Queen stealers, the Queens, and the not-so-crazy-anymore "fleet"

She backtracked. What was that about a poetry contest?

A symmetrically featured woman with thick black hair that curled down past her shoulders exhorted her audience: "Send us your best protest poems. What should these protestors be saying? How best can they say it? The winning poems will be read live to our nightbird audience."

Melissa's headlamps swiveled, burning excess energy into the surrounding cold. That was perfect! She could write a poem and make the true situation clear, have the rebels' voices be heard.

Except that her poems were still terrible.

She liked to think she was improving, finding better imagery and focusing on the right details.

She pinged her five Hive mates. "I'm going to enter a poetry contest."

Alan was the first to answer her conference call, and he choked on the air. "What? Now? *How* is that the best use of your time?"

She rolled her avatar's eyes at him. "Because it's a worldwide contest that'll get our story on the news. That's what Rhiannon wants, isn't it? To inform the populace."

As if summoned by her name, Queen-Commander Ceridwen joined in the chat with Gavin standing next to her. "And be acknowledged, yes. If the people *understood*—"

"But a poem," Gavin interrupted. "You're our bard, Melissa, but that's not, ah..."

Victor volunteered the entire Hive. "We'll all help."

With the Hive working together, it shouldn't take too long to make a functional poem. Melissa already had a short outline of what should go into the poem from her list of things Dyfed needed to know. She could start by breaking that up into random lines, some shorter and others longer to create a pleasing arrangement on the page. Besides, she had just successfully called on her goddess and received *awen* (maybe).

"We should use a traditional structured format," said Alan, nodding with his own suggestion. "Nothing too complicated. A nice *cyhydedd hir*, perhaps."

Luciano, signal strong from the *Ceridwen's Cauldron*, offered, "I can pull up the rhyming dictionary."

The last time Melissa had suggested using one of those, Gavin accused her of having no poetry in her soul.

"A sonnet!" Gavin pitched.

Victor took a deep breath, smile growing with every moment of inhalation. "Gods, I adore poetry contests."

Gee, thanks for that helpful bit of knowledge, Vic.

Melissa sent out another song to Saberhawen, and the void ate up her digital sound waves. But no ideas sprang forth immediately in her spherical head or mechanical heart, so she would have to make do with less divine methods of improving her blank verse report. Perhaps she could borrow symbols and juxtapositions from the Garden Station inscriptions.

She began with the section detailing the usurpers' first appearance.

```
The newest ship in town
Kneels into no wind, races with no
        equals. It belongs to
A would-be shadow government
        (listen to the darkness)
Who steals our Queens and knows
How to break bonds
        (smell the virus on the air)
```

Rhiannon twisted loose hair ends around her fingers, tugging her scalp out of place like an abstract painting Melissa had seen on John Wayne Station. "What if the government decides to silence the protestors in a more permanent way? We shouldn't be encouraging them into danger."

Victor scoffed and bent in over his tablet more tightly, giving them all a good view of his nose. "Just from our poem? They would never."

"That couldn't happen with hundreds of protestors, not even on Nuova," Luciano agreed.

"But on Garden Station—"

Victor disappeared from his tablet's picture and his voice moved to come from Rhiannon's microphone. "We're *home*." He sounded pleased about the fact, which he certainly hadn't been before.

She would mull that over later. For now she had a poem to write.

Melissa shared with the group's tablets what she had so far.

Luciano hummed. "We could rhyme ship with blip, or crazy with maybe."

"What was wrong with the *cynhydedd hir* format?" Alan demanded to know. "Something like: *All these harmless crews / Are much like all yous / But crazy from flus. / Don't fear the fleet.*"

Silence.

"It rhymes..." Luciano said eventually. Which was really all a person could say about it. Even Melissa knew Alan's effort there was subpar.

"No," said Rhiannon.

And her word was final, so that saved them from further Alan-poems.

Victor laughed, his mouth gaping wide. "How did you ever pass out of primary school with such abysmal poetry skills?"

Melissa tweaked her poem, added a line about "dripping Devoted dropping down into dust," then cut it because it made no sense, even if it did have some lovely alliteration. As Alan had proven, form and poetic conceit weren't everything.

Gavin tilted his head, considering the latest version she'd uploaded to their tablets. "Well, it's a factual poem at least. We could change this line about the space craziness to *stars shining their madness into the brain through ears and nose and mouth until all that stirs the soul is light and light and light with no substance*, though."

Melissa rolled all her shoulders in her sockets. *And no one would have any idea what that meant if they didn't already.* It was her poem, and Gavin shouldn't be trying to change it.

Alan pounded on whatever surface he'd rested his tablet on. It made the picture jump and sent thudding pleas for attention through the channel. "I know Melissa can translate this into Cymraeg. If we want to be taken seriously, it has to be in Cymraeg."

"Nmm-mm." Victor shook his head forcefully enough to send his hair flopping. "More people will understand it in English."

Melissa had been happy at first to allow the tweaking and suggesting. But now she saw the truth. If she was a bard, then her work had to stand on its own, to be loved or reviled, but not to be improved upon without her say.

"Real Cymric poetry is in Cymraeg," Alan was insisting. "To suggest otherwise is to diminish our heritage."

Luciano raised his hands in possible supplication to his God. "To demand Cymraeg from a poet whose first language is something else only stifles the creative process."

While they continued to bicker, Melissa sent her poem to the news channel. She was the Hive's bard, and this was her poem. It was as done as it was going to get.

She could only hope it was good enough.

Protest News – The Outtake

Dyfed, News Station 3

A young woman with black curls smiles at the screen. She's barely past twenty, working the graveyard news shift while she earns her way to a better hour. Her teeth are a flash of white in the night dark, illuminated by electronics and bare bulbs.

"I'm here live at the biggest protest in the last fifty years where News Station 3 brings you up-to-the-moment coverage." She might be exaggerating, but there's no one awake to fact-check a late-night field reporter doing human interest pieces. This protest is the best thing yet for her career, as proven by her evening's ratings compared to the last two months'.

"I'm already receiving entries to our Protest Poem contest." She juggles her pad and anachronistic microphone. The equipment bangs together, making crunching noises for her greater-than-usual number of viewers. Mouth and mic unaligned, her "sorry, sorry" seem muffled.

The microphone is forgotten as she reads something on her pad screen. She gulps, loud enough to be heard on worldwide news. Then she swears.

"Whoa," she says when she has the microphone in front of her mouth again. "That's... not what I thought this protest was about."

Chapter Thirty-Eight

The Great "I Am," part 2

The Iâr Du, *auditorium HQ*

Rhiannon liked to think she was good at waiting. She'd waited for the usurpers to address their own issues, before doing it herself. She'd waited for Olivia to wrap up her arguments before taking over the conference again.

Maybe she was terrible at waiting.

On a more successful note, she'd waited for Melissa's poetry contest gambit to cause some effect. A whole ten hours she'd waited so far. Mostly while massaging her cheek against the hemlock green couch she'd fallen asleep on.

Awake-ish, she kept her eyes closed. *Waiting is easier when you're napping.* She turned over to get out of the way when a finger poked between her knuckles, clunking against the bones.

"My lady." The poke escalated to words. "Queen-Commander Ceridwen. You have a message."

This guy wasn't giving up. She didn't even know his name. She squeezed her eyes tighter. She *didn't even know his name,* and still she needed to protect him from all the evils that would tear him apart. From the shadow government who'd stolen his Queen, from the Senedd who were ready to declare all the victimized Hives as dangerous traitors, from herself if she didn't give him enough attention.

So she'd sworn, after all.

"My lady."

Her stomach clenched and her eyes opened. She couldn't leave him squirming. "Good morning." There, that was appropriately friendly without betraying her ignorance of his name.

"Melissa is calling, my lady. She says it's urgent."

Of course it was. Rhiannon gave a long, slow blink. It cleared some sleep from her eyes and gave her a few seconds to tamp down rising bile. She twisted her mouth into a semblance of a smile and took the pad her Devoted proffered.

"Hello, Melissa." Rhiannon pushed a messy tendril of hair from her face, the better to observe her companion on the pad's small screen.

The Devoted man who'd woken her rematerialized at her side—when had he been gone?—with her crown in his hand. She must have taken it off for sleeping. The gold circlet's coated leaves bit into her fingers, and she slung the accessory onto her head with practiced ease. She didn't even need two hands for the adjustments, though she'd managed to catch a disheveled hair in her mouth. She blew to un-trap it from her lips.

"...as soon as you can." Melissa's visor flashed white then back into blue.

"Sorry, I missed some of that." Rhiannon needed to clear the sleep fuzz from her brain before it got her amalgamated Hive dissolved or blown up.

"The poem worked," Melissa said. It had repetition's practiced tone. "I have a journalist who wants to interview you. Live. In"—her image blinked out, replaced by a ticking cartoon clock—"three minutes."

A journalist! Rhiannon's heart rate kicked up into a wakeful gear and then some. "Yes. Yes, of course!" Her body jolted forwards and she clutched the edges of her pad. *The plan is back on.* She could talk to the journalist, reaching all Dyfed's people, and letting them decide what to do about the rebels and the cryptocracy and the changes necessary to the century-long Hive experiment. But, "Can you keep the communication open for long enough? Gavin said you were stuck out there."

"I've got this," said Melissa. They were the same words she'd spoken right before she flew in like the Cavalry and saved Rhiannon's ship from floating silently through space. "I'll put the journalist on your tablet and the news feed on the main screen." Two of her arms stretched up over her head and behind, opening up her thoracic area like a puffing bird. "Don't worry about which direction you're looking."

Three minutes, now two, wasn't a lot of time. But it was enough to scrape her hair off her face—not into a freshly woven series of knots, though—and back under her circlet. Enough to swish her mouth with water, wake up the other sleepers, and tell everyone to try and keep quiet while she talked with the planetary reporter.

The large screen lit. A blond woman with a chin-length bob and a chunky black necklace sat behind a dark wooden desk. Next to her hung a still image of Rhiannon's fleet surrounding Kendrick's ship.

The woman's eyes went larger and she smacked her lips once. "Good morning. This is the Early Machynlleth News. I'm your host, Gretchen Wyn. Last night, our Evening Edition colleagues uncovered a disturbing allegation concerning the ships above our planet.

"This morning, we're speaking with Queen-Commander Ceridwen on the *Iâr Du*"—her accent was perfect, but what else could Rhiannon expect from a woman named Wyn?—"in hopes of learning more. Queen-Commander, are you there?"

Rhiannon's stomach pulsed, threatening to vomit. Her face went hot and slick, and she could imagine the crown sliding to a crooked angle over frizzing hair. *No way to go but forward.*

"Good morning, Ms. Wyn." The image on the auditorium screen split to be left-half Wyn, right-half Rhiannon. Rhiannon looked away from it, not wanting to evaluate the sickly qualities of her own smile. Melissa had said she'd take care of such things, after all.

"Please, call me Gretchen."

"Thank you... Gretchen." Rhiannon couldn't offer a different name or title for herself in return. Not without losing ground.

Gretchen didn't pause to get one either, clearly comfortable interviewing Queens. "Last night, your Hive sent in a poem to our Protest Poetry contest explaining that the ships in orbit are not dangerous and never were. Would you expand on that, please?"

Rhiannon's stomach quivered again, and she was glad it was pre-breakfast empty. "I wouldn't call anyone harmless, exactly; you're not so harmless yourself." They shared a laugh, and Rhiannon went on to talk about the subfaction of the Senedd trying to set itself up as the supreme authority (a description which allowed the well-meaning not to be tarred with Kendrick's brush).

While Rhiannon explained about the tortured Queens and the horrible nonconsenting viruses and what Queen-craziness could lead to in Devoted, the large screen showed stills and clips to back up her words. Sickening though it was to see what exactly had been done to the abductees, the footage—*good work in your historian role, Melissa!*—could not be ignored.

"Once I personally took control over the staggering ships up here, this shadow government could not be a credible threat."

Melissa showed a clip of Rhiannon acquiring the Devotion of a man being held down. He went from bucking body and wild eyes to sobbing and gentled. Too intimate for a news report. Too disturbing to watch if you'd personally been there. Yet everyone in the auditorium was riveted. This was *their* story. Their Hive and their Queen.

Rhiannon watched in respect for her Devoted's choices.

"You personally?"

All right, that descriptor may have been a bit heavy, come across as too arrogant. But she *had* managed it without outside help. Gods above, but it was her Hive(s) and her work that led to defanging Kendrick's fleet.

What's more, she needed to be famous. She needed to be too prominent to disappear. If she couldn't make the majority of Dyfed's news-watching populace care—both about her Hive and about the entire rebel cause—while they were briefly giving their attention to this program, her Hive could be jailed or at least disbanded. The usurpers would win, and society would easily tear itself apart as the marginalized (who made up too many people to maintain that title) rose up against those who had systemic power.

"Me personally," she echoed. She had to be a figurehead that viewers would remember and appreciate and love. She had to protect her world, her culture, and her Devoted—new and old—from complete dissolution.

"Aren't you a little young?" Wyn asked.

Rhiannon's shoulders tightened up into her neck. This was exactly the aspect that had lost her credibility with the Senedd's negotiators. No matter what she did, it came back to her youth for these people. She had to find a way around it.

Other than the poetry, why should anyone listen to me?

In the auditorium, her twenty-two Devoted murmured to each other, frustration weighing the air. None seemed to take the journalist's stance that Rhiannon's youth should preclude her effectiveness as a Queen.

Holly vibrated in her chair, biting her lip and staring intently at the screen.

If Rhiannon couldn't convince a friendly journalist, if this interview went wrong, she'd have to go back to the life they'd had five days ago. Of her core circle, Melissa (female), Alan (otherwise employed), and Luciano (long disaffected) wouldn't necessarily follow her down that retrograde path. They could leave, the way that Gwyn had.

Would they be better for it? She didn't think so.

Rhiannon's shoulders loosened. *My Hive loves me and trusts me to speak for them.* "My youth doesn't matter," she told the journalist. On the screen, Melissa zoomed in to Rhiannon's resolved face, close enough to see pale freckles on her pointy nose. Rhiannon had never liked those freckles. They made her imperfect, but *everyone* had a bit of imperfection in them. "Just like my being a Queen doesn't matter."

Rhiannon reached up and slid her fingers along the metal crown. She felt every mighty ounce when she lifted it off her head. On the screen, she saw pinkened indents where the weight of constant wear pushed it against her skin. She smiled to see the proof of her position and her Devoted's love; even uncrowned, she bore their marks.

She said, "My deeds and my heart, these are what matters. *I am one of you.*" More true than Wyn knew. If she hadn't cheated the Test all those months ago, she'd never have worn a crown at all. "I am Tested, yes, but not all of my Hive are. I am Welsh, yes, but that did me no good in America and China. I am a woman, yes, and so is my Devoted who made this broadcast possible."

If she hadn't been looking into her own dark brown eyes on the oversized screen, she'd never have seen the brief flash of Melissa's female avatar waving to the people of Dyfed, smiling as if loving her moments of fame.

It had been so long since Rhiannon had seen Melissa's body as anything other than metal, and it threw her for a moment in which she wondered, *who is that?* Yes, it was the avatar Melissa had chosen, but the woman was far too proud of her PRob heritage and shock-rated armor to ever want a human body for anything more than a short visit.

Victor's hand came heavy and warm when it curled around Rhiannon's arm. "And Melissa wasn't the first woman in our Hive. When we first came together..." For the first time of his own volition, Victor talked about Gwyn and how she didn't belong in Dyfed's Hive system either.

When Victor's story ended, Melissa changed the main picture to Luciano on the *Ceridwen's Cauldron.* "My name is Luciano Totti, and I'm from the mining colony Nuova—some of you call it Dyfed3."

Until this point, he could've been anonymous, gone home in Cantor's wake as a hero or a victim in need of help, but here he was: speaking up for himself and his people. With his name out there and this appearance on public television, Luciano would be forever associated with Rhiannon and her strange Hive and this unstable moment in planetary history.

Luciano's intense brown eyes flattened till only the pupils were visible. "My accent isn't the same as yours, and I got mocked often when I came to study on Dyfed. My religion is still misunderstood, even by my Hive. How many Nuovan Devoted can you name?"

Luciano's head tilted upwards with his tone, displaying a firm jaw that Rhiannon knew meant he was working through fear. "Some may say I don't belong, but Queen-Commander Ceridwen and the rest of her Hive accepted me, and I have had the chance to do many useful things. I have patched up bullet wounds and interned with American doctors. I have been first-shift pilot on our ship since we first left Dyfed. I *do* belong."

Rhiannon wished Luciano were in the same room so that she could hug him. She settled for looking down at the floor and hugging herself. At his last words, she cleared her throat so that Melissa would know to transfer the transmission back to her on the *Iâr Du*. If Rhiannon gave the others the chance at this point, they'd all tell their personal stories, and this wasn't the time for that. This was the time to drive her message home.

"As you can see, my Hive is very unorthodox." Rhiannon's forehead was cold where the circlet had been. Cold and so light, like gravity had been turned off. "And it's worked well. We've discovered the shadow government's plot. We saved the people on these ships—Devoted and Queen alike. We've found love in our hearts and our Hive for even the most unorthodox of our members, and that would be the Devoted who made this broadcast possible."

Rhiannon hoped Melissa wouldn't mind this; they hadn't had a chance to discuss it ahead of time. When would they? "In fact, Melissa, would you say hello again to our watching audience?"

Gretchen Wyn interjected here, "Yes, please!"

Rhiannon had almost forgotten about her.

Melissa's avatar came up on the screen again, an unremarkable woman in her forties made of all browns and symmetry, doing the same wave as before.

"No, Melissa," said Rhiannon. "What you *really* look like."

The picture changed to a still image from Victor's birthday party. In it, Melissa's vest was soaked with water from when the bucket had been knocked over in challenge. The droplets glistened on her silvery hide, and her visor was a pale, happy sky blue. Two arms behind her head forced her chest out like a peacock's.

Into Wyn' sputtering surprise, Rhiannon said, "When my Hive left Dyfed, we chose to see the universe and learn remarkable things. In so doing, we were forged and made stronger, strong enough to best the cryptocracy trying to take over our home planet... and strong enough to share our stories with you."

Rhiannon reached out imploringly, and Melissa marvelously managed to catch the gesture for the broadcast. "You too can make your own choices." She infused her voice with all the hope and seriousness she could. "Just because the system has worked this way for generations, doesn't mean it's the best way anymore."

Gretchen Wyn waited a few beats before taking charge of the interview again. The woman was a professional who knew good theatre when she saw it, and Rhiannon had learned theatre in unexpected places. "Queen-Commander, we're getting questions from the public that I hope you'll be willing to answer."

"Of course." Rhiannon dipped her head, not even caring how many frizzes the motion bared to Dyfed's watching population.

"This question from a Jillian Thomas in our very own Machynlleth. She thinks you're a part of this shadow government. What do you have to say about that?" It should have been a hard-hitting question, but Wyn ruined that illusion by confiding, "She called in earlier this week to accuse the station of making up the orbiting fleet altogether, so don't be too alarmed."

Rhiannon bared her teeth in what she hoped could be considered a friendly smile. Didn't anyone have more relevant questions? If they were going to doubt her truths, they should ask for proof of the virus or that she truly controlled Holly's rebel flagship.

But this Jillian Thomas had asked a question, and, by Ceridwen, Rhiannon would answer it. "How am I different from the usurpers, I think you're trying to say." She found that reframing a question sometimes led to better data, and this was a good question. Even if Jillian Thomas hadn't quite intended it.

"The shadow government wants you to know there are ships in orbit, and to think that they can save you from the crews. They can't. I already did."

Across the bottom of the screen, a scrolling ribbon read: *Queen-Commander Ceridwen Popularity Poll.*

"How am I different from the Senedd? The Senedd want you to believe everything they do is transparent. It isn't."

The ribbon now read: *Do we trust her? You say YES 77%. NO 13%.* A red bubble in the lower right corner obscured Rhiannon's left elbow in the zoomed-out picture. *Tell us your thoughts! No fee to call or write in.*

"The protestors want to tell you what the Senedd is hiding."

The ribbon said: *Stay tuned for more on the Machynlleth protests after this segment.* And then it returned to the *Queen-Commander Ceridwen Popularity Poll.*

"I'm here to say that it's all shockingly true. Not just to give Ms. Wyn a good headline"—Wyn chuckled here, then stifled her mouth with her hand—"but because we all deserve more. We deserve choices and the chance to grow into the people we want to be." Rhiannon's eyes looked directly into the camera, wherever the camera was. "Who do you want to be?"

Do we trust her? You say YES 92%. NO 6%.

Rhiannon had never expected people would appreciate her so much. She had planned to live in relative obscurity, maybe do some good for a little segment of the world and for whoever her Hive members were, and then die fulfilled in a century or two. This was more than she'd ever expected to do, to be, to affect.

"Erherrm, well." Gretchen broke into the intense silence in Rhiannon's speech's wake. "Let's go to the next caller."

Rhiannon felt her cheeks appling up in a smug sort of way. She was totally in charge of this. She had it under control and knew all the answers. No one could ask a question about this situation she wasn't prepared for. Her limbs loosened, and she swung her circlet from hand to hand before tucking it into her belt. *Let the next question come.*

A man's face filled the half screen next to her own, and it was familiar. *From the Senedd's negotiating team.* All her once-loose limbs locked in place. He wore a grimace that she somehow knew she'd caused, like an unruly teenager whose parent has to smooth feathers to keep it out of trouble.

Only this was not her father, and she'd done nothing wrong. It had all looked so very right until he showed up.

A stray thought bubbled: *I wonder if my father is watching this.*

Rhiannon's facial muscles melted into horrified positions that shouldn't be broadcast to the world. From smile through flat, through frowning, through so horrified her mouth hung open to display a few tooth tops. She supposed she should be glad her fingers were too numb to tug at her tunic sleeves and mess up the lines of her outfit on air.

"Queen-Commander Ceridwen," the Senedd man grated out her name through gritted teeth.

The sound scratched down her spine. This was it, then. Arresting her or discrediting her, and for the entire viewership of Early Machynlleth News to enjoy live.

"Queen-Commander Ceridwen, the Senedd would like to request your Hive's presence to award you medals for bravery. You have"—he paused here to swallow and shuffle his pad across his desk and back again—"you have saved our planet from malign influences, and such service to Dyfed will be rewarded."

Rhiannon's lips went numb to match her fingers. Was this a trick? She'd go down with her Hive and they'd all be arrested, unable to escape to the life they'd had five days ago? Grounded in all ways.

The journalistic professionals had far fewer problems figuring out how to spin this to their own benefit. "Early Machynlleth News is pleased to be the first to report this historic moment, when our fair government recognized the accomplishments and sacrifices of Queen-Commander Ceridwen and her Hive," Gretchen Wyn said.

Gretchen's face, blond bob sleek and perfect because no force could destroy her polished appearance, appeared in side-by-side contrast with the man. "We'd like to take a moment to thank our viewers for making this the most highly rated show in its time slot, and to suggest that we would be the perfect crew to document this awards ceremony."

Across the black ribbon at the screen's edge: *Which medals will Queen-Commander Ceridwen receive? Write in your suggestions and find out! Here on Early Machynlleth News.*

Rhiannon ran a hand through her loose hair. The strands felt strange and slippery, wrong without the crown and the knot-weave to stop her from doing exactly that. With Gretchen Wyn on scene, and her own broadcast crew in Melissa's hardware, the Senedd couldn't abduct her and hide her away forever. Everyone would know where she ought to be. News viewers would ask after her.

Probably.

After far too long in silence, Rhiannon made her throat work. "We would be honored." She'd established herself as part of the system—a Hive Queen—*and* part of the rebel movement. If she represented all the populations, the privileged and the don't-call-them-peasants, then clearly a peaceful path could merge the best parts of the old system with the egalitarian desires of the proletariat.

And that path must be achieved on the planet itself. She had to trust some adults to make it work, but she'd learned her lesson on John Wayne and Garden Station and from Llewellyn. She'd only trust adults as far as she could monitor them. "My Hive and I will come to you in Ms. Wyn's presence in time for the morning news tomorrow."

She bowed to the room, and Melissa translated that into a humbling before the nations of Dyfed rather than a gesture to the Senedd man. It was better that way.

The connection cut. All the screens went dark.

"Good timing, Melissa," she praised her communications expert. "I'd only have caused trouble if I kept talking."

Melissa's husky voice vibrated with the pleased recognition of a job well done. "The station suggested we wouldn't want to go over twelve minutes without a break, my lady."

"I hope all of you are ready to make friends with Senedd officials," she said to the room at large.

Gavin raised his hand, ecru silk sleeve brushing against his nose, but didn't wait for her to call on him. "I, for one, am ready to go home."

Which was not a sentiment she'd expected to hear from Gavin in relation to Dyfed. Ever.

A new Devoted raised his own hand in imitation of Gavin's gesture. She didn't laugh. She'd just have to explain later that Gavin was posing and she didn't demand that kind of turn-waiting. Though maybe she should. Her Hive had grown exponentially since reentering Cymraeg space. She nodded, freeing him to speak.

"I hate for you to go alone, but... would it be all right if I stayed up here?"

A murmur of agreement ran through the room. Another Devoted said, "The last time I went down to a planet, my Queen was stolen."

On one level, Rhiannon would have expected them to forbid her from going without them or to demand she stay up here. On another, she hoped the reduced clinginess meant her newest Devoted were becoming capable of caring for themselves without her intervention.

On a third level, they might be rejecting her as their Queen. Her glutes clenched so hard that her legs turned out into a ballerina's first-position posture.

"Oh, no, no, my lady." The Devoted rushed to her side, jostling each other at first, then slamming right and left to make pathways. It was the most well-meaning mosh pit ever. "If it's only me staying behind"—a chorus of "and me's" rose up—"then you'll still be safe; I'm just not ready."

Victor tugged her behind him, out of the way of the oncoming oxen-Devoted. "I'll be with our lady. But the rest of you should think about going planetside once we've determined it's safe. Real nature—the trees and meadows—will do you good."

Nodding and a general rocking-back greeted this pronouncement. Rhiannon supposed she should take it as a good thing that they were no longer lunging for her in such a comfortingly disturbing manner.

Victor shooed them away to their corners and benches and other duties. Rhiannon patted his shoulder in thanks. Victor and Gavin had been wonderfully helpful here in the *Iâr Du*'s auditorium. Melissa had gone far beyond what was expected in making repairs, even if she hadn't been a historian-bard. Luciano had chimed in from the *Ceridwen's Cauldron* too.

But Alan had been conspicuously silent since helping with the comms. With his personality, perhaps it was better if he stuck to physics and left the interpersonal truth telling to the rest of them.

"Queen-Commander," a voice cut through the hubbub.

Cantor. She'd wanted to forget about him. Was he planning to arrest her on behalf of some planetary faction who'd given him secret orders while she'd been busy with the news?

"Yes?"

He looked more disheveled than he had before. His sleeves, tight in the forearms like all scientists wore, scrunched up and pinched the skin beneath his elbows. His face bore deep lines, making him seem older than the mere seventy-ish years he usually looked. "I'm sorry."

A simple statement, which could have applied to so many things that Rhiannon felt herself growing angry. She pulled her head back on her neck, getting a wider range of view, and raised two sardonic eyebrows. She didn't even have to say *oh really?* or *for which offense?*

"You made connections I didn't. Couldn't. And I'm sorry I couldn't handle that. I was trained…" He trailed off as if realizing his apology held more excuses than remorse.

She didn't have the luxury of holding grudges, not when she needed to keep him as firmly hers as a non-Devoted could be. He still had the clout to champion her cause, her Hive, to the authorities.

"I forgive you," she said.

He hastened to follow up with praise. "You chose your own path, a different one than I would have, and it looks like you may have successfully created a bloodless revolution."

From his mouth to Ceridwen's ears. And to Manawyddan's and Llyr's and any other god's. Even the new goddess Saberhawen's.

Please let us have done something good for our world.

Chapter Thirty-Nine

Late-Arriving Trains Still Arrive

Dyfed – the Senedd building, inside the front doors

Rhiannon had been back on her home planet for an hour. It was the first time she'd been on a planet in months, and so far she hadn't seen much of it. Only this little vestibule where she waited for the Senedd to give her recognition—or a trial, honestly.

Oh, she'd glimpsed buildings and protest signs on the way from the spaceport to the Senedd and a prisoner transport following behind with all the bad guys in it. But that was all the excitement she'd been allowed.

Now she and her Hive loitered in a small not-quite-a-room. Only Victor and Luciano had seats at the moment, because the area was equipped with two chairs.

Two chairs weren't enough for a six person Hive to wait for an hour. They'd been taking turns.

The floor was alternating geometric grey zigzags of dark and light stone. A chandelier dangled from the ceiling; it wanted to look like a crown but seemed more like a mass of tangled wires with spikey light bulbs cropping up at intervals. From the right location—right in front of the sad sooty fireplace—she could see the front doors. To the sides, archways opened onto other halls. These would lead to places where important people did governmental things.

Cantor had gone off in one of those directions and told the Hive to wait here.

Rhiannon was getting bored with waiting. So long as it was waiting for good things. If they wanted to spirit her away and throw her in a dungeon after all, she could wait a little longer. Compared to a dungeon, she rather enjoyed the fake plants on the fireplace mantle.

"Can I interest anyone in a round of truth or dare?" asked Victor.

Alan waved a wild hand. "I dare you to give me your chair."

Victor turned it over with good grace. "Luciano, truth or dare?"

"I don't know this game," Luciano said. He was lying, of course. Rhiannon grinned. Nuova wasn't *that* far off from Dyfed, and they'd all attended the same classes and events for the year prior to taking the Test. The question was: would Victor call Luciano on it or attempt to teach the rules?

The Senedd couldn't keep her Hive mewed up in here forever, could they? At some point they'd have to make good on their promises of rewards and to acknowledge her before an audience of cameras and documentarians. Then she couldn't be punished like the cryptocrats she'd brought home. Couldn't go unmourned like the Chinese scientists.

If she wasn't released from this vestibule soon, Rhiannon would have to call the Senedd's bluff. If that's what it was. But would making a fuss in order to get recognition be the thing that destroyed her positive reputation? Gods knew the Senedd would leap at the chance to discredit her.

At least, she thought they would.

Melissa's four shoulders rose and fell on a fabricated sigh. "Gavin, truth or dare?" She didn't wait for him to pick. "When was the last time you gave someone a courtship gift?"

Face hot, Rhiannon twisted her fingers in her tunic sleeves. She couldn't watch him. She had to know. She'd been so confused. The miniature landscape, the poem...

"I was in third year," Gavin replied. Rhiannon's eyes shot up, no longer too embarrassed to watch as he opened his arms expansively, showing off his sleeves and puffing out his chest. "The other kids loved me, and I had a thing for a girl in the front row who wielded glitter like a weapon."

Rhiannon swallowed against a sinus drip. *This is good.* She nodded along with herself. *I wasn't looking forward to turning him down.* That much, at least, was true.

A bustle at the entrance door made Rhiannon's heart tick up. Her Devoted surged to their feet. But it was just a woman, maybe Rhiannon's father's age, in a black tunic with silver knotwork buttons and tight black trousers under a long red coat that brushed her knees. Her aquiline nose was a blade ready to cut her enemies.

Alan groaned and slumped. His recently appropriated chair cushioned him, and Rhiannon's pulse pounded faster. Alan was always moving. But not now. Now he was a lump of sadness, trying to hide in the sparse furnishings.

The woman at the door spotted Rhiannon's Hive crammed into the vestibule and speed-walked in their direction. Rhiannon hugged the fireplace wall. If this woman wanted to cut through the waiting area to reach another hallway, Rhiannon wasn't going to get in her way. She'd get run over. Or run through.

But the woman did not pass. She came to a halt directly in front of Alan's chair. Her toes tapped the stone floor. Rhiannon's mouth thinned. If this woman wanted the chair, she'd have to ask for it politely. Even then, Rhiannon wasn't going to let her just *steal* it out from underneath her Devoted.

Rhiannon cleared her throat. "Excuse me." Her tone did not beg excuses.

The woman waved a disinterested hand somewhere around her ear. Rhiannon snorted, not bothering to hide her less civilized impulses in this rude woman's presence. If Alan came back to his normal temperament, she'd enjoy watching him face off against this stranger. They could make giant arm gestures at each other. Gavin might also work his way into the arm-waving, and his sleeves were a definite advantage.

"Well." The woman's toes were still tapping. "Are you going to introduce me to your friends." It wasn't a question.

Alan didn't look up at the woman towering over him. "Hi, Mum."

The woman's sharp nose went even sharper on a deep inhale. "We'd heard you were back. And a hero for the moment."

Now that Alan had pointed out the connection, Rhiannon could see the resemblance. The same hazel eyes were set in the woman's charcoal-skinned face, a darker version of Alan's space-and-laboratory paleness. They had the same excitable mannerisms. The same penchant for dismissing anyone not in their league.

"Yes," said Rhiannon. She let her annoyance at needing to introduce herself to the conversation for a *second* time color her voice a darker shade of quiet. "He's been very valuable to me." Alan's mother turned slowly, and Rhiannon was surprised to realize they were the same height. The older woman had a much taller presence. "Hello, I'm Queen-Commander Ceridwen."

The two Queens regarded each other until Melissa broke the standoff.

"Do Queens often have biological children?"

Alan's mother seized with her whole body, then turned the force of her glare onto Rhiannon's metallic Devoted. "We have the option, like everyone else. Who are you?"

Alan vacated his chair to hover behind his mother's shoulder. "Mum, this is one of my Hive mates. Melissa. Melissa, this is my mother, Queen Brenda."

He should have been standing with the rest of the Hive, not with his mother. Rhiannon's eyes felt too dry to betray any emotion about the slight. But that was just planet air. It had been too long since she'd dealt in anything other than perfect climate control.

"Oooh." Queen Brenda stood on tiptoe and peered at a seam on Melissa's neck. Her voice was... disturbed sounding. Possibly closer to *eeew* or *uuug*. Rhiannon's lungs strangled the air inside them. What if Brenda threw a fit because Melissa was a woman? What if she hated Americans? This was the first adult Rhiannon's Hive had encountered so far in the Senedd, and if she caused trouble before they could get their broadcast appearance in... "An intelligence without a body! What do you think of cognitive science research? Would you like to collaborate with an entire Hive of experts?"

Rhiannon's breath whooshed out. *Nope, not a Melissa-hater. Apparently she wants to steal all my Devoted.*

Gavin grasped Melissa's arm, an upper one in Queen Brenda's line of sight. "Melissa is with us."

So Rhiannon wasn't the only one who'd picked up on the potential for Devoted-stealing. Gavin had grown protective of Melissa lately, as though his authority issues had washed away with each lesson taught in poetry or spirituality or what it meant to be from Dyfed.

"Well," said Queen Brenda, "If you change your mind."

Alan waved his arms above his head, grabbing his interfering mother's attention. His squarish eyebrows pulled together and quirked upward at the innermost corners, creating three horizontal ridges on his forehead. "What're you doing here?"

"Can't I come see you while I'm in the capital on business?" Queen Brenda reached out as if to pat his cheek, but remembered that he was Rhiannon's just in time and pulled back.

"What *is* your business?" Victor slouched against the doorway she'd come through, both black-clad legs and grey-clad arms crossed.

The older Queen looked at his scuffed boots, trailed her eyes up all the way to the messy dark brown top of his head. She looked away, not acknowledging his query.

To Alan she decreed, "Of course, once this little experiment is over, you'll be joining my Hive. It will be good for you to have this experience with outsiders first."

Rhiannon's fingers tugged hard at her shirt cuffs. *We are not the outsiders here.* She could feel her lower jaw push forwards into that belligerent position that nobody worries about on teenagers but runs away from in the middle-aged.

Luciano sidled up to Victor at the door column. He whispered, "I knew he had a mother, but this explains... pretty much nothing. Why wouldn't he go with her?"

The question was meant to be overheard by anyone in the tiny, echoing space. And it was probably meant to shame Queen Brenda into wondering the same.

But Alan replied instead of his parent, whispering, "Would *you* want to Devote to *your* mother?"

Alan's mother dared to pat her son on the shoulder. "I can wait," she said before she swanned off down a side corridor, just as some officials *finally* showed up, trailed by what seemed to be the entire office of Early Machynlleth News.

Gretchen Wyn halted at the now-closed entrance doors, briefing her team.

The Senedd's Presiding Officer, Mohammad Crewe, bent shallowly at the waist in front of Rhiannon. She'd seen him on broadcasts before, surrounded by the same Assembly-person retinue as followed him this day. "Privately, I want to say thank you for saving both our planet and my job."

He paused so that she could laugh with him. Once upon a time, she might have. High and nervous and desperate to please. These days, strange adults in positions of power had to earn the right to her reactions—whether mirth or freely displayed discomfort.

He continued into the stilted silence, "That said, running away from Dyfed the way you did was very wrong. You stole a government ship." Rhiannon raised her eyebrows; that wasn't how she remembered it, and she could call in the previous Queen Ceridwen to debate the point. "And you also stole a number of good Dyfed citizens. Male *and female*."

She knew this already. He knew it too, but he was posturing for his hangers-on, who all gasped.

"Now I can't split you up"—Rhiannon's heart slowed down to speeds she hadn't realized were normal since these months of wondering what would happen if she ever set foot on her home planet again—"not when you did so well and have truly come together as a Hive. There are laws against splitting up Hives.

"But there will need to be acknowledgement of the way you've flouted conventions. It might be for the best that you left your female member behind. She can't detract from you. Though you appear to have added another."

He'd as good as told her that he had no power over her. She could not be separated from her Hive, and she was about to gain even more fame. He might not be happy with her. Maybe no Senedd man or woman was happy with her. But he couldn't *do* anything about that. All this? Just posturing.

So she could posture right back. She leaned in to him, intending to give him a dose of intimidating Queenliness and deep-voiced intimacy. But that was when Gretchen Wyn came up beside her and reminded Rhiannon that getting what she wanted was far more important than showing up some old man, ineffectual and lost without her to do his work for him.

"Yes," she said, loud enough to be overheard. "We are pleased to include Melissa in our Hive. She's a brilliant asset in terms of intercultural cooperation and space safety. Not to mention that she's a very evocative poet." Rhiannon gestured to the oncoming news crew. "As Ms. Wyn can attest."

The woman in question bobbed her head. "Your ladyship."

"Hello again, Ms. Wyn." Cultivating a positive relationship with the press could make a Queen's reputation. "Forgive me. Gretchen."

The journalist bowed lower than the mere dip of moments before. "A pleasure to see you again, Queen-Commander Ceridwen."

"I'm afraid you'll have to call her *Queen-Commander Rhiannon Jones* from now on, Ms. Wyn," said Presiding Officer Crewe. "I hear she plans to stay on Dyfed for the next year or so while her Devoted undertake research and studies."

Rhiannon hadn't thought her name would change. Her forearm skin bumped up with pimples. Somehow having the layer between her ship and her self had given her extra security. A different kind of security than being famous. "It will be nice to hear my own name again," she said.

She'd be using that fame to check up on Holly, who'd been whisked away to a research lab of her own. The woman had offered up her own desire for penance before Crewe could stick her in a hole and leave her there, and it seemed like things were going the repentant scientist's way. But gods knew even fewer people would be watching to guarantee Holly's safety than Rhiannon's own Hive's.

Crewe's mouth twisted, as though he knew her thoughts and resented her power. "If you'll follow me onto the steps, we'll make the presentations."

"I've got cameras out front as well as here with the sound equipment. Don't worry, we won't miss a thing."

Melissa made a throat-clearing rumble. "Neither will I." Her deep blue visor was angled at Crewe as she said it, but he had already turned his back.

"Queen-Commander!" An out-of-breath Assembly woman fell in step beside her. "Is it hard for you being back? When all you've really experienced is the American frontier, how will you relearn to be civilized?"

Wyn dropped into place with a sound screen already in her hand, scenting provocative questions on the air.

Rhiannon contorted her face into the confused and annoyed look common to her age set everywhere in the known universe. She should possibly have tried to stay calm and serene-looking, but the question was ridiculous. "I lived here until last year. I'm a *Queen*."

Wyn choked beside her, turning her face away from the sound screen to do it.

And then she was on the front steps.

Sunlight gleamed on the stone columns and into Rhiannon's squinting eyes. A cheering roar came up from the crowd. People held signs with slogans on them, and Rhiannon caught one that sported a line from Melissa's poem. Something about keeping an eye on the truth of the nation because when the blossoms fall from the branch, its naked lines are... something. The end of that stanza had been hotly contested before Melissa took full ownership.

Women and men. Children and adults and teenagers, so many teenagers. A group held a banner showing off her own institution's ash tree symbol.

"Good morning, my people." Presiding Officer Crewe pushed down with his hands from shoulder height to waist. The crowd hushed.

The ceremony took an hour and a half. In that time, Rhiannon got Crewe to promise to listen to the revolutionaries. On worldwide broadcast, mandatory Testing was abolished and women were guaranteed admission to Devoted programs.

There was a touchy moment when Crewe suggested, "Now that you've experienced a wider view of the universe than most people your age, would your Hive be interested in re-Testing?"

Perhaps it would be comforting to admit her duplicity. *Yes, I cheated! I'm not supposed to be a Queen.* But if they took her Devoted away...

Cantor intervened. "This Hive is such a symbol of what can be done," he said. "Any changes would be unwise as well as false."

Rhiannon's *prize* then—which may have been intended as a disciplinary ultimatum—demanded that she and her Hive undergo more schooling. With Cantor as Alan's champion, she knew they wouldn't be slighted.

Somehow, she'd received everything she'd ever wanted when she'd first cooked up her scheme to game the Test. She was a Queen. She would have an in-depth education in what that meant. She had five Devoted with strong interests who could work together smoothly. And she'd also affected her whole world for the better.

The system was changing.

⟍ Epilogue ⟋

Early Machynlleth News Redux

Dyfed, News Station 3

A blond woman sits behind a wooden desk. Her smile is genuine, her bobbed hair is mussed from its usual precision, and a mascara smudge mars the skin under one eye.

"Good morning," she bubbles. "This is Early Machynlleth News. I'm your host, Gretchen Wyn. For all the school-aged viewers and their parents, you'll be interested to know that our entire planet-wide school and university system has changed. This year's Test-takers-to-be will want to relax their study schedules since joining a Hive or becoming a Queen is now an optional side track."

The space next to her shoulder changes to a framed picture of women marching on the Senedd with homemade signs in their gloved hands. "These protestors don't think optional is good enough." A close-up of one sign shows the slogan *Phase Out or Drop Out!* "They want to abolish the Hive system completely, no options allowed. Later this morning, we'll have a field reporter interview these protes-tors about their plans."

The picture disappears.

"Let's go to Huw in the studio, where he's interview-ing an octogenarian who's demanding the Devoted virus. Huw?"

"Thank you, Gretchen..."

Author's Notes

Regarding the Chinese station –

Yin He Yuan (Garden Station)'s layout is inspired by Suzhou-style gardens. I've visited many, and much of this station is based on Portland's Lan Su Yuan with reinforcement from Vancouver's Dr. Sun Yat-Sen Classical Chinese Garden... both of which are driving distance from my residence in Seattle. Thank you to the many tour guides who told wonderful stories and answered my bizarre questions. (Also thanks to the helpful book *Listen to the Fragrance*, all about Lan Su Yuan's inscriptions and poems, by Charles Wu.)

Thinking about the Western future is hard enough. Trying to create an Eastern one is harder. (Maybe I should've picked Japan instead of mainland China; at least I have an academic background in that.) Thankfully, some amazing Chinese science fiction books have been translated into English, and I used those to craft much of my vision for the Chinese future. (If you're going to build a future society based on a contemporary one, you should maybe see what the contemporaries are making, right?)

I was particularly inspired by *The Fat Years* by Chan Koonchung, which is a near-future novel of Beijing. As with my Welsh future, though, I pulled heavily from historical sources and let my desired setting (the Scholar's Garden) shape much of this fictional society.

Note about the name: in the drafting phase, I had simply named the Mandarin Chinese station "Garden Station." At nearly the last moment, my wonderful college friend Maria Luk suggested Yin He Yuan, and that was that. In her honor, I've named the dead scientist "Lu Zhi" for an ancestor of hers who (lucky happenstance) turns out to be from Suzhou. (There's a Wikipedia page about him, if you're curious. He's pretty interesting.)

Inscriptions inspired by –

Listen to the Fragrance, all about Lan Su Yuan's inscriptions and poems, by Charles Wu.

'Drinking by the Lake: Clear Sky at First, then Rain' -'Yin hushang chu qing hou yu' 飲湖上初晴後雨 by Su Shi 蘇軾 – a poem of the West Lake (http://www.china heritagequarterly.org/features.php?searchterm=028_ graham.inc&issue=028)

On Gavin's quotes in this volume –

For some reason, Gavin quotes and misquotes *Volpone* (by Ben Jonson) a lot in this book. Possibly because when I was a high school junior/senior—like he is here—I read it for the first time. (I lucked out later in the year when it turned up on the AP English exam, and I knew what the sample passages were all about.)

Other quotes are from Shakespeare, *The Satyricon* (by Petronius, Nero's "Arbiter of Elegance"), other books by me, and stuff I've made up. Probably there are more, but I don't remember them all. Also, I refrained from ever quoting the bible (or other religious texts) because that seemed disrespectful with the way Gavin uses quotes.

More on Melissa's change from male to female—

I wanted to try and stay true to the trans experience with this one. To that end, I read blogs and books by trans individuals and spoke with a lot of people. I'd like to particularly thank Jordan and Graham Blair for their specific suggestions of particularly masculine actions that could freak out my mis-gendered robot.

Particularly wonderful non-fiction resources used in my research –

Anglo-Welsh poetry
Urgency and Identity edited by David T. Lloyd
The Dragon Has Two Tongues by Glyn Jones
Frontiers in Anglo-Welsh Poetry by Anthony Conran

Neuroscience
Brainwashed by Sally L. Satel
The Brain Science Podcast with Ginger Campbell, MD
(audio)

About the Author

Photo by Jeremy Barton

Janine A. Southard is the IPPY award-winning author of *Queen & Commander* (and other books in The Hive Queen Saga). She lives in Seattle, WA, where she writes speculative fiction novels, novellas, and short stories... and reads them aloud to her cat.

All Janine's books so far have been possible because of crowdsourced funds via Kickstarter. She owes great thanks to her many patrons of the arts who love a good science fiction adventure and believe in her ability to make that happen.

Get a free piece of fiction when you sign up for Janine A. Southard's newsletter (http://bit.ly/jasnews). The newsletter will keep you current on things like her latest release dates (and fun news like when her next Kickstarter project is coming). Usually, this is once a month or so, but sometimes goes longer or shorter. Your address will never be shared, and you can unsubscribe at any time. Plus: free ebook! (Rotating freebies mean I can't tell you what the work is right this second.)

You can hang out with Janine online where she's crazy about Twitter (@jani_s) and periodically updates her website with free fiction and novel inspirations (www.janine southard.com)